Let the blood flow and laughter reign—
because when it comes to facing our deepest, darkest fears,
a little hu[illegible]

BL[illegible]

D1014064

Kelley Armstrong [illegible]
Don D'Ammassa Charlaine Harris Nancy Holder
Sherrilyn Kenyon Nancy Kilpatrick
J. A. Konrath and F. Paul Wilson Joe R. Lansdale
Will Ludwigsen Sharyn McCrumb
Mark Onspaugh Mike Resnick Steven Savile
D. L. Snell Eric James Stone Jeff Strand
Lucien Soulban Matt Venne Christopher Welch

"This **toothsome** anthology of twenty-one **funny-scary** stories from members of the Horror Writers Association arrives **just in time for Halloween.** On the **humorous** end, Matt Venne's 'Elvis Presley and the Bloodsucker Blues' re-creates Presley's voice with pitch-perfect swagger and sets the record straight on how he really died, while Charlaine Harris's 'An Evening with Al Gore' depicts a novel way to deal with environmental criminals; both tales are **truly outstanding.** In a **creepier** vein, Steven Saville's 'Dear Prudence' finds a conflicted man repeatedly revising a note where he details **gory** plans for his significant other, and Nancy Holder's 'I Know Who You Ate Last Summer' features **stomach-churning** 'rock star cannibals.' Big names like Jim Butcher and Sherrilyn Kenyon will have comic horror fans **grabbing this anthology off the shelves.**"

—*Publishers Weekly*

The Horror Writers Association

presents

BLOOD LITE

AN ANTHOLOGY OF HUMOROUS HORROR STORIES

Edited by Kevin J. Anderson

Pocket Books

New York London Toronto Sydney

The sale of this book without its cover is unauthorized. If you purchased this book without a cover, you should be aware that it was reported to the publisher as "unsold and destroyed." Neither the author nor the publisher has received payment for the sale of this "stripped book."

Pocket Books
A Division of Simon & Schuster, Inc.
1230 Avenue of the Americas
New York, NY 10020

This book is a work of fiction. Names, characters, places, and incidents either are products of the author's imagination or are used fictitiously. Any resemblance to actual events or locales or persons, living or dead, is entirely coincidental.

Copyright © 2008 by The Horror Writers Association, Inc.

All rights reserved, including the right to reproduce this book or portions thereof in any form whatsoever. For information address Pocket Books Subsidiary Rights Department, 1230 Avenue of the Americas, New York, NY 10020

First Pocket Books paperback edition October 2009

POCKET and colophon are registered trademarks of Simon & Schuster, Inc.

For information about special discounts for bulk purchases, please contact Simon & Schuster Special Sales at 1-866-506-1949 or business@simonandschuster.com.

The Simon & Schuster Speakers Bureau can bring authors to your live event. For more information or to book an event, contact the Simon & Schuster Speakers Bureau at 1-866-248-3049 or visit our website at www.simonspeakers.com.

Photo © Radius Images

Manufactured in the United States of America

10 9 8 7 6 5 4 3 2

ISBN 978-1-4391-4840-2
ISBN 978-1-4165-7027-1 (ebook)

Page 469 constitutes an extension of this copyright page.

Contents

BLOOD LITE

The Ungrateful Dead

Kelley Armstrong

I see dead people. Unfortunately, they also see me.

One of the first lessons a necromancer learns is the art of playing dumb. When strolling down Fifth Avenue, searching for that perfect pair of shoes, pay no attention to the guy in the Civil War uniform. If he notices the glow that marks you as a necro, he will attempt to make conversation. Pretend you don't see him. With practice, you'll learn to finesse the act—pursing your lips, tilting your head, murmuring "Hmm, I thought I heard— Oh my God, would you look at those darling Jimmy Choos!"

Eventually, the ghost will decide you're untrained—or just plain stupid—and wander off before getting to the part that begins with "Say, could you do me a favor . . . ?"

Of course, one problem with playing dumb is that it seeps into your everyday life. But that has its advantages too. No one ever asks me to help with their taxes.

Now, as I stood behind the stage curtain, I searched for signs of any otherworldly presences. Nothing screws up a séance like the appearance of a real ghost.

In the theater, my intro began: "This is their world. A world of peace and beauty and joy. A world we all wish to enter."

I tensed, flexing my calf muscles.

"Jaime . . ." Brett warned as he fixed my hair. "Stand still or this piece is going to wave like a bug antenna."

Achieving an artlessly windswept updo is, truly, an art form, but it was part of the "sexy librarian" look I used for my shows. The pinned-up red hair, the modestly cut but curve-hugging dress and, of course, the wire-rimmed glasses. Admittedly, at forty-six, I was ramming the limit of how much longer there would be any "sexy" in my librarian. Keep the house lights low, though, and I looked damned hot.

My cue came. I walked to the curtain, cheeks twitching as I struggled to keep my smile in, reminding myself I'd need it for the next two hours.

As I stepped onto the dimly lit catwalk, I could hear the breathing of the sold-out crowd. Their excitement ignited mine and my grin broke through. I bit my cheek and set out.

"Come with me now," my recorded whisper snaked through the hushed theater. "Let me take you into their world. The world of the spirits."

I stopped. The speakers hissed as the recording switched to a man's voice.

"The Globe Theater proudly presents . . . internationally renowned spiritualist . . ." Another hiss as the volume swelled, the house lights rising with it. "Jaime Vegas!"

"I'm getting a male relative," I said to Patty, a round-faced woman with big tortoiseshell glasses straight out of the eighties. "His name starts with *N* . . . no, wait . . . *M*. Yes, *M*."

Statistically speaking, *M* is one of the most common first letters for male given names. Somewhere in Patty's mental file, she'd find a deceased Mike, a Matthew or . . .

"Mort!" she shrieked, like she'd correctly answered the Double Jeopardy question. "My uncle Mort."

"Yes, that's right. Your moth . . ." I drew out the word, watching for her reaction. At her frantic nod, I said decisively, "Your mother's brother."

Interpreting cues was the key to cold reading. Sometimes it was only a slight widening of the eyes or a faint involuntary nod. Then I'd get people like Patty, so eager to praise and encourage me that I felt like a puppy who'd finally piddled outside.

I spent the next few minutes postponing the inevitable message, with "Wait, he's fading . . . no, here he comes . . . I think he's trying to say something . . ." It's a two-hour show.

I was in the midst of "reeling" Mort back when a voice said, "You called?"

I glanced behind me. There stood a sixtyish bald man with a round face, bearing a striking resemblance to Patty. Uncle Mort. It doesn't matter that I rarely summon ghosts onstage. Sometimes they just show up.

"Mortimer!" I beamed a smile as his gaze nestled in my cleavage. "How wonderful. I thought I'd lost you."

"Uncle Mort?" Patty bounced, clearing her seat by a good three inches. "It's me, Patty."

Mort squinted. "Patty? Shit. I thought you said *Pammy,* her sister." His eyes rolled back as he smiled. "Mmm. Pammy. She was always the cute one, but after she turned sixteen? Boom." He gestured to show what part of Pammy's anatomy had exploded.

"Uncle Mort would like to tell your sister, Pammy, that he's thinking of her."

"Ask her if Pammy's still hot," Mort said. "Last time I saw her was at my funeral. She wore this lacy little black number. And no panties." He chortled. "That's one good thing about being a ghost—"

"Uncle Mort remembers that black silk dress Pammy wore to his funeral."

If Patty bounced any higher, she was going to take flight. "What about me? Does he remember me?"

"Yeah," Mort said. "The fat one. Even as a baby she was a little tub of lard—"

"Uncle Mort says he remembers what a beautiful baby you were, so cute and chubby with red cheeks like apples."

Patty spent the next few minutes telling Uncle Mort about Cousin Ken's cataracts and Aunt Amy's arthritis and little Lulu's lazy eye. Uncle Mort ignored her, instead peppering me with questions about Pammy.

"Are you even listening to me?" Mort said finally.

"Uncle Mort appreciates the update," I said. "And he'd like you to pass on a message in return. Tell everyone he misses them dearly—"

"Miss them? One more Christmas with those people, and if the cancer didn't get me—"

"—but he's gone to a good place, and he's happy."

"Would I be *here* if I was happy? I'm bored out of my frigging skull."

I crouched beside Patty, clasped her hands and wished her all the best. Then I returned to the catwalk. "Uncle Mort has left us now."

Mort jumped in front of me, waving his arms. I walked through him.

"She's ignoring you," another voice said.

"I'm waiting for a new spirit to make contact," I continued. "I can sense them just beyond the veil." I pretended to scan the room, to get a look at the new arrival without letting on I'd heard him. More secrets of the successful spiritualist.

A young man had climbed onto the catwalk. Dressed in a striped Henley shirt and cargo shorts, he was about twenty, stocky, with manicured beard stubble. A frat boy, I guessed. A ghost, I knew. The fact that no one noticed him sauntering down the catwalk gave it away.

I continued to survey the room. "A spirit is trying to break through the veil . . ."

"Don't bother, buddy," Mort said to the other ghost. "She may be a necromancer, but she needs some serious remedial training."

"Actually, I hear she's very good. Comes from a long line of powerful necros."

"Yeah? Well, it skipped a generation."

"I have a name," I intoned, eyes half-closed. "Is there a Belinda in the audience?" In seat L15, if my sources were correct.

"See?" Mort said. "She doesn't even know we're here."

"Oh, she knows." The frat boy's voice carried a burr of condescension. "Don't you, Red?"

"Do I have a Belinda in the audience? Hoping to contact her father?"

A bingo-hall shriek as an elderly woman—in L15—leapt up. I made my way over to her. Mort stomped back to his afterlife. The frat boy stayed.

After the show, I strode down the backstage hall, an icy water bottle pressed to my cheek.

My assistant, Tara, scampered along beside me. "We have a ten a.m. tomorrow with the *Post Intelligencer*, then a two o'clock pretape with KCPQ. Friday's show is totally sold-out, but you can plug the October one in Portland."

"Will do. Now, can you find Kat? Let's see if we can't get that sound system fixed before Friday."

I slipped into my dressing room, closed the door and leaned against it. A slow clapping started across the room.

The frat boy slid off my dressing table. "Okay, show's over. You done good, Red. Now it's time to get to work. Be a real necromancer."

I uncapped my water and chugged.

"Cut the crap," he said. "I know you can—"

"—hear you. Yes, I can." I mopped my sweaty face

with a towel. "But a dressing-room ambush really isn't a good way to get my attention."

His full lips twisted. "Oh, please. You think I'm going to peep at you undressing? You're, like, forty."

"I meant it's rude." I tossed the towel aside and grabbed my hairbrush. "If you'd like to talk, meet me at the rear doors in twenty minutes."

"Um, no. I'm going to talk to you now, and I'm not leaving until I do."

Rule one of "how to win favors and influence necros"? Never threaten. I'd say if you're lucky enough to get one to listen, you should fall on your knees with gratitude. But that might be pushing it. A simple "okay, thanks" will do.

I'm not heartless. In fact, in the last few years, I've made a real effort to listen to ghosts, and I'd had every intention of hearing this one out. But he was fast blowing his chance.

I turned to the mirror and brushed out my hair, pins clinking to the floor.

"Don't turn your back on me," the ghost said.

"I'm not. I said I'll be ready in twenty minutes."

He walked through the dressing table, planting himself between the mirror and me. "Fine. How about this?"

He shimmered, then shot back, clothing drenched with blood, stomach ripped open, safety glass shards studding his intestines. A brain-splattered metal rod protruded from his ear. One eye bounced on his cheek.

I fell back. "Oh my God! No, please. Not the death body. I'll do whatever you want!"

I recovered and reached through his intestines for my cold cream. "Do you really think you're the first spook who's tried that? I've seen decapitations, burnings, drownings, bear maulings, electrocution . . ." I leaned to see my reflection past the rod sticking from his head. "A couple of years ago, there was this one ghost who'd been cut almost in half. Industrial accident, I guess. That one *did* give me a start. But car accidents? *Pfft.*"

I met his eyes—or the one still in its socket. "Did you see that segment on E! last month? About celebrities addicted to plastic surgery? They talk and it's like watching a ventriloquist dummy. Only their mouths move. *That* scares me."

I went into the bathroom to wash my face. The ghost followed. He changed back to his regular body, but stood behind me, arms crossed. Now, I've played this game before, and I could usually hold out longer than any ghost. But then my cell phone rang.

Even without the special ring tone, I'd have known it was my boyfriend Jeremy. He always called me after a show to see how it went and he always timed it perfectly, giving me a chance to wind down but catching me before I headed out for a postshow talk with my staff.

The call also reminded me that he was coming to Seattle after my Friday show. Our schedules only allow weekend visits every couple of months, and there was no way in hell I was spending this one with a ghost in residence.

So I told Jeremy I'd call back, then said to the ghost, "What do you want?"

"My cousin died in the same accident as me. I want you to open his coffin."

"I'm not a grave digger."

"He isn't in the ground. Our family has a mausoleum."

"And why would I want to open his coffin?"

He looked down his nose at me, not easy when he was no more than my five foot six. "Because I said so. You're a necromancer. You serve the dead. I'm dead. So serve."

Of course, I said no, in increasingly descriptive ways. Of course, he didn't let it go at that.

The problem with refusing a ghost's request is that you can't just walk away. Wherever you can go, they can go. At my staff meeting, Frat Boy stood between me and my staff and shouted the Pledge of

Allegiance. When I called Jeremy back, he mocked and mimicked my conversation. In the rented limo, he sat on my lap and switched in and out of his death body.

Being unable to touch anything in the living world squashes a ghost's threat potential. But they can be damned annoying. And this guy was a pro, making me wonder how many other necros he'd hit up before finding me.

When it came time for my shower, I declared war. I've had enough ghostly Peeping Toms to get over any modesty, but Frat Boy would do more insulting than ogling, and as healthy as my ego was, I didn't need a twenty-year-old studying me for signs of sagging and cellulite.

So I filled a censer with vervain, set it alight and banished him. A temporary measure that worked until 4:10 a.m., when the herbs burned up and I woke to him screaming the Pledge in my ear. I added more vervain and went back to sleep.

When I woke, there was no sign of Chuck. I had no idea what the ghost's name was, but he looked like a Charles Willingham the Third or something equally pretentious—he reeked of money and privilege, too much of both, the smell as strong as BO and just as offensive. If he was a Charles, I'm sure he'd be Chas. I'd call him Chuck.

Not seeing him that morning, I hoped that meant he was gone and naming him was premature. The last bit of vervain still smoldered, though. When it disappeared, he'd come back.

I added another pinch, then noticed I was getting low. That happens when I'm on tour. There's a limit to how much dried plant material you can take on a plane. Even if I explain I'm a spiritualist and produce documentation, a satchel of dehydrated herbs begs for a trip to the little white room and a visit from Mr. Hand.

Half of my remaining vervain gave me time to dress and escape. But as I walked into the TV station that afternoon, Chuck found me, and I spent the next half hour with a ghost prancing naked between the interviewer and me. Though I kept my cool, I knew my distraction would show—eyes a little too round, gaze darting a little too often, laugh a little too shrill. That wouldn't do. Part of my appeal is that, yes, I can be spacey, but in a ditzy C-list celebrity way, not one that screams "I just got my day pass."

Afterward, sitting in the cab, listening to Chuck do a standup routine of sexist jokes, I envisioned him harassing me through my Friday show and into my weekend.

I can take abuse, but there are two things no one interferes with: work and Jeremy. The warning shots hadn't scared this guy away. Time to haul out the howitzer.

Normally, my "big gun" comes in the form of a sword-wielding, ass-kicking spirit bodyguard. Eve is a half-demon and a part-time angel, proving even the afterlife has moved to nondiscriminatory hiring practices. But when Eve is on a celestial stint, she's incommunicado.

So I had to do this myself. That meant the heavy-duty banishing ritual, one that required a lot of time, effort and ingredients. The last was the sticking point. Vervain wasn't the only herb I was low on. So I placed a call to my West Coast supplier.

Paige is a witch who lives in Portland and has everything a spellcaster or necromancer could need. She doesn't sell the stuff. She's just better organized than me . . . or anyone else I know.

It was still late afternoon, and Paige never went home early, so I called the office.

"Cortez-Winterbourne Demon Hunters," a voice sang. "Get 'em slayed before you get flayed."

"That's new."

"Yeah, needs work, though. The rhythm's off." A pause and a double thump, and I imagined Savannah leaning her chair back, feet banging onto the desk. "So how's the celeb necro biz?"

Savannah was Paige's nineteen-year-old ward and

Eve's daughter. From the way she answered the phone when she recognized my number, I knew Paige wasn't there, so I chatted with Savannah.

"Lucas is off in Chicago defending a client," she said. "Paige and Adam are in San Fran with Cass, checking out a vamp problem. Guess who's stuck behind answering the phone? I told Paige that's why God invented voicemail. But now I have a feeling my week is looking up. So what kind of trouble are you in? Kidnapped again?"

"Ha-ha. No trouble. I just need ritual supplies from Paige. Do you have access to her stash now? Or does she still keep it under lock, key and security spell so you don't blow anything else up?"

"Ha-ha. The shed was an accident. So what's the ritual for? Summoning or banishing?"

"Banishing." I listed what I needed.

"Ooh, big-ass banishment. What did your spook do to deserve that?"

"The usual. Tormenting me. Insulting me. Blasting me with the Pledge of Allegiance."

"Allegiance assault? The bastard."

"It's probably the only thing he'd ever memorized. Anyway, if you could courier the stuff to Seattle—"

"Seattle? You're just around the corner."

"A hundred and fifty miles around the corner."

"I'll be there by seven."

"No! I appreciate that, but really—"

"Staying at the Olympic, as usual?"

"Er, yes, but—"

"Seven it is. Don't eat without me."

Savannah arrived at 7:20, bearing pizza and beer. I wasn't asking how she got the beer. With Savannah, I'm better off not knowing.

She kicked off her knee-high boots, peeled a slice from the box and folded her long limbs into a chair, feet pulled up under her. "So, what does he want?"

"Who?"

"Your spook. Does he have a name?"

"Probably. I call him Chuck."

"So Chuck presumably asked you for a favor. You couldn't do it. He's making your life hell. You need to banish him. Which is why you shouldn't let them ask in the first place."

"It was more of a demand, really. But I have been trying to listen more often, help with little things like passing on messages."

"Uh-huh. How's that working out for you? Or I guess that—" She jabbed her pizza slice at the burning vervain. "—answers my question. About Chuck, though. What does he want?"

I took a beer and sat on the sofa. "He and his cousin

died in a car accident. They were interred in the family mausoleum. He wants me to open his cousin's casket."

"And . . ."

"There is no 'and.' Apparently, as a servant to the afterlife, it's not my place to question the will of the dead."

"Asshole." She chugged half her beer. "If he's got a mausoleum, that means he's got money—or his family does. I bet there's something valuable in that casket, and jerkwad is just too stupid to realize it won't do him any good, being dead. So, if we did find something, we'd need to keep it."

"No, I'd give it back to his family."

"Shit. Jeremy's finally rubbing off on you, huh?"

"There's no treasure in that casket."

"Then why does he want you to open it? Aren't you curious?"

I wasn't. Another necromancer lesson: Never stop to question. There are too many opportunities. Like the residual in Savannah's house—a woman forever watching out the window. I should wonder what she's looking for, why it was so emotionally powerful that the image of it is seared forever within those walls. But necromancers can't afford idle curiosity. They'll go mad chasing questions whose answers don't really matter. That doesn't keep me from feeling like I *should* be curious, though.

"It is odd . . ." I said finally.

"Good." Savannah smacked her bottle down. "Let's go take a look and get rid of this spook, so you can skip the nasty banishment ritual. You don't want to be wiped out when Jeremy's here, right?"

I hadn't thought of that. One problem, though . . . "If I do it, he wins. I'll have ghosts lining up to scream the Pledge of Allegiance at me."

"I'll handle that." She tamped out the burning vervain with her fingertips. "Yo, Chuck!"

After a moment, he appeared. "Who the hell is Chu—?" He saw the pizza and beer. "A party for me? How nice." His gaze moved to Savannah. "Whoa. You even brought party favors. Sweet."

Savannah's gaze followed mine and fixed on a spot near the ghost. "Sit down, Chuck. Grab a beer." She sucked back the rest of the bottle, eyes rolling in rapture. The pizza came next, which she dangled over her mouth, twisting the cheese strands around her tongue. "*So* good. Want some?"

His eyes slitted. "Teasing little—"

"He appreciates the offer," I said, "but respectfully declines."

She set down the pizza. "Come here, Chuck. I have a proposition I think you'd like."

Hope glimmered in his eyes, then guttered out as he remembered his noncorporeal state.

"We're going to open your cousin's casket. No, you didn't wear Jaime down. I'm curious so I talked her into it. Give her any grief, though, and she has the shit now to do a full banishment. And, later, if you ever come around again? Or tell anyone we did this for you?" She recited a spell. A fireball appeared at her fingertips. "I'll replace your balls with these."

"Bitch."

"He agrees to your terms," I said, "and thanks you for your help."

She pulled on her boots. "Off to the graveyard we go then. My first mausoleum break-in." She paused at the door. "Actually, my second, but if Paige asks . . ."

"It was your first."

It wasn't the first mausoleum break-in for me. Or the second. A practicing necromancer needs "artifacts of the grave" and the easiest way to get them is from bodies in crypts.

Between grave robbery and graveside summonings, I'd been in enough cemeteries to write a guidebook. I could also write a security manual for cemetery owners. I rarely encountered more than floodlights and an hourly rent-a-cop drive-by.

This cemetery had taken the extra step of locking the gates after dark . . . a gate attached to a fence with gaps you could ride a horse through. They'd splurged on lights too, and from a distance the place looked like a runway. But all the lighting in the world doesn't help when you're outside the city limits, a mile from the nearest house.

As we'd driven up in Savannah's car, I'd suspected Chuck had played us—this cemetery looked too small and new for family mausoleums. Apparently, though, it'd been designed by someone with a background in real estate, creating "mixed-dwelling" communities. Here, you had your apartments (columbaria), single-family dwellings (graves) and McMansions (mausoleums). The latter targeted families with too much money, too high an opinion of themselves and too little time to actually check out the product before plunking down cash. The buildings were little more than faux Greco-Roman sheds.

Savannah picked the lock and we stepped inside to what looked like a camp bunkhouse, stinking of damp wood, the walls lined with berths and a few coffins.

"So which—?" I began.

Chuck motioned for silence and made me relay it to Savannah.

"Um, okay," she said. "But someone should tell him 'waking the dead' is only an expression."

And, it seemed, we were the only ones supposed to stay silent. Chuck kept up a running commentary as we cast our flashlight beams around. When Savannah approached his cousin's casket, he got louder.

"Do you hear that?" Savannah asked.

"I can't hear anything with Chuck yapping." Which I began to suspect was the point.

"Something's in here." She bent to unlatch the coffin. "Are mice scavengers? If so, I think we have a nest of them chowing down at the body buffet."

My "wait!" came out like the squeak of a mouse, which must be what she mistook it for, because she threw open the lid. The corpse leapt up like a jack-in-the-box, shrieking and gobbling, fingers worn through from battering the casket, bone tips clawing the air, flesh tatters waving.

I'd seen this coming, but I still fell back. Even Savannah did, punctuating hers with a "holy fucking shit!"

At the sound of her voice, the zombie went still. His head swiveled toward her. Then, with the grace of a landlocked hippo, he lurched over the side of the casket. Savannah stepped back and the zombie—his internal bits and bones out of whack—hit the floor, limbs sprawled.

"Dude, chill." Savannah brushed a stray bit of flesh from her jeans. "Do we look like grave robbers? Your cousin brought this nice necromancer here, and I'm guessing he wanted her to help you out of your predicament."

The zombie looked around but, of course, couldn't see the ghost, who'd taken a seat on an empty berth and watched, arms crossed, waiting for me to get on with my job.

After a moment, the zombie got up. It wasn't easy. His left leg had evidently been broken in the accident and coroners didn't reset bones on dead people.

He propped himself against the berth and looked at us, his gaze keen and very human. A real zombie isn't the shambling brain-chomper of movie myth. It's a ghost returned to its corpse. Simple . . . and simply horrifying.

"So how did this happen?" I asked.

"What the fuck does it matter how it happened?" he shouted, voice garbled, wheezing through a hole in his throat. "Get me out of this rotting corpse!"

"You know, it shouldn't be rotting," Savannah said. "Someone went cheap with the embalming, dude."

"Stop calling me that."

"Would you prefer 'decomposing hunk of stinking meat'? Speaking of which, he is damned ripe, Jaime. Can we crack open the door before I hurl?"

I motioned for Savannah to tone it down and made a mental note to give her zombie sensitivity training later.

"Again," I said, "how did you—?"

"And again, what the fuck does it matter, you dumb twat."

He did not say "twat." The word he used made Savannah grab him by the suit collar and shake him.

"Show some respect, dickwad. She's trying to help you." A sharper shake. "That right hand looks a little loose. If I smack it off, it ain't growing back."

I motioned for Savannah to release him. Zombies are notoriously unhygienic.

"The reason I'm asking," I said calmly, "isn't to satisfy my curiosity. I don't really care how you got in there. But until I know, I can't get you out." I swept off a dusty berth and perched on the edge. "Why don't I take a guess? You and Chuck—"

"It's Byron," said the ghost.

"You and your cousin. You die in a car accident. You come back as ghosts. You find a necromancer. You demand something and you won't let up, so he teaches you a lesson by shoving you back into your body. Am I close?"

The zombie tried unsuccessfully to cross his arms. "I only wanted him to bring us back to life."

"And he did," Savannah said.

"I didn't mean like *this.*"

"That's the only way it can be done," I said. "I'm sure he tried to tell you that. You didn't believe him. So he showed you. Now he'll let you stew for a few days before setting you free." I took my flashlight from the berth. "I'll go talk to him and get this sorted. Where is he?"

"Why?" Chuck said. "Not good enough to do it yourself, Red?"

"No, I'm not 'good enough' to free another necro's zombie. It can't be done."

The zombie turned on me. "What? No way."

"It doesn't matter. I'm sure I can persuade this guy—"

"He's gone," Chuck said.

"Gone where?"

"If I knew, do you think I'd bother with you?"

When I asked what had happened, the cousins each gave their own rambling account, drowning out and often contradicting each other. After wading through the bullshit that blamed everyone but themselves, I figured out two things: One, some people never learn; two, I wasn't getting Chuck's cousin un-zombified any time soon.

After their pestering led the necromancer to return the cousin's soul to his body, Chuck decided the best way to fix it was to pester the guy some more. The necro had opted for an impromptu vacation to parts unknown.

"Okay," I said. "I have a lot of contacts, so tell me everything you know about him and, hopefully, in a few days—"

"A few days!" the cousins said in unison, then launched into rants that could be summed up as: "You're useless and stupid, and if you don't get him out of that body, you'll regret it." After a few minutes of this I began to think that, while I never thought I'd condone zombification, I could see the other necromancer's point.

If I could have stuffed Cousin Zombie back into his casket, I would have, but getting him there meant risking a noxious scratch or bite. So I agreed to attempt a soul-freeing ritual. And I kept attempting it for an hour before I gave up. That's when Savannah mentioned she knew a spell that might work.

"Why the hell didn't you say so?" the zombie said.

"A spell for freeing souls?" I said. "I've never heard of that."

"Because it's not meant for zombies. I'm thinking outside the box."

"Thinking?" the zombie said. "Must be a new experience for you."

"Do you want back *inside* the box? Nailed shut?"

"So, this spell," I said. "The real application is . . ."

"Knocking the soul out of a living person."

"Temporarily, I hope."

"Supposedly . . . but that's why I haven't tested it. Lack of volunteers."

The zombie cleared his throat, air whistling through

the hole. "This is all fascinating, ladies. But in case you haven't noticed, this body isn't getting any fresher."

Savannah looked at him. "I want to be clear that this is an untested, very difficult, very dangerous dark magic spell, intended for use—"

"Oh, for God's sake. Do you want me to sign a fucking liability waiver?"

"No, but I happen to be a mixed-blood witch," Savannah said, switching to a tone that sounded eerily like Lucas's legalese-speak. "That means when I cast a spell, the results can be more vigorous than intended. I'm trying to become a more responsible spellcaster by considering the ramifications—"

"Rotting here . . ."

She glanced at me.

I nodded. "If anything goes wrong, I'll tell Paige you read him the disclaimer."

Savannah cast the spell. The first two times, nothing happened, and the cousins started their heckling. By the third cast, her eyes were blazing as she spit the words, and I probably should have stopped her, but when I saw the zombie's skin balloon and bubble, like a pressure cooker, I thought his soul was about to pop free. Something did pop. His left eyeball shot out, bounced across the floor, then came to rest, optic nerve quivering like a sperm tail.

Cousin Zombie screamed, breaking it off in a string

of profanities long enough to hang someone with, and from the looks he shot Savannah, there was no doubt who he'd hang.

"Hey, I warned you." She prodded the eyeball with her boot. "You know what they say. It's all fun and games until someone loses—"

He lunged at Savannah. She hit him with a knock-back spell, sending him smacking against the wall, the flimsy building trembling. He bounced back, fists swinging.

"Watch out," Savannah said. "That hand is really wobbling."

He ran at her. She caught him in a binding spell.

"Damn, this isn't easy," she said through clenched teeth. "It doesn't work as well on zombies."

"Nothing does."

"We've got about ten seconds before he breaks it. And he's really pissed."

"No kidding!" yelled Chuck/Byron, who hadn't been silent, just ignored. "You popped out his eye, you incompetent—"

I returned him to ignore mode.

"Should I try the spell again?" Savannah asked, face straining with the effort of keeping the zombie bound. "I think I was close."

I looked from Cousin Zombie, frozen in a savage snarl, to Chuck/Byron, spitting dire vows of vengeance, and I decided that at this stage, "close" wasn't really an issue.

"Go for it," I said.

It worked the first time. That is, the spell worked in the sense that it didn't fizzle. It didn't release his soul either. Just that loose hand, which sailed off and flopped like a trout at my feet.

"Did anyone *not* see that coming?" Savannah asked.

The zombie broke the binding spell then and Savannah showed off her single year of ballet lessons by pirouetting and skating out of his way as he lumbered after her.

"Forget her!" Chuck/Byron shouted. "Get the necromancer. She's old and slow."

Great advice, if only zombies could hear ghosts. His cousin kept dancing with Savannah, who, after a few rounds, zapped him with another binding spell. Caught off balance, he tottered and fell sideways.

She whisked off her belt. "Are you over this 'I should be more helpful' shit yet?"

"In general, no. In this case, as you may recall, I was done with it long ago. Then you convinced me to open Pandora's casket." I walked closer, skirting the zombie in case the spell broke. "We aren't getting this guy back in that box without a fight. Even if we manage it, someone could find him, and I'll be the only council delegate who's ever had to haul her own ass before a disciplinary committee."

"Molly Crane."

I stared at Savannah.

"You remember Molly." She looped the belt around the zombie's ankles.

"Dark witch? Your mother's contact? You sent me to her for information, she knocked me out, dragged me into the woods, tried to torture me and dump my remains in a swamp? I vaguely recall her, yes."

"So what do you think?"

"About what?"

She untwisted her scarf. "Molly would *love* to babysit this guy for you. Not only does she get a slave, but the bits that fall off are gold on the black market. Then, when you've found that necro, he can de-zombify this guy, preferably after Mom's back to deal with him."

Again, I could only stare.

"What?" she said as she gagged the zombie with her scarf.

"Last time you saw Molly Crane you were leaving *her* gagged and bound."

"I didn't gag her. And she'll be over it." She knotted the scarf. "If not, then this is the perfect olive branch. She'll be happy for the excuse. I'm Eve Levine's daughter. Having me in her contact book is almost as valuable as those zombie bits. Of course, there is an alternative. We can put him in my trunk, take him to your hotel . . ."

"Do you still have her number?"

"Right here." She took out her BlackBerry.

Chuck/Byron leapt from his perch, where he'd been listening. "Am I hearing this right? You're going to sell my cousin into slavery?" He strode over to me, switching to his death body for effect. "You do this, and you will regret it. You think I was bad before? That was nothing compared to what's coming. I'll haunt you every minute of every day, and there's nothing you can do about it."

"Nothing?" I said softly.

He crossed his arms. "Nothing."

I took a slow step back toward the middle of the mausoleum.

A smirk rippled his defiant scowl. "So, Red, I'd suggest you start speed-dialing those contacts of yours."

"Uh-huh." I scanned the crypt, walking the perimeter.

"That's right. Find a place to get comfy. It's going to be a long night."

I stopped at a casket and my gaze settled on the plaque. Byron Carruthers. "Your name's Byron, right?"

"That's what I said. And you'd better start using it. No more of this 'Chuck' shit. Got it?"

I unlatched the casket.

"What the hell are you doing?"

"Just getting a look." I heaved it open. "Seems you've rotted even worse than your cousin. That's not good."

"Yeah, so?"

I retrieved my Gucci makeup bag of necromancy supplies. "Savannah?"

She pulled the phone from her ear. "Hmm?"

"Tell Molly we have a special today. Two zombies for the price of one."

I knelt beside the casket and started the ritual.

Mr. Bear

Joe R. Lansdale

For Michelle Lansdale

Jim watched as the plane filled up. It was a pretty tightly stacked flight, but last time, coming into Houston, he had watched as every seat filled except for the one on his left and the one on his right. He had hit the jackpot that time, no row mates. That made it comfortable, having all that knee and elbow room.

He had the middle seat again, an empty seat to his left, and one to his right. He sat there hoping there would be the amazing repeat of the time before.

A couple of big guys, sweating and puffing, were moving down the aisle, and he thought, Yep, they'll be the ones. Probably one of them on either side. Shit, he'd settle for just having one seat filled, the one by the window, so he could get out on the aisle side. Easy to go to the bathroom that way, stretch your legs.

The big guys passed him by. He saw a lovely young woman carrying a straw hat making her way down the center. He thought, Someone has got to sit by me, maybe it'll be her. He could perhaps strike up a conversation. He might even find she's going where he's going, doesn't have a boyfriend. Wishful thinking, but it was a better thing to think about than big guys on either side of him, hemming him in like the center of a sandwich.

But no, she passed him by, as well. He looked up at her, hoping she'd look his way. Maybe he could get a smile at least. That would be nice.

'Course, he was a married man, so that was no way to think.

But he was thinking it.

She didn't look and she didn't smile.

Jim sighed, waited. The line was moving past him. There was only one customer left. A shirtless bear in dungarees and work boots, carrying a hat. The bear looked peeved, or tired, or both.

Oh shit, thought Jim. Bears—they've got to stink. All that damn fur. He passes me by, I'm going to have a seat free to myself on either side. He doesn't, well, I've got to ride next to him for several hours.

But the bear stopped in his row, pointed at the window seat. "That's my seat."

"Sure," Jim said, and moved out of the middle seat and out into the aisle to let the bear in. The bear settled in by the window and fastened his seat belt and rested his hat on his knee. Jim slid back into the middle seat. He could feel the heat off the bear's big hairy arm. And there was a smell. Nothing nasty or ripe. Just a kind of musty odor, like an old fur coat hung too long in a closet, dried blood left in a carpet, a whiff of cigarette smoke and charred wood.

Jim watched the aisle again. No one else. He could hear them closing the door. He unfastened his seat belt and moved to the seat closest to the aisle. The bear turned and looked at him. "You care I put my hat in the middle seat?"

"Not at all," Jim said.

"I get tired of keeping up with it. Thinking of taking it out of the wardrobe equation."

Suddenly it snapped. Jim knew the bear. Had seen him on TV. He was a famous environmentalist. Well, that was something. Had to sit by a musty bear, helped if he was famous. Maybe there would be something to talk about.

"Hey," the bear said, "I ask you something, and I don't want it to sound rude, but . . . can I?"

"Sure."

"I got a feeling, just from a look you gave me, you recognized me."

"I did."

"Well, I don't want to be too rude, sort of leave a fart hanging in the air, though, I might . . . deer carcass. Never agrees. But I really don't want to talk about me or what I do or who I am. . . . And let me just be completely honest. I was so good at what I do . . . well, I *am* good. Let me rephrase that. I was really as successful as people think, you believe I'd be riding coach? After all my years of service to the forest, it's like asking your best girl to ride bitch like she was the local poke. So I don't want to talk about it."

"I never intended to ask," Jim said. That was a lie, but it seemed like the right thing to say.

"Good. That's good," said the bear, and leaned back in his seat and put the hat on his head and pulled it down over his eyes.

For a moment Jim thought the bear had gone to sleep, but no, the bear spoke again. "Now that we've got that out of the way, you want to talk, we can talk. Don't want to, don't have to, but we can talk; just don't want to talk about the job and me and the television ads, all that shit. You know what I'd like to talk about?"

"What's that?"

"Poontang. All the guys talk about pussy. But me, I'm a bear, so it makes guys uncomfortable, don't want to bring it up. Let me tell you something, man, I get plenty, and I don't just mean bear stuff. Guy like me, that celebrity thing going and all, I can line them up outside the old motel room, knock 'em off like shooting ducks from a blind. Blondes, redheads, brunettes, bald, you name it, I can bang it."

This made Jim uncomfortable. He couldn't remember the last time he'd had sex with his wife, and here was a smelly bear with a goofy hat knocking it off like there was no tomorrow. He said, "Aren't we talking about your celebrity after all? I mean, in a way?"

"Shit. You're right. Okay. Something else. Maybe nothing. Maybe we just sit. Tell you what, I'm going to read a magazine, but you think of something you want to talk about, you go ahead. I'm listening."

Jim got a magazine out of the pouch in front of him and read a little, even came across an ad with the bear's picture in it, but he didn't want to bring that up. He put the magazine back and thought about the book he had in the overhead, in his bag, but he hated to bother. Besides, the book was the usual thriller, and he didn't feel like bothering.

After a while the flight attendant came by. She was a nice-looking woman who looked even nicer because of her suit, the way she carried herself, the air of authority. She asked if they'd like drinks.

Jim ordered a diet soda, which was free, but the bear

pulled out a bill and bought a mixed drink, a Bloody Mary. They both got peanuts. When the flight attendant handed the bear his drink, the bear said, "Honey, we land, you're not doing anything, I could maybe show you my wild side, find yours."

The bear grinned, and showed some very ugly teeth.

The flight attendant leaned over Jim, close to the bear, and said, "I'd rather rub dirt in my ass than do anything with you."

This statement hung in the air like backed-up methane for a moment, then the flight attendant smiled, moved back and stood in the aisle, then looked right at Jim and said, "If you need anything else, let me know," and she was gone.

The bear had let down his dining tray and he had the drink in its plastic cup in his hand. The Bloody Mary looked very bloody. The bear drank it in one big gulp. He said, "Flight drinks. You could have taken a used Tampax and dipped it in rubbing alcohol and it would taste the same."

Jim didn't say anything. The bear said, "She must be a lesbian. Got to be. Don't you think?"

The way the bear turned and looked at him, Jim thought it was wise to agree. "Could be."

The bear crushed the plastic cup. "No 'could be.' Is. Tell me you agree. Say, *is.*"

"Is," Jim said, and his legs trembled slightly.

"That's right, boy. Now whistle up that lesbian bitch, get her back over here. I want another drink."

When they landed in Denver, the bear was pretty liquored up. He walked down the ramp crooked and his hat was cocked at an odd angle that suggested it would fall at any moment. But it didn't.

The plane had arrived late, and this meant Jim had missed his connecting flight due to a raging snowstorm. The next flight was in the morning and it was packed. He'd have to wait until midafternoon tomorrow just to see if a flight was available. He called his wife on his cell phone, told her, and then rang off, feeling depressed and tired and wishing he could stay home and never fly again.

Jim went to the bar, thinking he might have a nightcap, catch a taxi to the hotel, and there was the bear, sitting on a stool next to a blonde with breasts so big they were resting on the bar in front of her. The bear, his hat still angled oddly on his head, was chatting her up.

Jim went behind them on his way to a table. He heard the bear say, "Shid, darlin', you dun't know whad yer missin'. 'Ere's wimen all o'er 'is world would lige to do it wid a bear."

"I'm not that drunk yet," the blonde said, "and I don't think they have enough liquor here to make me that drunk." She got up and walked off.

Jim sat down at a table with his back to the bar. He didn't want the bear to recognize him, but he wanted a drink. And then he could smell the bear. The big beast was right behind him. He turned slightly. The bear was standing there, dripping saliva as thick as sea foam from his teeth onto his furry chest.

"Eh, buddy, 'ow you doin'." The bear's words were so slurred, it took Jim a moment to understand.

"Oh," he said. "Not so good. Flight to Seattle is delayed until tomorrow."

"Me, too," the bear said, and plopped down in a chair at the table so hard the chair wobbled and Jim heard a cracking sound that made him half expect to see the chair explode and the bear go tumbling to the floor. "See me wid dat gal? Wus dryin' to roun me ub sum, ya know."

"No luck?"

"Les'bin. The're eberyware."

Jim decided he needed to get out of this pretty quick. "Well, you know, I don't think I'm going to wait on that drink. Got to get a hotel room, get ready for tomorrow."

"Naw, dunt do 'at. Er, led me buy ya a drank. Miz. You in dem tidht panss."

So the waitress came over and the bear ordered some drinks for them both. Jim kept trying to leave, but no go. Before he knew it, he was almost as hammered as the bear.

Finally, the bear, just two breaths short of a complete slur, said, "Eber thang 'ere is den times duh prize. Leds go ta a real bar." He paused. " Daby Crogett killed a bar." And then the bear broke into insane laughter.

"Wen e wus ony tree . . . three. Always subone gad ta shood sub bar subware. Cum on, eds go. I know dis town ligh duh bag ob muh 'and."

They closed down a midtown bar. Jim remembered that pretty well. And then Jim remembered something about the bear saying they ought to have some companionship, and then things got muddled. He awoke in a little motel room, discovered the air was full of the smell of moldy bear fur, alcohol farts, a coppery aroma, and sweaty perfume.

Sitting up in bed, Jim was astonished to find a very plump girl with short blonde hair next to him in bed. She was lying facedown, one long, bladder-like tit sticking out from under her chest, the nipple pierced with a ring that looked like a washer.

Jim rolled out of bed and stood up beside it. He was nude and sticky. "Shit," he said. He observed the hump under the sheet some more, the washer in the tit. And then, as his eyes adjusted, he looked across the room and saw another bed, and he could see on the bedpost the bear's hat, and then the bear, lying on the bed without his pants. There was another lump under the blanket. One delicate foot stuck out from under the blanket near the end of the bed, a gold chain around the ankle. The bear was snoring softly. There were clothes all over the floor, a pair of panties large enough to be used as a sling for the wounded leg of a hippopotamus was dangling from the light fixture. That would belong to his date.

Except for his shoes and socks, Jim found his clothes and put them on and sat in a chair at a rickety table and put his head in his hands. He repeated softly over and over, "Shit, shit, shit."

With his hands on his face, he discovered they had a foul smell about them, somewhere between working-man sweat and a tuna net. He was hit with a sudden revelation that made him feel ill. He slipped into the bathroom and showered and redressed, this time putting on his socks and shoes. When he came out the light was on over the table and the bear was sitting there, wearing his clothes, even his hat.

"Damn, man," the bear said, his drunk gone, "that was some time we had. I think. But, I got to tell you, man, you got the ugly one."

Jim sat down at the table, feeling as if he had

just been hit by a car. "I don't remember anything."

"Hope you remembered she stunk. That's how I tracked them down, on a corner. I could smell her a block away. I kind of like that, myself. You know, the smell. Bears, you know how it is. But, I seen her, and I thought, Goddamn, she'd have to sneak up on a glass of water, so I took the other one. You said you didn't care."

"Oh God," Jim said.

"The fun is in the doing, not the remembering. Trust me, some things aren't worth remembering."

"My wife will kill me."

"Not if you don't tell her."

"I've never done anything like this before."

"Now you've started. The fat one, I bet she drank twelve beers before she pissed herself."

"Oh, Jesus."

"Come on, let's get out of here. I gave the whores the last of my money. And I gave them yours."

"What?"

"I asked you. You said you didn't mind."

"I said I don't remember a thing. I need that money."

"I know that. So do I."

The bear got up and went over to his bed and picked up the whore's purse and rummaged through it, took out the money. He then found the other whore's purse on the floor, opened it up, and took out money.

Jim staggered to his feet. He didn't like this, not even a little bit. But he needed his money back. Was it theft if you paid for services you didn't remember?

Probably. But . . .

As Jim stood, in the table light, he saw that on the bear's bed was a lot of red paint, and then he saw it wasn't paint, saw too, that the whore's head was missing. Jim let out a gasp and staggered a little.

The bear looked at him. The expression on his face was oddly sheepish.

"Thought we might get out of here without you seeing that. Sometimes, especially if I've been drinking, and I'm hungry, I revert to my basic nature. If it's any consolation, I don't remember doing that."

"No. No. It's no consolation at all."

At this moment, the fat whore rolled over in bed and sat up and the covers dropped down from her, and the bear, moving very quickly, got over there and with a big swipe of his paw sent a spray of blood and a rattle of teeth flying across the room, against the wall. The whore fell back, half her face clawed away.

"Oh, Jesus. Oh my God."

"This killing I remember," the bear said. "Now come on, we got to wipe everything down before we leave, and we don't have all night."

• • •

They walked the streets in blowing snow, and even though it was cold, Jim felt as if he were in some kind of fever dream. The bear trudged along beside him, said, "I had one of the whores pay for the room in cash. They never even saw us at the desk. Wiped down the prints in the room, anything we might have touched. I'm an expert at it. We're cool. Did that 'cause I know how these things can turn out. I've had it go bad before. Employers have got me out of a few scrapes, you know. I give them that. You okay, you look a little peaked."

"I . . . I . . ."

The bear ignored him, rattled on. "You know, I'm sure you can tell by now, I'm not really all that good with the ladies. On the plane, I was laying the bullshit on. . . . Damn, I got all this fur, but that don't mean I'm not cold. I ought to have like a winter uniform, you know, a jacket, with a big collar that I can turn up. Oh, by the way. I borrowed your cell phone to call out for pizza last night, but before I could, I dropped it and stepped on the motherfucker. Can you believe that? Squashed like a clam shell. I got it in my pocket. Have to throw it away. Okay. Let me be truthful. I had it in my back pocket and I sat my fat ass on it. That's the thing. . . . You a little hungry? Shit. I'm hungry. I'm cold."

That was the only comment for a few blocks, then the bear said, "Fuck this," and veered toward a car parked with several others at the curb. The bear reached in his pocket and took out a little packet, opened it. The street-lights revealed a series of shiny lock pick tools. He went to work on the car door with a tool that he unfolded and slid down the side of the car window until he could pull the lock. He opened the door, then said, "Get inside." The bear flipped a switch that unlocked the doors, and Jim, as if he were obeying the commands of a hypnotist, walked around to the other side and got in.

The bear was bent under the dash with his tools, and in a moment, the car roared to life. The bear sat in the seat and closed the door, said, "Seat belts. Ain't nobody rides in my car, they don't wear seat belts."

Jim thought: It's not your car. But he didn't say anything. He couldn't. His heart was in his mouth. He put on his seat belt.

They tooled along the snowy Denver streets and out of town and the bear said, "We're leaving this place, going to my stomping grounds. Yellowstone Park. Know some back trails. Got a pass. We'll be safe there. We can hang. I got a cabin. It'll be all right."

"I . . . I . . ." Jim said, but he couldn't find the rest of the sentence.

"Look in the glove box, see there's anything there. Maybe some prescription medicine of some kind. I could use a jolt."

"I . . ." Jim said, and then his voice died and he opened the glove box. There was a gun inside. Lazily, Jim reached for it.

The bear leaned over and took it from him. "You don't act like a guy been around guns much. Better let me have that." The bear, while driving, managed with one hand to pop out the clip and slide it back in. "A full load. Wonder he's got a gun permit. You know, I do. 'Course, not for this gun. But, beggars can't be choosers, now can they?"

"No. No. Guess not," Jim said, having thought for a moment that he would have the gun, that he could turn the tables, at least make the bear turn back toward Denver, let him out downtown.

"See any gum in there?" the bear asked. "Maybe he's got some gum. After that whore's head, I feel like my mouth has a pair of shitty shorts in it. Anything in there?"

Jim shook his head. "Nothing."

"Well, shit," the bear said.

The car roared on through the snowy night, the windshield wipers beating time, throwing snow wads left and right like drunk children tossing cotton balls.

The heater was on. It was warm. Jim felt a second wave of the alcohol blues; it wrapped around him like a warm blanket, and without really meaning to, he slept.

"I should be hibernating," the bear said, as if Jim

were listening. "That's why I'm so goddamn grumpy. The work. No hibernation. Paid poon and cheap liquor. That's no way to live."

The bear was a good driver in treacherous weather. He drove on through the night and made good time.

When Jim awoke it was just light and the light was red and it came through the window and filled the car like bloodstained streams of heavenly piss.

Jim turned his head. The bear had his hat cocked back on his head and he looked tired. He turned his head slightly toward Jim, showed some teeth at the corner of his mouth, then glared back at the snowy road.

"We got a ways to go yet, but we're almost to Yellowstone. You been asleep two days."

"Two days."

"Yeah. I stopped for gas once, and you woke up once and you took a piss."

"I did."

"Yeah. But you went right back to sleep."

"Good grief. I've never been that drunk in my life."

"Probably the pills you popped."

"What?"

"Pills. You took them with the alcohol, when we were with the whores."

"Oh, hell."

"It's all right. Every now and again you got to cut the tiger loose, you know? Don't worry. I got a cabin. That's where we're going. Don't worry. I'll take care of you. I mean, hell, what are friends for?"

The bear didn't actually have a cabin, he had a fire tower, and it rose up high into the sky overlooking very tall trees. They had to climb a ladder up there, and the bear, sticking the automatic in his belt, sent Jim up first, said, "Got to watch those rungs. They get wet, iced over, your hand can slip. Forest ranger I knew slipped right near the top. We had to dig what was left of him out of the ground. One of his legs went missing. I found it about a month later. It was cold when he fell so it kept pretty good. Wasn't bad, had it with some beans. Waste not, want not. Go on, man. Climb."

Inside the fire tower it was very nice, though cold. The bear turned on the electric heater and it wasn't long before the place was toasty.

The bear said, "There's food in the fridge. Shitter is over there. I'll sleep in my bed, and you sleep on the couch. This'll be great. We can hang. I got all kinds of movies, and as you can see, that TV is big enough for a drive-in theater. We ain't got no bitches, but hell, they're just trouble anyway. We'll just pull each other's wieners."

Jim said, "What now?"

"I don't stutter, boy. It ain't so bad. You just grease a fellow up and go to work."

"I don't know."

"Nah, you'll like it."

As night neared, the light that came through the tower's wraparound windows darkened and died, and Jim could already imagine grease on his hands.

But by then, the bear had whetted his whistle pretty good, drinking straight from a big bottle of Jack Daniel's. He wasn't as wiped-out as before, not stumbling drunk, and his tongue still worked, but fortunately the greased weenie pull had slipped from the bear's mind. He sat on the couch with his bottle and Jim sat on the other end, and the bear said:

"Once upon a goddamn time the bears roamed these forests and we were the biggest, baddest, meanest motherfuckers in the woods. That's no shit. You know that?"

Jim nodded.

"But, along come civilization. We had fires before that, I'm sure. You know, natural stuff. Lightning. Too dry. Natural combustion. But when man arrived, it was doo-doo time for the bears and everything else. I mean, don't take me wrong. I like a good meal and a beer"—

he held up the bottle—"and some Jack, and hanging out in this warm tower, but something has been sapped out of me. Some sort of savage beast that was in me has been tapped and run off into the ground . . . I was an orphan. Did you know that?"

"I've heard the stories," Jim said.

"Yeah, well, who hasn't? It was a big fire. I was young. Some arsonists. Damn fire raged through the forest and I got separated from my mom. Dad, he'd run off. But, you know, no biggie. That's how bears do. Well, anyway, I climbed a tree like a numb nuts cause my feet got burned, and I just clung and clung to that tree. And then I seen her, my mother. She was on fire. She ran this way and that, back and forth, and I'm yelling, 'Mama,' but she's not paying attention, had her own concerns. And pretty soon she goes down and the fire licks her all over and her fur is gone and there ain't nothing but a blackened hunk of smoking bear crap left. You know what it is to see a thing like that, me being a cub?"

"I can't imagine."

"No, you can't. You can't. No one can. I had a big fall, too. I don't really remember it, but it left a knot on the back of my head, just over the right ear. . . . Come here. Feel that."

Jim dutifully complied.

The bear said, "Not too hard now. That knot, that's

like my Achilles' heel. I'm weak there. Got to make sure I don't bump my head too good. That's no thing to live with and that's why I'm not too fond of arsonists. There are several of them, what's left of them, buried not far from here. I roam these forests and I'll tell you, I don't just report them. Now and again, I'm not doing that. Just take care of business myself. Let me tell you, slick, there's a bunch of them that'll never squat over a commode again. They're out there, their gnawed bones buried deep. You know what it's like to be on duty all the time, not to be able to hibernate, just nap? It makes a bear testy. Want a cigar?"

"Beg your pardon?"

"A cigar. I know its funny coming from me, and after what I just told you, but we'll be careful here in my little nest."

Jim didn't answer. The bear got up and came back with two fat black cigars. He had boxed matches with him. He gave Jim a cigar and Jim put it in his mouth, and the bear said, "Puff gently."

Jim did and the bear lit the end with a wooden match. The bear lit his own cigar. He tossed the box of matches to Jim. "If it goes out, you can light up again. Thing about a cigar is you take your time, just enjoy it, don't get into it like a whore sucking a dick. It's done casual. Pucker your mouth like you're kissing a baby."

Jim puffed on the cigar but didn't inhale. The action

of it made him feel high, and not too good, a little sick even. They sat and smoked. After a long while, the bear got up and opened one of the windows, said, "Come here."

Jim went. The woods were alive with sounds, crickets, night birds, howling.

"That's as it should be. Born in the forest, living there, taking game there, dying there, becoming one with the soil. But look at me. What the fuck have I become? I'm like a goddamn circus bear."

"You do a lot of good."

"For who, though? The best good I've done was catching those arsonists that are buried out there. That was some good. I'll be straight with you, Jim. I'm happy you're going to be living here. I need a buddy, and, well, tag, you're it."

"Buddy."

"You heard me. Oh, the door, it's locked, and you can't work the lock from inside, 'cause it's keyed, and I got the key. So don't think about going anywhere."

"That's not very buddy-like," Jim said.

The bear studied Jim for a long moment, and Jim felt himself going weak. It was as if he could see the bear's psychosis move from one eye to the other, like it was changing rooms. "But, you're still my buddy, aren't you, Jim?"

Jim nodded.

"Well, I'm sort of bushed, so I think I'll turn in early. Tomorrow night we'll catch up on that weenie pull."

When the bear went to the bedroom and lay down, Jim lay on the couch with the blanket and pillow the bear had left for him, and listened. The bear had left the bedroom door open, and after a while he could hear the bear snoring like a lumberjack working a saw on a log.

Jim got up and eased around the tower and found that he could open windows, but there was nowhere to go from there except straight down, and that was one booger of a drop. Jim thought of how easily the bear had killed the whore and how he admitted to killing others, and then he thought about tomorrow night's weenie pull, and he became even more nervous.

After an hour of walking about and looking, he realized there was no way out. He thought about the key, but had no idea where the bear kept it. He feared if he went in the bear's room to look, he could startle the bear and that might result in getting his head chewed off. He decided to let it go. For now. Ultimately, pulling a greased bear weenie couldn't be as bad as being headless.

Jim went back to the couch, pulled the blanket over him, and almost slept.

Next morning, Jim, who thought he would never sleep, had finally drifted off, and what awoke him was not a noise, but the smell of food cooking. Waffles.

Jim got up slowly. A faint pink light was coming through the window. The kitchenette area of the tower was open to view, part of the bigger room, and the bear was in there wearing an apron and a big chef's hat. The bear turned, saw him. The apron had a slogan on it: IF MOMMA AIN'T HAPPY, AIN'T NOBODY HAPPY.

The bear spotted him, gave Jim a big-fanged, wet smile. "Hey, brother, how are you? Come on in here and sit your big ass down and have one of Mr. Bear's waffles. It's so good you'll want to slap your momma."

Jim went into the kitchenette, sat at the table where the bear instructed. The bear seemed in a light and cheery mood. Coffee was on the table, a plate stacked with waffles, big strips of bacon, pats of butter, and a bottle of syrup in a plastic bear modeled after Mr. Bear himself.

"Now you wrap your lips around some of this stuff, see what you think."

While Jim ate, the bear regaled him with all manner of stories about his life, and most were in fact interesting, but all Jim could think about was the bear biting the head off that hooker, and then slashing the other with a strike of his mighty paw. As Jim ate, the tasty waffles with thick syrup became wads of blood and flesh in his mouth, and he felt as if he were eating of Mr. Bear's wine and wafer, his symbolic blood and flesh, and it made Jim's skin crawl.

All it would take to end up like the whores was a misstep. Say something wrong. Perhaps a misinterpreted look. A hesitation at tonight's weenie pull. . . . Oh, damn, Jim thought. The weenie pull.

"What I thought we'd do is we'd go for a drive, dump the car. There's a ravine I know where we can run it off, and no one will see it again. Won't even know it's missing. Excuse me while I go to the shitter. I think I just got word there's been a waffle delivery called."

The bear laughed at his own joke and left the room. Jim ate a bit more of the waffle and all the bacon. He didn't want the bear to think he wasn't grateful. The beast was clearly psychotic. Anything could set him off.

Jim got up and washed his hands at the sink, and just as he was passing into the living room, he saw the gun they had found in the car, lying on a big fluffy chair. Part of it, the barrel, had slipped into the crack in the cushions. Maybe the bear had forgotten all about it, or at least didn't have it at the forefront of his mind. That was it. He'd been drunker than a Shriners' convention. He probably didn't even remember having the gun.

Jim eased over and picked up the weapon and put it under his shirt, in the small of his back. He hoped he would know how to use it. He had seen them used before. If he could get up close enough—

"Now, that was some delivery. That motherfucker probably came with a fortune cookie and six-pack of Coke. I feel ten pounds lighter. You ready, Jimbo?"

In the early morning, the forests were dark and beautiful and there was a slight mist, and with the window of the car rolled down, it was cool and damp and the world seemed newborn. But all Jim could think about was performing a greased weenie pull and then getting his head chewed off.

Jim said, "You get rid of the car, how do we get back?"

The bear laughed. "Just like a citizen. We walk, of course."

"We've gone quite a distance."

"It'll do you good. Blow out the soot. You'll like it. Great scenery. I'm gonna show you the graves where I buried what was left of them fellows, the arsonists."

"That's all right," Jim said. "I don't need to see that."

"I want you to. It's not like I can show everyone, but my bestest bud, that's a different matter, now ain't it?"

"Well, I don't . . ." Jim said.

"We're going to see it."

"Sure. Okay."

Jim had a sudden revelation. Maybe there never was going to be a weenie pull, and as joyful as that perception was, the alternative was worse. The bear was going to get rid of him. Didn't want to do it in his tower. You don't shit where you eat. . . . Well, the bear might. But the idea was you kept your place clean of problems. This wasn't just a trip to dump the car, this was a death ride. The bear was going to kill him and leave him where the arsonists were. Jim felt his butthole clench on the car seat.

They drove up higher and the woods grew thicker and the road turned off and onto a trail. The car bumped along for some miles until the trees overwhelmed everything but the trail, and the tree limbs were so thickly connected they acted as a kind of canopy overhead. They drove in deep shadow and there were spots where the shadows were broken by light and the light played across the trail in speckles and spots, and birds shot across their view like feathered bullets, and twice there were deer in sight, bounding into the forest and disappearing like wraiths as the car passed.

They came to a curve and then a sharp rise and the

bear drove up the rise. The trail played out, and still he drove. He came to a spot, near the peak of the hill, where the sun broke through, stopped the car, and got out. Jim got out. They walked to the highest rise of the hill, and where they stood was a clean, wide swath in the trees. Weeds and grass grew there. The grass was tall and mostly yellow but brown in places.

"Spring comes," the bear said. "There will be flowers, all along that path, on up to this hill, bursting all over it. This is my forest, Jim. All the dry world used to be a forest, or nearly was, but man has cut most of it down and that's done things to all of us and I don't think in the long run much of it is good. Before man, things had a balance, know what I mean? But man . . . oh, boy. He sucks. Like that fire that burned me. Arson. Just for the fun of it. Burned down my goddamn home, Jim. I was just a cub. Little. My mother dying like that . . . I always feel two to three berries short of a pie."

"I'm sorry."

"Aren't they all? Sorry. Boy, that sure makes it better, don't it. Shit." The bear paused and looked over the swath of meadow. He said, "Even with there having been snow, it's dry, and when it's dry, someone starts a fire, it'll burn. The snow don't mean a thing after it melts and the thirsty ground sucks it up, considering it's mostly been dry all year. That one little snow, it ain't nothing more than whipped cream on dry cake." The bear pointed down the hill. "That swath there, it would burn like gasoline on a shag carpet. I keep an eye out for those things. I try to keep this forest safe. It's a thankless and continuous job. . . . Sometimes I have to leave, get a bit of recreation . . . like the motel room . . . time with a friend."

"I see."

"Do you? The graves I told you about. They're just down the hill. You see, they were bad people, but sometimes, even good people end up down there, if they know things they shouldn't, and there have been a few."

"Oh," Jim said, as if he had no idea what the bear was talking about.

"I don't make friends easily, and I may seem a little insincere. Species problems, all that. Sometimes even people I like, well . . . it doesn't turn out so well for them. Know what I'm saying?"

"I . . . I don't think so."

"I think you do. That motel room back there, those whores. I been at this for years. I'm not a serial killer or anything. Ones I kill deserve it. The people I work for. They know how I am. They protect me. How's it gonna be an icon goes to jail? That's what I am. A fuckin' icon. So I kinda get a free ride, someone goes missing, you know. Guys in black, ones got the helicopters and the black cars. They clean up after me. They're my homies, know what I'm saying?"

"Not exactly."

"Let me nutshell it for you: I'm pretty much immune to prosecution. But you, well . . . kind of a loose end. There's a patch down there with your name on it, Jimbo. I put a shovel in the car early this morning while you were sleeping. It isn't personal, Jim. I like you. I do. I know that's cold comfort, but that's how it is."

The bear paused, took off his hat and removed a small cigar from the inside hat band, then struck a match and took a puff, said, "Thing is, though, I can't get to liking someone too good, 'cause—"

The snapping sound made the bear straighten up. He was still holding his hat in his paw, and he dropped it. He almost made a turn to look at Jim, who was now standing right by him, holding the automatic to the bump on the bear's noggin. The bear's legs went out. He stumbled and fell forward and went sliding down the hill on his face and chest, a bullet snuggling in his brain.

Jim took a deep breath. He went down the hill and turned the bear's head using both hands, took a good look at him. He thought the bear didn't really look like any of the cartoon versions of him, and when he was on TV he didn't look so old. Of course, he had never looked dead before. The eyes had already gone flat and he could see his dim reflection in one of them.

The bear's cigar was flattened against his mouth, like a coiled worm. Jim found the bear's box of matches and was careful to use a handkerchief from the bear's paw to handle it. He struck the match and set the dry grass on fire, then stuck the match between the bear's claws on his left paw. The fire gnawed patiently at the grass, whipping up enthusiasm as the wind rose. Jim wiped down the automatic with his shirt tail and put it in the bear's right paw using the handkerchief, and pushed the bear's claw through the trigger guard, closing the bear's paw around the weapon so it looked like he had shot himself.

Jim went back up the hill. The fire licked at the grass and caught some more wind and grew wilder, and then the bear got caught up in it as well, the conflagration chewing his fur and cackling over his flesh like a crazed hag. The fire licked its way down the hill, and then the wind changed and Jim saw the fire climbing up toward him.

He got in the car and started it and found a place where he could back it around. It took some work, and by the time he managed it onto the narrow trail, he could see the fire in the mirror, waving its red head in his direction.

Jim drove down the hill, trying to remember the route. Behind him, the fire rose up into the trees as if it were a giant red bird spreading its wings.

"Dumb bear," he said aloud. "Ain't gonna be no weenie pull now, is there?" And he drove on until the fire was just a small bright spot in the rearview mirror, and then it was gone and there was just the tall, dark forest that the fire had yet to find.

Hell in a Handbasket

LUCIEN SOULBAN

The basket sat at the foot of the Inferno's red-hot, iron-wrought gates, below the steaming plate that read ABANDON ALL HOPE, YE WHO ENTER HERE! The ominous warning was wasted on the ebony-skinned baby, however, and it continued babbling. A burp followed; it giggled and cooed and the whole of the Underworld paused for a moment, pitchforks held frozen and tortures forgotten in media res.

"What the Hell was that?" a few demons were heard to whisper. But nobody wanted to be the chump to go and find out. Nobody volunteered in Hell. That, and sing-alongs, were frowned upon.

The ever-vigilant Cerberus, Guardian of the Gates of Hell and Angry Mutt of Damnation, padded up to the basket and looked around, confused and perhaps even surprised. He never saw who'd deposited the basket or why. Two of Cerberus's flanking heads peered around, while the middle one sniffed the basket carefully.

Yup . . . baby, most definitely, the heads agreed.

Cerberus's middle head considered swallowing the child whole.

"Do it, do it!" the left head whispered gruffly, obviously not interested in taking the risk itself. "You know you want to. All soft and juicy . . . just like we like 'em."

"I wouldn't do that," the right head counseled in a singsong tone, admonishing the left head. "Who leaves a child at the Gates of Hell? Or better yet, why? No, we should hand it off to someone who doesn't think with their stomach. Prudence is the better course here."

The middle head sighed and decided it best to delegate this chore to someone else; the three heads craned upward and Cerberus unleashed a ghastly howl. The gates opened slowly.

Roiling clouds of steam emanated from the cracks in the brass sidewalks of Dis; the screams of the damned and a thick blood clot of humidity saturated the air. Basket in hand, the demon Mastema, slayer of Egypt's firstborns, walked along, his cloven hooves sending sparks from the metal ground and scattering tinny echoes across the already noisy avenues. His once-perfect flesh remained scored and cracked from his plummet down, while the remnants of blackened feathers and scorched bones dangled from the shattered tree of his wings.

Mastema walked into the Great Assembly Hall, past several of Hell's senators and into the amphitheatre-style council chambers where Gressil, Devil of Slothfulness and Vile Slacker of the Pits, had convened a session. Only Gressil wasn't present; he was slacking off somewhere, much to nobody's surprise. Gressil's calls for a council were a national holiday in Hell, and everyone looked forward to propping their hooves up for the day.

That left the chambers relatively empty of all but a dozen damned. Mastema dropped the basket on the central dais of iron, immediately attracting the attention of those present.

"Anyone order this kid?" Mastema asked the assembled throng.

"Kid?" a voice asked.

Mastema looked up to see the human-looking Gaap hanging upside down from the ceiling's cathedral rafters. Bat wings unfurled from his human form, and he dropped to the floor with frightening grace.

"What d'ya know," Gaap said. "It *is* a kid. What happened, Mastema? Miss one of the Pharaoh's first-born?"

"One, he's not Egyptian," Mastema said. "Try to stay current. And two, I was following orders."

By now, the remaining devils and demons moved to the dais, craning their long necks and clucking to gain a better view of the child. The baby appeared delighted by the attention.

"Right," Gaap said, ribbing a fellow demon with his elbow. "Following orders. I think there's a few Nazis in the Seventh and Eighth Circles still singing that tune."

"The Egyptians invented beer," Mastema said. "I got nothing against them."

"Good point," Gaap replied.

"So," Mastema said. "Anyone order the kid?"

"Ooh, I did, I did." The demon deer Furfur spoke this time, He of the Unholy Venison, jumping up and down with cloven delight.

"Yeah?" Mastema asked, looking into the basket. "If you ordered him, what's he look like?"

"Small 'n black 'n soft," Furfur said, licking his chops.

"Sounds about right," Harpy said, looking inside

the basket. She lifted the baby's diaper and stole a peek inside. "Ohhh. Sorry, Furfur. Did Mastema say 'he'? You almost had it right except for that pesky genitals thing. It's a 'she.' "

"Darn."

"Well, how am I supposed to tell?" Mastema grumbled. "I'm about as anatomically correct as a Barbie doll."

"And they sent you down to kill the firstborn sons?" Gaap said with a barking laugh.

"Shut up," Mastema replied. "I got most of them, didn't I?"

"What have we here?" a new voice asked. Everyone turned as Vassago, Demon of Prophesy and the Kool Kat of Hell, walked up to the group. His large red wings melted into his back and vanished out of sight; otherwise, he looked human with his charming smile and combed-back brown hair. He was sporting a gray blazer and trousers.

"You order this kid?" Mastema asked.

A grin crept across Vassago's face and he pushed past the others to peer inside the basket. "Well . . . isn't she a cutie," he said, genuinely delighted. "Who she belong to?"

Mastema shrugged.

"Maybe we should split her," Gaap said, running his scalpel-like claws across the sides of the basket.

"That's your answer for everything," Vassago said, tickling the baby's dimpled chin. She cooed and grabbed his finger.

"Seriously, Gaap," Harpy said. " 'Let's split Hitler,' you said. All I got was his pinky; at least you got a leg."

"I got his mustache," the wolf-headed Mammon said, stroking the 'stache on his upper lip.

"Looking good, Mammon," Harpy replied.

"Well, I think I should eat her," Mammon said. "As the Demon of Avarice, it would be bad for my image if I didn't."

"Nobody's eating her," Vassago said.

A cacophony of voices broke out in dissent and a few demons began pushing each other away. Vassago decided to end the argument.

"Fine . . . we'll settle this according to the Old Ways, the Dead Ways," Vassago said. A hush fell over the chambers.

"Fight to the death," someone whispered.

"No! Choose a champion to battle for her meat," someone else countered.

Vassago shook his head and picked up the child. "Older than that," he replied. He licked her exposed tummy with his snaking tongue. She giggled. "There . . . I licked her, she's mine now."

"Since when is that a rule?!" Harpy protested.

"Fine, if you don't care about the Old Ways and the traditions set by the Ancient Ones, then go ahead and take her," Vassago replied casually. Several hands and claws reached out for the child, but it was Harpy that snatched her away by the legs with a triumphant shriek. The infant, however, seemed not the least discomforted being in her iron claws or upside down. A few demons seemed ready to tackle Harpy, however, infant and all.

"Of course," Vassago said, his words smooth, "you are running a risk here."

"What d'ya mean?" Furfur asked.

"Oh, I don't know. Like what if someone else ordered the child?" Vassago asked with a shrug. He began walking away. "Like Belial . . . or Asmodeus."

"Oh yeah," some of the demons whispered.

"Asmodeus . . . I forgot about him," Furfur said. "He's a mean drunk."

"Best you left the girl in my care," Vassago said.

"Thanks, but no thanks," Harpy replied. "She's mine to devour."

Vassago slowly walked away, nonplussed in demeanor but listening carefully to the exchange at his back.

"Stop touching her, Beelzebub. You're getting flies all over her," Harpy said.

"ZZZZzzzzz!"

"Oh, for the love of . . . ! Does anyone here understand what Beelzebub is saying? Mastema?"

"No. And the last time I tried talking to him, he regurgitated all over me," Mastema replied.

Quickly, the sounds of discord echoed through the Great Assembly Hall, the gathered and growing throng of demons fighting with Harpy for the child. And through the angry voices and the shouting and screaming, Vassago knew the baby would come to him eventually. Only he knew what she was, and only he knew how to deal with her.

Harpy tore through the air, the infant in the iron-clawed talons of her feet. Other demons tried flying after her, but she was faster and more cunning than them all. She darted in between the spires and thorny pinnacles of Dis's cathedral roofs, through broken windows and back out again, each time losing more pursuers. Finally, she soared high into the sky, heading for one of the abandoned churches growing down from the cavern's ceiling. Harpy settled into the crumbling niche of a red tower, behind the wailing statue of a demonic saint.

Satisfied nobody had followed her, Harpy held the child up with both hands. She smiled, her shredding, malicious grin stretched from ear to ear. The infant girl, however, chirped and cooed, much to Harpy's discomfort. Her large black eyes seemed to suck in everything around her.

"You're too stupid to be afraid, aren't you?" Harpy whispered. "Oh yes you are, oh yes you are," she said in a suddenly playful voice before pursing her lips against the infant's stomach and blowing mouth farts against her satin skin. "Who's a silly little girl!" Harpy chirped. "You are! You are!" Harpy and the child laughed out loud.

The smile, however, quickly vanished from Harpy's lips. "Wait," she said. "What am I doing?" For a moment, she felt displaced, seven leagues from the center of herself. This wasn't her. She should be tearing into the flesh of this infant, not playing with her, not engaging in nonsensical talk.

Harpy strengthened her resolve and stared at the infant with all the cruelty and malice she could muster. She would tell the child the horrible fate about to befall her, the hellish torture awaiting her. Harpy would explain in visceral detail how she was going to skin the screaming baby and suck up her strands of flesh like spaghetti. She smiled at her own cruelty and opened her mouth to speak.

"Cootchy cootchy coo!" Harpy hissed. Her eyes widened and she tried talking again. "Boobiwooboo," she said, her words trapped in babyspeak.

The child obviously approved; she giggled and jumped up and down in Harpy's grasp.

"Stop it!" Harpy wanted to say, but more nonsense spilled out instead. She tried to squeeze the infant to stop her from laughing, but the little girl giggled as Harpy tickled her with nary a scratch from her dagger talons.

"Cotchy coo!" Harpy screamed. She tried to let go of the laughing baby, to watch her plummet, but could not. The young girl was somehow glued to her hands. She tried to shake the child loose, but instead bounced her up and down gently.

I know, Harpy thought, her mind twisting and slipping in panic. *I'll corrupt the child!* After cradling the baby in her feathered lap, Harpy slid one sharp talon across her own wrist, drawing out her tarlike blood. It boiled and bubbled against the demon's skin, and she reveled at the thought of blistering the child's flesh. The infant opened her mouth expectantly and Harpy squeezed her own arm to force the turgid blood to flow quicker.

White droplets fell into the baby's mouth instead.

Harpy shrieked and stared at the ivory blood flowing from her wrist.

Milk! she realized in horror. *My blood's turned to milk.* Before Harpy could stop the little girl, the child latched her mouth onto one of her calloused nipples and began feeding. Harpy was lactating, and she couldn't pull the defenseless child from her breast.

She shrieked again, a wail that pierced the very corridors of Dis.

Vassago crossed the shag-carpeted floor of his creamy yellow bachelor pad. A Sinatra record, spinning out the best of the Vegas hits, played softly in the background, and his home smelled of sandalwood and a fresh ocean breeze. A cool wind filtered through the white curtains, and the rapid knocking persisted.

Hell's Suave Playboy opened the door to the tempest and infernal heat of Dis; the glamours filling his house shuddered slightly but held against the realities of the Underworld. Outside his door was Hell. Inside was Hollywood, circa 1960s. *A golden time,* he thought.

"Why, Harpy," Vassago said, smiling at the demon at his door. "How nice to see you."

"Bite me!" she said, thrusting the child in his direction. "You take her."

"Certainly," Vassago replied. He cradled the child and raised an eyebrow at Harpy. "You look . . . radiant. Motherhood agrees with you."

"I'm *lactating*!" she moaned. She grabbed one breast and pointed it at him. Milk dribbled down from her exposed nipple.

"Thank you, but I'm not thirsty," Vassago said.

"Furfur wants a sip!"

"Who wouldn't! Don't dribble on the carpet, dear," Vassago said kindly.

"Wait!" Harpy protested, looking for some trade to make good on giving the baby away, but Vassago closed the door with his foot as he turned around. The door slammed in her face and the smell of brimstone evaporated.

"Aren't you the cute one," Vassago said, stroking the baby's chin. She giggled in return, her Afro still wild and untamed. He sat in a molded chair, its white cushioned pads arched up the high back, and played with her for a while.

"Now," he said, a knowing grin splashed across his face, "do I call you Eve? Or the Serpent?"

The infant girl clapped her hands in approval and bounced in his grip.

"Right, Eve . . . of course. The serpent is our domain, isn't it?" he said, and continued to play and laugh right alongside her.

Eve slept on the wide-lipped couch, her tiny fists bunched up at her chest, her face filled with innocent trust. Vassago smiled at her. He may have had his shortcomings, but he genuinely liked humans.

They were a delightful species and highly inventive. In fact, after Applegate with Eve pulling a Yoko Ono on Adam and the Garden of Eden, Vassago came to appreciate humans all the more. They were no longer chimpanzees with souls.

The knocking persisted.

Vassago took a moment to compose himself before opening the door. Koka and Vikoka, the twin demon generals of Kali, stood waiting. They towered above the door, their once feral and fearful countenances surprisingly shy and darting. They appeared nervous and uncertain in their posture, which was unlike the twin ambassadors from the Realm of Hungry Ghosts. Koka played with the skulls wrapped around his neck; Vikoka looked even more crimson and fidgeted with the weighted and bloodied yellow sash around his waist.

"Yes?"

"Hello, Mr. Vassago," Koka said. "We, uh . . . we heard you have a human infant?"

News travels fast, Vassago thought. Soon his house would be inundated with demon callers trying to woo Eve out of his charge and onto their dinner plates. "Yes, she is," Vassago said.

"Can she, uh, come out to play?" Vikoka asked, beaming with a nasty grin. Bits of hair and flesh from his last meal lay wedged between his teeth and tusks.

"I'm afraid not," Vassago said. He tried closing the door, but Koka gently stopped it with his hand.

"Well, I'm sure as you know, we serve Kali," Koka said earnestly.

"And as you also know," Vikoka added, "we need sacrifices to keep her sated, lest she awakens in a terrible bloodlust."

"She's *not* a morning person," Koka confided with a whisper.

"Yes, yes," Vassago said, massaging the bridge of his nose. Each ritual murder was supposed to forestall the arrival of Kali by one millennium and blah blah blah. Western Hell had enough of its conditions and qualifications to distract a demon for a lifetime without throwing Asia's into the mix. It was, after all, the original bureaucracy. "Yes, well, when Kali rises, I'll be sure to bid her good morning and match her armies against my Legions. Until then, the child stays here. Good-bye."

No sooner had Vassago closed the door than the doorbell rang again. Vassago sighed and opened it; at this rate, it would take hours for the glamours to fully shroud the reek of brimstone again.

The Succubus twins, Lilith and Naamah, had taken Koka and Vikoka's places. They were much more pleasant to look at, their naked bodies taut and covered in a skin of oil and dewlike sweat. They undulated against each other, a form of greeting Vassago highly appreciated. Why, it almost brought a black tear to his eye, but he remained suspicious. Hell was like a trailer-trash family reunion on *Jerry Springer.* If demons weren't fornicating with each other like country siblings, they were feuding and squabbling . . . sometimes in the middle of intercourse.

The succubae offered Vassago their best lascivious smiles and ran their fingers across each other's erect nipples.

"Hiya, Vas," they said in unison, Lilith trying to entice Vassago with her come-hither-and-anywhere-else-you-like look while Naamah stole glances into the apartment.

"Ladies," Vassago said, offering them a flat smile.

"Remember when you said you'd invite us over to your place for dinner sometime," Lilith said.

"No, not rea—"

"Well, I brought dessert," Lilith replied, pushing her smiling companion forward. "There's enough of her for both of us to, uhm . . . eat."

Naamah smiled and sent her forked tongue across her lips.

"Unfortunately, I already devoured the mortal infant," Vassago said.

"Well . . . pooh. Isn't there anything left?"

"I'd settle for sucking out her marrow," Naamah said with a hopeful smile.

"Sorry. All gone," Vassago said. "Phew!" He unbuttoned his pants to emphasize how full he was.

"Okay, fine," Lilith replied, rolling her eyes. She shimmied down to her knees, obviously misunderstanding Vassago's pantomime.

"Whoa, ladies!" Vassago said, prying his zipper out from her claws and backing away. "That's not what I meant . . . well . . . okay, maybe later." He jetted out his gut. "I was trying to say, 'I'm full.'" He patted his stomach. "And lo, she was tasty."

With that, Vassago closed the door. He hesitated, and then opened it again. Sure enough, Hecate stood there now, one hand poised over the door to knock, the other hand filing her iron teeth.

"Hi, Vassago, you tricky devil," she said. "Is—"

"No."

"Can I—"

"No."

"But—"

"Go away," Vassago said with a sigh and shut the door. Before anyone else could knock, he quickly erected another glamour to silence the doors and windows. Satisfied at the momentary quiet, he absently swatted at a fly. He paused.

Why is there a fly in my home? he wondered suddenly.

In fact, the smell of brimstone should have started vanishing. He shook his head and headed for the couch. A sigh escaped his lips. Little Eve was gone and one of the windows was open.

A flash of momentary annoyance stabbed Vassago, and his human features slipped a touch. The umber of burnt skin and the ghost of long horns shimmered through, but he caught himself. His features returned back to human and Vassago went into the kitchen to fix himself a martini. The child would likely find her way back to him soon enough. He knew who had stolen her and doubted they'd last all that long.

"Did you get her?" Lilith asked. Both seductresses walked down the twisting Escher-like stairs into the basement dungeon. Their arrival was greeted by the wailing chorus of the damned so long chained to the walls that they were half-melted into them. The souls of the tortured writhed horribly; a legion of maggots covered their bodies and ate at their eyes and the nubs of their tongues, swelling their throats and stomachs with their squirming mass.

At the center of the stained stone floor was an altar of iron, set between two braziers lit with the dying embers of souls. Presiding over the altar was none other than Beelzebub, Lord of the Flies and winner of last year's Dancing with the Damned—where unwilling souls were forced to salsa, mambo, and lock pop with Hell's luminaries.

Beelzebub stood over the blood-and-excrement–crusted altar where baby Eve lay. His head was that of a giant fly, his body covered in the torn robes of a defrocked pope, and his skin a thick mass of millions of flies and squirming maggots. From his back emerged two tattered fly wings and stunted fly legs. In his maggot-coated claw, he held a curved iron dagger, the blade dark with rust and caked viscera.

"Bzzzzz!" Beelzebub chanted, ignoring the two succubae until they slithered up alongside him. The demonesses eyed the child and licked their lips, eager for the slaughter. The child smiled up at them, and her ignorance of her fate excited the three devils even more.

"I want one of her chubby little legs," Lilith said.

"Bzzz?" Beelzebub suggested. He stroked Lilith's thigh with his slimy hand.

"But we distracted Vassago for you!" Naamah complained.

"Zzz! Zz!"

"Fine," Lilith replied, flicking away the maggots that he'd left behind on her leg. "But the last time, you left fly eggs inside us both. We were itching for weeks. This time you wear protection."

"Trojans are good," Naamah suggested.

"They complain too much, more so than the Athenians," Lilith replied. "So, Beelzebub, agreed?"

"Bzz," Beelzebub said, agreeing to the terms. The flies covering his body buzzed louder in anticipation.

Beelzebub returned his attentions to Eve. He raised his blade, ready for the sacrificial plunge . . . and froze. A beautiful purple and red butterfly rose into the air before them. It fluttered momentarily before rising higher and vanishing. The three hellish hosts eyed one another. Lilith shrugged. The Lord of the Flies prepared a second time to plunge the knife into Eve.

Another butterfly, this one yellow and green, flitted up. This time, the two succubae backed away from a confused Beelzebub. More butterflies fluttered up into the air, their wings a brilliant collage of bejeweled hues, each prettier than the last. Eve clapped and chirped at the sight. Beelzebub, however, dropped the dagger and stared at himself. The butterflies were emerging from *him*. Blue and green bottle flies, houseflies, horseflies, and an assorted other myriad pests were turning into monarchs, blue morphos, goliath birdwings, peacocks, swallowtails of all ilks, and a dozen more species of Amazon flare and brilliance.

Even maggots weren't spared the touch and, within seconds, Beelzebub screeched at the butterflies that bloomed from his skin by the thousands. He was aflame in color. He spun and batted at his arms and legs, but the flies continued transforming.

"Stop, drop, and roll!" the succubae cried urgently, but the butterflies continued to fill the air with their kaleidoscopic wings.

Even the maggots devouring the gauze bodies of trapped souls joined the rainbow cloud. The tortured and harrowed cries diminished and for the first time in eons, the souls felt the forgotten sensation called relief.

Beelzebub, however, cried even louder in his fly voice, his own wings betraying him by adopting the mottled emerald and ivory patterns of the marble butterfly. His body continued to dissolve into a beautiful mosaic of color, and the two succubae ran from the chamber, abandoning him to the hiccupping laughter of Eve and the gorgeous swarms that floated above her like painted clouds.

News filtered in slowly, like war reports telegraphed back from the frontlines. First Beelzebub had her, but he was now somewhere in South America or Asia, collecting flies for his new body. Harpy had been charging the other demons for a sip of fresh milk from her teat before her wells finally curdled. Greedy Mammon was said to have taken Eve next, until he was seen running from his palace of gold and bones in a red suit and white beard, crying "ho ho ho" in frightened desperation.

It wasn't until Vassago opened his door, however, that he knew the game was at an end.

Towering well above him was Satan himself, his half-naked body cut to Spartan envy, his skin ruby red, and his long, slender horns swept upward.

From two of Satan's taloned fingers dangled the baby basket. Inside it, Eve giggled in delight.

"Is this *thing* yours?" Satan asked, his voice slipping over Vassago like warm honey. Curiously, he sounded like Tim Curry.

Someone's a fan of Legend, Vassago thought. "Mine? No, no," Vassago said, taking the basket. "But I approve of the jest," he amended.

"Hm," Satan replied, his attention equally focused and distracted. "See you return her with a little jest of our own."

"Of course," Vassago said as he bowed. He peered inside the basket and took the doll from Eve's arms. It was a stuffed animal . . . a bipedal deer with horns. "You gave her a plushy of Furfur?" Vassago asked and cocked his eyebrow higher.

"That *is* Furfur," Satan replied, obviously annoyed. He nodded to Eve. "It's her doing."

Vassago noticed the large tear across the doll's rump and the stuffing coming out of it. "And the orifice?" he asked.

"I was bored," Satan said. "And it's a lesson to Furfur for being so easily beguiled by the child. In fact, Furfur is the first stop of many today."

"It was all rather funny," Vassago said, smiling.

Satan harrumphed and walked away, the bronze ground trembling with his cloven footfalls. Vassago closed the door, allowing Billie Holiday's voice to flush through the house and a salted breeze to wash away the sulfur. He sat on the couch and let baby Eve play with her Furfur plushy before announcing, "Sorry to see you go, sweetheart. It's time for you to return home. But first, I have something to prepare. Now," he said to himself, "where's that umbrella?"

The clouds were immaculately white and cotton-candy fluffy. The Golden Gates gleamed and sparkled, the metal burnished to mirror sharpness. Saint Peter, Heaven's DMV clerk, didn't bother looking up from his pedestal; he dipped his quill in the inkwell and held it poised over his giant ledger. "Next!" he cried impatiently, shaking the long white beard that clung to his chin.

"Hey!" one of the spirits cried, "no cutting."

A dozen more voices protested in unison.

"It's okay," Vassago said as he strode past the long line of recently departed. "I'm a demon. I'm supposed to cut."

That managed to shut everyone up. Saint Peter, however, glanced up with a look that proclaimed, *I'm perpetually annoyed.*

"Vassago," Saint Peter said; he went back to studying his book. "Is it the End Times already?"

"Hardly," Vassago said with a smile. "Is this a bad time?"

"What do you want?" the saint asked.

"Nothing," Vassago replied. "I'm just here to drop this off." He deposited the basket on the pedestal before turning on his heels and heading back down the line, off to the brass-and-oak–paneled escalators poking up through the clouds.

"What's this?!" Peter shouted after him.

"Ask Haniel," Vassago replied over his shoulder. "It's his practical joke."

He of God's Joy (and just a touch too much of a bon vivant to be straight), Haniel stood over eight feet tall with his long golden hair fluttering and his four feathered wings of silver spread out behind him. He stood gossiping with the other angels at the marble-

and-gold fountain, Heaven's own watercooler. With casual indifference, he flicked his glorious hair and a thousand people in the world felt a grateful breeze cool their hot skin.

"I can't believe you left the Spirit of Innocence at the Gates of Hell," an angel said, laughing.

"What if something happens to her?" another angel asked.

"She's fine," Haniel said, waving away their concerns with an immaculately sculpted hand that sent a thousand artists into a mysterious inspirational frenzy. "She's the Spirit of Innocence. Nothing bad can happen to her. In fact," he pronounced, sweeping his hand toward an irate Saint Peter as he strode up to them with the basket in tow. "Back already!" Haniel exclaimed. "Who returned her?"

"Vassago," Saint Peter said. He then stopped. "Don't you mean *them*?" he asked, peering into the basket.

Haniel cocked a perfect eyebrow, and a thousand people across the world gasped at the beauty of the setting sun. He peered inside the basket to find the sweet perfection of the Spirit of Innocence cooing back at him . . . as well as a second child, a white boy, lying beside her. The second child was pale and fretful, his face furrowed with a strange intensity that suggested he was either about to cry or . . .

"He looks like he's concentrating," one angel said.

"Or about to take a—"

A ripe and snaking fart pierced the air and echoed off the clouds like wet thunder. All the angels across the nine spheres of Heaven paused in their holy works. A million harps screeched to a halt.

"What in the Creator's name was that?" a few angels were heard to whisper. But nobody moved to find out. In Heaven, everyone had a role and the angels were sure that someone would be on top of that little faux pas. Accordingly, as cultured agents of divinity, they decided the best course of action would be to ignore it.

Haniel held the strange infant up by the armpits. The baby began wailing, a miserable and uncomfortable cry that squeezed his face like a mouthful of lemons. More flatulence followed and Haniel realized the child was growing heavier.

"His diaper's swelling!" an angel cried, his wrists limp as he shook out his hands. "Jesus! Do something!"

"Do what?" the Messiah asked, sauntering up to the group with his hippie haircut, his golden halo, and his two fingers held up like, at any moment, those artistic paparazzi of Rembrandt, Michelangelo, and da Vinci might ambush him and paint him.

"You were human once," Haniel exclaimed, quickly

handing off the child to the Son of God. "Do something!"

The Messiah's eyes widened at the child, whose diaper was ballooning and browning at the touch of some ungodly stain. Everyone's eyes watered at the stench that reached deep into their stomachs. "I never had children!" Jesus protested, holding the child away from himself and trying to bury his nose into his shoulder.

"Yeah, right," one of the angels quipped before groaning.

The diaper had swelled like a brown beachball and the Velcro began ripping open under the strain.

"It's gonna blow!" one of the angels screamed over the bansheelike wails of the demon child.

The ripping explosion was heard up and down the funnel of the Nine Layers of Hell. What followed was the panicked shrieks of angels, what could only be described as the Heavenly Choir singing Guns N' Roses . . . off-key. All the demons paused and studied the storm clouds gathering overhead. A few devils nervously remarked how the clouds seemed more brown than purple. Stranger still, the discoloration was spreading like an ink stain in water, overtaking the silver lining of Heaven.

Vassago, however, whistled as he navigated the

bronze avenues of Dis and clicked his heels a couple of times along the way. The human-headed snake, Geryon, slithered after Vassago, entreating him to stop.

Geryon took a moment to catch his breath and glanced uneasily heavenward. "Vassago," Geryon said. "The river of excrement in the second Bolge is draining . . . someone said you took the plug. Where is it?"

Vassago grinned. "I put a glamour on it," he said proudly. "But don't worry. The river will soon fill again." He opened the umbrella hanging from his arm and pointed upward with his thumb. "Their cup overfloweth, and shit has a tendency to trickle down."

With that, Vassago walked home under the cover of his umbrella, leaving a confused Geryon behind. A moment later, Heaven rained its unfavorable bounty down upon Hell.

The Eldritch Pastiche from Beyond the Shadow of Horror

CHRISTOPHER WELCH

I went through the motions, the ritualistic motions I had done hundreds of times. But this one was special.

I printed out a standard cover letter along with my freshly edited story, "The Scarlet Horror from Beyond Space." I placed both with an SASE in an envelope addressed to the top professional horror-fiction market. I threw on my favorite coat—a faux letter-jacket from Miskatonic University—left my apartment, and strolled into the cool air of the night, a night that seemed darker than . . .

No, stop it.

I *cannot* think that way anymore. The night sky was simply the night sky, not some infinite brooding sentience with a conspiratorial agenda to reveal indescribable terrors to a timid dreamer. I will not believe in monsters.

I walked a few blocks to the nearest mailbox and dropped the envelope through the slot. I felt good about the story. I think this one had a *really good* chance of being accepted for publication. But then again, maybe I'm just crazy to believe that.

This one was special, though. This one was my last. This was the equivalent of a last drag of a cigarette on New Year's Eve, before quitting cold turkey for the New Year. I needed help, and with the wonderful information I found on a special Internet forum site, "Ignoring the Dark Places and Others," I found presumed salvation from my problem . . . from my addiction.

I walked through the city . . . and it was *just a city,* I told myself. It was not an uncanny multitude of honeycombed fears. It was not the domain of sinister machinations directed by the malformed hand of an inhuman puppeteer.

Just a city—it's just friggin' Janesville, Wisconsin, for Pete's sake!

After a few blocks, I found the old brick building I was looking for. The unremarkable structure was of standard Euclidian architectural practices. Its entrance was shadowed, a grim entrance to an unknowable . . . stop it! I cannot think like that. It is ruining my life.

The door was open and I entered the building. My heels clicked on polished floor tiles of squamous decor. A small light escaped from the only open interior doorway at the end of the long, dank hall. I slowly approached. I argued with myself.

Should I? Should I not?

I decided I truly needed self-control back in my life. My problem . . . my addiction . . . had cost me too much already, in terms of jobs, friends, and romantic relationships.

I had reached bottom. I needed *help*.

I came to the door and peered into the room. A single uncovered bulb, like a cyclopean eye, hung from the ceiling. There was a circle of a dozen folding chairs. Sitting in each one was a man, some younger and some older than me, but all had the same look about them: baggy eyes behind ill-fitting spectacles, unruly hair, and all about thirty pounds overweight.

"Is this your first time here?" the man at the front of the room asked me.

I did not see him at first glance. He was at a podium, and obviously had been talking to the congregation of men who all looked a little too much like . . . me.

"Yes," I finally answered. "I need help. I can't control myself."

"Welcome, friend. I'm Tom," he said as he shook my hand. "I have just finished telling my story. Please, tell us yours. We all have this addiction. But with group support, we can overcome it."

I stood behind the podium and Tom sat down nearby.

After swallowing hard, I finally uttered, "Hi, my name is Chris, and I write Eldritch Pastiche from Beyond the Shadows of Horror."

"Hi, Chris," everyone said in unison.

"It started when I was in middle school. That is when I first discovered H. P. Lovecraft and his Cthulhu Mythos. After reading his stories, I was addicted."

"Sounds right," someone in the audience muttered, followed by acknowledging nods.

"I mean, I had to read everything—*everything*—that made even the briefest of references to Cthulhu, Yog-Sothoth, Azathoth, and Nyarlathotep."

"How come everyone forgets Ithaqua," someone in the circle mumbled. "We live in the cold waste of Wisconsin, for crying out loud, yet everyone forgets Ithaqua the Wind-Walker."

"You hush, Artie," Tom admonished.

As Tom spoke, I noticed one figure was sitting in the back of the room, outside the circle of chairs. The figure blended with the corner shadows so perfectly that he was almost imperceptible.

"Please continue, Chris," Tom said.

"I hunted down every author—Derleth, Lumley, Campbell, Leiber, Smith, Howard, Ligotti—I read every story, every book, and every back issue of *Weird Tales* I could locate. I even found authors outside of the 'normal' realm of Mythos writers. I mean, I even finished Umberto Eco's *Foucault's Pendulum* just for its single Mythos reference."

"If you finished *Foucault's Pendulum,* you must really have a problem, Chris," Tom said.

"But I did not stop at authors, oh no," I continued. "I played every adventure of every role-playing game based on the Mythos. I played every video game and every collectable card game. I even played LARP."

There was a collective gasp of shock.

In that dark corner, I heard a faint chuckle.

"But then, at some point, I realized I had consumed everything—books, games, even DVDs. I had to have more. Then it hit me. I had to create the next generation of Mythos literature."

Again, a round of acknowledging nods. This group really did understand my problem, and it felt nice to know that I was neither alone nor mad, finally.

"That is when I wrote my first Eldritch Pastiche from Beyond the Shadows of Horror story. It was a quick tale, less than a thousand words. I called it 'The Beast from Beyond Terror.' It was about a necromancer who summoned an Elder Beast that was more powerful than he, so it ate him immediately."

More nods. "Yes, textbook predisposition," a man in the audience muttered with ivory-tower arrogance. He had white hair and apelike features.

Did I hear another chuckle from that veiled figure in the corner?

"I wrote nearly two stories a week, in those early days," I said. "I remember my titles clearly: 'The Thing Beyond Horror,' 'The Monstrosity from Nega-Time,' 'The Colors from Beyond the Shadows,' 'The Eldritch Witch Elders,' and 'The Madness at the Center of Eternity.' "

"Oh, I like that one," a chubby middle-aged man whispered. He received a collective scorn.

"Of course, I had to mention every Elder God in every story," I said. "I had to mention awesome Cthulhu; the gatekeeper Yog-Sothoth; Shub-Niggurath, the Black Goat of the Woods with a Thousand Young; the blind idiot-god Azathoth, who lives at the center of the universe; and Hastur, the Unspeakable."

"And Ithaqua."

"The tomes. I had to mention the tomes in every story, as well: the dreaded *Necronomicon* by the Abdul Alhazred was always mentioned first, of course, followed by *De Vermis Mysteriis* by Ludvig Prinn, von Juntz's *Unaussprechlichen Kulten, The Pnakotic Manuscripts,* and *The Book of Eibon,* as well. I could not continue to write anything unless I inserted this litany into my cosmic melodramas at some point before the real thrust of the story began."

"You forgot Comte d'Erlette's *Cultes de Goules,*" said Artie. He was immediately smacked in the back of the head by the person sitting next to him.

"You're not helping," the smacker said.

"I mailed my stories off to the top horror-fiction magazines and anthologies," I continued. "For three years, I got nothing but rejection letters. Every editor said the same thing—I was writing pastiche.

"I realized that they were only partly correct. I was writing Eldritch Pastiche from Beyond the Shadows of Horror, a very special and unique literary art form, if art it be. But I knew that if I persevered, I would, one day, be able to add my name to the Mythos Canon, that I would be up there in the highest echelon of Eldritch Pastiche from Beyond the Shadows of Horror authors. At least that was my dream . . . my obsession . . . my addiction.

"I tried new approaches," I added. "Instead of having my protagonists always being eaten, I thought maybe they could live, but just go insane. At the time, I thought that was an original ending."

"We all thought that once," Ape Face said.

"Then I tried having my protagonist become the monster he most feared, which I also thought was an original idea. But, after years of this, I have come to realize that I have no new ideas. I knew I could only write the same basic idea over and over, I would just go on and on and on and on and—"

"Yes, we all know that Ramsey Campbell story, Chris," Tom interrupted. "Continue."

"I'm sorry. Thank you. I know I should stop thinking in Eldritch Pastiche from Beyond the Shadows of Horror terms, and that is why I am here tonight. I need help. This whole Mythos thinking has invaded my daily life—my job, my relationships, everything.

"I have realized that this world, this universe, does not need another author like me, an author who feels compelled to write this type of literature that is so rightly rejected and can only find a home on my personal website. I still hope someone will visit the site once they discover its link on HorrorFind."

"You have all the support you need here," Tom said. "Together, we can help you get through this difficult time in your life."

I had to fight back the tears welling in my eyes. "Thank you."

"Would someone else like to speak?" Tom asked.

I sat down and I listened with rapt attention to three more testimonies of how the insidious disease of

Eldritch Pastiche from Beyond the Shadows of Horror addiction was ruining their lives, as well.

However, I sometimes found myself staring into that dark corner. I swore somebody was there while I was speaking, but now there was just empty darkness.

After the meeting, Tom gave me two pamphlets to read, "The 12 Steps of Eldritch Pastiche from Beyond the Shadows of Horror Recovery" and "So You Think You Can Write Something Scary, Eh?"

I left the meeting feeling uplifted. I was not alone and drowning in madness. The monsters were at bay.

As I was walking home by the dim light of a gibbous moon, I heard footsteps behind me. I turned to look. A few dozen yards behind me was a tall figure with noble yet ancient features. An overwhelming sense of dread chilled my veins.

When he saw me, he chuckled. I recognized that laugh; it was the same one from the meeting.

I turned back around and continued on my way.

He was following me, pacing me.

I could hear his heavy footfalls. Were those boots or hooves?

I could feel him behind me. I took another quick glance back. His shadow was stretching toward me. The low night sky, previously brooding in its pitch, now seemed to be a blazing quasar compared to his heatless shadow, which was an elongated pool of demoniacal darkness.

I ran down the street, away from this horrible but unnamed menace.

I turned one corner, and then another—when I plowed right into his chest as he seemingly just materialized in front of me. I fell to the ground, short of breath. I rose, and instinctually felt the need to retreat at full speed.

"Wait," he said, with a voice that sounded . . . a lot like James Earl Jones.

"Who are you?"

"You know very well who I am."

I had to admit it, though my mind screamed at the impossibility. It was undeniable. The Pharaoh-like features, the multiple infinities twirling in the eyes, the unshakable fear inspired by his presence. There was no doubt.

I could barely speak, yet I uttered, "Nyarlathotep."

"Who else?"

"Impossible . . . you're not real . . . you're just a fictional character . . . it's all made up."

"Of course I am real," he said through a contemptuous snarl. "We are all real. We are not some postmodern metafictional trope awaiting deconstruction as a metaphor for metrosexual Freudian angst from an untenured professor.

"No, we are *monsters.* If there is one thing I know about you, Chris, it is that we are *real* monsters to you. You *believe* the pastiche. It is your Holy Litany. You recite pastiche chapter and verse, author and publication date. You believe in the Word of the Almighty Pastiche. You are the door-to-door proselytizer of the pastiche. You want us Old Ones to be real—and so we are."

"What do you want from me?"

"Want? I want nothing from you. I came to warn you."

"Warn me?"

"Yes." He took a deep breath. "Look, this meeting you attended tonight. You can't go to one ever again. Ever. Do you understand?"

"But, I have to. I have this addiction. I can't control it. I have to continuously write Eldritch Pastiche from—"

"—Beyond the Shadows of Horror. Yes, yes. I get it."

"But it's like alcohol or narcotics. It is ruining my life, and I have no control over it anymore."

"You have never had control over your life, human," Nyarlathotep said with a sneer. "And you never will. But that is not the point. Well, not the entire point. You see, you hold a special place in the universe, Chris. A very special place that only one person in a generation can hold."

"What are you talking about?"

"Your work. Your stories. Your whole Eldritch yadda-yadda bit. You must continue to write more of it."

"Why?"

"Because you are unique, Chris. Your work achieves a level of recognition rarely seen in the entire writing industry, nay, the very universe itself."

My heart skipped a beat. A lump formed in my throat. Was my literary skill being recognized by beings that are higher than a mere mortal? Was I getting the ultimate acceptance letter?

"You mean you like my fiction?"

"Like it?" Nyarlathotep laughed, and all of Janesville trembled in fear. "I have read every single syllable you have written, and I can't stand it! Your work is the most unoriginal, unimaginative, most derivative, overwrought use of *any* language I have read since Captain Obed Marsh wrote love sonnets to his wife."

I was speechless. This was like a rejection letter from reality itself.

"I mean, have you ever really thought about your titles? 'The Thing from the Asteroid'? 'The Nega-Space Beyond Time'? 'The Horror from Pluto's Shore'? 'The Haunter Called from the Shadows'? I mean, c'mon now!

"And your so-called plots." He made quotation marks with his fingers. "You are the literary equivalent of a Family Dollar store coloring book."

I remained speechless. How could I say anything?

"Let me ask you something, Chris. Do you know the definition of *insanity*?"

I was not sure how to respond. It is not every day the Crawling Chaos asks you to define *insanity*. Finally, I said, "Do you mean doing the same thing over and over again and expecting a different result each time?"

"Correct."

"You're saying I'm crazy, right? That because I write Eldritch Pastiche from Beyond the Shadows of Horror over and over again, I am insane. Because no one will ever publish my work, but I think that some day, some way, it will get published? I mean legitimately published, like with an editor and an ISBN number, and not just uploaded to my website."

"That is only half of the answer."

"I don't understand."

"Of all the pastiches that you have read, what was the single most important philosophy, as a whole literary body, they encompass?"

"That humanity is insignificant to the rest of the universe, and that once humanity understands that, the terrifying vistas beyond our world will drive us to the safety of a new superstition-driven dark age."

"That's more fact than philosophy, but I won't argue right now since you have the gist," Nyarlathotep said. "But, what—or who—are those terrifying vistas?"

"The Old Ones, like Great Cthulhu and Yog-Sothoth."

The Pharaoh motioned encouragement with one hand.

"And . . . who else?"

"Ithaqua?"

"Keep going . . ." More motion.

"Azathoth, the Demon-Sultan," I said. "He is the blind idiot-god at the center of the universe. He is the mindless Primal Chaos behind the Veil of Colors, which is beyond our comprehension. He is accompanied by an inhuman chorus of dancers and pipers; they are servitors as equally mad as himself." Then, as I spoke, it hit me: "He is pure, ultimate chaos; conventional laws of space, time, and matter fail to exist in his presence—he is total insanity made incarnate."

"Very good," he said and folded his hands. "And who am I again?"

"You're Nyarlathotep, the Black Pharaoh, the Dweller in the Darkness, the Mighty Messenger, the Crawling—" I stopped in midsentence. "You are the Messenger of the Old Ones. You converse with Azathoth."

"Very good. Now what messages do you suppose I take to him?"

"Necromancer's spells?"

"Yes. But remember, he is insane."

I did not like where this was going. I said nothing.

"He likes to do things over and over, and over and over," he reminded me. "Do you have any idea what he likes, being a mindless idiot?"

I swallowed nervously. "He likes to read Eldritch Pastiche from Beyond the Shadows of Horror?"

"Likes it? The crazy bastard *loves* it! He can't get enough of it. He loves to hear about humans being driven mad by encounters with horrors beyond space and time. When you are *literally* the center of the universe, your favorite subject *is* the center of the universe. And guess who gets to read these stories to him every damn time?"

"You?"

"Me!" Nyarlathotep thumbed his chest. "That's how I know that you are such an awful writer."

Nyarlathotep sighed in resignation. "You are not the only writer of pastiche I have had to read to him. Oh, no. There are many, many unskilled and unimaginative authors out there. Every single one of them thinks, like you, that they have the same vision, talent, and discipline as our original courier, Lovecraft. But they don't. They are merely chimpanzees aping behavior that has been carved onto the blank slate of their pubescent brains. Their literary incompetence is only surpassed by their laughable claims of literary superiority. Everything with them is always blacker than black, darker than dark, nighter than night, or whatever.

"These so-called authors come a penny a dozen,

and the Demon-Sultan loves to have each and every single one read to him, like a child having a parent read Dr. Seuss, over and over and over."

I said nothing.

"And Azathoth is like a child. These Eldritch Pastiches from Beyond the Shadows of Horror keep him soothed. And for the time being, it behooves me to keep him soothed. And that is where you come into the picture, Chris."

He looked me in the eyes and I saw twirling galaxies inside his.

"Out of all the thousands of literary hacks on this orbiting pebble, you, Chris, are the single most untalented, single most uninspired, single most formulaic one of this generation . . . and Azathoth is your biggest fan. You are prolific in your output. You write the same crap over and over, and I read it to Azathoth over and over, and he loves it over and over. But it keeps him calm. Relatively speaking, of course, because . . . well, he is such *vast* churning Primal Chaos and all.

"So that is why you must never attend another Eldritch Pastiche from Beyond the Shadows of Horror Anonymous meeting." Nyarlathotep pointed at me. "Your stories are needed to keep the universe glued together. You want to see a terrifying vista? You want to live in real madness? Then you tell Azathoth he doesn't get a bedtime story.

"Don't get me wrong, human," Nyarlathotep continued. "You view time and space in a strict linear manner, and one day, as you see it, I will destroy this world with a planetwide holocaust and a crushing flood of doom. And afterwards, Cthulhu will rise from his slumber, the one-millionth grandchild of Shub-Niggurath will be born, Yog-Sothoth will throw open the Final Gate, and yes, Azathoth will spew forth into this reality and all the Outer Gods will glorify this realm once more.

"But not at this moment. Right now I have another agenda, and I require keeping Azathoth's eyes closed for the time being."

"What agenda?" I asked.

"That is no concern of yours," Nyarlathotep said in anger. He seemed to grow in stature, and fear slithered down my spine.

"Enough," he said. "I have warned you. Do not stop writing Eldritch Pastiche from Beyond the Shadows of Horror. *Do not stop!*"

He was looming over me like a bear, when suddenly, he levitated into the air. His Pharaoh-like appearance melted into a formless mass of darkness, like a cloud or an oil slick. Something like wings, resembling a bat, or maybe a manta, sprouted from the mass, as did a solitary red eye with three lobes. With a screech like a carrion bird, Nyarlathotep flew into the brooding sky and faded into the black horizon. It was very CGI.

I know I stood at that street corner laughing for a long time at the mere idea that my overwrought gothic melodramas have such an important role to play in the universe; to entertain such an idea invited lunacy . . . the lunacy of an accursed cosmos . . . madness rides the sanguine howls between the stars . . . a subbestial bacchanalia baying across the void . . . the mind-annihilating truth, the victory of the macabre and grotesque . . . *I believe in monsters . . . Iä! Iä!—Cthulhu fhtagn—*

How long I laughed, I do not recall. I vaguely remember ripping the pamphlets into confetti and tossing them into the air. But how I made my way home, I have no clear recollection.

Once there, I found myself typing madly at my computer. In a blind and idiotic fury, I cranked out what I thought was my best, most original, and most inspired story yet, "The Pharaoh from Beyond the Shadow of Insanity."

I printed out a standard cover letter along with the story, and placed both with an SASE in an envelope addressed to the top professional horror-fiction market. I walked a few blocks to the nearest mailbox and dropped the envelope through the slot.

I felt good about the story. I think this one had a *really good* chance of being accepted for publication. But then again, maybe I'm just crazy to believe that.

Elvis Presley and the Bloodsucker Blues

MATT VENNE

For my favorite man in the world, my father, Joe Venne.

I. HOTTER THAN THE HINGES OF HELL

Well, ain't this just a kicker? Here I am, lyin' in a pile of my own mess on the goddamned bathroom floor, the life runnin' outta me faster than shit through a duck, my favorite silk pajamas twisted around my ankles—and I know what all you sonsuvbitches are gonna say: you're gonna talk about how I died takin' a shit . . . too many peanut butter and nanner sandwiches . . . massive heart attack . . . clogged arteries . . .

drug overdose . . . tongue all hangin' out and disgusting looking and all sorts of other bullshit not befitting the death of a king.

Well, let me just set the record straight here, folks: The King of Rock 'n' Roll didn't die on no shitter.

No siree, Bob.

And I sure as hell didn't die of no drug overdose, either. Contrary to popular belief, I didn't take goddamned drugs. Hell, I hated drugs. Wish I coulda wiped out every drug dealer on the planet. Even had a plan to lure 'em into Graceland, then have me and the rest of the Memphis Mafia (always *loved* that nickname, by the way) unload on 'em with a bunch of Uzis, but—alas—that plan never came to be: I moved on to a fleeting obsession with horses, bought me a whole ranch of 'em, and by the time I remembered the drug dealer thing, I'd sort of just . . . *moved on.*

But back to this little matter of my demise: Hard as it might sound to believe, the King of Rock 'n' Roll died from exposure to sunlight.

Same way all vampires do.

All the freaky shit started after I wrapped *Change of Habit*—and the less said about that picture, the better: I mean, Lord have mercy, there ain't enough lipstick in the world to gussy up that pig. *Change of Habit* ended up being the final movie I made, and it sure as hell wasn't a case of savin' my best for last. *Habit* was one of my worst pictures (I'd put it right up there with *Girls! Girls! Girls!* and *Harum Scarum* for those of you keepin' score).

After the critical and commercial beating the picture took I was feeling pretty low. Looking for some excitement in my life. A way to recapture something that I'd lost somehow, somewhere along the way. Something that'd make me feel like I did when Sam Phillips and Scotty Moore and Bill Black and me cut our first record at Sun back in '54; or like when the three of us did the Louisiana Hayride; or when the Colonel got me my first big record deal with RCA; or like watching nekked girls wrestle with each other and hopin' they'd kiss; or—hell—even the feeling I got as recently as the year before, when I made "The '68 Comeback Special." Christ Almighty, folks loved that show. Me? I thought it was just okay. Some of the musical numbers were pretty hokey, even by the standards of the time, but—boy oh boy—did the ladies flip for that black leather outfit Bill Belew designed for me. Thing was hotter than the hinges of hell, but it got me more poontang than most men see in three lifetimes.

Priscilla and I had fallen on hard times—I think she was datin' her dance instructor, and I was dating just about anything that had two arms, two eyes, and a fish taco between its legs—so I had started up the old ritual I had with the boys of renting out the Memphian for a bunch of all-night movie marathons that summer.

On this particular night, it was late May/early June of '68, I was in a funky kind of mood, so I had Hamburger James pick up prints of three fittingly offbeat movies: *Planet of the Apes* (man, I wanted to serve those damned dirty apes a helping of King-Fu), *2001: A Space Odyssey* (fuckin' thing made no sense—I think the reels were mixed up or somethin' because a giant kid was born at the end of the picture!), and *Madigan* (pretty good crime flick; little gritty for my taste, though).

By the time the credits were rolling on the last movie, it was almost five in the morning. The sun would be up soon, and we were all durn near exhausted—which might explain why I ignored the First Rule of Being Rich.

First Rule of Being Rich?

Never Do Something Yourself that You Can Pay Somebody to Do for You.

Yet me, Elvis Motherfucking Presley, one of the richest sonsuvabitches in America?

I ignored the rule.

And that's when the rest of the night—hell, the rest of my *life*—really started goin' south. You thought

Clambake was bad, what happened next made *Clambake* look like *Gone With the Fucking Wind.*

Hamburger James had split early—something about his wife goin' into labor or some shit like that—so that meant David Stanley, my second-in-command (and stepbrother), was supposed to return the film reels back to the guy we rented 'em from. But David was feeling under the weather, and I could tell he really didn't wanna make the trip. Looking back, I think I was just searching for something new to do—some new spin on old habits; some way to reconnect with something that was dead inside my soul—so I offered to drive the truck and return the canisters of film myself. You know, get away for a little while—even if it was only for an hour or so.

Everyone looked at me like I'd just sworn off pussy for a year, but I assured 'em it was something I wanted to do.

Alone.

You see . . . I was getting tired of the crowds of people always around me. I know, I know: I only had myself to blame. I was the one who put all my friends on payroll and made 'em leave their wives and kids to be at my beck and call 24/7, but still. A man needs some time to himself once in a while, and, like I said, there was something about that summer that had me in a bit of a funk. I was only thirty-four, but I felt old, baby. Like they say, it's the terrain not the mileage—and I had seen me some pretty rough terrain through the years.

So with no small amount of reluctance, the fellas packed the film canisters into the back of the truck, and I waved good-bye as I headed out into the darkness of early morning.

Lemme tell you something. It was thrilling.

There were no cars on the road, and it took me back to the days before I became the most famous man on the planet; took me back to almost fifteen years ago, when I was nineteen years old and driving a delivery truck for Crown Electric.

As the quiet highway spread out before me, the dark sky began to turn into the beautiful purples and pinks you only find in Memphis, and it was suddenly like . . . like time traveling or something. For a few minutes there I was that fresh-faced kid again, with a tender heart, big dreams . . . and no idea how quickly dreams turned into nightmares. Gone was the hardened man who could trust no one, including his friends and family. Life was normal—or at least what I imagined normal to be—and it felt like I was on my way home from a long night of making deliveries, my pretty little wife waiting for me in our modest house, our children fast asleep in their small but cozy bedrooms, the world unaware of my existence.

I smiled at the thought, looked out at the horizon as the sunlight began to swing its golden scythe across the fields in the distance, cutting down night into day.

Which is when I ran over him.

I saw the poor bastard standing in the middle of the road out of the corner of my eye and slammed on the brakes.

But not soon enough.

The scraggly-looking kid's body made a disgusting thud as the truck slammed into him, his face shattering the windshield, his body flipping end over end before finally landing on the pavement behind the truck like a sack'a moldy potatoes.

Since these are probably my last words before I leave this mortal coil, I guess honesty is the best policy: I have to admit, first thing I thought about was how royally this was going to screw things up. Last thing I needed was all the bad publicity running over some kid in the middle of the night was gonna bring me. I mean, shit, it's one thing to daydream about a life lived without riches, driving a truck for a living, renting a small house somewhere out in the middle of nowhere—but it's another to actually lose all of your riches, women, and earthly possessions.

No thank you. Me and my daddy and my momma

were dirt poor back in Tupelo, and the thought of goin' back to anything resembling that type of life was terrifying.

It's good to be the King, and I wasn't in no hurry to give up my crown just yet.

I stared in the rearview mirror at the dead body splattered across the pavement, and all I could think of was how bad I wished I was lying in my bed at Graceland, Grandma cooking up some eggs and bacon and sausage and taters and waffles and biscuits with gravy and grits and corned beef hash for breakfast.

I could feel my foot on the gas pedal, itching to hit the road. It'd be so easy to tap that sucker down real quick-like and drive away . . . but I'm happy to report that the angels of my better nature prevailed. I was a good ol' boy at heart, and rather than hightail it out of there, I turned off the ignition, got out of the truck, and wandered over to the kid to see if there was anything I could do to help him.

Lordy lordy lordy, was he was in bad shape.

Just lookin' at him gave me a case of the willies, and I knew it'd be a long time before I'd get the image of his splintered face out of my mind. It took everything I had to keep my nachos and hot dogs and popcorn and soda and M&M's down—and it was just when I thought I was gonna hurl all over the dead sonuvabitch that he opened his eyes.

Let me repeat that:

The fucker was dead, but he opened his mother-fucking eyes.

Which made him undead, see?

And before I knew what the hell was goin' on, he sat up straighter 'n my pecker right before a threesome and grabbed me by the neck. I tried a little of the old Elvis-Fu (the karate technique I tried, if you want to know, was Heavenly Ascent), but the kid was just too durned strong: my elbow glanced off his chin without him letting out so much as a yelp.

He got to his feet real quick-like, raising me up off the ground as if I was lighter than a box a doughnuts, and I tried some more karate, but it was pointless.

I ain't gonna lie to you: I was scared, man.

Real scared.

But even bein' afraid, I wasn't gonna cry like a little baby about it. Hell no. This sonuvabitch wanted to tussle, we was gonna tussle. I kicked him in the nuts, but the dude must've been wearin' a cup or somethin' because it didn't faze him; he just kept holdin' me two or three feet off the ground with that monstrously strong arm.

I'd finally had enough, looked the bastard square in the eyes: "You better finish this thing, baby, cuz I'm Elvis Aaron Presley; you don't kill me now, I'm gonna make your life a livin' hell!"

The fella cocked his head as if I was speakin' gibberish.

Was it possible there was somebody in the world—in Memphis, no less—who hadn't heard of me?

I was stunned—until his eyes flickered in dim recognition, and he uttered with vocal cords gravelly as kitty litter:

"The Kiiiiing!"

I nodded. "That's right, son, the King," and the excited look in the kid's eyes suddenly filled with fear. But after a few moments, I realized it wasn't me he was afraid of:

I followed his gaze over my shoulder, discovered that the dude was staring at the risin' sun on the horizon. He was freakin' out. Frankly, I didn't give a shit if it was my words or the damned sunlight that had put the fear a God into him; all I cared about was gettin' away from this creepy fucker.

He started to go weak in the knees—but right before we fell to the ground he opened his mouth real wide. I winced at the sight of his mouth full of teeth: there were just too many of 'em, and they were all pointy and sharp, like . . . like—

Oh shit.

This sonuvabitch was a vampire.

A real-life goddamned bloodsucker.

His wounds started to heal right before my eyes . . .

like . . . like he was Jesus Christ or something . . . and the wider his mouth opened, the more I realized he was about to turn me into an Elvis sandwich.

He moved forward, started to wrap his lips around my neck.

Last thing I remember before passing out was smackin' him real hard and tellin' him I wasn't into none of that gay shit.

II. The Mother of Invention

The Colonel was pissed.

How in the hell was I supposed to make any more movies if I couldn't be out in the sun? That was the whole formula: get me drivin' a race car or a motorcycle or a speedboat, pair it with a snazzy location (Hawaii, Acapulco, Florida, Arabia, what have you), and—*voilà!*—two weeks later you had yourself a motion picture.

But that was PV, baby: *Pre-Velvis.* Some of the fellas in the Memphis Mafia took to teasin' me about gettin' myself turned into a damned vampire, thought it was a real hoot to call me "Velvis, the Vampire Elvis." That might seem like a funny reaction to you, but David and Jerry and Red and Lamar and the rest of the boys—they were used to crazy shit happenin' all the time. Vampirism was just one more once-in-a-lifetime thing to add to their big old list of once-in-a-lifetime things that happened while hangin' out with yours truly. Besides, what were they gonna do? Quit? Hell, I paid all their bills, bought 'em houses and Cadillacs and all kinds of shit. They learned how to deal with the Big E bein' a vampire—with smiles on their goddamned faces.

But dealing with the Colonel was a different matter. All that fat old man saw was the bottom line—and there was no way I could be on location makin' movies since the sun did somethin' nasty to my skin. Twenty seconds out in the sunlight, and my damned flesh started to melt right off.

But, truth be told, I was kind of relieved.

I was tired of the movies anyway, and as long as we could keep the whole vampire thing out of the press (you have no idea how much shit we kept out of the press; this wouldn't be too difficult), I was glad to have me an out. Thirty-one pictures was a lot of celluloid, baby—only problem was the fact that about twenty-eight of 'em were crap.

But even though my body of work in the screen trade can best be described as "quantity over quality," good or bad, very few people have made more pictures than me.

It was time for a new chapter of my life to begin.

Velvis had turned the page.

• • •

So while the Colonel figured out how to keep the Elvis Train rollin', me and the boys started tryin' to make the whole "creature of the night" thing work for me. Tell you the truth, it wasn't much of a stretch. I'd essentially switched days and nights years ago, staying up all night and then sleeping all day, so I was used to being a night owl, and all the stores and restaurants and movie theaters all across the country would stay open all night for Elvis Presley and a few of his friends with one simple phone call.

Frankly, a vampire never had it so good.

But, sure, there were a few physical difficulties to get used to—like the time I didn't get to bed until after the sun was up (nevermind the fact that, as usual, I'd been inside all night): the light blasted through the windows in Graceland like a bucking bronco, and I had to take cover beneath a few passed-out groupies while the boys scrambled around to get all the windows closed and hang drapes over 'em and shit like that. The next night I had David and Red and Lamar hang a bunch of tinfoil on the windows to block out the sunlight the next morning—and we were happy as the devil at the crossroads to discover that it worked perfectly.

Within a few days the whole house was covered in

the stuff, and I'll be damned if Graceland didn't turn out to be the fanciest vampire coffin you ever saw. Tinfoil came to be sort of a precautionary habit with me, so if I had to be driven anywhere during the day the boys would tinfoil all the car windows the night before. Same with all the airplanes and hotel rooms and any other space I might need to use during daylight hours.

I also had to stop wearing the crosses I was so fond of, because they burnt something fierce against my skin. One time it got so bad, my chest started smokin', and Sonny had to blast me with a fire extinguisher. But, as my momma, Gladys, taught me to do so well, I eventually turned lemons into lemon meringue pie: I had Lowell Hays, my jeweler out in Beverly Hills, design me a bunch of TCB pendants to wear instead, and those went on to signify my personal style and sense of individuality better than some frumpy old crucifix. Hell, by that point in my life I wasn't even sure the ol' Gray Beard existed anyway, and the TCB thing seemed much more inclusive.

Another tough thing to get used to was the cravings. God Almighty, did I wanna suck me some blood. And I tried it once, but it made me puke all the waffles and sausage and pork rinds and Popsicles I'd had for breakfast right back up. I just couldn't never get used to bitin' into some poor chick's neck—and I sure as hell wasn't gonna bite into no dude's neck.

Yet, having all the money in the world enables you to get creative—which is where the drug rumors started. I decided that I'd just have my good friend Dr. Nick inject me with blood once every coupla days or so. It beat the hell out of suckin' blood, and it allowed me to prevent turnin' anybody else into a vampire, something that would be a pain in the ass for someone without my resources.

Only problem with the injections—aside from the drug rumors—was that it made me get all bloated after a bad transfusion a few years back. You think I didn't know I'd gotten fat, baby? You think if it was just a matter of cuttin' back on the cheeseburgers I wouldn't a done it? C'mon, give the King some credit. The blood transfusions took a toll, but it was the only way I could avoid eatin' some poor bastard, so I kept on doin' it—whether it made me fat or not.

But now I'm just complainin'; feelin' sorry for myself. Truth is, for a while there, the whole vampire thing was great. I was lookin' lean and mean, losin' weight faster than a hooker loses her panties, and I experienced an increase in my physical abilities. I mean, let's face it: before I was turned into a vampire, I wasn't exactly the world's greatest karate master. Yeah, I tried hard, and practiced all the time (and paid Ed Parker and Kang Rhee a shitload of money to make me an eighth-degree black belt), but you look at those pictures where I was tryin' to show my stuff—pictures like *Blue Hawaii* or *Speedway*—and you can tell: I wasn't exactly a natural.

Now take a look at the concert footage of my acts in Vegas—after I'd been "turned:" I'm like a whole different cat out there, baby. I'm the Tiger Man. I'm nimble and fast and able to bend my legs one way and my torso another and my arms still another. My strength and dexterity were superhuman. Literally. And for a year or two, I was grateful to be a *nosferatu.*

The Colonel knew the only way to keep the gravy train rollin' was to find some way for me to perform to a crowd in a controlled environment, where I'd be out of the sunlight, and able to stay indoors all day if necessary.

Sound familiar?

You said it, bubba: *Viva Las Vegas!* indeed.

It was perfect, really. Like my hairdresser, Larry Geller, used to say: Necessity is the mother of invention.

We woulda never played Vegas for all those years if it wasn't necessary for me to stay out of the sun. I'd a probably made another thirty pictures, and never had that great second-to-last (that's "penultimate" for all you college boys out there who think I don't have me a good vocabulary) chapter of my life before the infamous fall from grace. So, I don't know, even though my time in Vegas eventually brought me a bad case of the bloodsucker blues, I'm still grateful for the bumps in the road that led me there. And even though it was the whole vampire thing that led to my early demise, I'm still sorta glad for the experience.

The shows themselves? They were Fuckin' Great with a capital Fuckin'. Go look at the tapes—you'll see. Long as we made sure my microphone wasn't made of silver and room service didn't put no garlic on my burgers, I was a pelvis-gyratin', lei-wearin', kiss-givin', sexy sonuvabitch. A pure hunka hunka burnin' love if ever there was one.

But . . . a funny thing started happenin' during the shows. I can't really describe it any other way than to say I started to get something like . . . like a *Spidey sense* about other vampires (*Spider-Man* was my second favorite comic, by the way, right behind *Captain America.* Hot damn, I loved me that Captain America . . . even thought about having Bill Belew design me a shield or somethin' I could take out onstage and work into my act . . . but . . . level heads prevailed and I eventually dropped it . . .).

This Spidey sense—it was real odd: I'd be doin' my thing up onstage, and all of a sudden I'd start gettin' this . . . this . . . *buzzing feeling.* Like I'd just drank a pot of coffee on an empty stomach. I'd have to stop movin' my hips for a minute to get my balance, and the first time it hit me, I happened to look out into the crowd, and I focused in on a pack of scumbags sittin' in the cheap seats. They smiled at me kinda knowingly-like—

And that's when I noticed their fangs.

Now, just so you know, I was not into the whole fang thing. Talk about puttin' the brakes on the Pussy Express. Lemme tell you: fangs? Not attractive, baby. Not in the least. So along with doing my hair and personal grooming, Larry Geller also started filing my teeth down every two or three days. Again, like everything else, it was no big deal, and we just sort of made it part of our normal routine: hair, manicure, pedicure, teethicure. We found that a really coarse stock of sandpaper did the trick, and if we were really in a pinch, using a nail file also worked.

But these vampires in the cheap seats? They were livin' the *vida vampira* and they were damned proud of it. They made no attempt to hide their fangs—least, not from me—and even though I quickly realized they meant me no harm, I was troubled to read the papers the next day. Turned out a group of teens had been found murdered, their necks ripped open as if attacked by wild animals, their bodies drained of blood.

I knew those bloodsuckers I saw at my show were responsible, and it made me feel guilty about bein' one myself. I began to wonder if there was something I coulda done to save those poor kids.

I tried to put it out of my mind and carry on with the shows. But my Spidey sense (or "vamp vibe" as me and the boys started callin' it) would always remind me of the life I was leading. It would come and go depending on how close I was to a vampire or how many of them there were, but—just like my martial arts training—the more I studied the sensation of the vamp vibe, the more in tune with it I became . . . until I realized that there were vampires all around us all the time.

A whole army of bloodsucking *nosferatus.*

A *vampire nation*, if you will.

Like all things in life (especially for yours truly), after a while the Vegas routine got a little . . . *stale.* Even aside from my increasing awareness of vampires, there was some dark undertone to the gigs after a while. In a nutshell with chocolate on top? I got bored, baby.

The whole thing started to feel a little bit empty. Sure, Sammy Davis Jr. and Liberace and Tom Jones and Barbra Streisand and Kris Kristofferson and Brian Wilson and Muhammad Ali and all those celebrities a few rungs down the ladder from me would come and hang out and pay their respects and sing with me back in the penthouse after the show (none of 'em remotely aware that I was a bloodsucker), but . . . I don't know . . . it just got . . . well . . . *old.*

I began to resent the life bein' a vampire had forced me into. I yearned to quit the Vegas gig, maybe make another picture or two out in some exotic locale, and then play a game of football with the boys in the lawn behind Graceland, the afternoon sun baking our skin into a golden brown.

But those days were to be no more. All because some faggoty vampire had sucked on my damn neck. Hell, after a few weeks of stewin' on it, I realized I was downright pissed.

Things started comin' to a head one night in my penthouse suite. It was the middle of the night, the loneliest time in the world, between three and four in the morning. Everyone who came back to the room after the show had passed out long ago, and the sun wouldn't be up for another couple hours. I felt like Charlton Heston in that movie *The Omega Man;* felt like I was the last man alive on the whole goddamned planet. I went to my window, pulled the curtains back to get a good look at the world below. Seeing the neon planet so lonely and quiet and dark filled me with sadness and made me happy all at once. I felt at peace and unsettled. I was fully human in that moment ('least, as fully human as a vampire can be) . . . until I got a blast of the vamp vibe so strong it almost knocked me on my ass.

I glanced toward some flash of action in a dark alley

on the streets below, my attention drawn to some distant scuffle. I watched for a moment, wanted to see what would happen, quickly realized that some heavyset older woman was runnin' from a pack of mean-lookin' dudes.

There was somethin' about the woman that reminded me of my momma. I felt sorry for the poor gal, and I was horrified when the pack of dudes chasin' her opened their mouths wide . . .

Too wide . . . too familiar . . . then pounced on her.

Helpless, the woman could do nothing but let them feed on her, those chubby legs twitching spasmodically as they slammed her up against a Dumpster and started to drain her of her blood.

And it didn't help matters any when I looked out my window a few weeks later and saw that same chubby old gal wanderin' around outside, confused as a doughnut in a deli, shamblin' along in a blood daze, hungry for the red stuff, but without the means or the know-how to get herself any.

Turned.

It was like seein' my momma reincarnated as some kind of bloodsuckin' freak, and it pissed me off somethin' fierce.

All those vampire sonsuvbitches out there?

They were ruinin' lives left and right, without a care in the world for people's rights or good old-fashioned American decency.

And then it hit me, my "moment of clarity": Yeah, sure, I was doin' all right, takin' care of business, all that shit.

But look at me.

Look at what the vampirism had done to me beneath my perfect public persona: I was a mess, and I knew it. 'Cilla and I had finally called it quits a few years back, and I hardly ever saw my little girl because of the hours being a vampire forced me to keep.

Those assholes had ruined my life—'least, they put the last nail in the coffin, *pun intended.*

It was then—right then and right motherfucking there—that I decided to do somethin' about it. I decided to execute every last one of those leeches. I decided to turn myself into a steamroller, baby, and roll all over their scuzzy vampire asses.

III. Napalm Bomb with a Goddamned Pompadour

So we scrapped the Vegas act.

And for once the Colonel and the Memphis Mafia were in agreement with each other: everybody hated the idea of trading the life of Vegas penthouse luxury for the day-to-day rigors of the road.

But the road it was. My mind was set.

I couldn't sit back and let the vampires win without

putting up a fight, and a cross-country tour was the perfect cover for me to get out there and hunt those evil sonsuvbitches down. The Vegas gigs had cemented my reputation as the world's biggest entertainment draw, which allowed me to tour the country nonstop until the end of my days, no questions asked.

Life was basically the same as when we were in Vegas, only this time my penthouse became a tour bus, and rather than go back to the room at night, I'd go out huntin'.

Once in a while some of the boys would come with me, and it turned out that my stepbrother David had a real knack for vampire huntin'; he was real good at cuttin' their bloodsucking heads off after I shot 'em full of silver bullets, which is why I nicknamed him The Headhunter (thanks, again, to my private jeweler, Lowell Hayes, silver bullets were very easy to come by; as you might've guessed, Lowell even designed 'em with a bit of the ol' Elvis flare: they had little TCB insignias in their tips).

Mostly, though, the boys couldn't keep up: they preferred to load up my guns with those specially made silver TCB bullets and send me on my way. And who can blame 'em? A night of vampire huntin' was filled with all kinds of jumpin' and wrasslin' and kickin' and killin'. It wasn't work that appealed to ordinary human beings, and—even though the Memphis Mafia was an extraordinary group of guys—they were certainly still human.

And you know what? I really didn't mind goin' out alone. It gave me that solitude I'd been searchin' for over the years. That peace of mind. Aside from the blood and the carnage and the all-around mayhem, it was sort of . . . peaceful. Kind of . . . *Zen,* I guess you'd call it.

While we're on the subject of my vampire huntin', lemme ask you somethin': You've heard the stories about President Nixon taking a meeting with me, and then bestowin' the government's highest law-enforcement badge on me, right? You've seen the pictures, right? You know it really happened, right? That it ain't some bullshit myth in a life admittedly riddled with bullshit myths? Then lemme ask you: Why in the hell do you think the president gave me the badge in the first place?

It weren't for no sharp-shootin', lemme tell ya.

It was for exterminating vampires, kiddo.

The White House is almost as wired into the cultural landscape of these glorious United States of America as Graceland is, and so it was only a matter of time before the Powers That Be recognized they had a real vampire problem on their hands. Granting me the status of federal agent allowed me to carry a firearm on my person at all times, and to shoot a perpetrator in the line of fire. I see a vampire gnawin' on somebody's jugular? *Blam-o!* bloodsucker. No questions asked.

So President Nixon knew what I was up to, and I bet if you could find the time to sift through all of those tapes that paranoid sonuvabitch made, he'd mention something about it. I hope so—it sure as hell would clear up a lot about the last few years of my life for the fans out there. At least my little girl would know how her daddy really died.

And so the federal agent badge from the president . . . the weight gain from the blood transfusions . . . the superhuman improvement of my karate skills . . . even the addition of ". . . in a flash" to "Takin' Care of Business . . ." (which became my code for "blast those vampires with sunlight, baby!")—it all makes a bit more sense now, don't it? I mean, you really think I was dumb enough to sit back and blow holes through all my TVs because I was too lazy to change the channel?

Guess again, son.

Whenever shit'd get shot up, you can bet your ass I was in the midst of a fight for my life, blastin' bloodsuckers left and right, things gettin' squirrelly all around me.

Vampire huntin', baby. It's a bitch.

• • •

I'm happy to report that as my beloved tour bus zigzagged across this great country of ours, I sent thousands of those wretched leeches to their eternal damnation. I was like a napalm bomb with a goddamned pompadour, baby. My country 'tis of thee, sweet land of liberty, *bang-bang*, bloodsucker, go fuck yourself.

And like a lot of things about my career, I took a little "inspiration" from the black community (and don't you dare call it "stealing"). Huntin' those bloodsuckers, I saw myself as something of a honkey Shaft, which should also help explain why I got into the whole cape thing: it was my version of Shaft's trench coat; my version of a superhero, which is exactly what I was for the last several years of my life, keeping the streets clean, saving all of you unsuspecting citizens from those nasty fanged rodents.

Yet, as my daddy used to say, when you set out to drain the swamp it always starts out good, but eventually you realize you're up to your ass in alligators.

Like most everything I did with my life, my reputation began to precede me, and pretty soon every goddamned *nosferatu* sonuvabitch from here to Timbuktu heard that the King was kickin' ass and takin' names.

Things got real sketchy for a while there, and the Colonel and the boys thought it'd be a good idea for me to hang up my spurs for a few months, get some rest back at Graceland, recharge the ol' batteries for a little while.

I didn't like the idea of quittin' somethin' midstream, but everyone assured me I wasn't quittin' nothin'. This was just a little hiatus. I'd gained about seventy pounds from all the bad blood transfusions, and my eyes were more sensitive than ever to ultraviolet radiation (that's the shit that's in the sunshine, for those of you of a less "scientific" persuasion; and it's also the reason I was always wearin' those big-ass shades at the end of my life—again, everything has a reason, baby; I wasn't as loony as everybody thought).

This little hiatus was to be a time to lose a little weight, get back to some all-night movie marathons at the Memphian (there was this science fiction flick everybody'd lost their minds for called *Star Wars* that I was dyin' to see), and bang a boatload of broads to see if I couldn't force the ever-present thoughts of Priscilla outta my mind.

It was a good idea.

It was a great plan.

It was not to be.

• • •

August 16, 1977. The vampires finally got the last laugh. Like I said, I'd become so prolific at exterminatin' bloodsuckers they'd finally had enough. They got together and decided it was time to put an end to my shenanigans: They sent a pack of southern-fried *nosferatus* my way, and, bein' vampires and all, they didn't have any trouble sneakin' past the front gates and creepin' into my bedroom at Graceland.

It was about four in the morning, and I'd just finished reading a great book called *The Necronomicon,* which was all about Egyptian lore and methods for battling deadly creatures (contrary to popular belief, I loved to read, and I'd devoured just about everything pertaining to the undead).

As I'm sure you're well aware, as luck would have it, heading into the final hours of my demise, I had to relieve my damned bowels.

And it was while takin' a blue ribbon shit that I got a mean ol' case of the vamp vibes, and heard a commotion in the bedroom outside the bathroom door. The girl I was seein' at the time, Ginger, let out a quick scream, but it was immediately muffled, like by a pillow or somethin'.

Silk pajamas still wrapped around my ankles, I jumped off the commode and busted from the bathroom—only to find my little honey pie knocked out on the bed. I was puzzled, whispered, "Ginger?"

She didn't say nothin' back—but my eyes went wide when out of the shadows of the bedroom I heard a familiar curdled voice: "*The Kiiiiiiing!*"

I turned toward the voice, but was a little too late: a group of redneck bloodsuckers hit me over the back of the head and knocked me to the ground.

And then, wouldn't you just know it? That same fugly (that's "fuckin' ugly") sonuvabitch who'd turned me into a vampire all those years ago was leaning over me.

He was smiling as he got real close to my face and taunted me: "*The Kiiiiing is dead.*"

Yep. "Et tu, Brute?" and all that shit. I mean, yeah, like I said, my reputation had spread from sea to shining sea, and it didn't really surprise me that a small faction of the vampire nation would eventually band together to eliminate me—it's just that I never thought they'd take me down in my own house, man.

That's just . . . *rude,* you ask me.

But . . . anyway . . . (I'm gettin' all worked up just thinkin' about it), Fugly and his minions hog-tied my ass, then dragged me across the cold tile floor of my bathroom. And it was with a sense of horror that I realized what they were doin': sun was gonna be up in about half an hour or so, and they were placing me right beneath the skylights in my bathroom's ceiling. They ripped down the tinfoil from the skylights, made sure I was tied down right beneath 'em, then scurried from my beloved bedroom—my goddamned sanctuary through all the years of madness and mayhem—and left me, Elvis Aaron Presley, the King of Rock 'n' Roll, to die alone on my dirty bathroom floor.

Ginger was knocked out cold—and after a few worthless attempts to wake her by callin' her name, I finally just got myself comfortable (comfortable as you can get when you're hog-tied), and turned to face the skylights as the sun began to poke its head over the dark horizon of night.

I was ready for the end. And it was coming faster than a fart after a plate of fried sausage and cornmeal mush.

IV. Daddy's Bound to Die

Last concert I ever performed was for an audience of one.

Kind of fitting, really. Took me back to the days in Tupelo, when I sang simply for the love of music. When I'd pick out a few chords on Daddy's old acoustic guitar and sing the traditionals about Ol' Shep or workin' the fields or finding peace in the valley.

I'd always loved "An American Trilogy," and decided that was as good a song as any to end my life with. As I sang the middle verses, I thought about my beloved daughter, and knew—just *knew*—she'd be okay. She knew that her daddy was a pioneer (maybe she didn't know I'd gotten heavily into vampire huntin', and that I was—in fact—a vampire myself, but that's just semantics). And she also knew that sometimes pioneers get lost along the way. The machete gets dull, the foliage gets too thick, and the trail disappears on you after a while. Such is the life of a pioneer, and if Daddy was one thing, he was a pioneer, baby. Sold more records, made more movies, ate more food, bumped uglies with more chicks, and—above all else—had me more laughs than any sonuvabitch who came before.

I was the first, and I was the last.

The Alpha and the Omega.

Elvis Aaron Presley.

So . . . that's why I needed to set the record straight, let you know that I didn't die in the squalid circumstances you'd been led to believe. I died like I lived; a noble death befittin' a king. I died fightin' the vampire nation, and left the world a little bit better off because of my time here.

The sun is starting to spread across the sky, making the clouds look like sponges at a bloody crime scene. My eyes are filling with tears, because I haven't seen the simple beauty of a sunrise in years, and this is going to be my last.

My skin is starting to smoke and mottle. I manage to wriggle just a little bit out from beneath the direct path of the sunlight, but I can't get too far, and the UV damage has already been done. At least I won't completely incinerate, though. Thank God for the little things, right?

I reach for my shades, but they're too far away and my hands are tied too tight. Fuck it. I'm gonna meet this sucker head-on, lookin' death right in the eye until the very end.

I think about 'Cilla.

Think about Lisa Marie.

Smile sadly. Proud and happy and low all at once. Fully alive, baby. Fully alive.

I resume singing "An American Trilogy" with everything my meltin' vocal cords have to give (the acoustics in this bathroom suck, but hell: you take what you're given).

I can hear a chorus of angels pretty as the Jordanaires singing backup, and as the sunlight finally turns me into a rotten-lookin' hunk of meat, I smile, open my arms to the glories that await me (again, as much as a hog-tied sonuvabitch can open his arms), content that I've lived a life worth livin'.

Alas, it happens to us all.

The King is dead, baby. All hail the King.

Elvis has left the building.

No Problem

Don D'Ammassa

I swear I had good intentions. I know that sounds pretty weak, but it's the truth. Look, I'll tell it the way it happened and you can judge for yourself.

My name is Herbert Franken and I've been working toward a master's degree in biochemistry at Brown University for the past year. My parents wanted me to go into the family business, but I don't even like pizza and I wanted more for myself than a life sweating over pepperoni and tomato sauce. When the oven exploded and killed them both, as well as burning down the restaurant, I took it as a sign that I'd made the right choice.

Brown allocated space for its grad students in the laboratory building, but it was hard to concentrate there with people coming and going all the time. No problem. The insurance had left me pretty well-off, so I decided to clean out part of the basement and put together my own facility. I was working on monitoring rates of cell degeneration, so I didn't really need a lot of room.

That meant going through all the boxes and crates and trunks of family memorabilia that my parents had stored there, most of which they hadn't even looked at after shipping them all the way here from Europe. Some of it I threw out, and most of the rest went into a storage locker. The only thing I kept at the house in Managansett was a crate full of old journals that looked like family histories.

It cost more than I expected to outfit my laboratory, even with buying used equipment where possible, but it only took a few weeks to get everything delivered and installed to my liking. The only drawback was the ventilation. There were two tiny basement windows, but they didn't provide much circulation. No problem. By opening the bulkhead door that led up into the backyard I even had a refreshing breeze.

So now I guess I should tell you about Mrs. Williams. Gretchen Williams was my neighbor, an elderly retired nurse who had lived in the small cottage next door for as long as I could remember. She had to be at least seventy, but she might have been a lot older than that. Her skin was dark and wrinkled like the dried fruit you find in trail mix. My dad used to call her the "neighborhood inspector" because she walked up and down the streets every once in a while with a pencil and pad, looking for code violations she could report to the town hall—broken windows, visible garbage cans, peeling paint, things like that. Once when I was a kid, she caught a whiff of some concoction I'd cooked up with my chemistry set and came over to complain, and on another occasion she walked right into our house, demanding to know when Dad was going to trim the front hedge. She was an incredibly nosy woman, asked all sorts of personal questions, and either didn't realize how unpopular she was or just didn't care.

My parents had never talked much about our family back in Germany and I always suspected that they were involved with the Nazis or worked in a concentration camp or something like that. I remember one time Dad let something slip about the family castle, but he insisted he was joking and got mad when I pushed, so I let it go. The journals were likely to answer at least some of my questions. Once my first experiments were under way, I had to spend a lot of time waiting for dead organic matter to get even deader, so I pulled one of the journals out and started reading. They were in German, naturally. No problem. I'd grown up speaking German at home and English everywhere else.

They were pretty dull, actually, at least until I found

my multiply great-grandfather's oversize, brass-bound account of his experiments. The name inscribed inside the cover was a bit of a shock: Viktor Frankenstein. I thought it must be some kind of elaborate joke, but there was no question about the age of the journals, and when I read through the first few pages, I felt a flicker of excitement. His observations were crude by contemporary standards, but there were hints of an acute intelligence and an almost supernatural insight into the processes of life. I was struck by some coincidental similarities with my own work, and read on far into the night.

The next morning, I threw out the cultures I'd started, ordered some new equipment, and began rearranging the lab.

Please don't get the impression that I had suddenly turned into some kind of mad scientist. I had no intention of digging up dead bodies at midnight, erecting a lightning rod on my roof, or stealing brains from Brown University. Nor were there any hints of such madness in the journal. The experiments described there were limited to rats and other lab animals. Contrary to the story promulgated by Mary Shelley, who may have known my ancestor socially, there was no suggestion that Viktor ever experimented on human subjects. At least not in the journals in my possession, which ended abruptly in 1816.

With modern equipment, I was able to duplicate

and improve on Viktor's work in a matter of weeks. I quickly confirmed what the journals had already suggested. The process could indeed generate vitality from dead cells, but there was no possibility of restoring the higher functions except on the most rudimentary level. A dead mouse's heart might resume its pumping, the tiny form might even stand and walk about and even go through the motions of eating or drinking, but it might just as easily begin gnawing on its own tail. Even among lower animals, the mind is more than just the physical structure of the brain.

One Saturday morning, I found Mrs. Williams's cat in my yard, chewing on a dead sparrow. After chasing the cat back over the fence, I examined the tiny corpse, which appeared completely undamaged, other than the missing head. I couldn't resist the temptation; I injected some of my serum into the cooling body, and was immediately rewarded by a slight fluttering of the wings. I hadn't anticipated the possible consequences, however, and I wasn't quick enough when it suddenly rose into the air and began flying around the basement. Its movements were random and had I thought to close the bulkhead door, I could have captured it in short order. Unfortunately, it blundered through the opening and quickly vanished. The stimulating effects of the treatment would wear off after a few hours, so presumably no harm was done.

A few days later I was preparing a new experiment when Mrs. Williams came boldly down the cement steps, demanding to know what I was doing. "I open the kitchen window this morning and what a stink! I thought something must have died over here." Her appearance was so unexpected that I didn't react until she was halfway across the basement. "What's this stuff, then? Are you making drugs down here?" She looked at the lab equipment suspiciously. "I'll bet the police would be interested to know about this, young man."

I stood up and advanced on her immediately, angry at the intrusion and concerned that she might damage something. "This is private property, Mrs. Williams. You have no right to come in here."

"Got something to hide then, do you?" She reached out toward my spectrometer and I caught her wrist reflexively. "How dare you!" Her face twisted in outrage. "How dare you lay hands on me!"

"Please get out of my house or I will call the police." My voice trembled. I felt like a child again, terrified of adult authority. I had never had the courage to so much as set foot on Mrs. Williams's property. For years I had been convinced that she was a witch, and that irrational fear quickened my pulse.

"Call them then! I'd like to see you explain all of this!" And she reached toward the bubbling vials where I was brewing a fresh batch of the revitalization serum.

I only meant to push her away, but she was a tiny woman and I'm not a small man.

She lost her balance and fell over so quickly that she never even cried out.

I heard the solid thud as her head struck the cement wall and I knew she was dead at that instant.

No, I didn't think that I could bring her back to life and send her home. Not exactly anyway. What I did next was a product of panic and guilt. It had been an accident, certainly, and she had been trespassing, as well. But I'm six feet tall, two hundred pounds, and here I was contemplating explaining to the police how an elderly one-hundred-pound woman received a fatal head wound in my basement. It would be inconvenient and embarrassing at best, possibly much worse. So I considered my options and came up with a plan.

No problem. I had plenty of serum. I lifted her onto the bench and half emptied a freshly filled hypodermic into her body. The results, if any, would be apparent within minutes. I have to confess that, despite everything, I was curious to see what would happen.

There was no thunderstorm, the lights didn't flicker, and I neither cackled nor rubbed my hands together in a sinister fashion. I simply waited until the serum had had time to be infused into the tissues. Although I tried to remain calm and collected, I have to admit that it gave me rather a start when she abruptly sat up on the bench.

To outward appearances, she appeared completely normal. Even the soft spot on the side of her head was hidden by her hair, and the small trickle of blood had completely dried. I couldn't help apologizing as I took her by the elbows and lifted her down from the table. She was a bit unsteady at first, but she followed docilely as I led her up the steps and out into the open. Her eyes were focused but I sensed no intelligence behind them. My earlier experiments had suggested that certain behavioral patterns remained intact, but no more. The sparrow had sought to escape into the open, crickets scurried toward dark corners, and one of the white rats had even remembered how to operate the feeding lever, then ignored the food pellet that dropped into the dish.

My plan was simple. I planned to take her back to her house and close her up inside, then call the police and tell them that I'd found her lying in her backyard, had assisted her into the house, but was concerned that she'd suffered a concussion. Which, of course, she had. No problem.

I even had a stroke of luck. Gus Robinson was watering his grass across the street. I waved when he glanced in our direction, and he nodded casually. I led Mrs. Williams, or her body anyway, up the porch steps, opened the screen door, and gently pushed her through. She advanced a few steps, then stopped. I waited, but she didn't move, so I let the door close and turned away.

Gus was coiling up the hose when I reached him. "Morning, Gus."

He raised his eyebrows. I guess I'm not the sociable type and it kind of surprised him that I'd initiated a conversation. "Morning, Herbert. What's the old biddy up to today?" He glanced at Mrs. Williams's house. He hadn't spoken to her since the day she reported him for putting up a flagpole that violated a town ordinance.

"She tripped over something and hit her head. I saw her lying in the garden and helped her inside. I'm wondering if I should call an ambulance or something. She might have a concussion."

"Her head's too hard for that."

I tried to smile, but it felt wrong. "Even so, I feel funny about not calling someone. I don't think she has any family in the area."

"Drove them all to suicide, most likely." Gus finished with the hose and took a tentative step toward his front door, as though he wasn't sure the conversation was over.

I decided not to push too far. "Maybe I'll just check on her later."

I waited for an hour, then went through the motions. I looked in through the screen door, but she was nowhere in sight. I rang the bell and then called her name, hoping one of the neighbors would hear me, then went back to my house and called the police, told them my version of the situation somewhat apologetically. A cruiser showed up ten minutes later and a uniformed officer rang the bell, rapped on the door, walked around peering in through the windows. I waited until he'd been at it for a few minutes, then went out and introduced myself.

"Is there anyone else living here?" he asked.

I shook my head. "Just Mrs. Williams. That's why I was so concerned." Something moved in the air at the periphery of my vision, a small dark blur. I glanced up to see a bird, or at least most of one, flutter past and slam into the trunk of Mrs. Williams's birch tree. "She didn't look good," I said hastily as Officer Tremblay's head began to turn. The bird, still twitching, fell out of sight.

He tried calling again, then opened the screen door. "Please wait out here, sir," he said firmly. I stood on the porch, shifting my weight nervously from foot to foot, rehearsing my lines over and over again. He seemed to take an awfully long time, but eventually he came back outside and shut the door.

"There's no one home."

Well, you can imagine how startled I was. "She has to be there," I insisted, perhaps a bit too strongly. "Maybe she wandered into a closet or something."

He shook his head. "It's a very small house, Mr. Franken, and I looked everywhere. She's not home. Maybe she took herself off to see a doctor, or felt well enough to go shopping. I don't see a car." He glanced toward the driveway.

"She doesn't drive."

"Then maybe she asked someone to drive her or called a taxi."

I knew how impossible that was, but I couldn't very well say anything. "I guess you're right, officer. I'm sorry if I wasted your time."

"That's all right, sir. Better safe than sorry."

I probably should have left it at that. Mrs. Williams, or her body at least, would turn up eventually. But I had to know what had happened to her. Somewhere, deep in the recesses of my mind, was the sudden fear that she hadn't been dead after all, that she'd recovered her wits and would tell someone what I'd done to her. The blow to the head I could explain, but how could I justify injecting strange substances into her body? No, I couldn't rest until I knew what had happened.

She couldn't have gotten far, not without help, so I set out to find her, methodically working my way around each separate block. I saw a few people outside, and I even ventured to ask some of them whether they'd seen an elderly woman wandering about, but no one was helpful. I was almost ready to give up and go home when I turned onto Burkett Street and heard the hammering.

I need to tell you about Bert Sanderson. Bert was Mrs. Williams's nemesis. She'd complained so many times that his dog was barking, the animal control officer finally threatened legal action. Bert had been so enraged that he'd assaulted the officer, and was lucky to have gotten a suspended sentence and a hefty fine. A week later he had been caught throwing eggs at Mrs. Williams's windows one night after a few too many beers, and she'd pressed charges, which had been added to resisting arrest and another assault charge. Bert spent six months in prison and lost his job. There had been a few more incidents of vandalism since his release—someone had twice sprayed her garden with weed killer—but Bert had not been proven responsible, and the truth was, Mrs. Williams had made a lot of enemies.

Although I only knew Bert casually, I'd heard that their latest run-in had involved the utility shed he'd built in his backyard. Apparently it was three inches taller than allowed by town ordinances, and Mrs. Williams had objected when he'd applied for a variance. The last I'd heard, he had removed the roof and was remodeling. I had almost passed his property when the hammering stopped and I heard him shouting angrily.

"Get out of here, you senile bitch, or I swear I'll use the hose on you!"

I knew who it had to be and started in that direction. As I passed the corner of the house, I saw Mrs. Williams standing near the unfinished shed while Bert stalked toward the garden hose that lay in the grass near his stockade fence. I hesitated, trying to decide how to proceed, never guessing that I'd just lost my chance to prevent a tragedy.

Mrs. Williams stooped to the bright red toolbox at her feet and picked up a claw hammer. I was momentarily paralyzed with astonishment because it seemed such a purposeful act that my earlier fear, that she wasn't dead after all, came back full force. Then she was moving and her arm was going up and I realized what she intended and started after her, but of course it was too late. She hit him from behind and I didn't think she could have exerted enough force to do much damage, but Bert slumped forward on his face with a grunt. He wasn't moving.

When I reached his side a second later, he wasn't breathing, either.

Mrs. Williams was just standing there, her face neutral, and she didn't resist when I took the hammer from her hand. Then I realized my mistake, took out my handkerchief, and wiped the handle to remove my fingerprints. "Mrs. Williams?" I asked, barely above a whisper. She didn't answer, didn't even seem to hear me.

I thought about taking her away and returning to my original plan. I could tell the police I'd spotted her while out for a walk. But Bert complicated things. His death was obviously no accident. I didn't think anyone had seen me there, but I couldn't be certain. For a minute or two I stood, unable to think clearly, and then the sound of children shouting somewhere close by made me panic. The back door to Bert's house was unlocked. I took Mrs. Williams by the elbow and brought her inside, shut her in the bathroom. Then I carried Bert in through the kitchen to the garage. His station wagon was there and a few minutes of searching turned up his keys. I bundled his inert body into the back and covered it with a blanket.

I wasn't thinking clearly, obviously, but I wanted to buy some time. Bert's wife would be home from work in another hour or two and I didn't want her, or anyone else, to find the body until I had a plan. I collected Mrs. Williams, who was perfectly docile now, and put her in the backseat. It was taking a chance to drive Bert's car but I hoped to have it out of sight before anyone took particular notice. Five minutes later it was inside my garage, and I had closed the curtains on the windows so that no one could look in and see it. No problem.

I went inside to look for some clothesline, intending to restrain Mrs. Williams, but before I could find any, the doorbell rang. It was Gus Robinson, who wanted to tell me that a squad car had stopped by looking for me.

"Why are they looking for me?" My voice trembled.

Gus shrugged. "He didn't say, just asked me to tell you that he'd stop back later." Gus seemed to want to talk, maybe hoping I was privy to some delicious secret, and I didn't want to make him suspicious by being too anxious to have him leave, so it took another couple of minutes to get rid of him. Even so, I was forced to be rather abrupt, and there was an odd look on his face when he left. I found the clothesline and went out to the garage.

Mrs. Williams was gone.

I ran quickly from room to room and noticed that the patio doors were open. I was sure I had closed them so I went outside, resisting the temptation to call her name. She wasn't likely to respond to it anyway, and someone might hear me. I ran around to the side yard, slowed when I saw Gus across the street. I didn't think he'd seen me, so I retreated around the corner of the house quickly. Then I went next door, climbing the fence so I couldn't be spotted, and searched the cottage. There was no sign of Mrs. Willliams.

I went back inside, telling myself that it wasn't a

problem. If she was gone, I could just revert to my original plan. She'd collapse in a few hours anyway and there was nothing to connect me with her death. Bert was a separate problem. As soon as it was dark, I could drive the car to Breakneck Hill, prop him behind the wheel, and send him over one of the drop-offs, then set fire to the wreck. It would be a long walk back, but I could stay in the woods for most of that distance. No one would be likely to see me there. No problem.

Once I'd decided on a plan, I felt better, but then I started to worry again. What about rigor mortis? What if the body was so stiff that I couldn't get it into position? Maybe I should prop it up in the passenger seat now. I started for the garage.

And heard something move.

Was it possible that Bert hadn't been killed after all? I opened the door to the garage with my heart in my throat, then felt a mixture of relief and shock. It wasn't Bert who was moving; it was Mrs. Williams. Somehow I'd missed her and she'd come back. She was standing at the rear of the station wagon, staring down through the open rear window at Bert's inert body. I walked around to stand beside her, already working on a new scenario.

Something glittered in her right hand. It was a hypodermic needle. One of mine. In fact, it was the same one I'd used to inject her with serum. I'd only used half but it was almost empty now.

Bert rolled over and sat up.

My chest began to hurt and I realized that I was laughing, great gasping sobs of laughter. I forced myself to calm down. Bert's body seemed content to remain where it was, so I turned to Mrs. Williams, relieved her of the hypodermic, and led her away. She didn't struggle while I tied her to the tool bench. I would have to find some way of restraining Bert next, but I'd barely begun to consider that problem when the doorbell rang again. I went into the house, closing the garage door behind me.

It was Officer Tremblay again. "Would you mind if I came in a moment, sir?"

I offered him a seat, which he politely refused. "I'm following up on your neighbor, Mrs. Williams. You haven't seen her since your first report, have you?"

"No," I lied.

"Well, we've had a call from a Mrs. Pereira a couple of blocks from here. She said an elderly woman who fits the description walked past her house about two hours ago. She said the woman had blood on her face and seemed dazed. If she'd called in at the time, we might have been able to find her, but she kept quiet until her conscience started to bother her.

We just wanted to make sure that we're not looking for two separate women." He read a description of Mrs. Williams's clothing from his notebook and I confirmed that she'd been dressed identically when I'd last seen her.

"Thank you for your assistance, Mr. Franken."

"I just hope it helps," I said with mock sincerity. Officer Tremblay turned toward the door and I started forward to open it.

There was a loud thump from the garage. We both heard it, but I pretended not to. "Are you alone here, Mr. Franken?"

"Yes, I am, officer. Something must have fallen over. It's nothing to worry about."

"I'm sure that's the case, but I was wondering if it might be the missing lady wandering again."

"The garage door is locked." Something in my manner must have betrayed me because he was immediately suspicious.

"Would you mind if I had a look, sir?"

I searched for a rational reason to object, but Tremblay didn't wait for one. He started toward the kitchen and I was forced to trail along in his wake. My heart sank and I knew this was the end. He'd see Mrs. Williams as soon as he stepped into the garage.

He wasted no time and I saw the way his head snapped up as the door opened. His hand was dropping to his weapon as he spun around to face me. "Please raise your hands, Mr. Franken."

I slowly began to do as I was told, but I never completed the movement. A crowbar flashed through the air, bouncing off his skull, and Officer Tremblay dropped like a stone. It was Bert, of course. Even dead, he hated the police with a passion. The crowbar rose and fell twice more before I ran forward and took it away from Bert. By then Mrs. Williams had untied herself, and she was staggering around the garage, apparently trying to stab Bert with the hypodermic, which she'd retrieved from the shelf where I'd put it.

So there I was with three dead bodies, two of them still moving around, and two cars to dispose of, one a police cruiser. I sat down for a while to think things through and decided that the first priority was to get rid of the cruiser. I couldn't carry Officer Tremblay's body down to it in the daylight, so I'd have to dispose of that separately. No problem. Bert was still wandering around, so I found some more clothesline and tied him to one end of the bench. He didn't seem to mind. By then Mrs. Williams was stabbing the dead policeman over and over with the empty hypodermic. I took it out of her hand and she sat down heavily. The serum was obviously starting to wear off.

I was just catching my breath when the doorbell rang. It was Gus from across the street.

"Hi. I saw the cop car out front and wondered if there'd been any news about Mrs. Williams."

I didn't invite him in. The noises from the garage had stopped, but I had a dead policeman and two reanimated corpses to deal with. It wasn't an appropriate time for entertaining.

I opened my mouth, intending to tell him that there'd been no news, that Tremblay was using the bathroom and it wasn't a good time, but before I could say anything, his eyes widened and he looked past me. "Mrs. Williams! We were all worried about you."

Somehow she'd found the strength to come into the house. I was paralyzed with indecision, and of course Gus decided to brush past me.

She didn't like Gus particularly, either, so she stabbed him with the hypodermic. He gave a surprised little cry, dropped to his knees, and fell headlong. There was no more serum, so at least he wasn't likely to get up anytime soon. I decided to consider that my luck had finally changed for the better.

Mrs. Williams had collapsed by the time I had finished dragging Gus into the garage. Officer Tremblay was moving around a little; apparently there'd been enough of the serum left to cause some reaction, but he couldn't stand up. He was pawing at his weapon and I took it away from him just to be safe. I carried Mrs.

Williams out next. She barely moved, so that was no problem.

It was later than I had realized. The day had gotten away from me. As soon as it was fully dark, I was going to carry the bodies next door, then move Bert's car out onto the street. I'd set fire to the house, wait until it was going pretty well, then call in the alarm. Let the police interpret the four bodies however they wanted after that.

By the time I was willing to risk it, Mrs. Williams was completely still, and the other two were obviously winding down. Tremblay was still pawing at his holster but he couldn't stand up, so I ended up carrying all four of them, one at a time. Then I went down to the basement and arranged some rags and other combustibles near the oil tank. It was harder to get the fire going than I expected, but eventually I was satisfied.

I decided to have one last look around upstairs before leaving and that was my last mistake. When I stepped through the doorway into the kitchen, I felt something brush against my leg.

There was a click and I looked down just in time to see Officer Tremblay fasten the free end of a pair of handcuffs to the foot of Mrs. Williams's antique cast-iron stove.

The other cuff was around my ankle.

I stood there, astonished that he'd been able to crawl all the way from the opposite end of the kitchen, and by the time I understood what had just happened, he'd moved beyond my reach, finally slumping inertly against a row of cabinets.

He and the handcuff key are out of my reach. The stove is too heavy for me to lift or move. There are wisps of smoke drifting up from the basement and I can hear the flames licking at the steps.

I think I have a problem.

Old School

Mark Onspaugh

"And arise!"

Everyone stood back from the corpse except Meg, who wanted to see whether the eyes would pop open like they always did in the movies.

The dearly departed, a crossing guard who had been struck down by a school bus, just lay there, like . . . well, like a stiff.

We waited thirty minutes, which seemed more than enough time for any self-respecting necromancer, then Dean hit Mal with his cap.

"Fuckin' retard—I knew that book was a load of shit."

The book was old and covered in stained leather that Mal had promised was the skin of some wizard from fourth-century Persia or some such nonsense. He had gotten it off eBay from a dealer in Bakersfield. The fact that it was written in English had made us doubt its authenticity. It wasn't even Old English like Chaucer or something. More like that Robin Hood–speak you hear in bad sword and sorcery flicks. Lots of "thee" and "thou" and "ye."

"Let's get her back to the office," I said wearily. "My boss has a nasty habit of dropping in after nine."

We loaded the battered civil servant into the back of my Subaru. Dean had put pennies on her eyes, which only he had found funny.

I smiled at Meg, but I could see she was disappointed. She was the only reason I had agreed to this in the first place. There was something about her pale skin and bat tattoo that made me feel feverish. The way the chrome stud in her tongue winked in the sun. The hints that her pale flesh held even more wonders hidden from prying eyes. Marvels that I had yet to be privy to.

The starter made a grinding noise and the car finally started with a belch of exhaust. The thing was a piece of shit but none of the others had a ride. We bounced off the dirt track that led to the Carl Milton campground and back onto the main road to Baylor Brothers Funeral Home, where I worked part-time.

The moon was coming up as we passed the cemetery, and Meg's skin looked silver and luminous. I tried to think of something clever to say, something that might eventually lead me into her cool embrace.

She beat me to it.

"There're a lot of fresh graves out there."

I looked, and saw several holes in the earth. But not the fresh excavations of men with equipment and a practiced hand. More the frenzied eruptions of someone making their way . . . out.

I stopped, which turned out to be a major mistake, and demanded to look at Mal's book. Nervous, he opened it to the resurrection spell and handed it to me. The dome light on my car had burned out long ago, so I used a lighter.

The spell read as he had recited it, up until the end.

*. . . and arise———!**

Dropping down to the bottom of the page, I read:

**Recite here ye name of the deceased, lest thee raise every corpse within the sound of thy voice.*

"You didn't follow the asterisk?" I asked. By this time, Meg was screaming at the shapes looming outside, just as Dean was trying to subdue the surprisingly strong crossing guard.

"What's an asterisk?" Mal asked, his brow crinkling in a road map of confusion.

As the car began to rock under the assault of the hungry undead, I regretted many things.

I regretted I would never taste Meg's tongue stud as it clicked across my teeth.

I regretted I would never take that surfing trip to Australia.

I regretted being so close to a large cemetery like Forest Lawn.

But most of all, I regretted we had attended such shitty public schools.

The Sound of Blunder

J. A. Konrath and
F. Paul Wilson

"We're dead! We're freakin' dead!"

Mick Brady, known by the criminal underground of Arkham, Pennsylvania, as "Mick the Mick," threw the remains of his shrimp egg foo yung across the cellar, then held a shaking fist in front of Willie Corrigan's face. Willie recoiled like a dog accustomed to being kicked.

"I'm sorry, Mick!" Willie said through a mouthful of General Tso's chicken.

Mick the Mick cocked his fist and realized that smacking Willie wasn't going to help their situation.

He smacked him anyway, a punch to the gut that made the larger man double over and grunt like a pig.

"Jesus, Mick! You hit me in my hernia! You know I got a bulge there!"

Mick the Mick grabbed a shock of Willie's greasy brown hair and jerked back his head so they were staring eye to eye.

"What do you think Nate the Nose is going to do to us when he finds out we lost his shit? We're not going to be eating takeout from Lo's Garden, Willie. We're both going to be eating *San Francisco Hot Dogs.*"

Willie's eyes got wide. Apparently the idea of having his dick cut off, boiled, and fed to him on a bun with a side of fries was several times worse than a whack to the hernia.

"We'll . . . we'll tell him the truth." He shoved a handful of fried noodles into his mouth and crunched out, "Maybe he'll understand."

"You want to tell the biggest mobster in the state that your Nana used a key of uncut Colombian to make a pound cake?"

"It was an accident," Willie whined. "She thought it was flour. Hey, is that a spider on the wall? Spiders give me the creeps, Mick. Why do they need eight legs? Other bugs only got six."

Mick the Mick realized that hitting Willie again wouldn't help anything. He hit him anyway, a slap across his face that echoed off the concrete floor and walls of Willie's basement.

"Jesus, Mick! You hit me in my bad tooth! You know I got a cavity there! Hey, did you eat all the duck sauce? Is duck sauce made from duck, Mick? It don't taste like duck."

Mick the Mick was considering where he would belt his friend next, even though it wasn't doing either of them any good, when he heard the basement door open.

"You boys playing nice down there?"

"Yes, Nana," Willie called up the stairs. He nudged Mick the Mick and whispered, "Tell Nana 'yes.' "

Mick the Mick rolled his eyes, but managed to say, "Yes, Nana."

"Would you like some pound cake? It didn't turn out very well for some reason, but Bruno seems to like it."

Bruno was Willie's dog, an elderly beagle with hip dysplasia. He tore down the basement stairs, ran eighteen quick laps around Mick the Mick and Willie, and then barreled, at full speed, face-first into the wall, knocking himself out. Mick the Mick watched as the dog's tiny chest rose and fell with the speed of a weed whacker.

"No thanks, Nana," Mick the Mick said.

"It's on the counter, if you want any. Good night, boys."

"Night, Nana," they answered in unison.

Mick the Mick wondered how the hell they could get out of this mess. Maybe there was some way to separate the coke from the cake, using chemicals and stuff. But they wouldn't be able to do it themselves. That meant telling Nate the Nose, which meant San Francisco Hot Dogs. In his twenty-four years since birth, Mick the Mick had grown very attached to his penis. He'd miss it something awful.

"We could sell the cake," Willie said.

"You think someone is going to pay sixty thousand bucks for a pound cake?"

"I dunno. Maybe. Some people ain't so bright."

Truer words were never spoken, Mick the Mick thought.

"No junkie is going to snort baked goods, Willie. Ain't gonna happen."

"So what should we do? I—hey, did you hear if the Phillies won? Phillies got more legs than a spider. And you know what? *They catch flies, too!* That's a joke, Mick."

"Shaddup. I need to think."

"Okay. I don't think I like the Phillies anymore. Are they called Phillies because they're all named Phil? I think—hey, we got fortune cookies. Lemme see my fortune."

He cracked open a cookie and pulled out a slip of paper.

"Look, it says, 'You are very wise.' I always think it's funny to add 'in bed' after a fortune. That means mine is, 'You are very wise *in bed*.' Ain't that funny, Mick?"

"A freakin' riot, Willie. Now let me think."

Willie tossed Mick the Mick a cookie. "Open yours, Mick! Open yours!"

"How about instead I open your skull with a ball-peen hammer?"

"Do I got a fortune in my skull, Mick?"

Mick the Mick cast his eyes about the basement for some sort of bludgeon, but the basement was unfortunately bludgeon-free. So he decided to open the damn cookie. Anything to shut Willie up.

"What's it say, Mick?"

" 'You will change the world.' Yeah, right."

"No!" Willie shouted. " 'You will change the world *in bed*'!"

Mick the Mick couldn't think of an appropriate response, so he rabbit-punched Willie. Even though it didn't solve anything.

"Jesus, Mick! You hit my kidney! You know I got a stone there!"

Mick the Mick turned away, rubbing his temples, willing an idea to come.

"That one really hurt, Mick."

Mick the Mick shushed him.

"I mean it. I'm gonna be pissing red for a week."

"Quiet, Willie. Lemme think."

"It looks like cherry Kool-Aid. And it burns, Mick. Burns like fire."

Mick the Mick snapped his fingers. *Fire.*

"That's it, Willie. Fire. Your house is insured, right?"

"I guess so. Hey, do you think there's any of yesterday's pizza left? I like pepperoni. That's a fun word to say. 'Pepperoni.' It rhymes with 'lonely.' You think pepperoni gets lonely, Mick?"

To help Willie focus, Mick the Mick kicked him in his bum leg, even though it really didn't help him focus much.

"Jesus, Mick! You know I got the gout!"

"Pay attention, Willie. We burn down the house, collect the insurance, and pay off Nate the Nose."

Willie rubbed his shin, wincing.

"But where's Nana supposed to live, Mick?"

"I hear the Miskatonic Nursing Home is a lot nicer, now that they arrested the guy who was making all the old people wear dog collars."

"I can't put Nana in a nursing home, Mick!"

"Would you rather be munching on your vein sausage? Nate the Nose makes you eat the whole thing, or else you also get served a side of meatballs."

Willie folded his arms. "I won't do it. And I won't let you do it."

"Woof!"

Bruno the beagle sprang to his feet, ran sixteen laps around the men, then tore up the stairs.

"Bruno!" they heard Nana chide. "Get off the counter! You've had enough pound cake!"

Mick the Mick put his face in his hands, very close to tears. The last time he cried was ten years ago, when Nate the Nose ordered him to break his mother's thumbs because she was late with a loan payment. When he tried, Mom had stabbed Mick with a meat thermometer. That hurt, but not as much as a wienerectomy would.

"Maybe we can leave town," Willie said, putting a hand on Mick the Mick's shoulder.

That left Willie's kidney exposed. Mick the Mick took advantage, even though it didn't help their situation.

Willie fell to his knees. Bruno the beagle flew down the stairs, straddled Willie's calf, and began to hump so fast his little doggie hips were a blur.

Mick the Mick began searching the basement for something flammable. As it often happened in life, arson was really the only way out. He found a can of paint thinner on a dusty metal shelf and worked the top with his thumbnail.

"Bruno, no! Mick, no!"

Mick couldn't get it open. He tried his teeth.

"You can't burn my house down, Mick! All my stuff is here! Like my comics! We used to collect comics when we were kids, Mick! Don't you remember?"

Willie reached for a box, dug out a torn copy of *Amazing Spider-Man* #146, and traced his finger up and down the Scorpion's tail in a way that made Mick the Mick uncomfortable. So he reached out, slapped at Willie's bad tooth. Willie dropped the comic and curled up fetal, and Bruno the beagle abandoned the calf for the loftier possibilities of Willie's head.

Mick managed to pop the top on the can and he began to sprinkle mineral spirits on some cartons labeled "Precious Photos & Memories."

Willie moaned something unintelligible through closed lips—he was probably afraid to open his mouth until he disengaged Bruno the beagle.

"Mmphp-muummph-mooeoemmum!"

"We don't have a choice, Willie. The only way out of this is fire. Beautiful, cleansing fire. If there's money left over, we'll bribe the orderlies so Nana doesn't get abused. At least not as much as the others."

"Mick!" Willie cried. It came out "Mibb!" because Bruno the beagle had taken advantage. Willie gagged, shoving the dog away. Bruno the beagle ran around Willie seven times, then flew up the stairs.

"Bruno!" they heard Nana chide. "Naughty dog! Not when we have company over!"

Willie hacked and spit, then sat up.

"A heist, Mick. We could do a heist."

"No way," Mick the Mick said. "Remember what happened to Jimmy the Spleen? Tried to knock over a WaMu in Pittsburgh. Cops shot his ass off. His whole ass. You want one of them creepy poop bags hanging on your belt? Freaks me out."

Willie wiped a sleeve across his tongue. "Not a bank, Mick. The Arkham Museum."

"The museum?"

"They got all kinds of expensive old stuff. And it ain't guarded at night. I bet we could break in there, get away with all sorts of pricey antiques. I think they got like a T. rex skull. That could be worth a million bucks. If I had a million bucks, I'd buy some scuba gear, so I could go deep diving on shipwrecks and try to find some treasure so I could be rich."

"You think Tommy the Fence is going to buy a T. rex skull? How we even gonna get it out of there, Willie? You gonna put it in your pocket?"

"They got other stuff, too, Mick. Maybe gold and gems and stamps."

"I got a stamp for you."

"Jesus, Mick! My toe! You know I got that infected ingrown!"

Mick the Mick was ready to offer seconds, but he stopped midstomp.

"You ever been to the museum, Willie?"

" 'Course not. You?"

"Nah."

But maybe it wasn't a totally suck-awful idea.

"What about the alarms?"

"We can get past those, no problem. Hey, you think I need a haircut? If I look up, I can see my bangs."

Willie did just that. Mick the Mick stared at the cardboard boxes, soaked with paint thinner. He wanted to light them up, watch them burn. But insurance took forever. There were investigations, forms to fill out, waiting periods.

But if they went to the museum and pinched something small and expensive, chances are they could turn it around in a day or two. The faster they could pay off Nate the Nose, the safer Little Mick and the Twins.

"Okay, Willie. We'll give it a try. But if it don't work, we torch Nana's house. Agreed?"

"Agreed."

Mick the Mick extended his hand. Willie reached for it, leaving his hernia bulge unprotected. Now that they had a plan, it served absolutely no purpose to hit Willie again.

He hit him anyway.

• • •

"I don't like it in here, Mick," Willie said as they entered the great central hall of the Arkham, Pennsylvania, Museum of Natural History and Baseball Cards.

Mick the Mick gave him a look, which was pretty useless since Willie couldn't see his face and he couldn't see Willie's. The only things they could see were whatever lay at the end of their flashlight beams.

Getting in had been a walk. Literally. The front doors were unlocked. And no alarm. Really weird. Unless the museum had stopped locking up because nobody ever came here. Mick the Mick had lived in Arkham all his life and never met anyone who'd ever come here except on a class trip. Made a kind of sense then not to bother with locks. Nobody came during the day when the lights were on, so why would anyone want to come when the lights were out?

Which made Mick the Mick a little nervous about finding anything valuable.

"It's just a bunch of rooms filled with loads of old crap."

Willie's voice shook. "Old stuff scares me. Especially *this* old stuff."

"Why?"

" 'Cause it's old and—hey, can we stop at Burger Pile on the way home?"

"Focus, Willie. You gotta focus."

"I like picking off the sesame seeds and making them fight wars."

Mick the Mick took a swing at him and missed in the dark.

Suddenly the lights went on. They were caught. Mick the Mick feared prison almost as much as he feared Nate the Nose. He was small for his size, and unfortunately blessed with perfectly shaped buttocks. The cons would trade him around like cigarettes.

Mick the Mick ducked into a crouch, hands above his head. He saw Willie standing by a big arched doorway with his hand on a light switch.

"There," Willie said, grinning. "That's better."

Mick wanted to punch his hernia again, but he was too far away.

"Put those out!"

Willie stepped away from the wall toward one of the displays. "Hey, look at this."

Mick the Mick realized the damage had been done. Sooner or later someone would come to investigate. Okay, maybe not, but they couldn't risk it. They'd have to move fast.

He looked up and saw a banner proclaiming the name of the exhibit: ELDER GODS AND LOST RACES OF SOUTH CENTRAL PENNSYLVANIA.

"What's this?" Willie said, leaning over a display case.

Suddenly a deep voice boomed: *"WELCOME!"*

Willie cried, "Whoa!" and Mick the Mick jumped—high enough so that if he'd been holding a basketball he could have made his first dunk.

Soon as he recovered, he did a thorough three-sixty, but saw no one else but Willie.

"What you see before you," the voice continued, *"is a rare artifact that once belonged to an ancient lost race that dwelled in the Arkham area during prehistoric times. This, like every other ancient artifact in this room, was excavated from a site near the Arkham landfill."*

After recovering from another near dunk, plus a tiny bit of pee-pee, Mick noticed a speaker attached to the underside of the case.

Aha. A recording triggered by a motion detector. But the sound was a little garbled, reminding him of the voice of the aliens in an old black-and-white movie he and Willie had watched on TV last week. The voice always began, "People of Earth . . ." but he couldn't remember the name of the film.

"We know little about this ancient lost race but, after careful examination by the eminent archeologists and anthropologists here at the Arkham, Pennsylvania, Museum of Natural History and Baseball Cards, they arrived at an irrefutable conclusion."

"Hey," Willie said, grinning. "Sounds like the alien voice from *Earth Versus the Flying Saucers*."

"The ancient artifact before you once belonged to an ancient shaman."

"What's a shaman, Mick?"

Mick the Mick remembered seeing something about that on TV once. "I think he's a kind of a witch doctor. But forget about—"

"A shaman, for those of you who don't know, is something of a tribal wise man, what the less sophisticated among you might call a 'witch doctor.'"

"Witch doctor? Cooool."

Mick the Mick stepped over to see what the voice was talking about. Under the glass he saw a three-foot metal staff with a small globe at each end.

"The eminent archeologists and anthropologists here at the Arkham, Pennsylvania, Museum of Natural History and Baseball Cards have further determined that the object is none other than an ancient shaman's scepter of power."

Willie looked at Mick the Mick with wide eyes. "Did you hear that? A scepter of power! Is that like He-Man's Power Sword? He-Man was really strong, but he had hair like a girl. Is the scepter of power like a power sword, Mick?"

"No, it's more like a magic wand, but forget—"

"The less sophisticated among you might refer to a scepter of power as a 'magic wand,' and in a sense it functioned as such."

"A magic wand! Like in the *Harry Potter* movies?

I love those movies, and I've always wanted a magic wand! Plus, I get crazy hot thoughts about Hermione. She's a real fox, Mick. Kinda like Drew Barrymore in *E.T.* Hey, why does the wand have a deep groove in it?"

Mick the Mick looked again and noticed the deep groove running its length.

"Note, please, the deep groove running the length of the scepter of power. The eminent archeologists and anthropologists here at the Arkham, Pennsylvania, Museum of Natural History and Baseball Cards believe that to be what is knows as a fuller . . ."

A fuller? Mick thought. Looks like a blood channel.

". . . which the less sophisticated among you might call a 'blood channel.' The eminent archeologists and anthropologists here at the Arkham, Pennsylvania, Museum of Natural History and Baseball Cards believe this ancient scepter of power might have been used by its shaman owner to perform sacred religious ceremonies—specifically, the crushing of skulls and ritual disemboweling."

Mick the Mick got a chill. He hoped Nate the Nose never got his hands on something like this.

"What's disemboweling, Mick?"

"When someone cuts out your intestines."

"How do you dooky, then? Like squeezing a toothpaste tube?"

"You don't dooky, Willie. You die."

"Cool! Can I have the magic wand, Mick? Can I?"

Mick the Mick didn't answer. He'd noticed something engraved near the end of the far tip. He leaned closer, squinting until it came into focus.

Sears.

What the—?

He stepped back for another look at the scepter of power and—

"A curtain rod . . . it's a freakin' curtain rod!"

Willie looked at him like he was crazy. "Curtain rod? Didn't you hear the man? It's, like, a magic wand, and—hey, what's that over there?"

Mick slapped at Willie's kidney as he passed, but missed because he couldn't take his eyes off the Sears scepter of power. Maybe they could steal it, return it to Sears, and get a brand-new one. That wouldn't help much with Nate the Nose, but Mick the Mick did need a new curtain rod. His old one had broken, and his drapes were attached to the wall with forks. That made Thursdays—spaghetti night—particularly messy.

"*WELCOME!*" boomed the same voice as Willie stopped before another display. *"What you see before you is a rare artifact that once belonged to an ancient lost race that dwelled in the Arkham area during prehistoric times. This, like every other ancient artifact in this room, was excavated from a site near the Arkham landfill."*

"Hey, Mick, y'gotta see this."

After some biblical thinking, Mick the Mick spared the rod and moved along.

"We know little about this ancient lost race but, after careful examination by the eminent archeologists and anthropologists here at the Arkham, Pennsylvania, Museum of Natural History and Baseball Cards, they arrived at an irrefutable conclusion: The artifact before you was used by an ancient shaman of this lost race to perform surrogate sacrifices. (For those of you unfamiliar with the term 'shaman,' please return to the previous display.)"

"I know what a shaman is, 'cause you just told me," Willie said. "But what's a surrogate—?"

"A surrogate sacrifice was an image that was sacrificed instead of a real person. Before you is a statuette of a woman carved by the ancient lost race from a yet-to-be-identified flesh-colored substance. Note the head is missing. This is because the statuette was beheaded instead of the human it represented."

Mick the Mick stepped up to the display and immediately recognized the naked pink figure. He used to swipe his sister Suzy's and make it straddle his rocket and go for a ride. Only Suzy's had a blonde head.

"That's a freakin' Barbie doll!" He grabbed Willie's shoulder and yanked him away.

"Jesus, Mick! You know I got a dislocating shoulder!"

Willie stumbled, knocking Mick the Mick into another display case, which toppled over with a crash.

"WELCOME! What you see before you is a rare tome of lost wisdom that once belonged—"

Screaming, Mick the Mick kicked the speaker until the voice stopped.

"Look, Mick," Willie said, squatting and poking through the broken glass, "it's not a tome, it's a book. It's supposed to contain lost wisdom. Maybe it can tell us how to keep Nate the Nose off our backs." He rose and squinted at the cover. "*The Really, Really, Really Old Ones.*"

"It's a paperback, you moron. How much wisdom you gonna find in there?"

"Yeah, you're right. It says, 'Do not try this at home. Use only under expert supervision or you'll be really, really, really sorry.' Better not mess with *that.*"

"Oh yeah?" Mick had had it—really had it. Up. To. Here. He opened to a random page and read. " 'Random dislocation spell.' "

Willie winced. "Not my shoulder!"

" 'Use only under expert supervision.' Yeah, right. Look, it's got a bunch of gobbledygook to read."

"You mean like 'Mekka-lekka hi—'?"

"Shaddap and I'll show you what bullshit this is."

Mick the Mick started reading, pronouncing the gobbledygook as best he could, going slow and easy so he didn't screw up the words like he normally did when he read.

When he finished, he looked at Willie and grinned. "See? No random dislocation."

Willie rolled his shoulder. "Yeah. Feels pretty good. I wonder—"

The smell hit Mick the Mick first, hot and overpowering, reminding him of that time he stuck his head in the toilet because his older brother told him that's where brownies came from. It was followed by the very real sensation of being squeezed. But not squeezed by a person. Squeezed all over by some sort of full-body force, like being pushed through a too-small opening. The air suddenly became squishy and solid and pressed into every crack and pore on Mick the Mick's body, and then it undulated, moving him, pushing him, through the solid marble floor of the Arkham, Pennsylvania, Museum of Natural History and Baseball Cards.

The very fabric of reality, or something like that, seemed to vibrate with a deep resonance, and the timbre rose to become an overpowering, guttural groan. The floor began to dissolve, or maybe he began to dissolve, and then came a horrible yet compelling farting sound and Mick the Mick was suddenly plopped into the middle of a jungle.

Willie landed next to him.

"I feel like shit," Willie said.

Mick the Mick squinted in the sunlight and looked around. They were surrounded by strange, tropical trees and weird-looking flowers with big fat pink petals that made him feel sort of horny. A dragonfly the size of a bratwurst hovered over their heads, gave them a passing glance, then buzzed over to one of the pink flowers, which snapped open and bit the bug in half.

"Where are we, Mick?"

Mick the Mick scratched his head. "I'm not sure. But I think when I read that book I opened a portal in the space-time continuum and we were squeezed through one of the eleven imploded dimensions into the late Cretaceous period."

"Wow. That sucks."

"No, Willie. It doesn't suck at all."

"Yeah, it does. The season finale of *MacGyver: The Next Generation* is on tonight. It's a really cool episode where he builds a time machine out of some pocket lint and a broken meat thermometer. Wouldn't it be cool to have a time machine, Mick?"

Mick the Mick slapped Willie on the side of his head.

"Jesus, Mick! You know I got swimmer's ear!"

"Don't you get it, Willie? This book *is* a time machine. We can go back in time!"

Willie got wide-eyed. "I get it! We can get back to the present a few minutes early so I won't miss *MacGyver*!"

Mick the Mick considered hitting him again, but his hand was getting sore.

"Think bigger than *MacGyver*, Willie. We're going to be rich. Rich and famous and powerful. Once I figure out how this book works, we'll be able to go to any point in history."

"You mean like we go back to summer camp in 1975? Then we could steal the candy from those counselors so they couldn't lure us into the woods and touch us in the bad place."

"Even better, Willie. We can bet on sports and always win. Like that movie."

"Which one?"

"The one where he went to the past and bet on sports so he could always win."

"The Godfather?"

"No, Willie. *The Godfather* was the one with the fat guy who slept with horse heads."

"Oh yeah. Hey, Mick, don't you think those big pink flowers look like—"

"Shut your stupid hole, Willie. I gotta think."

Mick the Mick racked his brain, but he was never into sports, and he couldn't think of a single team that won anything. Plus, he didn't have any money on him.

It would take a long time to parlay the eighty-one cents in his pocket to sixty grand. But there *had* to be other ways to make money with a time machine. Probably.

He glanced at Willie, who was walking toward one of those pink flowers, leaning in to sniff it. Or perhaps do something else with it, because Willie's tongue was out.

"Willie! Get away from that thing and try to focus! We need to figure out how to make some money."

"It smells like fish, Mick."

"Dammit, Willie! Did you take your medicine this morning like you're supposed to?"

"I can't remember. Nana says I need a stronger subscription. But every time I go to the doctor to get one, I forget to ask."

Mick the Mick scratched himself. Another dragonfly—this one shaped like a banana wearing a turtleneck—flew up to one of those pink flowers and was bitten in half, too. Damn, those bugs were stupid. They just didn't learn. He scratched himself again, wondering if the crabs were back. If they were, he'd be really angry. When you paid fifty bucks for a massage at Madame Yoko's, the happy ending should be crab-free.

Willie said, "Maybe we can go back to the time when Nate the Nose was a little boy, and then we could be real nice to him so when he grew up he would remember us and wouldn't make us eat our junk."

Or we could push his stroller into traffic, Mick the Mick thought.

But Nate the Nose had bosses, and they probably had bosses, too, and traveling through time to push a bunch of babies in front of moving cars seemed like a lot of work.

"Money, Willie. We need to make money."

"We could buy old things from the past then sell them on eBay. Hey, wouldn't it be cool to have four hands? I mean, you could touch twice as much stuff."

Mick the Mick thought about those old comics in Willie's basement, and then he grinned wider than a zebra's ass.

"*Action Comics* number one, which had the first appearance of Superman!" Mick the Mick said. "I could buy it with the change in my pocket, and we can sell it for a fortune!"

Come to think of it, he could buy eight copies. Didn't they go for a million a piece these days?

"I wish I could fly, Mick. Could we go back into time and learn to fly like Superman?"

"Shh!" Mick the Mick tilted his head to the side, listening to the jungle. "You hear something, Willie?"

"Yeah, Mick. I hear you talkin' to me. Now I hear me talkin'. Now I'm singing *a sooooong, a haaaaaaaappy soooooong.*"

Mick the Mick gave Willie a smack in the teeth,

then locked his eyes on the tree line. In the distance the canopy rustled and parted, like something really big was walking toward them. Something so big, the ground shook with every step.

"You hear that, Mick? Sounds like something really big is coming."

A deafening roar came from the thing in the trees, so horrible Mick the Mick could feel his curlies straighten.

"Think it's friendly?" Willie asked.

Mick the Mick stared down at his hands, which still held the *Really, Really, Really Old Ones* book. He flipped it open to a random page, forcing himself to concentrate on the words. But, as often happened in stressful situations, or even situations not all that stressful, the words seemed to twist and mash up and go backward and upside down. Goddamn lesdyxia—shit—*dyslexia*.

"Maybe we should run, Mick."

"Yeah, maybe . . . wait! No! We can't run!"

"Why can't we run, Mick?"

"Remember that episode of *The Simpsons* where Homer went back in time and stepped on a butterfly? The point is, evolution is a really fickle bitch. If we screw up something in the past, it can really mess up the future."

"That sucks. You mean we would get back to our

real time but instead of being made of skin and bones, we're made entirely out of fruit? Like some kind of juicy fruit people?"

Another growl, even closer. It sounded like a lion's roar—if the lion had cojones the size of Chryslers.

"I mean really bad stuff, Willie. I gotta read another passage and get us out of here."

The trees parted, and a shadow began to force itself into view.

"Hey, Mick, if you were made of fruit, would you take a bite of your own arm if you were really super-hungry? I think I would. Wonder what I'd taste like?"

Mick the Mick tried to concentrate on reading the page, but his gaze kept flicking up to the trees. The prehistoric landscape lapsed into deadly silence. Then, like some giant monster coming out of the jungle, a giant monster came out of the jungle.

The head appeared first, the size of a sofa—a really big sofa—with teeth the size of daggers crammed into a mouth large enough to tear a refrigerator in half.

"I think I'd take a few bites out of my leg or something, but I'd be afraid because I don't know if I could stop. Especially if I tasted like strawberries, because I love strawberries, Mick. Why are they called strawberries when they don't taste like straw? Hey, is that a T. rex?"

Now Mick the Mick pee-peed more than just

a little. The creature before them was a deep green color, blending seamlessly into the undergrowth. Rather than scales, it was adorned with small, prickly hairs that Mick the Mick realized were thin brown feathers. Its huge nostrils flared and it snorted, causing the book's pages to ripple.

"I think we should run, Mick. I don't wanna be dinosaur poop."

Mick the Mick agreed. The tyrannosaurus stepped into the clearing on massive legs and reared up to its full height, over forty feet tall. Mick the Mick knew he couldn't outrun it. But he didn't have to. He only had to outrun Willie. He felt bad, but he had no other choice. He had to trick his best friend if he wanted to survive.

"The T. rex has really bad vision, Willie. If you stay very still, it won't be able to . . . Willie, come back!"

Willie had broken for the trees, moving so fast he was a blur. Mick the Mick tore after him, swatting dragonflies out of the way as he ran. Underfoot, he trampled on a large brown roach, a three-toed lizard with big dewy eyes and a disproportionately large brain, and a small furry mammal with a face that looked a lot like Sal from Manny's Meats on Twenty-third Street, which gave a disturbingly human cry when its little neck snapped.

Behind them, the T. rex moved with the speed of a

giant two-legged cat shaped like a dinosaur, snapping teeth so close to Mick the Mick that they nipped the eighteen trailing hairs of his comb-over. He chanced a look over his shoulder and saw the mouth of the animal open so wide Mick the Mick could set up a table for four on the creature's tongue and play Texas hold 'em, not that he would, because that would be fucking stupid.

Then, just as the death jaws of death were ready to close and cause terminal death, the T. rex skidded to a halt and squinted down at the dead little furry thing that used to look a lot like Sal from Manny's Meats, but now looked like Sal with a broken neck. The T. rex nudged it with its massive snout, as if it was trying to wake proto-Sal up.

"What's it doing, Mick?"

Mick the Mick had no idea. The dinosaur nosed the furry thing back and forth, back and forth. Like playing with a toy. Then it gently picked up proto-Sal and flung it across the jungle, toward Willie. It landed at his friend's feet.

"I think it wants to play, Mick." Willie picked up the limp animal. "Hey, you see this mouse thing? Looks like that butcher from Manny's. But smaller. And with a tail. And it don't got no tattoo that says 'Fillet the World.' "

"Throw it, Willie!"

Willie cocked his arm back, aiming at Mick.

"To the dinosaur, you moron!"

"Oh. Fetch, boy!"

Willie tossed proto-Sal, and the T. rex snatched it right out of the air, crunching on it like popcorn.

"He can catch, Mick! Let's throw him something else."

Mick the Mick scanned the jungle floor, quickly overturning a large, flat rock. Beneath it was a family of small rodents who resembled the Capporellis up in 5B—so much so that he swore one even said, "Fronzo!" when he broke its little furry spine. Mick the Mick scooped it up, raising his arm to throw. But the lizard was no longer staring at them. Instead, the creature was bent over and sniffing one of the big pink, fishy-smelling flowers.

"Throw it to me, Mick! We'll play monkey in the middle!"

The 'saur stuck out its queen-size-bed tongue for a lick, and the flower chomped down on it. This sent the T. rex into a screeching, stomping, spitting fit, crushing the flower beneath gigantic talons. Then it sniffed out a similar flower and gave that one a lick.

"Now's our chance to get away, Willie. Willie!"

Before Mick the Mick could stop him, Willie yelled, "Catch!" and chucked a fallen tree branch at the dinosaur. It smacked against the T. rex's head with a painful-sounding thud. The T. rex locked eyes on them and roared.

"He don't want to play no more, Mick. I don't, neither."

They ran. The thunder lizard lunged after them and gained quickly—no surprise, what with it being able to cover a dozen of their steps with only one of its own.

As Mick the Mick whipped through the jungle, overwhelmed with bladder-squeezing panic, he tried to force lucidity and make his very last thought something profound and revelatory. Instead, all he could think of was that *Brady Bunch* episode in Hawaii when Greg found the cursed tiki idol.

Not a brilliant last thought, but everyone had to admit that was one of the show's best episodes.

"Mick! It's not following us anymore!"

Mick the Mick chanced an over-the-shoulder look and indeed the T. rex had once again abandoned pursuit. It simply stood there, staring off into the jungle, as if in deep thought. Then it dropped to the ground like it had been shot, the impact a sound of thunder.

Had some caveman killed the dinosaur? Or perhaps some rich hunter from the future on some kind of prehistoric hunting expedition? Or Nate the Nose, who had come back in time to get his money?

But another look at the Tyrannosaurus dispelled

any such notion. The thunder lizard wasn't dead. It was licking itself between its legs. Really going at it, too, like a giant Jurassic dog.

"I wish I could do that," Willie said. "But he'd probably bite me."

After a good thirty seconds, the T. rex sighed loudly, balletically leapt to its feet, and became distracted by one of those dragonfly things, wandering off after it.

This T. rex was beginning to remind Mick the Mick of someone he knew. He just couldn't place who. But he was getting a flash of why the damned things were extinct.

Which gave Mick the Mick a great idea. An idea that would save their asses and make them even richer than *Action Comics* #1.

"Look for an egg, Willie."

"An egg, Mick? You hungry? I'm kinda hungry, too. I like my eggs sunny-side up, because they look like big yellow eyes. Then I make a smiley mouth out of bacon, and I call him Mr. Henry. Don't we need chickens to get eggs, Mick?"

"Dinosaur eggs, Willie. If we bring one back with us, we can grow a dinosaur. Just like that movie."

"Which one?"

"The one where they grew the dinosaurs."

"*The Merchant of Venice?*"

"Just find an egg, Willie."

"I get it, Mick. We grow a dinosaur, and we can feed it Nate the Nose so he won't kill us—"

"Shaddup and search for a damn nest."

"I'm searching, Mick. Hey! Look!"

"You find one?"

"I found one of those pink flowers that smell like fish and look like—"

Willie screamed. Mick the Mick glanced over and saw his lifelong friend was playing tug of war with one of those toothy prehistoric flowers, using a long red rope.

No. Not a red rope. Those were Willie's intestines.

"Help me, Mick!"

Without thinking, Mick the Mick reached out a hand and grabbed Willie's duodenum. He squeezed, tight as he could, and Willie farted.

"It hurts, Mick! Being disemboweled hurts!"

A bone-shaking roar from behind them. The T. rex had lost interest in the dragonflies and was sniffing at the newly spilled blood, his sofa-size head only a few meters away and getting closer. Mick the Mick could smell its breath, reeking of rotten meat and bad oral hygiene and dooky.

No, the dooky was all Willie. Pouring out like brown shaving cream. Willie's face contorted in pain.

"I think I need a doctor, Mick. Use your cell phone. Call nine-one-one."

Mick the Mick released his friend's innards and wiped his hand on his shirt just as the T. rex leaned over them and opened its maw, blotting out the sky. All Mick the Mick could see was teeth and tongue and that dangly thing that hangs in the back of the throat like a big punching bag. He could never remember what those things were called.

"Look, the dinosaur is back," Willie groaned. "Check out the size of his epiglottis, Mick. Like a big punching bag."

The book. It was their only chance. Mick the Mick raised the *Really, Really, Really Old Ones* and flipped open to the same page that had brought them here. Maybe if he read the passage again, it would take them back to their time. Or if he read a little earlier, maybe they could go back to before Nana made the cake, and prevent this incredibly stupid chain of events.

"I think my kidney just fell out." Willie held something red and squishy in his cupped hands. "It still hurts from when you punched me."

Mick the Mick concentrated. Concentrated as hard as he could, blotting out Willie and the T. rex and everything in this horrible prehistoric world except the words on the page.

"It looks like a kidney bean. Is that why they call them kidneys, Mick? Because they look like beans? I like beans."

Mick the Mick's hands shook, and his vision swam, and all the vowels on the page looked exactly the same and the consonants looked like pretzel sticks, but he began to read aloud.

"Is this my liver, Mick? And what's this thing? I should put all this stuff back in." Willie dropped to his knees and began scooping up guts and twigs and rocks and shoving everything into the gaping hole in his belly.

The T. rex lowered its mouth, about to swallow them both at once.

Sweat soaked his face and stung his eyes, and the hair still left on Mick the Mick's comb-over started to curl from the T. rex's breath as its jaws began to close, but he finished the passage, reading better and faster and harder than a homeschooled foreign kid who won spelling bees.

Nothing happened.

The fabric of reality didn't vibrate. The ground didn't dissolve. There was a familiar *pbbbbth* sound, but it was from Mick stepping on Willie's colon.

Willie flopped sideways and sprawled out onto his back, limbs akimbo, looking like he took a bath in lasagna. Mick the Mick ducked down next to him, narrowly escaping the snap of the dinosaur's bite. The Tyrannosaurus grunted, then opened wide for a second try.

"Mick . . ." Willie panted, his breath fading. "Read . . . read the part . . . that sent us here . . . but . . . read it backward."

The T. rex snatched both of them into its jaws like a giant bulldozer, if bulldozers had jaws and could snatch people. The *Really, Really, Really Old Ones* book fell from Mick the Mick's grasp, and the dagger teeth punched into his legs and chest with agonizing agony, but for the first and only time in his life his dyslexia paid off, and with his last breath he managed to cry out:

"OTKIN ADARAB UTAALK!"

Another near-turd experience and then they were excreted into a room with a television and a couch and a picture window. But the television screen was embedded—or growing out of?—a toadstool-like thing that was in turn growing out of the floor. The couch looked funny, like who'd sit on that? And the picture window looked out on some kind of nightmare jungle.

And then again, maybe not so weird.

No, Mick the Mick thought. Weird. Very weird.

He looked at Willie.

And screamed.

Or at least tried to. What came out was more like a croak.

Because it wasn't Willie. Not unless Willie had

grown four extra eyes—two of them on stalks—and sprouted a fringe of tentacles around where he used to have a neck and shoulders. He now looked like a conical turkey croquette that had been rolled in seasoned bread crumbs before baking and garnished with live worms after.

The thing made noises that sounded like, "Mick, is that you?" but spoken by a turkey croquette with a mouth full of linguine.

Stranger still, it sounded a little like Willie. Mick the Mick raised a tentacle to scratch his—

Whoa! *Tentacle?*

Well, of course a tentacle. What did he expect?

He looked down and was surprised to see that he was encased in a bread-crumbed, worm-garnished, turkey croquette. No, wait, he *was* a turkey croquette.

Why did everything seem wrong, and yet simultaneously at the same time seem not wrong, too?

Just then another six-eyed, tentacle-fringed croquette glided into the room. The Willie-sounding croquette said, "Hi, Nana." His words were much clearer now.

Nana? Was this Willie's Nana?

Of course it was. Mick the Mick had known her for years.

"There's an unpleasant man at the door who wants to talk to you. Or else."

"Or else what?"

A new voice said, "Or else you two get to eat cloacal casseroles, and guess who donates the cloacae?"

Mick the Mick unconsciously crossed his tentacles over his cloaca. In his twenty-four years since budding, Mick the Mick had grown very attached to his cloaca. He'd miss it something awful.

A fourth croquette had entered, followed by the two biggest croquettes Mick the Mick had ever seen. Only these weren't turkey croquettes, these were chipped-beef croquettes. This was serious.

The new guy sounded like Nate the Nose, but didn't have a nose. And what was a nose anyway?

"Oh no," Willie moaned. "I don't want to eat Mick's cloaca."

"I meant your own, jerk!" the newcomer barked.

"But I have a hernia—"

"Shaddap!"

Mick the Mick recognized him now: Nate the Noodge, pimp, loan shark, and drug dealer. Not the sort you lent your bike to.

Wait . . . what was a bike?

"What's up, Nate?"

"That brick of product I gave you for delivery. I had this sudden, I dunno, bad feeling about it. A frisson of malaise and apprehension, you might say. I just hadda come by and check on it, *knome sayn*?"

The brick? What brick?

Mick the Mick had a moment of panic—he had no idea what Nate the Noodge was talking about.

Oh yeah. The *product.* Now he remembered.

"Sure, Nate, it's right in here."

He led Nate to the kitchen, where the brick of product lay on the big center table.

Nate the Noodge pointed a tentacle at it. One of his guards lifted it, sniffed it, then wriggled his tentacle fringe that it was okay. Mick the Mick had expected him to nod, but a nod would require a neck, and the guard didn't have a neck. Then Mick the Mick realized he didn't know what a neck was. Or a nod, for that matter.

What was it with these weird thoughts, like memories, going through his head? They were like half-remembered dreams. Nightmares, more likely. Pink flowers, and giant lizards, and stepping on some mice that looked like a lot like the Capporellis up in 5B. Except the Capporellis lived in 5B, and looked like jellyfish. What were mice anyway? He looked at Willie to see if he was just as confused.

Willie was playing with his cloaca.

Nate the Noodge turned to them and said, "A'ight. Looks like my frisson of malaise and apprehension was fer naught. Yer cloacas is safe . . . fer now. But you don't deliver that product like you're apposed to and it's casserole city, *knome sayn?*"

"We'll deliver it, Nate," Willie said. "Don't you worry. We'll deliver it."

"Y'better," Nate said, then left with his posse.

"Where we supposed to deliver it?" Willie said when they were alone again.

Mick the Mick kicked him in his cloaca.

"The same place we always deliver it."

"Ow!" Willie was saying, rubbing his cloaca. "That hurt. You know I got a—hey, look!" He was pointing to the TV. "*The Toad Whisperer* is on! My favorite show!"

He settled onto the floor and stared.

Mick the Mick hated to admit it, but he was kind of addicted to the show himself. He settled next to Willie.

Faintly, from the kitchen, he heard Nana say, "Oh dear, I was going to bake a cake, but I'm out of flour. Could one of you boys—oh, wait. Here's some. Never mind."

A warning glimp chugged in Mick the Mick's brain and puckered his cloaca. Something bad was about to happen . . .

What had Nate the Noodge called it? "A frisson of malaise and apprehension." Sounded like a dessert, but Mick the Mick had gathered it meant a worried feeling, like what he was having right now.

But about what? What could go sour? The product was safe, and they were watching *The Toad Whisperer.*

As soon as that was over, they'd go deliver it, get paid, and head on over to Madame Yoko's for a happy ending endoplasmic reticulum massage. And maybe a cloac job.

The frisson of malaise and apprehension faded. Must have been another nightmare flashback.

Soon the aroma of baking cake filled the house. Right after the show, he'd snag himself a piece.

For some reason he thought of an odd-shaped cookie with a prediction inside. What was it called? A prediction pastry? No, something else, something similar.

Who cared? Predictions never came true. The only thing you could count on was Nana's cake. That was always good.

An Evening with Al Gore

CHARLAINE HARRIS

Toddy Makepeace had seen Al Gore speak the previous spring, and a year later she hadn't gotten over it. Toddy, born and bred a realist, was quite aware the former vice president hadn't particularly noticed her when he'd shaken her hand, though he'd looked slightly startled that her grip was so firm. But he'd nodded in approval when she'd told him she intended to join in his fight against people who trashed the planet.

Toddy's husband, Mark, joined in Toddy's new crusade with fervor. He'd seen too many changes in the world to deny that Earth was being damaged and polluted at an alarming rate. Mark and Toddy had no plans to have children, but they did hope to continue enjoying their happy life together. A big part of that happy life was the pleasure they took in their extended exploration of the Earth's remaining wilderness. Having plenty of forests left in the world, preserving an environmentally safe wilderness, was vital to the Makepeaces.

Through the years, Toddy had gradually assumed the role of moral compass for the pair, while Mark had slipped into a more logistical role. They played to their strengths. Toddy had been recycling newspapers, cans, and plastics for years, she rode a bicycle while she went about her errands in their historic New England village, and she and Mark shared a shower quite often to cut down on the amount of water they used. Mark made sure the accumulated recyclable material made its way to the correct collection site, kept the bicycle in good repair, and enjoyed the showers very much.

Toddy was both thorough and conscientious, and after her inspiring connection with Al Gore, she decided it was time to step up her slapdash "green" efforts a notch or two. Or three. She began passing out leaflets at the nearest mall. She put indignant handwritten notes under the windshield wipers of gas-guzzling SUVs. She established a compost heap at the back of the lawn of the charming Victorian house where she and Mark lived.

When Mark was sure Toddy wasn't around, he made a face at the smell of the compost heap. He quietly hired a teenager who lived nearby to come and turn the compost, a job Toddy had assigned to Mark. (Same difference, Mark figured. He'd been charged with getting the job done, and it was.) Perhaps Mark wasn't quite as passionate about confronting litterers and polluters as his wife, but he was always present to haul her out of the resultant trouble. Toddy had no problem at all pouncing on a woman who tossed her cigarette butt to the sidewalk; in fact, Toddy had no problem tackling the CEO of a local company that had been caught dumping industrial waste into a remote pond.

Since Toddy had followed litterers, pointing out their transgressions at the top of her lungs, and also had quite literally tackled the CEO, the police had come to call at the Makepeaces' house more than once. Every time, Toddy's appearance always bought her some grace without Mark's having to intervene. Toddy was five feet tall, pleasantly round and bosomy, and had a head full of red curly hair. She certainly didn't look her age; in fact, Toddy looked like a naughty teenager who might need to be spanked for her own good.

Following the tackling incident, as Mark watched two patrolmen fall under Toddy's spell in ten minutes, he had a hard time concealing his smile. He'd been watching men fall for his wife for years. How could he blame them? Mark, who was tall and dark and unremarkable, thanked his lucky stars that he and Toddy had found each other in a most unlikely encounter. They'd been separately hiking the Appalachian Trail, and in a remote area they'd happened across a wounded deer some careless hunter had neglected to kill. Their eyes had met over the pitiful bleeding animal, and they'd been together ever since.

On this cool evening, when the policemen had departed, the Makepeaces settled in their gazebo with a bottle of wine. Some couples who'd been together as long as Mark and Toddy had lost the spark, but the two had the good fortune to still find each other exciting. They enjoyed the evenings they got to spend alone together. It was dark, and they lit the candles on the table. The backyard of the old house wasn't huge, but it had been carefully planted to provide privacy.

"I feel confident Fenton won't press charges," Mark said after they'd each had a sip from their glasses. It was a cool Massachusetts evening, and their cobblestoned village, Bracefield, was quiet and serene, just the way they liked it.

Toddy laughed as if such a concept was ridiculous. "Of course he won't," she said. "Think of how silly he would look if he did." She took a deep breath and her smile faded. "Mark, I have to confess. I'm getting bored with Bracefield, even with town," she said, and Mark sat up straighter at the change in topic.

Bracefield lay outside Boston, which was very convenient for shopping trips. There was a state park within easy driving distance where the two spent a lot of time, and they'd made a network of friends in the area. But Toddy seemed quite serious.

"We've been here a long time. Maybe we need a change of scene. We might have been more aware of this global crisis earlier if we lived in a more enlightened country, or if we were in less of a rut. Why don't we try living somewhere with a more positive attitude toward 'green' issues?"

"Like where?" Mark set down his glass. Toddy, as always, was challenging him to rise to the occasion.

"Oh, I don't know . . . one of the Scandinavian countries. They're much greener than the USA. Sweden?"

"That's an idea," Mark said slowly. "We'd have to learn the language. But we could do that." He found himself unexpectedly enthusiastic. How long had they lived in Bracefield? At least twenty years, he thought. As much as he adored the old house they'd restored, maybe it was time for a change. And as long as they were making a change, why not make it a really big one? Why move to somewhere equally predictable, like Miami or Seattle? "In fact, Toddy, that's a wonderful idea," he said and watched his wife's face glow. The more Mark considered the excitement of learning a new country, coping with daily living there, making new friendships and achieving new goals, the more stimulating he found the prospect.

"But I don't want to just slink away," Toddy said. Mark understood they'd entered phase two of the conversation. "I want to leave with a big bang. Like Bilbo in *The Lord of the Rings.*"

"You want to slip on an invisibility ring and disappear in a giant explosion?"

Toddy laughed and refilled their glasses. "No, Mark. Not exactly. I want to do something for America before we go. I've always been a patriot, you know that."

"What form do you want this service to take? You know I'm willing to help you do whatever you want."

"You're so sweet," Toddy said. She laid her hand on his. "I'll think about it and let you know."

While Toddy considered her patriotic duty, Mark began to wind down the Makepeaces' extensive financial affairs. He knew Toddy; she wouldn't change her mind.

One evening after their housekeeper, Mrs. Powers, had left, Toddy put her arms around Mark's neck. "We're going to have a party," she told Mark. "A really special party. I think we'll need Purcell and Deena Collville to help us."

Mark raised his eyebrows at that. Purcell and Deena were old friends they hadn't seen in . . . well, years, Mark realized when he thought about it. "That'll be nice," he said, though rather doubtfully. The Collvilles were almost as wealthy as Mark and Toddy, and they were an attractive couple, but Mark had never been as fond of the two as Toddy was. Deena and Purcell were a little cold-blooded for his taste. But since he loved Toddy, he began thinking of practical arrangements.

"Tomorrow morning, I'll ask Mrs. Powers to make up the guest bedroom. And to put those extra-heavy drapes up so they can sleep in." The Collvilles might have changed in the years since the Makepeaces had seen them, but their sleeping habits were surely going to be the same.

"Thanks, darling," Toddy said. "Oh, please tell Mrs. Powers not to disturb anything on our office table. That's where I'm working this week."

The next time Mark went into the office to take care of his e-mail, he found the round table in the center of the room covered with lists. Toddy had moved her laptop from her desk to the table, and she was staring at the screen with an air of preoccupation. She was searching for something on Google, and when she found it, she read intently.

"No, not quite," she muttered and Mark smiled. Toddy talked out loud when she was hot on the trail of a project. She was so engrossed in her research that she didn't even notice when Mark left the room after making a few phone calls and sending some e-mails.

When Purcell and Deena drove in that night, they were treated to the best bottle of wine Mark's cellar could produce, and Toddy continued to be generous with the drinks all evening. Purcell and Deena were even more upscale than Mark and Toddy; in fact, sometimes Mark thought the two verged on pretentious, though he'd never tell Toddy that. Purcell was tall, slim, and gray-haired. He generally wore striped dress shirts, starched and rolled up to his elbows. He thought this made him look egalitarian. Sometimes he even tied his sweater sleeves around his neck as if he were posing for a J.Crew ad. Deena carried a purse that cost eight hundred dollars. Mark and Toddy knew this because Deena told them.

Despite the Collvilles' affectations, they were good company, all in all. Mark found himself enjoying their visit more than he'd anticipated. While their guests took a stroll down the town's well-lit streets, Toddy popped *An Inconvenient Truth* into the DVD player. Mark could tell she was humming with anticipation. When Purcell and Deena returned to the house, relaxed and smiling, the moment was right.

"Toddy has something for you to watch," Mark said. "We think it'll interest you."

After the Collvilles had watched the film, Deena said, "I had no idea. Purcell, I think we're horribly out of touch."

Purcell nodded, looking rather self-consciously grave and thoughtful. "What do you want us to do?" he asked Toddy.

She began to explain.

By the time she'd finished, the Collvilles were on board with Toddy's plan of providing a grand gesture to mark the end of the Makepeaces' years in the United States.

Preparations began in earnest the next day.

Toddy had assigned Mark the job of looking for a house in Sweden. This was the kind of challenge Mark relished, so soon he was knee-deep in small boxes from Rosetta Stone and packets of papers from real-estate agents. He and Toddy had agreed that they'd wait to put their house on the market after they were out of it, which saved them a lot of grief. Mark reflected for the millionth time that having money smoothed out many jagged corners, as he examined a picture of a house for sale outside Malmö. Swedish homes tended to be wooden and barnlike, at least the ones he'd been viewing online. Mark thought Toddy would find them amusing. He was searching for a large home in the middle of a forest, which wasn't going to be easy to find.

Purcell was acting as social adviser. He was helping Toddy assemble the guest list and he was experimenting with the wording of the note of invitation.

Deena was working on assembling the paperwork Toddy and Mark would need in their new life. This involved a lot of trips into the city to consult with people who kept a very, very low profile. She was also arranging for the staff they'd need.

One night Mark went into the study to track down a crossword puzzle book, and Toddy called him over. "Darling, look at this man," she said, holding up a picture of a very heavy forty-year-old with big jowls and lots of blond hair. "Doesn't he look like he needs enlightening?"

"Of course," Mark said promptly. "And I'm sure he'd be honored to be on the guest list for your party. Isn't that James Jeffrey Jamison, who imports rare woods for luxury homes?"

"Yes, he's responsible for the clear-cutting of thousands of acres of rainforest," Toddy said grimly. But then she caught sight of Mark's worried face, and she smiled up at him, her blue eyes sparkling. "We're going to have a great party, we're going to show the film, and then we'll ask them for contributions. I know they'll be glad to write great big checks, even Jamison. We'll persuade them!"

Deena was sitting on the other side of the table

beside Purcell. She said, "Let's invite Catriona McHughes." She held up a magazine. "See? She's the editor. She's always printing articles about global warming for her readers, but she just flew from New York to Chicago in her private jet for a party! What a criminal waste of fuel!"

Purcell seemed to enjoy seeing his normally uninvolved wife on fire about a cause. Even a near narcissist like Purcell could be swayed by the passion of a beautiful woman. This was not the Collvilles' usual style, so the novelty of it intrigued both of them. They'd probably drop their new cause fairly quickly, but Mark realized their help was essential in ensuring the Makepeace farewell party's success. He would hate it if Toddy were disappointed the least little bit.

"Are we having the party here?" Mark asked his wife the next time he passed through.

"Oh no," she said. "We're making arrangements in the city. I don't think some of these people would come if they had to drive out to Bracefield. They don't know us, after all; though I'm sure they can find out we're rich. I'm counting on that. Anyway, we couldn't possibly handle all those cars. Deena, we need a competent driver for valet parking."

Mark was beginning to appreciate the scope of Toddy's planning. He didn't want to sound mistrustful, but he had to ask one final question. "You're asking them to bring the invitations with them?" he said.

"Oh yes," Toddy said. "It's the best means of preventing gate crashers."

"Have you hired the caterer?" Purcell asked. "They'll expect good food."

"I'm on it," Deena said. "Sweetheart, did you know Toddy and Mark are friends with *Anna Clausen*?" Purcell looked suitably impressed, though neither he nor Deena was a foodie. Anna Clausen was the hottest caterer in the Boston area.

"Is Anna Clausen an, ah, environmentalist like you two?" Purcell asked, conscious that Mrs. Powers was still in the kitchen.

Toddy nodded. "Yes," she said. "She sure is. In fact, she's donating her time to the cause."

When the guest list had been gone over with a fine-tooth comb, Toddy and Purcell tossed it on the table in front of Deena and Mark with an air of triumph. The list was short—only twenty-six names.

"Why so few?" Mark asked.

"No waste," Purcell said. "This is the maximum number we can persuade, I think."

"How'd you pick them?" Mark could think of many major offenders that weren't listed.

"They're not the most important figures, as you see, but they're all on the blacklist. Just, the B or C blacklist rather than the A. We had to pick people who would come without hangers-on or media. We want this to be a private affair."

Mark recognized most of the names, though Deena was looking rather blank. "Oh yes, the car manufacturer who won't look for alternative fuel," he told Deena. "Here's an EPA inspector who's under indictment for taking bribes . . . good choice. Bella Bordelon?"

"Her beauty products are tested on bunnies," Toddy said. Her face was stiff with indignation.

"Is that strictly a global-warming issue?" Mark asked, trying not to smile. "After all, you've eaten rabbit before."

"*Bunnies,*" Toddy said. "And I didn't torture them first."

By the time the big evening rolled around, a lot of things had changed in the beautiful Victorian home in Bracefield. Many of the Makepeaces' possessions had been sold or stored, Mrs. Powers had been bid farewell with a lovely large check, and Deena and Purcell had thrown their bags in the trunk of their car, since they'd be returning to their own place in Westchester immediately after the festivities. Mark had been at his town office ten hours a day for the past week, ensuring that when they arrived in Sweden they'd have a place to stay while they viewed homes, and a secure financial base.

Toddy and Mark were dressed to the nines: Toddy

looking delicious and elegant in silver-spangled vintage Dior, Mark in a very conventional but tailor-made tux. They stood in the living room of the home they'd shared for two happy decades. Toddy had trouble holding back tears.

"Come on, darling, the future promises buckets of fun," Mark said. Toddy was so seldom melancholy that he wasn't used to having to raise her spirits.

"I know," she said. "What a great evening this will be. Mr. Gore will be so proud of us. I started to put in the notes, 'Come share an evening with Al Gore.' Though that wouldn't have been entirely honest, because we have the film, not the man himself. Purcell said none of them would come if they thought Mr. Gore would actually be there."

"When he gets the checks," Mark said, in a gentle reminder that the former vice president would probably never know how much they'd personally contributed to environmental fund-raising, "he'll be so pleased."

"Yes, of course," Toddy said. "I've got the mailing envelope ready." If she sighed very gently, Mark was not going to offer any rebuke. His wife was amazingly optimistic, so much so that she'd already put stamps on the envelope. He was afraid she was in for a disappointment.

Their trip into the city in their Prius was a silent one. Deena and Purcell, dressed to the teeth in up-to-the-minute designer finery, followed in their own Lincoln Town Car. Mark was mentally reviewing all the arrangements, and perhaps Toddy was saying a quiet good-bye to the country she loved so much.

When they reached the outskirts of Boston, they followed the route to the venue. It had been chosen with some difficulty, and Toddy and Purcell had debated fiercely about the selection. The location had to be quirky enough to engage the invited guests, but the party couldn't be held in any of the beautiful hotels or restaurants Boston had to offer. Toddy had designed the evening to be an expression of her own nature, and crowded areas just didn't fit in with that expression.

Toddy had handwritten each invitation, following Purcell's model. After the correct opening salutation, each one read:

> *Mark and I hope you'll come to Mark's offices at the Huntleigh Building at eight o'clock on October 10. We'll provide further transportation after that. We have an evening of surprises for our very select group of guests! In addition to enjoying your company and an excellent meal, we're touting our favorite charity, so please don't forget your checkbook. We hope to see you then.*
>
> *Toddy Makepeace*

The Huntleigh was a respectable downtown Boston office building. Though this was an odd invitation, Toddy and Purcell were hoping the Makepeace name and fortune and the Huntleigh's staid but lavish appearance would stoke the guests' curiosity while making them feel secure. Not all of the twenty-six invitees had accepted; there'd been eight refusals, fifteen acceptances, and three of the proposed guests hadn't let the Makepeaces know one way or the other. "So rude," Toddy had told Mark, her sweet face looking anything but sweet for a moment. "But of course, the ones who've accepted are all bringing escorts. So, thirty for sure. And the most important guests have said yes."

After they arrived in the city, the Collvilles and the Makepeaces parked their cars at the party venue and got a ride to the Huntleigh from one of the hired staff members. When they stepped into the marble lobby, the rest of the staff was waiting.

The results of Deena's labor looked good. The people she'd hired were dressed in white serving jackets and black pants. They were all attractive and smiling. They'd been extensively prepped. At this pre-party pep rally, Toddy gave them even more careful instructions and handed them their paychecks in advance. The three women and the six young men, all apparently in their early twenties or younger, looked very happy.

Toddy got more and more anxious as the party time grew near. "Oh, Mark," she said, "I hope this all goes well."

"Darling, it's a win-win situation," Mark said. "If our guests see the error of their ways, we'll have a lot of checks to contribute to environmental issues. If they don't, well, we'll have the satisfaction of having done our best in our own way."

Toddy nodded, determination in every line of her rounded face. Then a car pulled up to the lobby door and Toddy prepared to greet the first guest.

To her delight, the first arrival was James Jeffrey Jamison, looking even more like a blond frog than he had in his picture. Jamison was accompanied by a ravishing young woman who was not Mrs. Jamison. Though Toddy realized this was an insult, she greeted Jamison with apparent delight and introduced him to Mark. Other guests arrived almost immediately on Jamison's heels. Unmarried EPA Inspector George Puffman arrived with a young man he introduced as Selim, who appeared to be Puffman's bodyguard. Puffman didn't seem to be relaxed. In fact, he looked around him with suspicion.

But Toddy greeted George Puffman, Selim, and all the subsequently arriving guests with an optimistic cordiality, and Mark, too, was at his best, asking all the right questions about their welfare, their business ventures, their sports opinions. Mark was quick to learn all the names and relationships of the guests' escorts, too. Toddy reflected, not for the first time, that she'd been incredibly lucky to find Mark. The Collvilles acted as backup hosts, stepping in when any guest looked abandoned. Deena and Purcell definitely had on their party faces; they were dazzling in their charm and animation. Deena herself made a point of collecting the invitation notes; to her pleasure each guest had remembered to bring it.

When all the guests had assembled and their cars had been parked in the building's garage, a gaudy bus pulled up to the doors. The guests exclaimed, in confusion or derision or good humor. "I don't think any of them have ridden in a party bus before," Mark murmured. He hadn't himself. He hadn't even known they existed until Toddy had shown him a brochure.

"Come on, friends, this is the easiest way to get you all to dinner," Toddy said gaily, and because they would have been embarrassed to do otherwise, the guests climbed on board the bus. The driver, a dark, almond-eyed young woman with dreadlocks whose name tag read MARCHESA, gave them a cordial nod as they boarded. Despite the presence of his mistress, James Jeffrey Jamison visibly appreciated Marchesa's appearance. He chucked her on the cheek as he passed. He said something to her that sounded to Toddy like,

"Hey, dark meat." That puzzled Toddy, who'd never heard the expression. Marchesa didn't seem to take offense; in fact, she looked pleased.

The hired servers had left at least fifteen minutes before the huge vehicle began to roll through the dark streets, the guests gaping around at the bus's cheerful disco lights and the liquor cabinet. Another server whose name tag read PAULA began passing around glasses of wine. Conversation between the guests began to flow more easily, and finally the party began cohering. The Makepeaces and Collvilles circulated like mad. In fact, the guests were already in the dingy warehouse area close to the water before they knew it. A few of them exclaimed at the "neighborhood."

"I thought this had all been gentrified," said a real-estate developer.

"There are pockets here and there that haven't been touched," Deena said. She'd searched hard for one of those pockets.

"Don't worry, friends," Toddy called. "You'll love our surprise venue."

One or two still seemed uneasy as the bus pulled up to an old warehouse, but once they'd been ushered inside the large rolling door they saw that the old place had been beautifully decorated. There were carpets strewn everywhere on the old wooden floor, and the walls had been camouflaged by swaths of hanging material in rich colors. The round tables were draped with white linen and the place settings were perfection. There was a centerpiece on each table, and a large movie screen was set up at a strategic point. The waitstaff was fully briefed. They began taking coats and carrying around yet more wine the minute the door had rolled shut behind the last guest.

Anna Clausen entered soon after. Clausen was a tall, angular woman with jet-black hair and a face like a hatchet. She was elegantly dressed in a severe gray-blue evening dress. All of the guests exchanged happy, anticipatory looks as she entered. Anna Clausen was well-known among the rich and nearly rich. None of them dreamed that Clausen had driven the catering truck herself. It was loaded with excellent food, though Clausen certainly wasn't used to delivering and serving it herself.

"Deena, Toddy! Beautiful as always!" Anna kissed their cheeks, shook the hands of Mark and Purcell.

Toddy said, "Anna, I can smell the wonderful aroma from here. You've become so famous you don't just feed the celebrities, you *are* a celebrity."

Clausen looked pleased. "When you called me to explain," she said in her heavily accented English, "I could hardly take in the audacity of the idea. The Makepeaces always think big. That Deena, she agreed with my menu completely." Anna was impressed with

Deena's intelligence. The truth was, Deena had never cared a thing about food. Prime rib, salmon, it was all one to her. But Anna was happy, that was the important thing.

"Thanks for agreeing to be one of the big draws for the evening," Mark said. "Thanks to our money and the reputation of your cooking, we're hoping this party will be a big success."

"I'm ready to start the evening," Toddy said. She looked around to make sure everything and everyone was in place. The waitstaff was circulating with a so-so choice of wines ("No reason to waste money," Mark had decided) and hors d'oeuvres. A CD of chamber music provided a soothing background. A lone man was stationed in front of the rolling door. There was another door at the back of the warehouse, but it was concealed by a swath of material.

Deena murmured to Toddy, "I notice that ass Jamison brought his mistress, not his wife."

Toddy shrugged. "Then he'd better be in a generous mood," she said, and Deena laughed.

Bella Bordelon had dressed for the evening in full warpaint, glistening and gleaming with every beauty product she could slather on her skin or in her hair. Bella was an aging beauty, and she had arrived on the arm of her latest husband, a man just old enough to keep her from being a figure of fun. She greeted Anna

Clausen as if they were very old friends. She didn't notice the gleam in Anna's eyes as she threw her arms around Anna's neck.

When the guests had had a few glasses of wine and a bacon-wrapped fig or two, Toddy took the microphone and tapped on it. The courteous silence was relaxed; a result of the alcohol, Toddy thought.

"I'm so glad you're all here tonight," she said sincerely. "Each of you is our very special guest, and we hope you'll join with us in our effort to save this wonderful planet. We chose this warehouse to meet to emphasize our commitment to reclaim buildings that are still usable, buildings that for tax reasons are allowed to fall down and become blights on the landscape. Throwing this dinner here cost a sixth of what it would have cost at a hotel. That's money we can use to scrub our planet clean!"

There was a murmur of comment. Mark, standing at the side of the crowd and keeping a sharp eye, could tell that the tone was contemptuous.

Toddy's smile never wavered as she met Bella Bordelon's scornful face. If anything, it brightened. "She's thinking of the bunnies," Mark whispered to Deena. "Do you think there's any way they'll be talked around?"

"No," said Deena. And she smiled a little herself.

"Before we serve your excellent meal, supplied by

the great Anna Clausen," Toddy said, "we'd like to show you a film that's made a huge impact on our lives. We hope it'll do the same for yours. I have a feeling it will." And the young man in charge of the movie equipment began to show *An Inconvenient Truth.*

At least the audience was quiet during the showing. But by the time the showing came to an end, the guests were hungry and restless, and the applause was lukewarm.

James Jeffrey Jamison was not being subtle about pawing his mistress, and she was struggling to keep a pleasant expression on her face. She wasn't drunk; she'd been quite careful in her wine intake. Bella Bordelon and her husband were more decorous. Bella was whispering to George Puffman, who'd been seated next to her, and Bella's young man fell deep in conversation with Selim, the bodyguard. As a whole, the audience of environmental offenders didn't seem to be showing the contrite attitude that Toddy had yearned for.

But she smiled and persevered. "My husband, Mark, the host of this wonderful event, will be passing among you with the proverbial hat, hoping you'll contribute generously to our cause."

"We're hungry," said George Puffman. "I'll write a damn check if it means you bring the food."

"Of course, Mr. Puffman," Toddy said.

There was not a wave of check writing. In fact,

as Mark passed through with a battered porkpie hat (which Deena had pronounced highly symbolic), the contributions came lightly, and when Toddy riffled through the collected checks, looking at the amounts, her sweet face fell. Mark was angry on her behalf, though he hadn't expected great things. The guests had been selected for their poor track record on environmental issues, and they were running true to form.

Toddy raised her hand in the air in the prearranged signal. She picked up the microphone for the last time.

"I'm sorry you didn't come through for the cause," she said sadly. "I had hoped this evening with Mr. Gore would persuade you. We planned our party so carefully, to give you all a chance to redeem yourselves."

Bella Bordelon called, "I don't need your redemption. I've done nothing for which I need to apologize."

"Give 'em hell, Bella," said Puffman. Jamison echoed the sentiment. His mistress, who was a canny young woman, looked around at the white-clad waitstaff. They'd moved to form a loose circle around the cluster of tables. She rose and excused herself quietly to go to the powder room. Instead, she walked as swiftly as her feet would carry her over to the big rolling door. The sharp-eyed waiter guarding it glanced at Toddy, a question on his face. Toddy gave a tiny nod of assent, and he rolled the door open just wide enough to permit the young woman to exit. She stepped outside with an unmistakable air of relief, and began walking quickly through the deserted warehouses on her high-heeled sandals as the door rolled closed behind her. She may have sensed someone following her for a few blocks, and she took care not to run.

But no one else in the warehouse seemed to pick up on whatever had spooked Jamison's mistress. In fact, the guests were beginning to look more and more restless and angry.

"Since you don't seem to feel the need to help the Earth, we've decided to give the United States a present before we leave these shores," Toddy said, her voice sad. "I'd hoped we'd have a huge sum to hand to the former vice president, and I'd hoped we'd all serve you a great meal and you'd get to go home replete with food and virtue. But now, I'm afraid, that won't be happening."

"NO FOOD?" bellowed Puffman.

"*We'll* eat," Toddy said gently. "See my teeth?" At that unexpected question, all the guests stared. Toddy Makepeace shucked her vintage Dior and parted her lips to show her white teeth, and the assembled crowd watched as they grew longer and sharper. Then Toddy bent over and jerked and spasmed, and when it was over, she was a huge wolf.

There was an appalled and unbelieving hush.

Then Toddy leapt on Bella Bordelon and ate her up.

It was a very noisy process.

Mark became an even larger wolf. Deena and Purcell stayed in human form, but their incisors extended and became needlelike. Deena yanked Puffman from his table, drew him into a loverlike embrace with superhuman strength, and sank her fangs into his neck. Purcell enjoyed the same pleasure with Puffman's bodyguard, Selim, whose gun never left its holster.

Most of the guests were still frozen in their seats for a few important seconds, unable to believe the sights in front of their eyes. But that didn't last long.

The guests that tried to run provided the most entertainment for the serving staff, some of whom had changed into animal form, and some who'd turned out to have fangs like the Collvilles. Marchesa took particular pleasure in hunting down Jamison. She said something before she bit him, something that might have been, "White meat."

The sounds in the old warehouse reached a crescendo of screams and growls and moans, broken by the occasional howl and crack of bone: this quite drowned out the chamber music.

A good time was had by all—at least by all the survivors.

After it was over, and the replete staff had heaped what remained of the guests in the middle of the warehouse (and had hosed themselves down outside and donned clean clothes), Anna Clausen left with the truck of excellent meals. She would take them to the homeless shelter downtown, so the food wouldn't be wasted. Two of the staff went with Anna to help distribute the meals. Three others returned to the parking garage to begin ferrying the cars left there to an automobile graveyard Purcell owned, where they'd be crushed and recycled.

Marchesa and her friend Paula searched the bodies for metal objects that fire might not consume. They assembled a bagful of disabled cell phones, belt buckles, jewelry, and the like. These identifiable objects would be tossed into one of the cars before it made its final trip through the crusher.

The cash from the bodies was tucked thriftily into Marchesa's pocket.

Paula, whose mouth was still bloodstained, had the job of stomping skulls. She was of the fanged persuasion, and terrifically strong. It would be better if the bodies were never identified, or at least not for a long time, and Paula went about her job with the enthusiasm of the young. Marchesa laughed when Jamison crunched under Paula's heel. Paula took extra care to pulverize him.

The young man who'd played the music and started the film had a new task. He was pouring the contents of a can of accelerant around the warehouse, making sure everything would be consumed. It would take a while for the fire trucks to get here.

Toddy hugged Deena and Purcell. "Thanks so much for helping out," she said, and hiccuped. She covered her mouth and giggled. "They'd had so much to drink," she said apologetically.

"It was a ton of fun. Sorry it turned out that way. I really hoped they'd see the error of their ways," Purcell said, not too sincerely. "I thought about using mind control, but I decided that really would have been cheating. They needed to earn their own redemption." He tried to look righteous.

"But you weren't counting on that," Mark said.

Purcell shrugged. "I was pretty hungry," he admitted with a charming smile. "It's been a long time since Deena and I hunted and drank our fill. Got to be so careful these days! Now we're full, and the environment is safer." He practically glowed with virtue and Selim's blood.

They all left out the concealed back door and emerged into the cool night. Their cars were parked there, ready for their departure. Toddy and Mark's Prius looked a bit prissy next to the Collvilles' Lincoln. The couples bade each other farewell, and Mark took a package of papers containing their new identities from Deena's hands.

Toddy and Mark, both full and exhausted, exchanged only the occasional comment on their way to the airport. They'd reluctantly decided to fly to Sweden rather than take a boat. All their possessions were in storage, to be retrieved some day in the very distant future. They'd narrowed their home search down to three ecologically friendly structures designed by forward-thinking architects. Despite her anticipation of a great new chapter in their lives, Toddy still had regrets.

"I'm sorry I couldn't convert them," she said sadly as they waited to board. "I did everything I could."

"At least they're being recycled," Mark said.

Dear Prudence

STEVEN SAVILE

Miller held the pen poised over the scrap of paper, thinking about what he would write.

> *My Dearest Darling Prudence,*
> *Just nipped out to the shop to buy a packet of cigarettes. I might pop into the pub for a quick pint, catch up with some of the lads and watch the second half of the game. You know me and football. So, if you come back and I am not here, don't worry, I'll be right behind you, singing and dancing if we win, sulking and in need of some TLC if we don't. Hope you had a great night out with the girls.*
>
> *Your fool in love,*
> *Miller*

No, that wasn't quite what he wanted to say.

My Darling Pru,
Just nipped out to the shop for a packet of cigarettes. I'm gasping here. I feel like I'm living in Old Mother Hubbard's house. There's nothing in the cupboard, not even a digestive to munch on. There was a time when twenty a day would do me, then I met you. Now I could smoke for England. Could there be a link? I think I'll drop into the pub on the way home, watch whatever's left of the match, have a smoke and listen to some idiots talking about how crap the game is while I drown my sorrows. You know me and football. I'd rather sit in a smoky bar in the company of drunken strangers than alone in the house while you gallivant here, there and everywhere. I'm sure we'll lose, so most likely I'll be a bear with a sore head when I get in. Not that you'll notice. You never do. I might as well be a Ken doll you can put away in his box when you're finished playing with him—only I'm not as flexible these days. I feel about as sexless, though. That's a form of torture in some countries, I'm sure. Melting the genitals. If it isn't, it ought to be. Women of the world could unite in emasculating their men.

Life in plastic. It's fantastic.

Your love toy,
Miller

Better, but still not right. There was so much more inside him he wanted to say.

Dear Prudence,
Won't you come out—no, I promised myself I wouldn't do that anymore. I used to think it was cute you were named after my favourite song. Now, I can think of so many more appropriate tunes, but the one that immediately comes to mind sounds like a love song but isn't. It's funny, it always ends up on these greatest love song collections but its evil. That's why it fits. "Feels Like Heaven." Only instead of love its about twisting the bones until they snap, the poor sod screaming without anyone being able to hear his pain. That's me. Screaming and snapping while you twist.

Well, you know what? I'm sick of it. This worm's turning, baby. Oh, hell yes. Screw romantic love songs for the bunch of crap they are. God, it's liberating to say that. No more pretending that ours is the great love.

I'm going out to buy some cigarettes and then I am going to the pub to drink myself into oblivion. You've driven me to it. Does that make you all warm and tingly, knowing you've reduced a grown man to drink? I'm hoping my liver perforates before the night is out, or I can suck down enough smoke to give a small third world country cancer. Right now drinking and smoking myself to death seems like a great way to go.

It's Monday so there should be a game on. Watching other people kicking seven shades of shit out of each other should serve to appease my need to do bodily harm.

Should, did you like the way I said that?

Your shrinking violet,

Miller

That brought a smile to his face, but it barely scratched the surface. He let his thoughts run down a different track.

Prudence, Bane of my Life,

I had one once, you know, a life . . . but that was before I met you. To think I used to love you. If I could hop back into a time machine and warn Young Me, I would, in a heartbeat. How sad is that? I'd go back to the day before I met you and spill my guts about all the vile things you do day by day to ruin what shred of self-worth I have left. I doubt I'd believe me, though. I'd be like Nostradamus predicting the end of the world, but without the cute poetry. "Tomorrow you will meet the devil," I'd tell myself earnestly. "You won't recog-

nize her because she wears human skin and speaks pretty words with her forked tongue, but don't be gulled by her words or flattered by her looks. They will fade. Her wickedness will not. When she smiles at you, run and don't stop running until your lungs collapse."

Prudence, Prudence, what is a boy to do?

Smoke a cigarette? Coitus Nicotinous? See, instead of a life all I have now is an addiction to nicotine and a need to drink myself into a stupor. Cigarettes without sex are like fish without bicycles. The feminist in you will understand that, I'm sure.

I remember when we first slept together, thinking I was the luckiest man in the world. I lay there all night just watching you snore and imagined all of the things I wanted to do with you. Now I watch you sleep and my head explodes with all of the things I want to do to you. Instead of climbing Machu Picchu and the observation deck of the Eiffel Tower, it's all about choking the life out of you until you turn blue. I imagine you kicking weakly at the bedsheets then lying utterly still.

All this excitement has given me quite a thirst. Don't wait up.

Miller
Prophet of Doom

Yes, that was what he wanted to say. Blue is the color of my heart. He smiled, ready to commit it to paper and banish forever the image of the doting husband, but even before he had set the first letter down, his mind was racing with another, more creative missive.

You Know Your Name, It Is Legion
Do you know what I want? Right now, more than anything I want to see you die. I'm simple to please like that.

Let's play a game. Let me count the ways:

By hanging, your feet dangling inches off the floor.

Drowning in a vat of acid. No, a bathtub, your hands slapping at my arms as I hold you down.

A silver bullet between the eyes.

A stake through the heart.

Sunlight and a crucifix.

A gypsy curse.

Set ablaze by a mob of angry villagers.

Defenestration. That's another great word, isn't it? See, all this thinking about you is good for my vocabulary.

Disembowelment.

Decapitation by a rusty chainsaw.

Fed into a wood chipper. How much Pru

would a wood chipper chip if a wood chipper could chip Pru? That's today's million-dollar question.

Eaten by a pack of hungry wolves is good.

Struck by lightning would do. I love the smell of ozone in the morning.

Anaphylactic shock. I'm not fussy and wasps have always frightened you, so that's a bonus right there.

Hell, even a good old-fashioned heart attack would raise a smile.

That's a lot of ways to die, some of them were good enough for Dracula, Frankenstein, the Wolf Man and all those other Universal Monsters, but shall I tell you a secret? Not one of them is good enough for you, Prudence.

Piranhas aren't good enough. Plague isn't good enough. Warts eating away at your genitalia, still not good enough. Mad cow disease? I pity the cows. A thousand cuts? Come on, there's got to be a more inventive way to do it.

How do you kill the Antichrist? Blessed flatware from the kitchen of the Lord?

Dull, dull, dull.

There has to be a better way.

Voodoo? Witchcraft? Sacrificing a virgin?

Sacrificing a wizened old hag (easier to come by around here)?

Nibbled to death by gerbils?

Hmm, I rather like that one. I wonder if the pet store is open at this time of night? I'll check when I'm picking up the victuals—cigarettes and alcohol.

If not, buried alive does have its charms.

Don't say I don't love you—I am always thinking about you. Even when you are not here.

M

He grinned, delighted with himself. Then doubt set in. Was it wise to reveal his hand so early? Forewarned, forearmed and all that. Could she find silver-bulletproof armor?

Slut Bitch Whore,

I have plans.

Such plans.

Oh yes.

Such plans.

Must remember to buy plastic sheets to catch the blood. I can get them now while I am out buying cigarettes.

Shall I tell you what I am going to do?

Oh yes.

Everything is better shared.

First I will gut you, then I will stuff you and stitch you back together and then I will have you mounted and put on display in the Met. I already know what the plaque will read: This Bitch Ruined My Life.

Your taxidermist,
Miller

He relished the image of his wife stuffed and displayed as an exhibit, but even as he felt the warm glow of freedom seeping into his limbs, those doubts solidified. He saw it now, laid out before him, chains of cause and effect. No, no, no.

Oh, Pru, You Clever, Clever Bitch,
I get it.

I understand your game. You think you are so much cleverer than me, don't you? You think you can play me like a . . . a . . . I was going to say radio, but that doesn't work, you're a passive listener with a radio, sure, you can twiddle the dials but essentially you're at the mercy of the DJ, then I was going to say a guitar but we both know you're tone deaf and about as musically inclined as a bag of nails. And you're the antithesis of sporty so let's forget football analogies while we're on. Chess! That's a miniature reflection of a war, black and white generals going at it head-to-head. That's perfect. You think you can make me your knight sacrifice, pushing me out to murder the queen only to get taken in turn.

Oh no, no, no. See, it's all about the long game, looking moves ahead. I'm no fool. You telegraphed your play. I can see it plain as the nose on your fat face. You'd give yourself up, driving me to murder, just so your specter could lurk behind The Chair and gloat as they juice her up . . . I get it. It's the ultimate, the queen sacrifice. Not only do you get to ruin my life, you get to sink your fangs into my afterlife. I don't think so. See, I'm too clever for you. As David Bowie sang, this is not America. We're civilized. We've done away with state-legislated murder. I know, I know, you think with this new lot in power they'll bring it back—just for me. Sorry to ruin your scheming, m'dear.

Check and mate,
Grandmaster Miller

But should he let her know he was on to her schemes? Could he somehow twist it for his advantage? Slowly, slowly, catchy monkey, as his mom used to say.

Prudence, Woman of My Nightmares,
I still think about you all the time. They were such loving thoughts. But times change. I still think of you

all the time but now my head is filled with all of these vicious, horrible, nasty things I want to do to you.

Familiarity breeds contempt, and all that.

I hear voices, goading me on, telling me to cut you, to hurt you, to punish you. They want me to do unspeakable things to your corpse. I try not to listen to them but when you leave me alone like this, they get louder and louder until I want to scream and it seems the only way to shut them up is to surrender and do what they say.

I am going out now to walk and to clear the demons out of my mind. In the words of Captain Scott: "I may be some time."

Call it an exorcism, only instead of a Bible and holy water I'm shooting for the purifying essence of cigarettes and alcohol.

Nomini patri et Philip Morris . . .

Father Confessor Miller

Finally, he wrote:

Dearest Prudence,

Got lonely without you, so I just nipped out to the shop to buy a packet of cigarettes. I'll be home soon. Hope you had a great night out with the girls. Been thinking about you. A lot.

All my love,

Miller

A Good Psycho Is Hard to Find

WILL LUDWIGSEN

At least with the Chainsaw Guy, you always knew where you stood. When he came lurching between the palmetto fronds, swinging that Husqvarna over his head, there was no question that he wanted to lop off your arms and send them flying in a bloody spray into the bushes. There was no debate, no discussion, no feasibility study or Microsoft Project resource allocation chart.

Nobody at EnAble Technical Consulting has the straightforward, no-nonsense attitude of the Chainsaw Guy. Like an algae-coated stone at the bottom of a shallow mountain creek, our CEO Mr. Wendell has been worn into a rounded disk of corporate pliancy: everything just flows above and around him. He deflects responsibility to people like me, still idealistic and energetic from college. Like him, everyone here is safe, friendly, professional. Worst of all, none of them have ever threatened to kill me with a garden tool.

The summer before I started here, I worked one last time as a counselor at Camp Soaring Osprey. Maybe it was my way of saying good-bye to my young adulthood. Maybe I also hoped for one more chance with Misty, the girl at the canoe paddock I'd always dreamed of helping to—well, fill a canoe, anyway.

When the Chainsaw Guy came to kill us, I got my chance.

The newspapers distorted the story. Yes, an escaped mental patient wearing camouflage fatigues hunted the children at Camp Soaring Osprey. Yes, the scalp of a diner waitress who'd spurned him hung from his belt. Yes, the *chug-chug-chug* sound of a chainsaw cranking up growled across the lake. Yes, children fled for their lives, and their camp counselors managed to stop him. But no, we weren't naked and making love in the moonlight on Rowboat Island. We'd just gotten there.

Mostly, I was pissed. Together, we had paddled across the lake after lights out. Beneath the moonlit sycamore leaves, I'd finally told Misty how I felt about her, and we'd started our negotiations—mostly with our hands. I'd just managed to unclasp her bra when that crazy asshat came stumbling out of the underbrush.

You'd think it would ruin the mood, but there's something existentially inspirational about the possibility of death. It's as though your genetic code knows it's now or never. I wish I could say I bravely stood up to fend him off, but frankly, my DNA still wanted to get as far as it could.

Misty, fortunately, had more sense. With her lovely left breast surging from beneath her shirt, she rose from the grass and took a swing at him with her canoe paddle. The screwball parried with the chainsaw, and sawdust salted the air.

Annoyed, I grabbed the other paddle and got in the perfect dueling stance I'd learned from watching *Star Wars.* I wondered which of us was Qui-Gon Jinn and which was Obi-Wan Kenobi while she lunged and jabbed toward the Chainsaw Guy.

I spun dramatically, swinging my paddle in a motion that was more Bambino than Jedi. The water-treated spruce thocked against his skull and he tumbled backward onto his ass. The Husqvarna fell against his chest, nearly cutting him. Misty squished his balls with her paddle, and we ran to the trails.

You saw the rest of the story re-created on *American Justice.* We got the kids together, hid in one of the cabins, and tried to wait out the night until the police came. They squirmed and sobbed, but we managed to keep them all contained—except for Gordon. We begged him to use a bucket, but he insisted on making a run for the latrine. We heard his scream echoing against the tiled walls followed by the slurp and smack of his fat-streaked giblets.

Enough was enough. We had to stop the maniac before he came looking for us.

Misty and I hatched a plan. She'd run out into the quad, lure him into the electrical shed, and I'd finish him off by shoving him into the old non-OSHA-compliant circuit breaker.

We left Reuben, the crazy tough redneck kid, in charge and stepped outside. There, huddled beside the door, I held her hands. "Are you sure he'll follow you?"

She grinned and unclasped her jeans. "I think I can persuade him."

In the movies, the psycho killer is a little smarter than to chase the panty-clad teenager into a trap, but ours was a dumb-ass. Misty had just passed the flagpole when he came staggering out from behind the dining hall, chainsaw snarling above his head.

She played her part well, prancing across the quad and stumbling to give him time to catch up. She shrieked a few times to seal the deal, begging for her life and clutching her breasts. She even made a token effort to close the electrical shed door before he zipped through it. She cowered and shielded her eyes as he raised the chainsaw, and she had to be scared. A little, anyway, despite the grin I saw just as I crashed through the split door.

If you've never pushed a guy into a zillion volts of electricity, let me recommend it to you. He stumbles back, stunned look on his face. Then he clatters against the panel, his skin turns black, and he sizzles. He literally sizzles. It rocks.

When the cops arrived the next morning, they were impressed. The medical examiner bagged up Chainsaw Guy's charred skeleton while they all laughed with us and reenacted the scene. We should have gotten a medal or the key to the city, but the camp administrators chose to focus on the one kid we lost instead of the thirty we saved. We preferred to think of the camp as ninety-seven percent full instead of three percent empty, but they didn't see it that way.

At least we had each other. When the Morning After occurs postmurder instead of postcoitus, you skip several levels of dating. Unfortunately, some of those are the fun ones. We jumped straight to the "something missing" stage.

We'd established some weird Pavlovian connection between groping and fighting for our lives, and nothing we could do ever got our hearts racing like they did that night. It was all anticlimax, if you'll pardon the expression.

When I took this job in the fall, managing regional sales representatives for a global e-business outsourcing firm, I discovered that it wasn't just the sex that was anticlimactic. It was everything. It was driving to work all belted in safely. It was drinking coffee from one of those cups with the extra-stable bases. It was sitting at an ergonomically calculated perfect height, distance, and angle from my computer.

It was working for levelheaded, evenhanded, mild-mannered Mr. Wendell. "Good morning, Chet!" he'd say, giving me the thumbs-up or the "OK" gesture or some other corny thing. "Ready to satisfy our customers today?"

Vrrrrrummmmmm! I'd imagine the chainsaw clawing for wood or flesh in the nighttime air and smell the burnt two-stroke engine oil that portended my coming death.

"We surely appreciate all your hard work, Chet," Gerald from Marketing would say, putting a hand on my shoulder that I wished was a hook. "You're an invaluable part of the team."

My veins ached for that rush of adrenaline you can

only get on a sweaty summer night when swinging a canoe paddle at a psychopathic assailant.

Why did I have to electrocute the only person who'd ever made me feel alive? Maybe the Chainsaw Guy and I could have come to some kind of agreement: We'd fight a little every night and then go our separate ways. He'd show up whenever Misty and I were on a date, remind us of our Darwinian duty to procreate, and then discreetly leave once Misty and I got our pulses racing.

The Chainsaw Guy couldn't be the only serial killer willing to ply his trade on us, could he?

Despite what the media tells you, there really aren't that many serial killers around. The best ones burn out quickly, and all the others are incompetent. Misty and I waited in every lover's lane within sixty miles for some disgruntled woman hater or sexual sadist to find us, but no dice. We wrote to some of the old Manson family members, but they just wanted to lecture us about saving the Earth. Hell, we even considered writing a controversial and blasphemous book challenging fundamentalist Islam, but, well, neither of us knew enough about it to provoke a good fatwa.

I tried hiring an actor to pretend to murder us, but it just wasn't the same. First of all, you know it's just an act in the back of your mind. Second of all, it's almost impossible to find a person who can convincingly portray a psychopath. The drama program at George Mason had some close candidates, but certainly no Christopher Walkens or Dennis Hoppers to really get the electricity sparkling across my neurons.

I even offered a mental patient some dough to come kill me in the middle of the night, but he got lost on the way and the police found him frozen to death by the Jefferson Memorial. To his credit, he was clutching a scythe in his hand, but I still probably would have taken him.

The truth is that a good psycho is hard to find. Pissing off a biker is too iffy, poking a bum in the eye will just get you panhandled to death, and even calling old high school enemies just shows you how much crazy people mellow with age.

Bungee jumping and race-car school didn't capture the same feeling. The risk was too arbitrary, accidental. I needed the personal touch of another human being going out of his or her way to kill me, not the capricious hand of fate.

Misty felt it, too. We talked about our boring jobs and our boring lives, about the strange void a dead serial killer tends to leave in your life after you kill him. Everyone else at the bar talked about their IRA accounts and their BMWs, but all we wanted to discuss was the best way to knock a murderer through a fiftieth-story plateglass window.

We'd imprinted on each other. The ancient test of

survival had proved us a worthy match, if only we could re-create the circumstances. Some couples try to regain their senior year of high school or a magical summer in Paris; we went to Lowe's and looked at the chainsaws.

We finally tried to make love the only way we knew how. She rode atop me, rocking back and forth with the chainsaw held high. I knew we'd never hurt each other, though, and the neighbors banging on the wall to shut it off distracted us anyway.

But the chainsaw itself gave us an idea. Dressed all in black, we snuck out of the apartment complex with it and slinked several blocks down the street to another apartment building. We mounted the emergency stairwell—unwisely left open—and climbed to a random floor. Then we tiptoed to the end of the hall, fired up the chainsaw, and rang the doorbell.

When that ten-year-old boy answered the door, we almost wet ourselves laughing. The expression on a kid's face when faced with the rapture of dismembering doom is something one of those Renaissance painters should have captured to hang in the Louvre. I think his freckles actually fled to the back of his head, that's how pale he was.

Still convulsing from laughter, Misty stumbled forward and just barely nicked the kid's forehead with the chainsaw. It cracked open and his brains sprayed in an arc like a pink Mohawk.

"Oh, shit," she said, still compulsively giggling.

The chainsaw by now had cleaved his skull, and his father shuffled barefoot to the door just in time to see his son collapse to the ground. I'd like to say the look on his face was priceless, too, but all I saw clearly was his .357. Misty and I ran for opposite exits and managed to evade the bullets shattering the drywall around us. His son probably distracted him from having better aim.

We wiped down the chainsaw and tossed it in the Dumpster. Then, making peace with our twitching hearts, we slithered home through the shadows. We didn't talk much. We were both scared and a little guilty about what had happened.

When we got back into her apartment and crawled into bed, though, we tangled beneath the sheets and made love, happy to still be together for just this one night, happy to have survived.

I guess that's how we started creepy-crawling the city. That's what we call it when we sneak into buildings with a chainsaw and scare the shit out of someone. It's best in neighborhoods with a lot of Bush stickers: they tend to be gun owners, and there's nothing as invigorating as a pistol leveled at you by an angry Republican anxious to prove the Second Amendment works.

It's a strange kink, sure. We try not to kill anybody,

but sometimes things get out of hand and we have to. There's something primal there, too. Something exciting.

Work isn't so bad anymore, especially since Mr. Wendell—poor, friendly, Christian-deacon Mr. Wendell—has been stalked from home to work at least twice by fiends the newspaper likes to call "Mr. and Mrs. Chainsaw."

Silly media. We're only dating.

One of these days, though, we might just tie the knot. The only question is whom we'll invite to the wedding.

And what we'll do to them.

High Kicks and Misdemeanors

JANET BERLINER

For Russell Markert,
founder of the Rockettes

Most things that happen in Vegas stay in Vegas because no one outside the city would believe them.

Typical of that is the truly tall tale of Willie and Legs Cleveland and the ostrich army. The story begins with two men killed under similar circumstances at Country Club Towers, a high-rise that Legs called home. One man, who lived in the apartment above Legs's, bled out in the elevator as the result of two deep gouges in his stomach. Legs, who discovered the body, noticed that he was wearing a "Say No to Yucca Mountain" T-shirt. Several days later, a handyman in Legs's employ was killed in the identical manner. The cops, only vaguely interested since the men had no particular claim to celebrity, failed to notice that the second man wore the same T-shirt.

Legs tried to point out the coincidence.

Instead of gratitude, they hauled him down to the station and badgered him to tell them what he knew about the dead men.

"You're not pinning this on me," he said. "Everyone knows I'm a lover not a killer." Not that he hadn't caused a few deaths in his time, like that gorgeous chorus girl in Memphis and the Zulu Dancers in Laughlin and . . . but that was different. He hadn't meant for anything to happen to them.

When the cops let him go, warning him not to leave town, he felt fear at the pit of his gut. It was not something he'd experienced often. For a few days, he tried focusing on his search for new clients. As a self-styled talent scout with a penchant for long-legged chorines, thus his nickname "Legs," his search took him to Strip shows and stripper shows, to secondary casino acts and bordellos, but for once his heart wasn't in it.

In need of company and sound advice, he went Downtown to find the only person he trusted—his great-granduncle "Way-Out" Willie, so called because he played by his own rules. He was beholden to none and trusted nobody, with two exceptions—himself and his ostrich spirit guide. He took pride in his full-blooded Piute heritage, even though he hadn't set foot on Indian territory since, at the age of twelve, he'd left his family to seek his spirit guide.

Willie loved Las Vegas, mostly because it was a city where the culture of anonymity was God. He shared his innermost thoughts with no one and kept to himself the business he did for Moe Dalitz of the Cleveland Mob. As a private joke between them, Willie—whose Indian name was Nattee-Tohaquetta—took on the name Will Cleveland. He drove for the Mob and learned where the bodies were buried, and was the most trusted and feared loan shark in town. Sometimes he gave loans and washed them away; other times he had bones broken.

Legs found Willie Downtown, playing in a small Texas hold 'em game. After a stint at the back of the Sports Book—Willie's office—he got the old man a complimentary corned beef sandwich from the deli, waited for him to be cashed out, and took him over to the Towers.

The day was November 16, 1999, which Willie swore was his one-hundred-and-fiftieth birthday. They sat on the balcony, looking at the Stratosphere and the Strip beyond while Willie chomped on his sandwich, washed it down with a bottle of dark beer, and listened to Legs.

"Nothing to worry about," Willie said.

"You think?"

Willie belched his confirmation and cleaned his teeth with his nail. When he was done, he took his black book of debtors out of his pocket and tore it into shreds.

"What the hell are you doing?" Legs asked, watching the gathering heap of outstanding markers from God, Satan, and half of the population of Las Vegas.

Willie laughed. "Now you listen to me," he said. "You don't have to worry about anything." He pointed at the shuttle to Area 51's Groom Lake. The pair watched it circle and head toward the Janet Air Terminal. "What you need to know is that my time is done. They're coming to get me. Keep the fifty K you skimmed from me, give the money in my mattress to our people, and stay away from the Road to Rachel." He laughed at Legs's expression.

"What happens to your ostrich?" Legs asked, treating the affair as a joke.

"Probably come to you," Willie said. "Treat him right or he'll get you. He can be mean and stupid. Kick a man to death right easy, run forty miles a' hour—"

"You know I don't believe in spirit guides," Legs said. "What if I don't?"

"You'll be knee-deep in shit," Willie said. "Ostrich shit."

Around midnight, a white Jeep Cherokee stopped in the street down below and let down a rear ramp. A tall, slender woman in camouflage coveralls stepped out of the Jeep and entered the building.

"Let her in," Willie said as the buzzer sounded.

Legs knew better than to argue, even when she wheeled Willie out of the apartment and, within minutes, pushed him up the ramp and into the truck.

As the Cherokee pulled away, the streetlight illuminated a decal of an ostrich on the back bumper.

By noon of the following day, Legs called Downtown to see if the old man had gone directly there, but no one had seen him. He decided that Willie was doing a favor for one of his Mob friends or there was always the possibility that senility had finally done what senility does. Besides, reporting a missing person was not a comfortable idea.

He remained mostly distracted by his own problems until, catching sight of the afternoon Janet Air Shuttle, he remembered what Willie had said when they'd last watched one together: *They're coming to get me,* adding later, *Stay away from the Road to Rachel.*

Never one to obey orders, Legs walked the mile or so to the closest car rental company and was soon on his way to Area 51, though what he hoped to do when he got there was anybody's guess.

Radio on full blast, he smoked part of a joint, munched on a candy bar, and enjoyed the winter sunshine. He felt good until he saw what looked like an unmarked cop car closing in on him. Glancing at the speedometer, he slowed down below the speed limit and veered onto Highway 375, which would take him to Groom Lake Road. The road was bumpy; the cop car stayed with him. After about twelve miles, with the cop still behind him, he swerved to the right down a narrow road, unmarked except for a broken-down shack and a sign that read DORA'S PLACE: GENTLEMEN WELCOME.

The car behind him made a U-turn. Legs gave a sigh of relief and kept driving until he saw a very large animal lying across the road. He put on his brakes and was about to get out of the car when a white Jeep Cherokee like the one that had taken Willie hurtled toward him.

He sat and watched the Jeep stop on the other side of the big bird.

The same tall woman he'd seen the night of Willie's disappearance stepped from the passenger side, holding a gun in her hand. To Legs, who knew little about guns, the weapon looked real. A man, also dressed in camouflage, stepped out of the driver's side, strode over to the animal, and kicked it. He realized suddenly that they were the Camo Dudes who patrolled Area 51, but since he had neither a camera nor a weapon, they would probably just ream him out and call the Lincoln County Sheriff's Department.

"This one's dead," the man said. "Told you he wouldn't make it to the road after what I shot into him." He looked at Legs. "Dead as you'll be if you don't do what you're told."

The woman pushed Legs toward the passenger side of his car and got behind the wheel. "You were supposed to stun it, not kill it," she said through the open window.

The man laughed. "What's one ostrich, more or less?"

The woman turned to Legs. "As for you, Mr. Cleveland," she said.

"How—"

"Maybe your uncle might have told you a little too much about our business. Know what I mean?" Her laugh was not pleasant.

The man roped together the legs of the dead ostrich and looped it around the bumper of the van.

"Hope you're into ostriches, Mr. Cleveland," the woman said. "Dumb creatures. With Willie gone, someone's got to take care of them."

Within twenty minutes, the van pulled up in front of a huge barn, barricaded by a wide iron bar. The man removed the bar and Legs was shepherded inside. Corralled in the middle was a large flock of ostriches.

The smell was gross. He gagged.

"You'll get accustomed to it," the woman said.

Legs prayed silently for the cop who had been following him, vowing to G-d that if he got out of this, he'd give Willie's money to the Piutes, never gamble again or booze, never—

"All right, Mr. Cleveland," the woman said. "Time to meet our soldiers. They've been restless of late. You'll have to calm them down so that they follow instructions. Who knows, if you're good at your job—if they don't kill you—maybe we'll show you our other brigades. Noah got it right when he saved the animals."

Hoping to control his fear, Legs turned and focused on the troop of birds. The ostriches looked calm enough to him. Most of them had their heads spread flat on the sand. The rest milled around in an almost listless manner, nudging one another occasionally. They were just like Willie had described during his interminable recounting of his misspent youth.

According to Willie, his search for a spirit guide had led him to Walker Lake. While sleeping under a bush, he was awoken from a peyote dream by the poking head of a strange and hideous animal nuzzling him in the armpit. The animal looked like a three-hundred-pound sage hen. Its skinny, long legs and blush pink neck were devoid of plumage, its large body covered by odd grayish-brown feathers, its undersized head marked by beady onyx eyes, which, he was to learn, were larger than its brain.

The bird, for that was what Willie determined it was, stared at him and refused to move. When Willie pushed at it, it skittered to one side, but made no attempt to fly. He would have understood if he'd known anything about ostriches. However, he did not, yet.

What he did know was that he could not embarrass his family by going home. Not then. Not ever.

Thus began a lifetime of adventure for Nattee-Tohaquetta, aka Way-Out Willie. First he walked to Austin, Nevada, where he met a pretty young woman by the name of Dora who gave him shelter at her place of employment—the larger of Austin's two whorehouses. He quickly became a favorite of the rental ladies, who were quite happy to feed him in exchange for yard work and Indian tall tales. On his sixteenth birthday, they even took it upon themselves to initiate him into manhood in the pleasantest of fashions.

Nattee and Dora became a couple. She continued plying her trade, but pleasured him on the side. In what spare time she had, she taught him to read, a skill that allowed him to learn about his ostriches. Of most significance to him was the fact that his spirit guide was not unique and he determined that he would earn the money to buy several more.

He did, and Willie's Ostrich Farm and Whorehouse was born.

All went well for him until his ostrich conspired to lead its fellows away from Willie's Farm and Whorehouse and onto the road that led from Austin to Belmont. Like a revolutionary army, sixty-three strong, they marched off, leaving Willie no longer the owner of an ostrich farm.

Rather than search for them, he sold his farm, split the money with Dora, who said nothing about being with child, and took off for Las Vegas to become a gambler.

The woman had called them "our soldiers," yet Willie had said they never attacked unless provoked.

Or trained? Legs thought.

Maybe he could find a way to free them, but what was the point if they killed whoever they'd been trained to kill? Or if they killed him.

Either way, it seemed to him, he was a dead man.

He was still staring at the birds when he heard a door open behind him. The man stood by the barn door they'd entered through while the woman stood near a storage closet he hadn't noticed before. She had stripped off her camo outfit and was standing in a pair of short shorts and pulling on one of those white suits that emergency workers wear when cleaning chemical spills.

"You got some pair of legs. Let me out of here and I'll make you a star."

Zippering the suit, she came toward him. She held a large syringe in her right hand. Praying it wasn't meant for him, he squinted at the name tag attached to her suit and said, "Ava. Perfect. Why would you want to be here when you could be a headliner?"

"You're a funny man, Mr. Cleveland." She came closer.

"Legs," he said. "Call me Legs."

"All right, Legs. Let's talk. What did Willie tell you about his work here?"

"Nothing."

"Nothing? That's hard to believe."

"Believe it."

For a moment, the woman was silent. Legs figured he had nothing to lose by asking what it was they were doing to the ostriches to turn them into killing machines and why they were doing it. He was as good as dead anyway. Might as well know what he was dying for.

"Willie told you nothing?"

"Nothing."

"Tell me something, Mr. Cleveland. Legs. Do you also have an ostrich spirit guide?"

Legs shook his head. "I don't believe in that stuff."

She looked at the syringe in her hand. "He did," she said. "It kept him safe in there."

Legs could feel the sweat running down his neck. "What did he do here?" he asked again.

"He worked with the ostriches. Taught us about them."

"Why?"

She held up the syringe. "He wanted to live to be old," she said, "and keep his own teeth. There was a price to pay and he paid it."

It was all Legs could do not to reach out and knock the syringe out of her hand. "I don't mind false teeth," he said.

She laughed.

"There has to be some other reason," Legs began.

"There was. Me. I'm Dora's great-granddaughter."

"Aren't you afraid I'll tell people—"

"What? That we're training an army of killer ostriches? You've got to be kidding."

"How much time do I have to spend here?"

"As much as we say."

In his mind, Legs heard old Willie telling him to behave. He saw only one realistic possibility open to him: He would work on Ava, which wouldn't be the worst punishment in the world. She did have great gams, and who knew, maybe she could sing.

She pointed at a loft over the barn. "There's a mattress up there, a pillow, a blanket and a computer. You can use one, I assume." Without waiting for an answer she said, "Start learning about ostriches. Oh, and say hello to Willie."

"Willie?"

The man grinned. "See you later, if there's anything left of you to see," he said, and he and the woman walked out of the barn.

Legs heard the bar falling into place and felt the warm trickle of urine down his legs.

He had forgotten how cold it could get out in the high desert at night. Shivering, he made his way up to the loft, followed by one ostrich. He lit the kerosene lamp they'd left up there, and covered himself with the horsehair blanket. The portable computer was on the mattress, along with spare batteries. Next to the lamp was an old brass urn. He opened it up, hoping it held liquor, but it was filled with ashes.

"I fucked up, Willie," he said, knowing at once that he was looking at what was left of his great-granduncle.

"That you did." Willie's voice came from the ostrich. "I told you not to take the Road to Rachel."

Legs knew he'd lost his mind. He was talking to a spirit guide and an invisible dead Indian.

"You're stuck with us now," Willie said. "The collected wisdom of our people has to be passed along. You'll have to be the conduit."

"You can pass on information about those things down there."

"Careful. Don't want to insult my buddy. How about you start checking the computer."

First, Legs found out why the ostriches were so silent. Apparently the males hissed and grunted, but just during mating season, when their necks turned blue. They could only kick forward, like the Rockettes. Their food was grasses and bugs and small pebbles to help their digestion. Their average weight was three hundred fifty pounds, yet they ran like the wind.

Legs was growing tired. Before turning off the computer, he looked at the day's local headlines. More than seven hundred Nevada Test Site workers or their survivors were reopening cases linked to radioactive materials here at this federal facility northwest of Las Vegas.

"Lovely," Legs said. "They'll stomp me to death or burn me to death."

Willie chuckled. "Sleep well, kid," he said. "Happy dreams."

He looked down at his charges. Two of them had separated from the others. The male's neck had turned blue. They were doing a bizarre dance around each other and, ugly as they were, they were clearly getting ready to mate. He laughed despite his circumstances, lay down, and fell into a heavy, dream-filled sleep.

The first was about his attempt to build a chorus line out of a group of Zulu warriors he'd brought from Africa. Their performance had become a bloodbath when their war dance, rooted in their collective unconscious, took over.

The second dream was Busby Berkeley's choreographed march through town from the Mickey Rooney–Judy Garland barn movie, *Babes in Arms.*

He awoke to an entrepreneurial epiphany: Ostrich Rockettes high-stepping it down Fremont Street to "The March of the Wooden Soldiers." Like Russell Markert's original Rockettes, they wore faux military uniforms designed by Vincente Minnelli: wide-legged white sailor pants, fitted red jackets and high black hats topped with jaunty white feathers. They moved in one perfect line. He could see them in his mind's eye, moving in precise circles to form shapes that fit together like a puzzle. Standing sideways, they acted as if they had been hit by a blast from a cannon and fell down one by one, each partially on top of the dancer in front. Like dominos, they descended upon one another until the final dancer fell onto a huge red velvet cushion.

It would be hypnotic.

"Hey, Uncle Willie," Legs said, looking over at

the urn and feeling only slightly ridiculous. He heard a soft chuckle, followed by silence. "You not playing speaks?"

Not sure what he was hoping to see, he walked over to the urn and looked inside at the ashes. Nothing moved, no voice rose to advise him. He waited a moment and gave up. He'd probably imagined Willie's voice. Anybody would get a little crazy under the circumstances.

The barn door rattled and Ava opened it. She held a steaming bowl in one hand and a cup in the other.

"Feeding time at the zoo, Legs," she said. "Come on down."

He did as she said and was handed coffee and oatmeal. "Eat it. That's as good as it gets. When you're done, you'll feed the herd and clean up the shit." She wrinkled her nose. "Stinks in here."

He took the meal and stepped hopefully toward the outdoors. She shook her head, then relented. "Okay, but don't try anything." She was back in fatigues, a whistle hanging from her neck and her pistol prominently displayed. He had no doubt she knew how to use it.

After he had gratefully eaten the oatmeal, he lit a cigarette, counted how many he had left and sipped the coffee. It was surprisingly good.

"I used to read stuff about UFOs around here.

There's a website, ufomind.com, sends me all kinds of information. Know anything about that?"

Ava shrugged. "The site's a mailing list for UFO and conspiracy nuts and it's being cut off on December eighteenth. That's all I know. It has nothing to do with my job."

"What is your job and what the hell do I have to do with any of this?"

"Guess it's time I tell you. Remember that dead body you found in the elevator at Country Club Towers and the fix-it man who died in your apartment?"

"I'm not likely to forget!"

"What do you think killed them?"

Legs remembered the double gouges in each of the men's bellies and the blood. Not a pleasant sight. "I have no idea. Cops said it must be some kind of gang ritual, probably the Twenty-eighth Street gang."

"No."

"Who then?"

"You mean *what.*"

Legs was getting annoyed and not a little antsy. Ava continued. "Didn't you read about the ostriches? The way they can kick a man—"

"—No way."

"Yes, way. Willie's guide did a perfect job."

"How—?"

"Listen to me. This is serious stuff. A military

experiment. We hope to turn the herd into Special Ops assassins. They'll be shipped to the Middle East to mingle with the camels and get the terrorists. They're being programmed."

Legs started to laugh. He couldn't help himself. What a gig. Ava was crazier than he was. "And my job is?" he asked when he calmed down.

"Like I said. You feed them, clean up after them. You saw the syringe I had yesterday. They each get one of those every day."

"Operation Ostrich," Legs said. "When is this supposed to happen?"

"Think millennium."

"If I go along with it—"

"There ain't no 'if,' kid. Now get moving."

After what was likely the worst day of his life, Legs returned to his mattress. For most of that night and the next, he formulated a plan. By the third day, he'd worked out the details. On New Year's Eve, he and as many of his ostrich buddies as he could muster would be off and running—not to the Middle East, but to the center of Las Vegas. He'd need to pick the ones who were in heat as his dancers.

Until then, the trick was to stay alive.

It took Legs another three days to get up the nerve to speak to Ava. He waited for breakfast, the only time he could actually talk to Ava, and put the beginnings of his plan into motion.

"What's your take on the Yucca Mountain nuclear waste debate?"

" 'Scuse me?"

"Seriously," Legs said. "Does anything about it impact our . . . um . . . squadron?"

"What do *you* think?"

Legs's answer had to come out just right. He took his time.

"I think you'd want to use the ostriches to deliver 'dirty bombs' from the Yucca Mountain nuclear waste to terrorist encampments."

Ava stared at him. "You're not as dumb as you look, Legs Cleveland," she said, and spoke of something else.

After a few more days, Legs said, more confidently, "I've been thinking about something we have to do with the soldiers. They need a trial run to see how they do as a team."

"All of them? Not possible."

"Right. But what about five or six?"

"What do you have in mind?"

Legs took a deep breath. "Ever seen the Radio City Rockettes?" he asked.

She nodded. "Of course I have. Think I've lived all of my life out here in the boondocks?"

"Good. Then think about this. On New Year's Eve day, there's going to be a major protest at Cashman Field against the Yucca Mountain project. What if we dress our soldiers as Rockettes and march them to town to pull for the project? They'll get all of the attention."

Ava laughed long and hard. Then suddenly she was quiet.

After several minutes, she said, "Be a lot of major politicians there and a couple of bands and fireworks."

Legs merely nodded.

The following morning, Ava reopened the subject. "Can you have them trained in time?" she asked.

"Sure. No problem."

"And you'll need what from me?"

"I'll need costumes so we can dress them like the Rockettes. One for you, too, if you want to dance with them."

She smiled.

"Told you I'd make you a star," Legs said.

And so the preparations began.

When the day came, everything was ready. Legs patted his pocket, making sure he hadn't forgotten Uncle Willie, whom he'd poured into a Baggie, figuring the old man wouldn't want to miss the show. With Ava's help, he piled five "Rockettes" into a large van with the backseats removed. He'd found two couples and a fifth who made everything possible: Uncle Willie's spirit guide, with whose help he taught them high kicks and tried the "Shuffle Off to Buffalo," though without much success.

Truth was, all he wanted was to cause enough of a ruckus to give him enough cover to leave town. He hadn't yet decided whether to sprinkle Willie on a poker table en route.

Legs sat in the back with the ostriches, each of which wore a banner reading WELCOME TO YUCCA MOUNTAIN. Ava drove, looking stunning in her costume. When they got Downtown to Cashman Field, Ava drove them through several roadblocks with a flash of her credentials. Parked near the loading docks, they assembled the troupe. When they were all set, they walked past hot dog stands and popcorn vendors. The soldiers would love the popcorn, he thought, as they headed into the stadium, where a local band playing loud rock held the attention of most of the security personnel assigned to the event.

While Ava and the ostriches waited in what was the visiting team's dugout when the Las Vegas 51s were playing baseball, Legs bounded onto the stage in the echoing last notes of one of the interchangeable rock anthems he abhorred. Taking the microphone, he said, "Thank you. Thank you. And now, a special surprise performance." The strains of "The March of the

Wooden Soldiers" started to play over the loudspeakers and Ava high-stepped out of the dugout, followed by the five costumed ostriches. As they reached the center of the field, the birds began a strange dance around the woman. Watching her gorgeous gams move in time to the music, Legs almost forgot to edge his way toward the home team's dugout, where he could make good his escape.

The crowd, at first stunned into silence, began to cheer and laugh. Legs felt rather than heard Uncle Willie's voice slip from his pocket up to his neck and into his ear.

"Run, Legs," it whispered.

But he was rooted to the ground. With enormous effort, he moved one foot, then the other.

Legs moved faster now. He reached the steps off the field and took the Baggie out of his pocket. It stuck to his fingers. Legs peeled it off his hand, along with a layer of skin. "Thank you, Nattee-Tohaquetta," he said.

He looked at his troop. Something was amiss. Ava twirled and pointed at a set of box seats behind home plate. He recognized several prominent senators from nearby states standing there, all of whom were staunchly opposed to the use of Yucca Mountain as a nuclear storage facility.

That was when the ostriches abandoned the dance

Legs had taught them and ran head-on in a vicious assault. Blood and brains flew into the crowd, raining onto the first few rows.

In his ear, he heard Uncle Willie's voice, clearer than the screams and the music. "I told you not to screw with my spirit guide, nephew."

From the middle of the carnage an ostrich, its red-and-white costume smeared with gore, came charging toward Legs. "It's still *my* guide," Willie's voice said. "Throw me away and it'll come to me."

An Indian war cry rose above the sounds of death and Legs was shocked to realize it came from his own throat. He flung the ashes into the path of the oncoming bird. It grabbed the Baggie from the air in its beak, stopped and whipped around, showering Willie onto the ground, on top of the peanut shells and popcorn and political flyers.

Legs turned to run and never looked back.

PR Problems

Eric James Stone

What annoys me the most about vampires and werewolves is their good PR. Not that I want a return to the days of villagers with pitchforks and torches, but all the romantic attachment to predators who hunt and kill humans makes me sick.

So when a cannibalistic serial killer started leaving the gnawed-on bones of his victims in public places, did the media label him a vampire? No. A werewolf? No.

The press called him the "Grove City Ghoul."

Those reporters had obviously never heard of fact-checking.

First, we ghouls are carrion eaters, not predators—hyenas, not wolves. Sure, we like to feast on human flesh, but we find bodies that are already dead and eat them, after they've had a chance to decay a bit. For some inexplicable reason, people seem to think that's more grotesque than the actual killing by vampires and werewolves.

Second, a ghoul wouldn't just gnaw on the bones, he would eat them. Besides being nice and crunchy, they're a good source of calcium. That's why ghouls never suffer from osteoporosis.

We ghouls just have bad PR. And the serial killer wasn't helping.

But what could I do about it? I worked as property manager for a high-rise apartment complex. Vampires might whine till daybreak about how their undead lives sucked, but it was vampires and werewolves who got the really cool jobs, like private detective or radio talk-show host. My crime-fighting experience was limited to stuff like catching the Nelson kids from apartment 4C spray-painting graffiti in the parking lot, while my radio experience consisted of listening, not talking.

And that's what I was doing the morning after the police found the sixth victim's bones: listening to the news on the radio while I mopped the floor of the lobby.

I was relieved when Olga Krasny from 8A came in the front door. Olga worked the night shift as a nurse, and from what I heard on the radio, all the serial killer's victims either worked or went to school at night. Each victim except the first had been taken the night after bones from the previous victim were found, which meant another victim would have been taken last night.

"Hey, Mr. Ahsani," said Olga, "my kitchen faucet has the leaky again."

If I were a vampire or werewolf, the moment would have been filled with sexual tension. Olga would be a slinky Swedish nurse rather than a stout Ukranian one, and "my kitchen faucet has the leaky" would be a euphemism for passion and desire.

"I'll come take a look when I finish here," I said. In this case, a leaky faucet was just a leaky faucet. With forty-eight apartments in the building, something was always breaking somewhere. Vampires and werewolves, I was fairly certain, didn't mop floors or fix faucets.

To my surprise, Olga's kitchen faucet did not, in fact, have "the leaky." But she wasn't trying to seduce me—she was merely wrong about the source of the leak. The water was coming through the wall under the sink from the kitchen of apartment 8B.

I knocked on the door of 8B and waited for Harvey Tanner to respond. Harvey seemed like a nice, quiet young man—which is always how the neighbors of serial killers inevitably describe them on TV after they are arrested. That didn't mean anything, of course. My neighbors would probably describe me the same way, and I had never killed anyone.

I knocked a couple more times, but there was still no answer. Under the lease agreement, an ongoing water leak was sufficient reason for me to use my master key and enter without the renter's permission. So I did.

As I got to the kitchen, I could smell the faint but tasty aroma of rotting human flesh. I might not have enhanced senses like a vampire or werewolf, but my ghoulish nose was pretty good at sniffing out potential food.

I wondered for a moment if maybe Harvey had died somehow, but then I remembered I had seen him yesterday, and what I smelled was more decayed than would happen in less than twenty-four hours.

I walked over to the sink and opened the cupboard doors so I could access the water shutoff valve. I turned off the water to stop the leak, and that's when I spotted the scraps on the floor—three strips, each about an inch long and a quarter of an inch wide, slightly rounded, like cheese that had been through a grater.

I sniffed at the scraps.

They were not cheese, but they were quite tasty.

Maybe Harvey had accidentally grated bits of himself while cooking dinner, but I had my doubts. Unfortunately, I didn't think about the fact that those scraps might be evidence until after I ate them.

I burped and considered what to do next. I couldn't call the police without any evidence, so I decided to see if Harvey had any skeletons in his closet. Literally.

All the apartments in the building have two bedrooms. Harvey lived alone, so I wondered what he used the extra bedroom for. I opened the door.

The room's windows were covered so that no light came in from outside. I flicked the light switch and was startled to see a young woman, gagged and tied to a folding metal chair, in the middle of the room.

She swung her head up to look at me, her eyes wild with panic.

Then someone grabbed me from behind and shoved a chemical-smelling cloth over my mouth and nose.

One of the more ridiculous myths about ghouls is that we are undead creatures. Just because we hang out around graveyards a lot doesn't mean we're undead. We're merely going where the food is. Would you assume someone was Italian just because he hangs out around a pizza parlor?

Of course, in this case, the disadvantage of not being undead was that after struggling to breathe, I sank into unconsciousness.

• • •

When I came to, I found myself in the same room, sitting on a chair. A piece of towel had been stuffed into my mouth, held in place by more cloth tied around my head, and I had to work hard to keep myself from gagging on the gag. My wrists were bound tightly together behind the back of the chair, and my feet were tied quite thoroughly to the bottom.

The young woman was watching me from her chair. It would be hard for me to free myself without showing my true nature, and I was afraid that might freak her out. On the other hand, she had been kidnapped by a serial killer, so how much more freaked-out could she get?

I want to make it clear that just because I can transform myself into a hyena does not mean I am a "werehyena." We ghouls have a long and proud tradition of being able to morph into hyenas. (You can look that up on Wikipedia, although the article is inaccurate in many other respects.) And unlike lycanthropes, we're not infectious. I really don't understand what the werewolves have to be proud about. Anyone can become a werewolf, just by being bitten by one. Essentially, lycanthropy spreads like rabies. We ghouls, on the other hand, reproduce in the normal human fashion. My family can trace its lineage back to the ancient Persian Empire.

In all modesty, though, the ability to become a hyena isn't very impressive. It's useful for feeding, because those hyena jaws are strong enough to bite through bone, but hyenas really don't get a lot of respect. Take *The Lion King,* for example: The hyenas don't even get to be the real villains, merely minions for an evil lion. Thus Hollywood continues to perpetuate the stereotype that carrion eaters are of lower status than predators.

After a few minutes of struggling with my ropes, I decided that transforming was my only option. I could only hope that if the young woman told anyone about my ability, they would attribute her story to hysteria.

I shape-shifted into my hyena form. Since it was smaller than my human form, the ropes loosened as I transformed. As soon as I was free, I changed back to human.

From behind her gag, the young woman made a half-choking cough of incredulity.

I knelt by her chair and set to work untying her. "Don't worry, I'll get you out of here."

Before I finished, the door opened. I rose to my feet and turned to find Harvey pointing a gun at me.

If there was one thing that the PR about vampires and werewolves was not overhyping, it was their magical resistance to harm. I envied that. It wouldn't take a wooden stake through the heart or a silver bullet to kill me: plain old lead bullets would do the trick. I raised my hands in surrender.

"I'm sorry, Mr. Ahsani," Harvey said, "but I couldn't have you running to the police. People might get the wrong impression."

"People already have the wrong impression," I said. "They're calling you a ghoul when you're actually a serial killer. It's very bad PR for—"

"I'm a vampire hunter, not a serial killer," said Harvey, still pointing the gun at me.

"What?" I said.

He motioned with his gun toward the girl. "Go ahead, check her pulse."

I put my fingers to her throat. There was no heartbeat, and her skin felt cool to the touch. "You really are a vampire," I said.

She glared at me. "So what? You're a—"

I stuffed the gag back into her mouth. "So why haven't you killed her yet?" I said as I backed away from her, which took me closer to Harvey and the door.

"I don't want the meat to go bad," he said. "It's much better when you slice it off fresh."

I didn't bother to express my disagreement verbally. There's no accounting for taste.

"Fortunately," he said, "vampires stay alive a lot longer than humans after you start cutting chunks off them."

"How do they taste?" I asked.

He smiled. "Much better than chicken."

For a moment, as I stood next to Harvey and we both looked at the vampire, I thought he and I could come to a culinary arrangement. I could eat the bones for him, at the very least. I guess the serial killer mentality made him taunt the police by leaving the bones lying around for people to find, but it really wasn't very smart.

However, before I could say anything, he added, "Vampire flesh isn't really human anymore, so it's not like I'm a ghoul."

Being looked down on by a serial killer was the straw that broke this ghoul's back. In one smooth motion I transformed my head into my hyena form and tore out Harvey's throat.

Hey, we may not be hunters, but that doesn't mean we're not dangerous when provoked.

After I untied her, the vampire and I looked down at Harvey's body.

"I suppose I should call the police or something," I said, "and let them know the serial killer is dead."

"Are you kidding?" said the vampire. "Let's just leave him and get out of here."

If I left the body for a few days, sealed up in this

room, it would get nice and ripe. And unlike my usual food, it wouldn't taste of formaldehyde. My mouth watered just imagining the meal.

"Let's go," I said.

As we got to the living room, she grabbed my hand and pulled me close. My heart beat faster.

"I've heard that werewolves are the greatest lovers in the world," she said.

I was about to express my annoyance at yet another example of good werewolf PR when I realized what she was implying. And despite being so dumb she couldn't tell a hyena from a wolf, she was very good-looking.

"Yes," I said as I embraced her. "Yes, we are."

Where Angels Fear to Tread

Sherrilyn Kenyon

"From humble beginnings come great things." Zeke Jacobson rolled his eyes as he read the strip of paper he'd just fished out of his broken fortune cookie. "Well, you can't get more humble than me," he muttered before the phone rang.

His stomach clenching in dread of the latest complaint, he picked up the receiver and glanced around his pale gray cube walls where he spent an average of fifty hours a week. There were times when he swore he could hear his life ticking away with every swipe of the second hand on the *Transformers* clock he'd inherited from his older brother. Optimus Prime stared at him from his perch next to Zeke's drab gray monitor.

"Good afternoon. Taylor Transportation. Claims Division. Zeke speaking. How may I help you?" The worst part of the job . . . he sometimes heard those words even in his sleep.

The irate woman on the other end laid into him over the fact that he'd rejected her dubious claim that their delivery truck had mowed down her mailbox and kept going. If she'd spoken to the driver the way she was speaking to him, she was lucky the driver hadn't mowed her down first.

Her voice held that high-pitched, nasal quality that went down a man's spine like a shredder. "You're a pathetic idiot if you don't believe your driver did that."

Zeke didn't speak as she continued shrieking at him.

And for the glorious honor of being bitched at constantly and the esteemed title of Claims Investigator, he'd given up five years of his life as he went to college, created a debt his great-grandkids would curse him over, and got the holy honor of MBA. More Bullshit Allowed. Unlike his more intelligent counterparts, he'd actually studied and graduated with honors, thinking he'd have a bright future . . .

Yeah, this was his life and he hated every minute of it.

Well, not *every* minute. But enough that he dreaded what more wondrous developments the future would hold.

You know, as a kid, I just didn't see this one coming.

When he'd dreamed of his future, never once had he seen himself sitting in a cube ten hours a day having people yell at him while he glibly took it for fear of losing his thirty-thousand-a-year salary.

The highlights of his life? Drinking beer and playing basketball on the weekends with his friends.

Damn, the woman's right. I am a pathetic idiot.

"Are you even listening to me?" she droned.

"Yes, ma'am. I understand what you're saying. But there's no evidence that our driver did that. I have a sworn statement from him that he didn't hit the mailbox."

"Fuck you, you stupid bastard!"

"Yes, ma'am. You have a good day, too."

She slammed the phone down hard enough for it to ring in his ear.

Zeke sighed before he put his head to his laminated desk and beat it against the cold, granite-look finish. *Maybe I'll get a concussion . . .*

The phone rang again.

He lifted his head to glare at Optimus Prime. It was only eleven in the morning. Was it too much to ask for one little brain aneurysm? Just one.

His stomach churning, he picked the phone up and repeated his work litany.

"Am I speaking to Ezekiel Malachi Jacobson?"

Zeke cringed at the name with which his grandfather, a devout Baptist preacher, had cursed him, the only grandson, at birth. God, how he hated hearing all that said at once. It was a name that had gotten his ass kicked on many an occasion at school. It had even caused one college roommate to move out of his dorm room before he arrived.

"That would be me." *God, don't let this be someone I owe money to.*

"My name is Robert West. I'm the attorney for your granduncle Michael Jacobson."

"Who?"

"He was your grandfather's youngest brother."

That was weird. He'd thought all of those relatives were long gone.

"I'm sad to say that your granduncle passed away a few weeks ago and named me as the executor of his will. Since he wasn't married and didn't have children, he's left everything to you."

"To me? What about my sister?"

"He only named you."

Oooo-kay . . . Zeke listened as the lawyer gave him more details.

• • •

"Can you imagine how lonely he must have been?"

Zeke paused at his sister Mary's question. At five ten, she was only a couple of inches shorter than him. And like him, she had straight black hair and creepy topaz-colored eyes that their grandmother used to call "the devil's gold."

He indicated the brass bed behind her that was covered with an old-fashioned quilt. "Yeah. The lawyer said he died in his bed. Three days before anyone found the body."

She jumped away from the footboard and scowled at him. "Ew! Thanks, Zeke. You're such a sick bastard."

"Apparently so, since that's all anyone ever says to me."

She ruffled his hair. "Oh, poor baby. We have to find you a better job one day."

"Never happen, sis. I sold my soul to the devil for thirty thou a year." Zeke glanced around the room, which was covered in ancient artifacts from Egypt, Persia and other cultures at which he could only guess.

"What was it Grandpa used to say? 'You may pawn your soul to the devil, but the good Lord will always bail you out'?"

"Something like that."

She paused at the desk by the door before she picked something up to look at it. "What's this?"

Zeke moved to peer over her shoulder. It was a round medallion with what appeared to be an angel and serpent fighting. There was some old-timey script that he couldn't read. "Looks like one of those things from a horror movie that someone uses to summon a demon or something."

She snorted. " 'Back, Manitou, back.' Do you remember that old movie?"

"I remember you making me watch it, then telling Mom it had a naked woman in it and getting my ass busted because of it."

Mary gave him a sheepish grin. "Oh, never mind. Forget I said anything." She handed him the medallion. "Maybe you should chant something over it."

"O great Manitou, I want another life. Something completely different than this one."

"Wouldn't it be freaky if the two of us exchanged places? You'd have to go home to my house and make out with Duncan."

Zeke covered his ears with his hands in mock horror. "Ah *gah*! Eye bleach. Don't put that shit in my head. You're my sister, for Pete's sake. Now I'm going to have to beat your husband the next time I see him for defiling you." He cringed. "I'd rather be at work."

"Oh, pooh. You always overreact to everything."

"So not true. Trust me. I live a life where people scream at me on an hourly basis and I take it without raising anything more than an ulcer."

She pressed the medallion to his chest. "One day, your life will change."

"Yeah." He took the medallion as she walked back toward the living room. "One day I'll also be in a pine box, six feet under." He followed her out of the bedroom and had to admit their granduncle was a weird old man. "The lawyer said Gramps here spent his younger years as an archaeologist and the last few decades as a total recluse."

Mary nodded as she scanned the bookshelves and tables, which were littered with even more artifacts. "It looks like he spent a lot of time bringing that stuff home. You could probably make a killing on eBay."

Zeke didn't really hear her as his attention was taken over by an odd coin that was partially covered on the coffee table. Frowning, he walked over to it. Bright and shiny, it looked brand-new and yet the markings on it appeared as ancient as everything else.

More than that, it actually felt warm to the touch. "What do you think this is?"

Mary shrugged. "More junk."

Maybe. Then again, a strange sensation went over him. "You think any of this crap could be possessed?"

"No. I think you're possessed of the spirit of creepiness. Put that down and let's go get dinner. This place makes me depressed."

Zeke nodded. He reached out to drop it, but couldn't make himself let go. It was as if the coin somehow called out to him. Whispered to him.

And before he knew what he was doing, he put it in his pocket and followed Mary out to her car.

You have been chosen . . .

Zeke looked up from his meat loaf sandwich in the cozy diner they'd found to see Mary chowing down on her burger. "What did you say?"

She swallowed before she spoke. "Nothing. I'm eating."

You have been chosen . . .

"You're not funny, Mary. Stop that."

"Stop what?"

"Throwing your voice."

"I'm not throwing my voice, but if you don't stop irritating me, I might be throwing a fry at your head."

You have been chosen . . .

Zeke looked around the small restaurant. All the tables around them were empty. The only other customers were seated at a bar, talking to the waitress. "You didn't hear that?"

Mary scowled at him. "Hear what?"

"You have been chosen."

"What are you? On crack?"

"Not yet, but I am thinking it might behoove me to find some, except that they make me take a urine test every other day for work, so no fun there."

"You're not right, are you? God, I hope that's not genetic since Duncan and I are trying to get pregnant."

"Again with the ick stuff. Stop!"

You have been chosen . . .

Zeke growled at the voice. "And that means you, too. Damn. My life is bad enough. The last thing I need is to be schizophrenic."

"I don't know. Given your job, schizo could be fun . . . 'No, lady, *I* didn't turn you down. That was the voices in my head telling you to shove that claim where the sun doesn't shine.' "

"I really hate you," he said with a laugh.

"I know. It's why you tried to feed me Drāno when we were kids."

He shook his head at the memory. "Yeah, but you're the one who traded me for a wagon."

"You do know that when you turned sixteen, Mom told me that we should have kept the wagon."

"I've no doubt."

You have been chosen . . .

Zeke raked his hands through his hair. "Call the shrink. I've lost my mind."

"Sweetie, you lost that a long time ago. Now eat your sandwich. The voices in your head are probably hungry."

Zeke rolled his eyes at his sister's curt dismissal. He'd just turned back to his sandwich when something that felt like an electric current went down his spine. It truly felt like a razor blade skimming his soul.

And something inside him raised up like the hackles of a dog. He turned toward the door at the same time a well-dressed man entered. Wearing a suit and tie, he looked completely respectable.

Cheats on his taxes and wife. Misappropriated funds from his clients earlier tonight. Beats his kids. Total douche bag. Will eventually spend ten years in jail for fraud. Damned to hell on his deathbed. Nothing will redeem him. His ego won't let it.

Zeke shook his head to clear out the strange voice that wouldn't let up.

"Richard Cheatham."

The man stopped next to him. "Do I know you?"

Zeke looked up and blinked. "Excuse me?"

"You just said my name. Do I know you?"

"I didn't say anything."

"Yes, you did. You said 'Richard Cheatham.' I heard you." His dark blue eyes narrowed dangerously. "Did my wife hire you?"

"Dude, I don't know you and I have no idea what you're talking about."

Richard started to grab him.

Zeke caught his hand and whipped it around, twisting Richard's body as he rose. He held Richard against him while the man struggled and cursed.

Stunned, he glanced to Mary, who was as shocked as he was.

He released Richard, who scurried out of the diner.

"What the hell was that action?" Mary asked.

Zeke had no idea. He didn't know how to move like that. How to defend himself. God knows his ass had been kicked enough in his life to prove it to him.

You have been chosen . . .

Chosen for what?

"I don't feel good, Mare." He pulled out a ten and dropped it on the table. "I think I need to go home and rest. Thanks for coming with me." He didn't give her time to say a word before he bolted.

He quickly got into his silver Nissan, parked beside hers, and headed home. For the entire two-hour trip back, he kept waiting for the voices to return.

They didn't.

But his car radio was whacked out. The CD player wouldn't work and every time he changed the station, some weird-ass song would play. AC/DC's "Highway to Hell." "Hells Bells." "Evil Walks." Godsmack's "Releasing the Demons." Papa Roach's "Roses On My Grave."

"What the hell is up with my radio?"

Every single station had something weird to do with death, demons or hell.

"Well, I know this damn car ain't Bumblebee." For one thing, he'd been driving it for over nine years. If it was an Autobot in disguise, surely it would have transformed before now.

No, this was like one of those *Twilight Zone* episodes they showed on the SciFi Channel.

Maybe his voices had possessed his car.

Yeah, right.

By the time he reached his house, he was really starting to freak himself out with psycho fears that the devil was after him or that aliens were about to pull him on board for an anal probe. His heart racing, he parked the car in the driveway and got out. Before he reached his door, the neighbor's dog came running up to him to hump his leg.

"What in the world is wrong with you?"

He pulled the dog gently from his leg, then ran like hell to his door. He fumbled for the keys while Tiny was trying to make time with his shoes. Opening the door, Zeke slid inside, then slammed it shut.

The dog whimpered on the other side.

"This is the weirdest day of my life."

"Just wait. It gets stranger."

Eyes wide, Zeke turned toward the deep, scary voice behind him to find what had to be a man, who was so beautiful he would have made a hot woman. Tall, thin and blond, he had eyes so blue they could only be called celestial. "Who the hell are you?"

"Wrong direction, actually. But my name is Gabriel."

Zeke tightened his grip on the doorknob, ready to bolt outside again. "And you would be in my house to . . ." *Rob me blind and kill me,* was the thought in his head.

"Explain the weirdness that surrounds you."

Call the cops, Zeke. Now.

That would only be a waste of your time.

He gasped at the sound of Gabriel's voice in his head.

"You have been chosen," Gabriel said in that same spooky voice he'd been hearing.

"For what?"

"To be an avenger."

Zeke tried to open the door, but before he could, it vanished. Anger and fear mixed inside him. "Yo, Hotel California, I want my door back."

"And so it'll return once we have this settled."

"Settled, my ass. I'm not Emma Peel and I'd look like shit in a black catsuit. Find her for your avenger. Now let me go."

Gabriel tsked at him. "You can't fight your destiny, Ezekiel. Besides, you asked for this. We couldn't have fulfilled Michael's choice had you been unwilling."

Zeke swallowed as he turned around slowly to face Gabriel. "How did I choose this?"

"You asked for your life to change. You wanted to be special. To make a difference. Michael heard and so he chose you to be his replacement."

"Michael's dead."

Gabriel shook his head. "After all these centuries of fighting, he's retired. You're the new seraph who will take on his duties."

Yeah, the dude was on crack. "What duties?"

"To maintain the natural order of the universe. Good versus evil. We allow evil a certain latitude to fulfill its part, but whenever the demons take their duties too far, we are the ones who rein them in."

"Bullshit!"

Zeke ran for his bedroom. He slammed the door shut and locked it, then froze as he caught sight of himself in the mirrored door of his closet.

His short black hair was now snow white and long. His clothes were gone, replaced by a black shirt and pants and a long, full, black leather coat. Three spikes stood out on each shoulder and a red chain was wrapped around his left arm.

On his right hip was the cross hilt of a sword that looked like an ancient cross. As he watched the hilt in the mirror, the center opened to reveal two pale blue eyes and a small mouth.

"You can call me Jack."

Zeke screamed, ripping the hilt off and throwing it to the ground. He turned to run to the window only to find Gabriel there.

"I see you met Jack. Don't worry. Most people scream like girls when he does that."

"This is a whacked-out dream. I'm going to wake . . ." He trailed off as "Jack" mutated from a cross hilt into a large metallic man.

"All seraph have a minion and a guardian. I'm yours."

Zeke's head whirled at what was happening.

"Breathe deep before you hyperventilate," Jack said.

"What are you?"

"I told you. I'm your guardian and your minion. Anything you need that's metal, from transportation to weaponry, I can be. When you need a hand fighting, I look like this." He indicated his armored human form, then pounded his hand against his breast. "The best armor in the world. Nothing, except a handful of demonic weapons, can mar me."

Gabriel clapped him on the back. "Welcome to the fold, Ezekiel."

Suddenly something warm swept through Zeke. It felt as if his very blood was on fire. His breathing ragged, he turned back toward the closet. His eyes were a vibrant red and his face was every bit as perfect and ethereal as Gabriel's.

Zeke lifted his armored arm to make sure it was him.

It was.

"What about my job?"

Gabriel looked a bit sheepish. "There's no payment for being a seraph. Sorry. But you will have a whole new set of skills. Just wait."

That sounded ominous.

"And there's one more thing."

Of course there was. "And that is?"

"Michael notwithstanding, the average life expectancy for a seraph is . . . two years."

Zeke laughed nervously. "Oh no, I definitely decline. You can take this crap and stick it."

Gabriel reached behind his ear and pulled out the coin Zeke had taken from his uncle's house. "The minute you willingly took the medallion, you sealed your fate. You have been chosen, my brother. The only way out now is death."

"You're shitting me."

Jack clapped him on the back. "But on the upside, your seraph form will never age. And the only way to die is by a demon blade. As long you survive fighting them, you're immortal to the things that would kill a normal human. Think of the money you'll save on medical bills."

That was so not an upside.

Gabriel gave him a gimlet stare. "And there's one more thing."

"Neutering?" That would be Zeke's luck.

Gabriel grinned. "No." He snapped his fingers. An instant later, a black mist appeared by his side. It swirled into the small form of a raven. No sooner had the bird appeared than it exploded into the form of a tall, gorgeous woman with long black hair and coal black eyes. Dressed all in black, she was striking and tough. "Ravenna is also your helpmate."

"Oh yeah, baby." He reached for her, only to have her grab his wrist and flip him onto the ground, where he landed with a painful *oof.*

She wrenched his arm and put one perfectly spiked heel on the center of his chest. "Keep your hands to yourself or lose them." She pressed the heel in, making him grimace. "And don't call me 'baby.' " Then she released him and moved away.

Gabriel's eyes danced with humor. "Ravenna is your contact with the other side. She's also your eyes and ears, both to me and to Lucifer's posse. You guys get acquainted. I have duties to attend." He vanished.

"But—"

"There are no buts," Jack said, laughing. "You, my friend, have been chosen."

Ravenna nodded her agreement. "Always be careful what you wish for. You just might get it."

Yeah, and in this one wish, Zeke had definitely been screwed.

A Very Special Girl

A Harry the Book Story

Mike Resnick

I am reading the *Daily Racing Form* in my temporary office, which is the third booth at Joey Chicago's 3-Star Tavern, and coming to the conclusion that six trillion to one on Flyaway in the fifth at Saratoga is a bit of an underlay, as there is no way this horse gets within twenty lengths of the winner on a fast track, a slow track, or a muddy track, and I have my doubts that even a rain of toads moves him up more than two lengths. I conclude that this horse cannot beat a blind sea slug at equal weights, even if he has the inside post position. Suddenly a strange odor strikes my nostrils, and without looking up I say, "Hi, Dead

End," because one whiff tells me that it is Dead End Dugan, who simply cannot hide the fact that he is a zombie.

He also is an occasional employee that I use when some goniff does not wish to honor his marker, and indeed he has just returned from Longshot Lamont's, where I had sent him to collect the three large that Longshot Lamont bet on Auntie's Panties to come in first, and indeed the filly does come in first by seven lengths, but she comes in first in the eighth race after she goes to the post in the seventh race thirty minutes earlier.

"So do you pick up the three large that Harry the Book is owed?" asks Benny Fifth Street.

"Of course he picks it up," says Gently Gently Dawkins. "After all, he is half as big as a mountain, and is covered by almost as much dirt, and how much can three large weigh anyway?"

They immediately get into one of their arguments, Gently Gently saying that a three-thousand-dollar diamond weighs less than a cigarette, and Benny replying that it all depends who is manning the scales, and that his cousin is the clerk of scales at Belmont and has been weighing Flyboy Billy Tuesday in at 120 pounds every day for years, even though the Flyboy has not topped 108 pounds since eating some bad chili three years ago. This drives Joey Chicago, who has been standing behind the bar, wild, because he has been betting against Flyboy Billy Tuesday's horses all year, and now he learns that they've been carrying twelve pounds less than they should, but Benny points out that it's okay, because 108 pounds of Billy Tuesday is more of a handicap to a horse than 130 pounds of most jockeys, and Joey Chicago has no answer for this, so he goes back to cleaning the bar around Dead End Dugan, which requires cleaning every time Dugan moves.

"So does Longshot Lamont pay with a smile?" I ask Dugan.

He gives me that puzzled expression—he doesn't think as clearly as he used to before he became a zombie—and says, "I thought you wanted money, Harry."

"Money is even better than smiles," I say to comfort him, and because it is also true. "I trust you have it with you?"

"Well, I *had* it," says Dugan. I was going to say "says Dugan uncomfortably," but the fact of the matter is that nothing makes him more uncomfortable than being dead, which is a permanent if not a stationary condition.

"If you do not have it anymore, you had better tell me where it is and why it is not in my hand right now," I say.

"I am in love," says Dugan. "I meet the most wonderful girl this afternoon on my way back from Longshot Lamont's."

"Is this not a bit early in the relationship for an exchange of three-thousand-dollar gifts?" asks Gently Gently.

"Do not be so fast to misinterpret," replies Dugan. "This girl is just half a step short of perfection."

"Then she will understand that that was not your money to give, and she will be happy to hand it over to me," I say.

"Uh . . . *that* is the half a step I was referring to," says Dugan, brushing away flies that are starting to play field hockey on his face, as they always do when he stands in one place for a few minutes.

I decide to be the reasoning father figure, partially because I am a saint among men, and primarily because I have not yet figured out how to threaten a man who is already dead, and I say, "Tell us about this remarkable lady who has won your heart."

"She has left my heart right where it has always been," answers Dugan. "She is much more interested in my brain and my soul."

"I can't imagine why," says Benny. "You never use the one, and you are no longer in possession of the other."

"She is kind of a collector," explains Dugan,

and it is the first time in my life I ever see a zombie swallow uneasily, or swallow at all, for that matter.

"What does she collect, brains or souls?" asks Benny, who has a healthy curiosity about such things.

"I get the impression that she is not all that choosy," answers Dugan.

"Where do you meet her?" I ask.

"I am passing Creepy Conrad's Curiosity Shop, and I see her through the window, nibbling on a little snack in a feminine way, and it is love at first sight."

"What kind of snack?" asks Gently Gently, who at 350 pounds and counting has a serious interest in such things.

"I cannot see through the window," replies Dugan, "but it is wiggling its tail just before she swallows it."

"But she swallows it in a feminine way," I say, though my sarcasm is lost on Dugan.

"Yes," he says. "She is just beautiful. And very precise. Why, she drains an entire fifth of Comrade Terrorist vodka and does not spill so much as a drop."

"I figure the tail accompanies both ears of whatever it was as a prize for her feminine appetite," says Benny.

"She should skip the Olympics and go pro," adds Gently Gently.

"Does she eat anything else we should know about?" I ask.

"Like what?" asks Dugan.

"Like small children," I say. "Or even big ones."

"You are speaking of the woman I love!" says Dugan heatedly.

"I am speaking of the woman who is holding three large that belongs to me," I say. "Maybe you should introduce me to both of them."

"Both?" asks Dugan.

"Your girl and my money," I say. "I will take it from there."

"All right," says Dugan. "I am dying to see her again anyway."

"Poor choice of words," notes Joey Chicago from behind the bar.

"But you have to approach her gently, Harry," continues Dugan, ignoring Joey's unfeeling if accurate remark. "She is a sensitive thing and takes offense easily."

"I will approach her so gently she will hardly know I am there," I assure him.

"She will know," he assures me. "She is very perceptive." He pauses. "I think it is the extra pair of eyes."

"She has four eyes?" I say.

"At the very least," says Dugan.

"Has she got four of anything else important?" asks Benny, suddenly interested.

"She comes equipped with all kinds of extras," says

Dugan. "This is why I have fallen in love with her. She is unique, even among women, who are all unique, each in their own alien way."

"What kinds of extras?" I ask.

"Teeth," says Dugan. "Claws. Eyes. Tails. Well, it is only one tail, but compared to everyone else it is extra."

"I cannot argue with that," agrees Benny.

"And how many women can lift an entire car?" says Dugan proudly.

"Six cylinders or eight?" asks Gently Gently.

"Why would she lift a car?" chimes in Benny.

"It is a very tight parking space, so she just walks out, picks up the car, driver and all, and sets it down in the empty space." Dugan smiles wistfully. "And she does not even break a sweat."

"I agree that she is unique among all the women of my acquaintance," I say. "Right up to the incident with the car, she is running neck and neck with a redhead named Thelma, but she has sprinted into the lead."

"That is nothing," says Dugan. "You should see her fly."

"Probably I shouldn't," I say. "I have enough trouble falling asleep as it is."

"She just flaps her arms and flies away?" asks Benny.

Dugan smiles. It is maybe the first smile anyone

has seen on him since he came back from the grave. "Nobody can flap their arms and fly," he says. "She flaps her wings."

"Does she imbibe anything besides vodka while you are with her?" I ask suddenly.

"Like what?" says Dugan.

"Like blood," I say.

"I will not dignify such a crude question with a response," responds Dugan.

"I doubt that there can be more than one of her," I say, "but just in case God has been asleep at the switch and there are two or more, what is she wearing so I will be able to identify her?"

"I will be right alongside you, Harry," he replies.

"True, but you are still a relative newcomer to the zombie trade, and what if you suddenly decide you don't like it? If I am to present a moldering corpse to the lady of your dreams, I at least should be sure I have the right lady. So what is she wearing?"

"I don't know," says Dugan. "I am so enraptured by her face, I never notice."

"Now I know for sure he's a zombie," says Benny.

"All right," I say, trying to hide my annoyance. "What color is her hair?"

"That's kind of difficult to say."

"How hard can it be?" I persist. "It is blonde, brunette, or possibly red."

"Well, it wriggles and hisses a lot, and it keeps changing colors under the lights," answers Dugan. "Sometimes it is red and sometimes it is green. I do not think it is ever blonde, but I could be wrong."

"Are you saying she is a Medusa?" I ask.

"No, I am not saying any such a thing," answers Dugan. "For one thing, her hair is friendly."

"How can hair be friendly?" asks Gently Gently.

"It chats with me, and it sings 'Ninety-nine Bottles of Beer on the Wall' while she is drinking the vodka."

"You talk to her hair?" says Benny disbelievingly.

"No," answers Dugan.

"Then you just made that up?" says Benny.

"I made nothing up," says Dugan sharply. "Her hair chats with me, just like I say. But I do not talk to it, because I am shy and tongue-tied in her presence."

"So she has extra eyes and teeth, and comes equipped with wings and a cold-blooded hairdo," I say. "I hope you will not take it askance, Dugan, but I think I am going to bring a little protection along."

"A gun?" he asks.

I shake my head. "I have a feeling that a hail of bullets would just annoy her," I say. "No, I will take Big-Hearted Milton."

"I do not see him," says Dugan, looking around.

"That is because you are not looking in his office," I say. "I will go and fetch him."

And with that, I walk to the men's room and enter it, and there is Big-Hearted Milton, my personal mage, sitting in his usual spot on the tile floor, surrounded by five black candles, which have all burned down to nubs.

"Hi, Harry," he says. "Be with you in a minute." He mutters a spell that has very little melody and even fewer vowels. As he says the last word of it, all five candles go out. "That'll show her," he says with a satisfied smile.

"What will show who?"

"Mitzi McSweeney," says Milton. "I take her to dinner last night, and just because I play a little itsy-bitsy spider on her thigh under the table she throws her soup in my face and walks out." He glowers furiously. "And I do not even like chicken gumbo."

"What have you done to the poor girl?" I ask.

"When she steps on the scale this morning, vain creature that she is, she will find out that she is ten pounds heavier than last night, and nothing will take the weight off except an apologetic phone call to me."

I decide not to point out that Mitzi is bordering on anorexic anyway and an extra ten pounds will fill her out nicely. I especially decide not to mention that she can probably pack more of a wallop at 115 pounds than at 105.

"Okay, Milton," I say, "if you are done with your just

and terrible vengeance, I have need of your services."

"I am the best there is at my trade," he says. "I put Morris the Mage in the shade. Spellsinger Sol cannot hold a candle to me. But I tell you up front, Harry, that even *I* cannot bring Flyaway home a winner at Saratoga tomorrow. I could put a saddle on *you* and you could spot him eight lengths and still beat him by daylight."

"That is not the particular service I need," I say. "It seems that Dead End Dugan has fallen in love, and has given his lady friend the three large that he picked up for me from Longshot Lamont. It is my intention to retrieve it."

"And you need my help taking your money back from a girl?" laughs Milton.

"Anything is possible," I say.

"Oh well, I have not been out of my office since I showed up to wash the soup off my face last night," he says. "A little fresh air will do me good. And getting your money back should be like taking candy from a baby."

I resist the urge to ask him a baby *what,* and a moment later we emerge from the men's room into the bar, and pick up Dead End Dugan, Benny Fifth Street, and Gently Gently Dawkins, and we are about to walk out the door when Milton asks Dugan what the name of the lady we are about to visit might be.

"Anna," he says.

"And her last name is Conda, right?" says Milton, laughing at his own joke.

"How did you know?" asks Dugan.

Creepy Conrad's Curiosity Shop is easy to find. You just see where all the terrified women and children are running away from, and follow the screaming to its source. On the day we go there, Conrad is having a sale on shrunken heads, but these differ from every other shrunken head I have ever seen in that they are still alive and are attached to nonshrunken bodies. They spend most of their time eating, because their mouths are so small and their bodies are so big.

Because he is on the outskirts of an Italian neighborhood, Conrad also sells a lot of full-size wooden crosses, with or without hammers and nails. His vinyl record section—he has not yet made the jump to CDs—sells mood music, providing that your mood is either morbid or panic-stricken. He is also having a special on surplus dialysis machines, and three pale, lean gentlemen, each wearing a velvet cape, are examining them.

The rest of the merchandise is *really* esoteric, especially the part that is still alive, but we have not come to enjoy a pleasant afternoon browsing through

Conrad's stock. We have come for Anna Conda and my three thousand dollars, but as I look around there is no morsel of femininity to be seen, nor is there anyone who matches Anna's description.

Finally Creepy Conrad emerges from a back room. He is missing one eye, and his left cheekbone protrudes through the skin, and those few teeth he still possesses are filed and discolored, and the nails on his hands are about an inch long and curve like those of a leopard, but aside from that he looks every bit as normal as Dead End Dugan, which is perhaps not really an apt comparison as Dugan still possesses his hair.

"Well, curse my soul if it isn't Harry the Book and his retainers," says Conrad. "What may I do for you fine gentlemen today? Could I perhaps interest the illustrious Mr. Dugan in a coffin?"

"You couldn't interest me no matter where you were," says Dugan. "We have come to see the delectable Anna Conda."

"Well, there is an Anna Conda on the premises," answers Conrad. "But a delectable one? Possibly you want Madame Bonne Ami's House of Exotic Comforts for the Recently Departed. They might have one."

"Watch your step, sir," says Dugan, drawing himself up to his full height. "You are speaking of the woman I love."

"Now, why would the woman you love be working for Madame Bonne Ami?" muses Conrad.

"Keep a civil tongue in your head," says Dugan ominously.

"I already have one," says Conrad, sticking his tongue out at us. "It belonged to a little old lady who only used it in church on Sundays."

"Where is she?" demands Dugan.

"The little old lady?" says Conrad. "She is long gone."

"Where is Anna Conda?" says Dugan.

"I heard you mention my name," says a voice that sounds kind of like a wirehaired terrier being combed against the grain, and a moment later Anna Conda steps out from one of the back rooms.

She is everything Dugan says she is, but Dugan does not say the half of it. He never mentions the cold reptilian eyes, the pointed ears, the reticulated greenish skin, or the four-inch dewclaws on each of her ankles. She offers us the kind of smile healthy cats offer to three-legged mice, and I can see that her tongue is black and forked.

"Hello, Mr. Dugan," she says, and her voice does not improve with proximity. "How nice to see you again."

"You are even more beautiful than before," replies Dugan, and Benny shoots me a look that says, *My God, what does she look like earlier in the day?*

"Who are your friends?" asks Anna.

"This is Harry the Book, my sometimes employer," says Dugan before I can whisper to him to make up a name, "and these are Benny Fifth Street, Gently Gently Dawkins, and Big-Hearted Milton."

"And what are you gentlemen here for?" she asks.

"It is Harry's fault," Dugan blurts out, so I figure I had better explain the situation.

"It would appear that Dugan, with the best will in the world, gives you a little keepsake that is not his to give," I say.

"I am just as happy to accept it from you, Harry," she says with a smile that makes me want to turn and race for the door and not stop running until I have reached Des Moines or Des Plaines or some other distant municipality beginning with "Des."

"I will handle this, Harry," says Milton, stepping forward. "Miss Conda, charming and beautiful as you are, I am afraid I must insist that you return the three large to Harry, though you can keep a couple of Ben Franklins for your trouble."

"It was given to me in all earnestness, and I am not inclined to give it back," she says, and I notice that blue vapor is starting to pour out of her nose, which means that either she is losing her temper or perhaps her spleen has spontaneously combusted, and I will give heavy odds on the former.

"Then I am afraid I shall have to resort to stringent means of recovering it," says Milton.

"You do that," says Anna.

"Very well," says Milton. "Do not say that you weren't warned."

And with that, Milton begins chanting something in a forgotten language, and making gestures in the air, and otherwise conjuring up all of the black arts at his command, and finally he ends it with a cry of "presto!"—and suddenly there are only four of us facing Anna Conda, and Big-Hearted Milton is nowhere to be seen.

"Where did he go?" asks Gently Gently.

"Beats me," I say.

"Get me the hell out of here!" says Milton's voice.

I look around, but there is no sign of him.

"Get you out of where?" I ask.

"This damned dimension that she hurls me into," says Milton's voice. "And hurry! It is cold and there is something very big sniffing at me and drooling on my face."

"I do not know how to magic you back," I say. "After all, you are the mage."

"Reach out and grab my hand, of course," says Milton.

"Reach *where*?" I say.

"Out!" yells Milton.

I reach my hand out, and sure enough a pudgy invisible hand takes hold of it. I give it a pull, and suddenly there is a *pop!* and then Milton is standing next to me, looking both relieved and annoyed.

He stares at Anna Conda with a combination of fear and awe. "Who does your protection?" he asks. "Whoever it is, he's *good*!"

"I need no protector," answers Anna.

"I can believe it," says Benny fervently.

"Enough of this chitchat," I say. "I still want my money."

Dugan walks over and stands next to Anna. "Enough!" he says. "I will not stand idly by and let you pester the love of my life."

"Actually, she is more the love of your death," Gently Gently points out.

"Whatever she is," I say, "I am not inclined to supply her with a dowry one hour after collecting it from Longshot Lamont." I turn to her. "I hope you and Dugan will be very happy, and can find a hotel that caters to both of whatever you are, and I will even pop for a flimsy nightgown if you are going to tie the knot, but I still want my three large."

"And if I do not agree to part with it, will you put a hit out on Dead End Dugan?" she asks with a cold reptilian smile, and I have to admit that the idea of putting out a hit on a dead man can best be called counterproductive.

"Milton," I say, "have you got any other tricks up your sleeve?"

"He has nothing up his sleeve except his arm," says Anna. "And if he tries anything, he will make me lose my temper. You will not be happy if I should lose my temper. The last time I lose it they blame what happens on Hurricane Katrina, and the time before that they invent Hurricane Andrew."

"Did you do Chernobyl, too?" asks Benny curiously.

"No," she says. "That was my kid sister."

"I am sure I will love her, too," says Dugan.

No sooner do the words leave his mouth than Anna gets all red in the face and lets out a shriek. All the windows break, my fillings fall out of my teeth, a bus half a block away veers and plows into a fire hydrant, and every dog within a mile begins howling.

"I am sorry," says Anna a moment later. "I have a jealous and passionate nature."

"To say nothing of 'cataclysmic' and 'catastrophic' and a lot of other words that begin with 'cat,'" I agree.

"I see your friend is sprawled out on the floor," she says, indicating Gently Gently. "I hope I did not do him irreparable damage."

"If he can survive eighty-seven million calories," I say as Benny and I heave him to his feet, "he can survive a jealous scream."

"Where am I?" mumbles Gently Gently. "Are we at war? What day is it? Wait! I have it! Flyaway won and the world came to an end!"

"You'll be all right," I say. "Just stand there and try not to think."

"That should be very easy for him," says Benny. "Not thinking is one of the things Gently Gently does best."

Anna Conda turns to Dugan. "I am sorry I have upset your friends so much. I cherish our relationship, and to prove it I will return Harry the Book's money."

"While those are words I have been longing to hear," answers Dugan, "the part about cherishing our relationship, not the part about Harry's money, I am mildly surprised as our total time spent in each other's company has been only ten minutes, give or take."

"That is about seven minutes longer than most of my relationships last," says Anna. "I will be back with the money in a moment."

She goes into one of the back rooms, and Benny walks over to Dugan.

"I would be very careful with this girl," he says confidentially. "For example, when she suggests you go out for a bite, I will give plenty of eight-to-five that she is not talking about patronizing a restaurant."

Anna comes out and hands me a bag containing the three thousand dollars. "It is all there," she says. "You can count it, if you wish."

"That is not necessary," I tell her. "Dugan would never cheat me, and if you would I prefer not to know about it, because then I will not have to do anything about it."

She gives me another of those smiles that are more frightening that a Gorgon's grimace. "You are wise beyond your years, Harry the Book."

"And you are formidable beyond yours, Anna Conda," I say, bowing low, but not so low that I can't jump back if she changes her mind and reaches for the money, or maybe my neck.

As we are leaving, Benny whispers to me: "I know love is blind, but until this minute I do not realize he is on life support."

And that is the story of Dead End Dugan's very special girl. I suppose their relationship was doomed from the start. I know that opposites attract, but there is nothing in the rule book about anyone quite as opposite as Dugan and Anna. They decide to go away for a weekend in the mountains. Dugan never mentions exactly what happens, except that he makes a mistake by remarking that the tour bus driver is very pretty, but

I am told that when the next edition of Rand McNally comes out Pikes Peak will now be Pikes Valley.

"I have learned a valuable lesson, Harry," Dugan tells me when it is all over. "From now on, I will stick to my own kind."

And so he does. The next afternoon I am sitting in the third booth at Joey Chicago's, reading the *Form*, and the smell of rotting flesh is twice as strong as ever. I look up and there is Dugan and his new girlfriend, sidling up to the bar.

"What can I get you and this beautiful young lady?" asks Joey Chicago, managing to string together three misstatements in just three words.

"What will it be, my dear?" says Dugan.

"It's been so many decades since I've drunk anything at all, I can't remember," says his companion. "Why don't we let the bartender decide?"

"I've got just the thing," says Joey Chicago, pulling out a pair of tall glasses and little paper umbrellas.

"And what is that?" asks Dugan.

"A pair of Zombies," says Joey Chicago.

Love Seat Solitaire

D. L. Snell

"Dude," Jess said, pushing up his glasses, "the kitchen table's floating again."

Sam looked up from the *Street Fighter* round he and Dave were playing on the love seat, Ken versus Chun-Li. "Fuck."

"Suuuure," Dave said, using the distraction to beat Ken into a corner with Chun-Li's unbeatable lightning kick. "Let me guess: the ghost is playing poker. And 'gullible' isn't in the dictionary."

"Casper doesn't play poker," Sam said. "He plays solitaire."

"And fifty-two card pickup," Jess added.

"Fucking ghost."

"And I'm sure he does card tricks, too," Dave said.

He won the round with Chun-Li and looked up. "So why'd the old man kill himself anyway?"

Sam threw down his controller. "He *didn't.* He drowned in the crapper."

"How the hell did he—?"

"Haven't you ever been drunk?"

Dave held up his soda can. "I only drink Coke," he said, smiling. He took a swig.

Sam stood up from the love seat and let Jess sit down to play.

"Scoot over, newbie," Jess told Dave. "You're in my ass-kicking zone." Dave moved to the other cushion, over far enough so his hairy leg wouldn't brush Jess's—they were both wearing shorts—but Jess sat down and rubbed their thighs together, making silly sounds like one of the Three Stooges.

"Stop it!" Dave said, smashing himself against the arm of the love seat. "I feel like a fag on this thing."

Sam picked up his pizza plate and beer mug from the milk-crate end table. "Well, it was free and I was poor," he said. "And you *are* a fag."

"Where are you going?" Dave asked.

"To take care of the ghost."

"Want me to come with you?"

"Why?"

"To protect you. And to see this spook you've been talking so much about."

"Be my guest."

Dave furrowed his brow as if considering it, but finally shook his head. "Nah. I'll take your word for it."

"Whatever," Sam said. As he stepped over a pile of dirty clothes and Red Bull cans to get to the kitchen, he heard Dave ask, "So when Casper drowned . . . was there shit in the toilet?"

And Jess, ignoring him, said, "No Cheat-Li this time, Dave. And no E. Honda, either!"

The kitchen table was indeed floating, an old rusty patio table hovering three inches off the linoleum. The crusty paper plates, soda cans, and credit card offers had slid to the floor to make room for Casper's game of solitaire. The cards floated, too: Casper was invisible.

"Goddammit," Sam said, picking up forks, spoons, and an experimental bong made out of a fishbowl and two eggbeaters. "Look at the mess you made."

He threw the silverware in the sink, and it rattled off the dirty plates back onto the floor. "Dammit." Sam ignored them and set the bong on the counter.

The fridge was a kegerator, with a keg inside and a tap on the door. Soda, mayonnaise, mustard, and ketchup lined the shelves; most of his food came from boxes in the freezer or from the deep-fat fryers at the closest Burger King.

He pulled the tap on the fridge and poured beer into his cup. "Why do you always do this when company's over?" he asked Casper. "Here I am trying to have a good time with my bros, and you try to screw it up. You're going to scare off Dave, you know, the same way you scared off Samantha. One friend down, one to go."

Casper ignored him and kept laying out cards.

Sam smirked. "Why do you play that game anyway? You never win. It's depressing."

The ghost paused, as if considering the question. Then he picked up the cards, shuffled, and dealt seven to himself and seven to the empty spot across from him; he laid the remaining stack in the middle and started sorting his hand.

"Go fish?" Sam said. "No thanks. I've got a life." He said it, but what would he be doing if he didn't have friends over? Playing *Street Fighter* by himself? He had done it before. And sometimes he slouched on the love seat, watching *Blades of Glory* or Ricky Bobby late into the night, feeling so empty he almost wept.

Casper threw a card at him.

"Queen of hearts," Sam said. "Coming out of the closet?"

The ghost threw a run of clubs at him: seven, eight, nine.

"So that's why six was afraid of seven. Spoooooky." The beer filled his cup to the top, surfaced with foam. He took a drink and sighed. "Ahhh. It's not quite like the head your momma used to give, but it sure is good."

Casper sprayed cards everywhere. He threw the patio table on its side, blasted open cupboards, and exploded boxes of Kix and macaroni. Sam's mug shattered and he dodged the amber waterfall, arching his back and holding the shattered cup away from his shirt and shorts. The cold brew splashed his feet; shards bounced off them.

Sam shut his eyes, furrowed his brow, and as loud as he could, shouted, "Beetlejuice, Beetlejuice, *Beetlejuice*!"

The spilt cereal, pasta, and paper crumples swirled one last time on the floor, and then Casper's wind disappeared.

Sam sighed. The skin beneath his eyes felt heavy. "I'm too old for this shit." He was twenty-five. He threw the broken glass in the trash can and dried off with a towel.

Back in the front room, Jess and Dave sat wide-eyed on the love seat. "What the hell happened?" Dave asked.

Sam smiled. "Casper's like a kid; he just wants attention. So you piss him off, insult his momma, and he makes a mess and leaves. It's almost impossible to keep the house clean."

"Check out what he did to your SNES," Jess said, straightening his glasses.

The vintage Super Nintendo, disconnected, sat on

its side against the far wall. Its wires hung out of the entertainment system, and the TV screen had turned blue. Jess and Dave held the unplugged controllers.

"I think Jess was just mad 'cause I was winning," Dave said, "so he yanked his joystick."

"You weren't *winning*." Jess put air quotes around the word. "You landed a few uppercuts and were jumping around like a dick, waiting for the timer to run out."

"Whatever," Dave said, "I pwn."

From the other side of the room, Sam's Frisbee flew into Dave's head—*thock!*

"Ow! What the—?!"

A pencil tried to stab his eye. He dodged and it stuck in the wall behind him. "Jesus—who the hell?"

"It's Casper," Jess said.

"Would you stop with that ghost bullshit? Who else is here?"

"No one," Sam replied, glancing around the room. The attacks had come from different places; Casper could have been anywhere. "He must be fucking pissed: he's never tried to poke out someone's eye before."

"Look," Jess said, pointing at the TV.

In the dust on the screen, words began to appear, as if the ghost was running a finger through the filth. He filled in letters at random, playing a three-word puzzle: one word on top, one in the middle, and one on the bottom, *Wheel of Fortune*–style.

Dave squinted and leaned forward. "Ha . . . r . . . wa . . . Ha-r-wa. What's that, Chinese? How are you doing that? With magnets or something?"

"There's more," Jess said as letters continued to develop. He took off his glasses, steamed them up with his breath, and cleaned them off on his yellow shirt.

"The middle one's 'or,' " Sam said. " 'Or' what?" he asked Casper. "And why'd you try to kill my Nintendo?"

" 'Harts,' " Dave said, reading the top line as it filled in. "What the hell's 'harts'?"

Jess put on his glasses and wrinkled his nose. "Dude, I think he means 'hearts.' "

Sam crossed his arms. "Illiterate spook."

The last few letters fell into place and the message was clear: "Harts," it said, "or war."

Sam shook his head. "Whatever, man. Cards are for losers. We're playing video games." He used his shirt to clean the TV screen, then stepped back and waited for Casper's outburst, waited for the lightbulb to shatter and the bunny ears to hop off the TV—waited for his dumbbells to fly at Dave's head.

The blue screen buzzed.

The house creaked.

Dave lifted his butt and farted.

"Aw, dude!" Jess exclaimed, plugging his nose and fanning the air.

"Jesus," Sam said, spraying some Febreze he found on the floor. "Sodomy Hussein *did* have weapons of ass-destruction."

Dave grimaced. "Sorry."

"Why don't you go dump that nuclear waste?" Sam asked.

"I don't know." Dave turned a little red.

"Afraid we'll hear the splash?"

"No."

"Afraid of Casper?"

"No." He picked up the controller and fiddled with the buttons. "I don't believe in that crap. I'm not a two-year-old."

"Yes, you are."

"No, I'm not."

"Yes, *you are.*"

"Nuh-uh."

Sam smirked and crossed his arms. "Don't worry, kiddo. Casper stays out of the crapper."

" 'Cause that's where he died?" Dave asked.

"No, 'cause that's where I shit. Of *course* it's because that's where he died. And if he *does* go in there, which will never happen in a million, billion, trillion years, just scream 'Beetlejuice' three times and he'll go away."

"How the hell does that work?" Dave asked. "Is that really some kind of ancient incarnation?"

"Aside from the fact that you're an illiterate douche," Sam said, "no. The landlord says Casper hates that movie, thinks you'll make him watch it."

"Not a big Michael Keaton fan," Jess added.

"But he's okay with the original *Batman* because of Jack Nicholson. Now would you just go?"

"Okay, okay." Dave excused himself to the bathroom and farted as he walked.

"Dude!" Jess vacated the love seat, plugging his nose.

After the stink had cleared, Sam hooked up the Super Nintendo and turned on *Street Fighter.* "Care for a quickie?" he asked.

"Sure, big boy."

"Ken versus Ryu?"

"You know it.

"Classic."

"Just like the old days."

"Carpet stretcher."

"Twat."

"Your momma."

"*Dave's* momma."

"Hey!" Dave called from the bathroom. *"For the last time, I'm not a fucking llama! I've just got a long neck!"*

Sam and Jess chuckled and tapped their controllers together as if they were toasting beer mugs, something they had done since middle school, back when they had bowl cuts and liked to play *Ninja Turtles.* Jess was his only friend the ghost hadn't run off. Not that he'd had many friends.

They went to sit on the love seat—and Casper shoved it out from beneath them; they landed in dust bunnies, a crusty sock, and a school of Goldfish crackers.

"Ouch," Sam said. "I think a Dairy Queen token's lodged in my ass."

"I—" Jess began. And then the love seat charged them.

Sam dodged.

Jess didn't.

The piece of furniture rammed into his shoulder. He fell over and the seat reared, its front leg poised over his head. It plunged—and Sam caught it, hands under the bottom as if he were lifting one side. "Move!" he yelled, muscles standing out on his neck, love seat bucking against him, dry-humping his leg.

Jess rolled away.

Sam let go of the love seat and it crashed down. It tried to head butt him. He and Jess sidestepped it and went for the front door, but Casper blocked it with the dresser where Sam stored his DVDs. Sam and Jess retreated to the kitchen doorway, crunching Red Bull cans and tripping in dirty clothes.

Something hit the door behind them. They jumped. Metal points stuck through the door at head level.

"Dude," Jess said, "is that . . . ?"

"A salad fork," Sam replied.

A cleaver hit and poked out of the wood. Plates shattered against the door, knives stabbed it. It was hollow. It wouldn't last long.

Puffed up with air, the love seat feinted toward them; it scooted left, then scooted right.

"What the hell is *its* problem?" Jess asked, rubbing his shoulder. "Dave's fart?"

Sam ignored him. He shouted, "Beetlejuice, Beetle-juice, *Beetlejuice*!"

The love seat paused. The racket behind the kitchen door came to a halt, and somewhere a faucet dripped. After a few seconds, Sam's muscles began to relax. "Phew, I think it's—"

The love seat reared and stomped; the knives continued to hack through the door. They were almost through.

"Shit," Jess said, "what do we do?"

Red boxer shorts lay tangled in the laundry. Glancing at the love seat, Sam grabbed for them. The love seat feinted again and he shot upright, freeing the shorts.

"Dude," Jess said; he pointed at the Ninja Turtle on the boxers and raised an eyebrow.

"Shut up," Sam said. "I've got an idea." He nudged Jess aside with his elbow and held the shorts out in front of the kitchen door like a matador taunting a bull.

The love seat scuffed its front legs on the carpet. It snorted out a cloud of hair and dust.

"*Toro,*" Sam said, staring it down, sweat on his brow. "*Toro,* you springy son of a bitch—your momma was an ottoman!"

That did it: the love seat charged.

Sam held his ground, held his ground—then leapt aside as the bull of wood and soiled upholstery smashed its head through the door. It lodged in the bottom panel, ripping itself on the jagged edges as it tried to pull out.

"The bathroom!" Sam shouted, grabbing Jess by the shirt. "Go, go, go!"

Sweaters and flannels groped for their legs, tried to trip them up in a tangle of sleeves. A pair of boxer briefs with a hole worn in the crotch flapped up like a green bat. It whipped Jess in the face, knocking off his glasses.

"Dude!" Jess bent to feel for them, and—*crunch*—stepped right on them.

With the crack of wood and the tearing of upholstery, the love seat finally freed itself from the door. It whirled around, stuffing billowing out of it like fatty tissue. And behind it, through the hole it had made, knives wandered. Knives—and the bong made of the fishbowl and the eggbeaters.

"Oh my God," Sam said. "No . . . *no.*"

Jess stood up, holding his broken glasses. Sam seized his wrist and screamed, *"Run!"*

In the narrow hall, Sam fumbled along the frame above the bathroom door. "Shit, shit, shit—where is it?"

The doorknob featured a hole through which you could pop open the lock. For a makeshift key, Sam usually used a straightened paper clip, hidden above the door.

"It isn't here!" he said, groping.

The fishbowl bong crept to the mouth of the hallway.

"Beetlejuice!" Sam exclaimed, but the bong just rotated its beaters, making a chuckling sound. It turned to the knives. They looked at each other and nodded.

"Dude," Jess said, clutching at him blindly.

"Found it!" Sam jammed the paper clip into the hole and popped the lock.

The knives darted forward—and lodged in the wood as Sam slammed the door.

"Hey!" Dave pulled up his pants to cover his lap. He still sat on the toilet, holding a copy of JC Penney's *Big and Tall.* "Fags!" He beat at them with the catalogue. "Get out!"

Sam grabbed the catalogue from him. "We *can't.* Casper's gone Michael Myers on us."

Dave raised an eyebrow. "That guy from *Austin Powers*?"

Sam whopped him over the head with *Big and Tall*, then threw it to the floor. "He tried to *kill* us," Sam said.

"Ooooh. Fags."

The bathroom was so small you could take a crap on the toilet and puke in the bathtub at the same time (Sam had done it before, the night Samantha dumped him because Casper had given her an atomic wedgie). With three people, the room was even smaller. So Sam stepped into the tub and made room.

Dave hopped up and down a little on the seat.

Sam frowned. "Done yet?"

He shook his head. "Dangler."

"It stinks like a bagful of assholes in here," Jess said. He put on his glasses, which sat crooked on his face, the right arm bent away from his head. One of the lenses had popped out, and Jess squinted with the affected eye. "How do I look?"

Sam smirked. "Like a dangler."

There was a plop, and Dave sighed. He reached for the toilet paper. "If there's really a ghost," he said, "why don't you move?"

Sam crossed his arms. "Because. I signed a *lease*. Besides, it's never been this bad. He was just a pain in the ass before."

"What's his problem anyway?" Dave asked, mummifying his hand in the paper; he was good at clogging toilets.

Sam ignored him and stared at his shampoo bottle. "I told you already: he's an attention whore."

"The landlord says he was a lonely old fart," Jess pitched in. "An old card shark. No friends, no family, just a goldfish: Gold Bond, or something like that. Dude, tell Dave about the goldfish."

Sam sighed and looked down at his hands. "Fine," he said. He sighed again, feeling that heaviness in his chest like the last time he'd told the story, or like those nights he sat on the love seat alone, watching *Ninja Turtles* or something. "Casper—I can't remember his real name, but . . . he liked to pour Coors or Smirnoff or whatever he was drinking into Gold Bond's fishbowl. Liked to shoot the shit with the fish, talk about the weather and the Seahawks—"

"Liked to argue with him about who'd do the dishes," Jess said.

Sam nodded. "Guess the landlord saw dirty forks and spoons in the fishbowl a couple times. And he found cards in there, too, an unfinished game of go fish.

"Anyway, one night Casper poured too much Everclear into the water and found Gold Bond belly-up—"

"The landlord heard all this from the police," Jess explained. "They kind of filled in what they didn't know."

"That's right. So Casper gets all smash-faced and decides to give Goldie a good old funeral flush. But before he can send him out to sea, he gets real sick, starts throwing up. He passes out, falls into the toilet, and—"

"Wakes up with a ghastly hangover," Jess said, grinning. "And the sad part is Gold Bond wasn't dead. Just blacked out."

"Really?" Dave asked, breaking off the toilet paper.

"Yeah," Jess continued, "the cops found him feeding on Casper's puke."

Sam nodded. "End of stupid, pointless, and totally depressing story."

Dave frowned at the floor, toilet paper still wrapped around his hand. "Damn," he said. "It's kind of like . . . *Romeo and Juliet.* So what happened to Gold Bond?"

Sam shrugged and picked at some soap scum on the shower stall, suddenly taking an interest in cleaning after months of ignoring the buildup.

"We don't know what happened to him," Jess said. "But we made a killer bong out of his fishbowl."

"And who really gives a shit?" Sam interjected.

"Well," Dave said, lifting one buttock to wipe, "Casper obviously gives a shit. Have you ever tried being nice to him? Maybe he just needs a friend."

Sam chuffed. "What he needs is a quick trip into Egon's containment unit. You know what? Just drop it. I don't want to talk about it anymore."

"Well," Dave looked at the strip of toilet paper he'd just used, "if this were my house and there really was a ghost, I'd give him a big old hug and—" He shot up off his seat, flipped, and landed headfirst in the toilet. The water bubbled and churned, muffling his scream. His bare ass poked up in the air.

"Crap!" Sam said. He stepped out of the tub, reaching for Dave's legs. Dave kicked aimlessly; his sneaker cracked the bridge of Sam's nose.

Sam stumbled, tears flooding his eyes, hot blood gushing down his chin and soaking his shirt. He cursed, slapped a hand to his face, tasted something coppery.

Holding his glasses on with one hand, Jess went to help Dave, as well. Dave accidentally kicked him in the throat. Jess fell against the wall, clutching his neck and wheezing. Sam's robe, hanging from a hook on the door, strangled Jess with its sash.

Sam's vision was blurry from the tears and the shock, but he couldn't let that stop him. He spit blood off his lips, reached for Dave.

The lid of the toilet tank flew at his head. He ducked and it shattered against the shower stall. The shower curtain wrapped around him like a flour tortilla. He wrestled one arm free.

Dave's legs thrashed less and less; the bubbles began to peter out. Jess was about to pass out, too.

Sam lurched forward—the shower curtain yanked him back. So he lunged, put all his weight into it, his free arm outstretched, and the shower curtain tore away from its hooks. He flew past Dave, his hand slammed the toilet handle, and then he fell between the toilet and the vanity, the plastic trash can jabbing his ribs.

The toilet flushed; Dave gasped and fell back, sitting his bare ass in the tub. The shower curtain loosened around Sam and the robe quit strangling Jess. The only sound was heavy breathing and water rushing into the toilet tank.

Sam lifted himself and shucked the shower curtain. Jess, his eyes a little watery, was picking himself up and rubbing his neck, hacking dryly. Sam went to Dave and bent over him.

"You okay?"

Dave glared; his hair dripped toilet water and brown smears sullied his cheeks—one of the smears resembled a penny, complete with Honest Abe. "Fuck you," Dave said. He pushed Sam out of the way and climbed out of the tub. He yanked up his pants.

"Dave," Sam said, "I'm sorry. He *never* comes into the bathroom, he—"

"I'm leaving," Dave interrupted. "I've had enough of your spook house." He shoved Jess aside and reached for the door.

"Dave, no!"

But he had already opened it.

Somewhere in the hall, the fishbowl rattled its egg-beaters. And suddenly knives darted into the room. Dave ducked and Sam dove into the tub, but Jess didn't react in time—he was too busy adjusting his glasses.

One of the blades stabbed into his arm. Two more sank into his belly. And the last one—the last one sliced open his neck and severed an artery. The blood, bright and red, sprayed the vanity mirror. Jess fell against the back wall.

Dave ran screaming and Casper didn't stop him. Sam heard his DVD dresser crash to the carpet, heard Dave run out the front door, screeching into the night.

Sam got out of the tub, his hands and knees shaking so badly he could barely stand. "Bro," he said, kneeling next to Jess. "Shit—hang in there, bro. I'm going to—shit, fuck—I'll get you an ambulance."

Jess stared at him, his eyes glazing, his body squirming less and less. He took Sam's hand, greasing it with blood, and pulled him closer. He opened his mouth as if to say something.

"What is it?" Sam said. "What?"

Jess started to speak but cleared his throat, choked up blood, swallowed, licked his lips, pulled Sam closer and closer and closer still, until Sam could smell iron in the blood, and with the whispery wisdom of those legendary last words, Jess said, "Twat." He exhaled and his head fell to one side.

"Jess," Sam said. "Jess!" He wanted to shake him, shout at him, rouse some life in him, but the eggbeater chortled and something pressed against Sam's throat: a steak knife.

He tensed and began to shudder and weep. "Please," he said, "I'll do whatever you want. Just—let me have one call. Just one. My friend"—*my only friend*—"he needs help."

There was a pause. Then in the scum and dust on the bathroom mirror, two words formed: "Beast frend."

"Yes." Sam nodded. "Best friend. *Please.*"

The knife pressed into his neck, forcing him to stand. It led him to the love seat, back in its original position. *Street Fighter* idled on the character select screen, cursors highlighting Ken and Ryu. And in Jess's ass-kicking zone, with both controllers floating in front of it, Gold Bond's fishbowl waited; a fish's skeleton, swabbed in cobwebs, floated in kegerator beer.

"Holy shit," Sam said. "You're . . . you're not Casper. You never were."

The bowl stared at him. It gestured for him to sit down.

"I need to call— I . . . my friend needs help."

The bowl just stared at him. The knife pressed into his throat and forced him to sit. He smashed himself against the arm of the love seat, trying to get as far away from the fishbowl as possible, but he still felt a chill, like a cold leg brushing against his—or like when something swims past you as you're wading up to your neck.

Working both controllers, the ghost began the match, Ken versus Ryu, the classic fight. The second-player controller floated over to Sam. He frowned at it, glanced at the phone sitting on the milk crate.

The eggbeaters growled and the house thrummed; the timer on the match counted down.

"Fucking carpet stretcher," Sam said. He took the controller and prayed Dave would bring back the cops, or the Ghostbusters, or John Edward, or that short lady from *Poltergeist*—*anyone* who could deal with a ghost.

The spirit held out its controller the way Jess used to do. Sam glowered. He tapped his against it, toasting. "I'm going to eat you for dinner," he said. And then, with a knife against his throat, tears on his cheeks, and blood on his shirt, he began to play with the goldfish.

I Know Who You Ate Last Summer

NANCY HOLDER

"That should be 'who*m*,'" Carla M. said, "and that's part of the problem. It's too convoluted and it puts the emotional throughline on the victim. And frankly, who gives a shit about her?"

"Whom. 'I Know Who*m* You Killed Last Summer'," Angelo read off the screen of Carla M.'s state-of-the-art flat-screen monitor in her cool North Hollywood bungalow; bitch thought she was all that. Which she was.

"Wow, you're right. It sucks," Angelo said happily.

"It's all about the Big Picture," Carla M. rambled on. "How all your artistic choices flesh it out."

Flesh.

"It's so obvious," Angelo cooed.

On the couch, away from the action, Dwight rolled his eyes. All Angelo had talked about on the drive from their Spanish Revival mansion in the Hollywood Hills was how great his title was. How much he loved it. Now he was betraying it because Carla M. had dropped it back into the Bottomless Well of Artistic Choices.

"Big picture. You're a genius. You're better than Robert McKee." Angelo gazed at her like she had invented the space-time continuum and tossed back his black shoulder-length curls.

Dwight stared at Angelo's hair and ground his teeth. Last night, Dwight got told by Tawni, the hairdresser who came to their mansion to style them and give them blow jobs, that shoulder-length curls were just too eighties rock star. It was almost too late to even go for the bald look, but luckily. . . .

So once Dwight was shaved like a fucking cue ball, in walked Angelo from somewhere he went alone and had *not* told Dwight. And then he proceeded to *laugh* at Dwight's head and get a curly perm like he was going to tape an infomercial for *A Tribute to Dan Fogelberg.*

And when it was all done, Tawni *ooh*ed and *aah*ed and spouted some bullshit about Angelo's sharp profile and rugged chin line; and wondered aloud if maybe she had been hasty about the death of curly and long. And by the way, *Dwight* should lay off the Botox injections and hire a personal trainer to correct his body mass index. She lectured him about colonics, which were *enemas.*

So after she left, Dwight made an ultimatum: his ego, her life.

"We can't eat her. She's the best haircutter in Hollywood," Angelo argued. "Plus, we gotta stay off the radar."

Dwight pouted and stared at his reflection in the mirror. He looked like a young Uncle Fester from *The Addams Family.* He was going to have to buy a wig.

Plus, he was starving. Angelo was so caught up in his movie thing that they hadn't devoured a chick in *forever.*

Sweating in his black leather pants, Dwight crossed his legs, put his dusty boots on Carla M.'s Danish modern "find" (as opposed to a "couch"), and text-messaged with the president of their fan club. God, he was so hostile. It would be nice to go to a therapist, but shrinks were clever bastards: *When did you stop eating your wife?* Rule Number One of the Cannibal Code was No One Knows.

Besides, wives were for wimps. Dwight had never

been married. It was just him and Angelo, not in a gay way, not even vaguely metro. When you were busy and famous, you had relationships with nobodies. And ate them, too.

Except now they were busy at the home of Ms. Somebody, who they had met in AA. Despite nearly losing her liver to booze, she was still a player. So Angelo played her. One minute they were listening to her war stories about Demon Tequila and the next, Angelo was informing her that he and Dwight wanted to be the next Rob Zombie, which was total news to Dwight.

And now they spent every single Saturday night at her trendy NoHo bungalow, working on Angelo's creative genius piece-of-shit serial killer movie while she groped Mr. Curly Top. Which was the most insane, self-destructive thing they could possibly do, because, hello? Cannibals? What about "No One Knows"?

"Also, since the Echo Park Killer is still at large, it looks like you're riffing off the murders. It comes off cheesy," Professor M. continued.

"Carly-car," Angelo moped. "Then we've got nothing." He sighed and glanced over at Dwight with his patented "Maybe you're right, maybe we should just eat her" look.

He shifted around on the find/couch, squishy with

sweat. He wished she had air-conditioning. Summers in LA could be brutal. All the chrome and glass; sometimes the freeways started to melt, no lie.

Rock stars like them couldn't be caught dead in shorts.

"Don't panic. This is the most exciting part of the creative process," Carla M. told the guy who was in the Songwriters Hall of Fame. "The artistic choices. There are so many."

"So little time," Angelo joshed. They put their heads together and chuckled. *What goes hahaha—thud? A cannibal cat laughing his head off.*

"You break it down, you build it up," Carla M. went on. And on.

You knock her out, you chew her up, Dwight thought.

CannibalDwight2CCatsPrezie: SHOUT-OUT 2 JACKIE ON HER BDAY!
CCatsPrezie2CannibalDwight: OMG!!!!!!!!!!!!!!!!!!!!! U remembered!

Then a new text message came in. Not from CCats-Prezie but from someone named Unregistered. What the heck; they had to be cool if they had his number. Dwight read it.

I NO WHO U 8 LAST SUMMER

Dwight nearly fell off the couch. Instead, he gasped as his phone clattered onto Carla M.'s state-of-the-now retro turquoise linoleum floor.

"Dwight?" Angelo asked, swiveling around on Carla M.'s desk chair. "Zup?"

The people with hair were both staring at him. Dwight bent down—his black leather pants needed to be let out a tad—grabbed up his phone, and very carefully did not look at the faceplate again.

"Wow. Sorry, dozed off, it's so fucking unbearably hot in here," he said.

Angelo gave him a look. Dwight wanted to return it. Dwight wanted to tell him to meet him in Carla M.'s bathroom, with her vintage Serenity Prayer plaque on the wall and a pair of Praying Hands from some little town in Tuscany called Nostromo or something like that. He wanted to tell Angelo they were either in big trouble or Angelo was a douche bag for sending him a tasteless practical joke.

However, he and Angelo had not survived decades of living as rock star cannibals without becoming very, very good at covering their tracks. You eat a couple little runaways or an insecure, unreliable backup singer, that's one thing. You accidentally devour the wife of the guy who runs your new label, that's quite another.

Yeah, and you gobble up Alice, the one girl in all the world who your partner loves. . . .

He knew he was panicking. His mind was zooming all over the inside of his skull like a pinball. Feigning a semiapologetic, mostly not-giving-a-shit look, he slipped the phone into his wretchedly tight leather pants and shrugged.

"We should go."

"*Dwight,*" Angelo said tiredly. "Dude, we're working here. Well, at least Carla and I are working."

Dwight's heart thundered. He didn't want to work here. His stomach was a bowlful of acid.

I NO

Dwight hadn't peed in his tight black leather trousers yet, but he was about to vomit all over them.

"Angelo, we have to go now," he blurted, and there went the expert covering of their tracks. He was too scared. He had to get out of there before he had a panic attack. "We really, really do."

"Maybe your blood sugar's low," Angelo said. "Maybe you need something to *eat.*" He waggled his brows. From where she sat, Carla M. couldn't see the smirk on Angelo's face; and for all her highly touted writer's powers of observation, she didn't even know there was a joke, much less that it was at her expense.

"It's not funny," he insisted. "I, uh, have a sudden emergency."

"Okay. Jesus." Angelo rolled his eyes at Carla M. "Musicians."

"Hey, at least you guys never go on strike," she replied, and they both chuckled.

Dwight was doing no chuckling. He didn't wait for Angelo to finish elbowing Carla M.'s boobs while he dug out the keys. He was out the door and down the walkway by the time Angelo caught up to him.

"What the fuck is your problem?" Angelo demanded. "We were closing in on a title!"

Dwight kept walking. Angelo beeped open the Jag and Dwight slid in, black leather on black leather. Angelo stomped around to the driver's side and despite everything, every single motherfucking thing, Dwight enjoyed seeing Angelo being pissed off by *him.*

"Okay, here it is," Dwight said. He reached into his pocket and pulled out his iPhone. He handed it to Angelo, who glanced down at it while he started the car. Baby purred. Angelo stared.

Then he said, "I know who you ate last summer?"

"I think that should be 'whom,'" Dwight said snarkily, which was stupid but he didn't care. He was shaking. "I have to throw up."

Angelo pulled over and Dwight leaned his head

out of the air-conditioning and into the overheated, smoggy night. Because they were rock stars, they had to pull over a lot. Their limo drivers were all trained to take it to the curb ASAP if they got the word.

But there was nothing to throw up. Dwight's dry heaves made him dizzy, but that was about it. Sighing and wiping his forehead, he slumped back into his seat and rolled up the window. The air-conditioning made his nipples hard.

Angelo resumed driving. He wasn't going anywhere near their Spanish Revival mansion up in the Hollywood Hills.

"Someone's watching us. Someone knows," Dwight said.

Angelo took his eyes off the road, not a good idea when you are going ninety-five. Worse when you are going a hundred and seven. They were rock stars. They had to speed.

"Dwight, if this is a misguided cry for attention . . ."

Dwight wanted to choke him. God*damm*it, sometimes he had just had it up to *here* with Angelo's condescension and his cooler-than-thou bullshit. Okay, okay, Angelo had been Angelo Leone back in Upper Mayonnaise, Iowa; and Dwight Jones had been the son of a man who had beat his wife to death, and was going to come after his kid next.

And Angelo was the one with the trust fund, who got him the hell out of there (without graduating from high school) and rented a mansion close to where the Grateful Dead lived; and bought them equipment and lessons and all the clothes.

But *Dwight* was the one who found out that living human flesh tasted better than any other delicacy on the planet. And *Dwight* was the one who had nearly devoured Angelo on not one but three separate occasions, and then relented and let him live. And of course self-absorbed, arrogant, *stupid* Angelo didn't have a clue, not a clue, that he had come so close to death at the hand—*make that teeth*—of Dwight "the Loser" Jones.

"Let's go to Maria Begsley's house and score some blow."

"Maria's in AA now," Dwight reminded him.

They had joined Alcoholics Anonymous as a metaphor, so they could stop eating people—okay, women—but Dwight had never wanted to—join, or stop. Raw human flesh was all he could eat anymore, and all he wanted to eat. Then Angelo had become addicted to making connections through their AA meetings, so they had to keep going.

Maybe that anonymity shit worked back in Sheboygan, but in Hollywood, if you were getting your act together, you wanted everyone to know it. You went to a party, you strutted around saying things like, "No alcohol for me tonight, thank you. I'll just have an Evian and some St. John's Wort. I am in the *program.* I am a *friend of Bill W.*"

"Is this for the movie?" Dwight asked. "Like, you sent me the message to see how I would react?"

Angelo flashed him a look. "Dwight, please, would I do anything so idiotic?"

Yeah, actually, you would, Dwight thought. And he also thought about that brain disease that Hawaiians or whoever got, *kurukuru,* from practicing cannibalism. It came from eating people's brains. There were parasites. It couldn't be Hawaiians. It happened in the 1960s. Okay, maybe it could be Hawaiians. Hawaiian hippies or something. Some Hawaiian hippies ate roadkill.

Kurukuru tossed you into the Well of Bad Judgment. Maybe Angelo had it.

"Did you text me?" Dwight asked. And before Angelo could flash him another "how dareth you question *moi*" look, he said, "Just tell me."

Angelo swerved around a slow-moving vintage Corvette and nearly took out a guy on a motorcycle. Guy looked like a Hells Angel. Flipped Angelo off.

"Who might know?" Angelo asked. "Hey, you didn't, like, tell your sponsor about us, did you?"

"Are you insane?" Dwight snapped. Then a horrible suspicion dawned on him. "*You* didn't tell Bob V., did you?"

Bob V. had been Angelo's AA sponsor. Who Dwight had managed to kill in a fire.

That should be 'whom.'

"Jesus, Dwight, give me some credit," Angelo said, but there was a catch in his voice. A guilty little catch.

He did. Dwight knew it as sure as he knew the words to "The Star-Spangled Banner," which they had sung last Saturday at Angels Stadium.

Angelo had told his sponsor that they were cannibals. Sponsors were these guys who took you through your Twelve Steps and overstepped your boundaries. Tried to become your new best friend.

"Anyway, he's dead," Angelo went on.

The Jag hurtled through an orange light and zoomed past the fountain in Echo Park. The fountain was on, spewing colored water the city really could not afford; but when you lived in Echo Park, you needed a little lift.

The drug dealers hanging around the fountain turned and stared in astonishment as Angelo zoomed back. Big hats, bling, sweatshirts, .357s. They glowered at the Jag, which was stupid because dudes in Jags could be customers. But a serial killer was after their bitches and sistahs, so long faces were probably more appropriate than signs that read BUY YOUR SHIT HERE.

Angelo made a choking sound. Then he threw back his head and started laughing as he cranked the wheel and started circling the fountain.

"Okay, truth time. But you already know I sent you that message as a test," Angelo said. "Because *I* thought *you* told Carla M."

Dwight stared at him. Horror and relief washed through him like wave upon wave of pastel dancing waters. It was a joke! A horrible example of terrible judgment, and so unbelievably mean and cruel, and *God,* he was pissed, and—

"*What?*" he said to Angelo. "Why would I do that?"

"Because you like her. You want to get into her pants."

"Dude, you have *kurukuru,*" Dwight said. Then he hit rewind. "And don't try to push this thing onto me. Jesus, you told Bob V. What the hell were you thinking?"

Angelo looked unrepentant. "I wanted to get better. You don't get better if you're not rigorously honest. He was my sponsor. We did the Fifth Step at Malibu: *Confessed to God, ourselves, and another human being the exact nature of our wrongs.*"

"Get better? At what? Dying by lethal injection?" Dwight shouted.

"Bob V. is dead," Angelo reminded him. "Having

a sponsor is like going to confession. They can't tell anybody jack."

"Priests can go to the police if it will solve a murder case," Dwight bellowed. "We just saw that on *CSI*."

"Stop freaking out. I was raised Catholic," Angelo said with a toss of his brand-new curls. "You're wrong."

The Jag was still circling the fountain. The localz were standing up, watching, fishing in their sweatshirts, probably for unregistered weapons. Angelo gazed thoughtfully at them.

"I want something," he said. "Meth or I don't know what." He giggled. "Blow. It's the other white meat."

And it was then, and only then, that Dwight realized that Angelo was already higher than a kite. He must have toked up or tanked up or shot up sometime during their creative Big Picture evening of Artistic Choices.

That was allowable. Dwight had shot up, too. In fact, he was probably higher than Angelo right now, because of the adrenaline racing through his body. He could feel his mind beginning to carom again, zinga-linging dangerously out of control.

"I was worried you might tell Carla M. to impress her," Angelo said again. "You know you want her. And not just for dinner."

And suddenly Dwight saw the *real* Big Picture:

Telling. *I Know Who Ate You Last Summer.* Forget perms and screenwriters with tasty parts; Angelo was going to start one-upping him with *the truth*. He was going to break Rule Number One with the gusto of the parasitically infected. Already had, in fact.

"You bastard!" he shouted at Angelo. Then who knew what possessed him, but he made a fist and slammed it against Angelo's temple. To his even greater surprise, Angelo's head slammed against the driver's side window, and the car roared straight for the fountain.

"Shit!" Angelo yelled. "What the hell did you do that for?"

I did it because you always humiliate me. I did it because you ate my girlfriend. I did it because if I don't do it to you, you're gonna do it to me.

Dwight saw red. He saw blood. He grabbed the wheel with his left hand and dug in the glove compartment with his right. Got out their .357 Magnum and whammed it against Angelo's head as hard as he possibly could.

Angelo slumped. His foot slid off the gas pedal. Dwight turned the wheel and they orbited the fountain like a ride at Disneyland.

The gangbangers looked on in amazement. Bling gleamed in the moonlight. Teeth, too. It was not every night boyz in the hood watched two guys in a Jag making like Lindsay Lohan.

Finally the car screamed sideways and stopped. The tires were smoking. Angelo was still unconscious.

Dwight got out of the car, stomped around to the driver's side, opened the door, unbuckled Angelo, and dragged him out.

"Hey!" he shouted at the desperado homeboys. "Hey, this dude killed that girl Maria!" He dug into the pocket of his tight leather pants and pulled out her ugly rhinestone LA County Fair necklace. He'd almost forgotten he'd ripped it off her neck after he'd bashed her head in with that very same .357 last Tuesday. And Ana-somebody-nobody, three weeks before that.

"Check it out!" He shook the necklace at them. M-A-R-I-A. Stringy. Addicts so often were. "I found this on him! He killed her!"

Faces black and brown looked at one another. Muttered. Someone purple-black and six-four started walking toward the car.

And bald. He was *bald*!

"Yeah! Bring it on! Payback!" Dwight flung down the necklace; it landed in the big gash in Angelo's head where the blood was pooling. Oh God, were those his brains? Eaten away by *kurukuru*?

Dwight stepped over him, piled into the car, and blasted out of there. Drove like a crazy man. A crazy man with a big secret that he had told no one, not even Angelo. No One Knows.

He called Carla M.

"Hey," she said drowsily. She must be in bed.

Ka-zoing! Dwight got hard.

"Yeah, hi. Angelo said he forgot something at your house. Okay if I come and get it for him?"

"Oh? Sure," she said. "What is it?"

"His emotional throughline," he replied. Then he hung up.

Laugh, cry? Plow the car into that oncoming retaining wall?

So many artistic choices, so little—

time.

Bitches of the Night

Nancy Kilpatrick

"Dis night, you vill take two each, a male and a female. And dis time, no AB negative!"

Istvan hated using the cheesy English-with-a-Transylvania accent. Sure, he'd been born in Transylvania, but his family had moved to what was now called Romania. He'd tried to teach these women his language—Romanian—but they were all too thick to learn. And although each spoke English, and their native tongue, of course, nothing worked as well at controlling them as the Englvanian. And Satan knew, they were hard enough to control. He felt lucky he'd stumbled on even one trick, which seemed to excite them sexually. At least when they were aroused they weren't thinking about wrestling power from his hands. They were perverse in the extreme, and he had to stay on top of his game or he was doomed; no wonder he felt perpetually exhausted! When was the last time he'd had a good day's rest?

"Am I understood?" he bellowed, Bela Lugosi–style, accompanied by Lugosi hand gestures.

The three females cowered, or two of them anyway. For the last century or so, he hadn't deluded himself that it was in real terror, but at least they played the game.

Sephora, the Spanish one, so voluptuous and juicy, the one who refused to cower, cocked her pretty head, dark eyes flashing, and positioned her fists on her ample hips. "Master, let me take two females. *She* can take two men." She jerked her head toward the willowy Céline, the French one, who arched a pencil-thin eyebrow and pouted her full lips until the tip of one snowy fang glistened against the crimson of that sensuous mouth.

"You think I want to take the men?" Céline snapped. "*Tabernace!*" she shouted, a Québécois curse word that had something to do with a church. "They are puny in this city. Their balls shriveled and their cocks hungry like a moose's snot."

They all stared at Céline blankly. Istvan wished she'd stop using those indecipherable and obscure French expressions. Her language skills were pathetic.

Morgana, of Celtic origins, or so she claimed, always

the impatient one, tossed back her long fiery hair and hissed at Céline. Céline clawed the air in Morgana's direction. Sephora cackled, a sound like fingernails on a blackboard.

Istvan's shoulders tensed. He felt a headache forming at his frontal lobes. They were driving him nuts! "Enough, bitches! I haf no time for your constant bickerings! I am busy man!"

"But Master," Sephora purred, moving close, and he became wary.

She smiled up at him and batted her eyes flirtatiously.

This was better. He snaked an arm around her waist. "Yes, my luf?" He cupped her chin.

"Master," she breathed seductively into his ear, "you are no longer a *man*."

And then the bitch cackled in his ear, so loud that headache pain flashed through his brain like lightning. The other two joined in. He shoved the Spanish bitch away, but that only made her laugh more.

"Poor Master," Morgana said, trying to run her hand up the hairs of his chest where his shirt was open to the navel and the gold chains dangled. He hated it when she did that, making him nearly lose it every time, and he knocked her claw away. "Are there not still kisses for all?" she went on sarcastically. "You said so yourself."

Great, he thought, now she's quoting from *Dracula*! Soon she'd be acting out a vampire-bride role from one of those stupid *Nosferatu* movies she runs continuously on the DVD player. She actually spent a thousand of his hard-earned dollars on a white wedding dress with a frilly lizard-neck ruff that imitated what Lucy wore in Coppola's *Bram Stoker's Dracula*. Would it never end?

How in hell did he ever get hooked up with these three? Each had seemed like a good idea at the time. He remembered fondly "acquiring" them one by one, turning them from the light toward the darkness, from day to night. He had loved each, in his way, according to who they were as individuals, their special beauty and unique talents. He'd spent much time and energy and had given considerable blood to change them. But all too soon they succumbed to what appeared to be the fate of the females of his kind—intense viciousness fueled by vindictiveness. And, unfortunately, familiarity did breed contempt and he was their main victim, or would be, if he let that happen.

He could see now he'd made a mistake, making three. One he could control. Two he could manage. Three . . . they had ganged up and nearly overpowered him!

"We want to go to the Vampire Lounge," Céline whined, her black eyes flashing, her newly bleached ponytail that hung to her waist swaying seductively.

Sephora's brown eyes twinkled, and the fun lover tossed her long black hair back over her bare shoulders.

Morgana's blue eyes narrowed into cool agates. She folded her arms across her pert bosom. "Chicken again? We just had that last night!"

"Sweet eighteen and all fake fangs," Sephora said.

"Well, at least they are tasty!" Céline snarled. "And they can still get it up!"

Did she just glance at him? The impertinence! She turned her head toward him full-face and smiled sweetly. Maybe he'd imagined it. But it was one of the huge drawbacks of their vampiric state. The females could still enjoy copulation, but Istvan could no longer function up to speed.

"They're salty, too," Sephora added. "They sweat when they drink so much beer." She licked her thick lips, flicking just the tip of her tongue around an incisor—he loved that tongue in his ear! It aroused him, or would have, if he still had an appendage that could be aroused.

"They swing like a monkey's finger from cheesecloth over a warm lake," Céline said dreamily.

Istvan blinked in incomprehension just before pain blasted his head anew. He turned toward the window, wishing he could either catch his reflection in the glass or turn into a bat and fly away. A rest or a change. He'd give his eyeteeth—well, one anyway—for either.

But all he saw was the empty parlor. No reflection of him. He had no fear that he wasn't there, though—he could hear the three airheads chattering incessantly like crows at dawn.

He glanced around the room as he saw it reflected. The Spanish wrought-iron screen, the French chaise longue, the antique Irish bellows and other fireplace implements . . . something for everyone. Anything to keep them happy and the bitching to a minimum! Maintaining such a large house and an extravagant style that would appease proved costly, not to mention the yearly moves to a new city—he'd been wise to invest money in various airlines for nearly a century. But they were insatiable when it came to makeup, hair treatments, manicures and pedicures and facials and massages, jewelry and fancy outfits, expensive restaurants where they ate no food, and theaters where they could be seen—it's a wonder they hadn't bankrupted him! Céline was tall and slim with feline grace, Sephora short, full-figured and emotive, Morgana in the middle with tight curves and high pert breasts, plus a quick wry wit. Their tastes, they'd informed him often enough, were distinctive—although they all usually dressed like Elvira clones—and they had assured him it was impossible to wear the same clothing more than once. Naturally it took them until midnight to dress—every closet and drawer was stuffed with black fabric and evening after evening he watched them toss piles of designer clothing onto the middle of the floor, searching for a particular piece. They didn't bother picking anything up, which forced him to do it because he had been cursed by being born to his mortal life a double Virgo and then being turned when the moon was in Virgo, and he needed order. And demon knew, a century and a half of nagging had not altered their messy habits. If anything, they were worse than ever. He couldn't find a surface unmarked by makeup the color of fresh blood or dead roaches!

They were still bickering, now about who would get to go first tonight. Morgana was asserting her rights, as the first turned.

Sephora said, "Well, you *are* the oldest."

"What's that supposed to mean?" Morgana snapped, eyes narrowing.

"You are the old bat!" Céline snarled out a laugh.

"At least I have style!" Morgana shouted. "You two are worse than hags."

"Oh, *we're* hags!" Sephora responded snidely. "At least I don't try to wear microminis up around my fangs!"

Céline was applying black kohl to her eyelids. "That is because, *chérie,* they do not sew them in your size!"

"And they don't make men in *your* size!" Sephora snapped. "Except what's on ten-year-old boys!"

Céline hissed. Sephora threw a black pillow at her, that the svelte Céline ducked. Morgana draped yet a seventh Celtic crucifix backed by a copper plate around her swanlike neck and poked a fourth copper-backed cross earring through the lobe of her left ear. Somehow she had learned this—"Druid," as she called it—trick of wearing crosses without harming herself, although everyone else in the room had to endure the violent light they emitted. Istvan turned away from her to protect himself.

Wearily, he wondered how many more centuries it would take before they drove him completely insane. The true death was looking better and better. Was there a way to get rid of them and recover the peace and quiet he longed for?

"I am hungry!" he shouted. A rerun of *The X Files* would be on in ten minutes and he wanted to get the pint he'd socked away, plop in front of the tube and relax until close to dawn, when they would come scuttling in, shrieking, drunk on too much vitae and more obnoxious than ever.

"Be gone!" he shouted, raising his arm dramatically and pointing to the door. Getting them moving always took so much energy.

The three backed out of the room submissively like vapors receding in a cheap horror flick. They loved theatrics. The door slammed and he heard them laugh derisively on the other side, but at least they had vanished from his sight. He watched out the window until he saw them depart the house giggling, arguing, touching one another like the whores they were, leaving the garden gate open, of course. Then they disappeared around the corner.

He took a deep breath and felt peace wash over him. Tonight, for the millionth time, he contemplated just leaving. But they would find him. Like iron filing to a magnet, the vampirized always found the creator. He would have found his if she hadn't met the ultimate fate. Another breath turned into a sigh of resignation.

It was hard now to remember his plan, and he'd had a plan. Once. Something to do with making existence easier, more fulfilling. Take three women, a blonde, a brunette and a redhead—he really should buy shares in Clairol!—turn them into submissive vampiresses, have them go out and hunt and then, when they came home, he could extract all he needed from each. A bit of fondling whenever he was in the mood. . . . Wasn't that every male vampire's dream? But the dream had quickly disintegrated into a nightmare. He hadn't anticipated that problems would develop because he could no longer perform sexually while they still possessed functioning equipment. And he had not bargained on them forming a unit and turning against him. If he were not an honorable man, or a reasonable facsimile of a man, he would have abandoned them long ago and taken his chances, fleeing as they pursued until they, hopefully, gave up the search. But he had made promises—of which they were only too eager to remind him—and he intended to live up to his commitments, even if it killed him, which it just might. *I will love you until the true death and beyond!* What a fool he had been to say that to each of them!

He opened his coffin and felt under the satin along the false bottom until he found the little indentation. He then pressed the button and a panel slid open. He reached inside the tiny refrigerated box for the Hellmann's jar of O positive. His fingertips slid along the cold metal. It must be here somewhere; the hidden compartment wasn't that large. But after feeling around for a few seconds, then tearing away the satin so his nocturnal vision could confirm what his hand already knew, he faced the grim reality—the blood was gone. It, as well as the double metal box that contained half a dozen consecrated wafers he kept for emergencies—he never knew when he'd have to stop one of his "brides" cold.

Damn those bitches! They had stolen his blood! And his wafers! Rage boiled in his empty veins. He trembled and regaining control of himself proved to be a struggle. He knew it was Sephora—she was always sneaking around, prying into his things, meddling. . . .

Well, when she got home there would be hell to pay! She would be severely punished! Black thoughts streaked through his mind in images of what he would do to the perpetrator. The tortures he would inflict. She had gone too far this time. No, he would not tolerate this!

He punched the TV's on button and sat down. There was still *The X Files*—the *TV Guide* said it was a repeat of the vampire episode, one of his favorites because in the end, the female gets her just desserts.

It was five seconds after the hour and he expected to hear the familiar whistling, see the opening credits . . . but the President of the United States was on television, giving a speech about war and budgets! He grabbed up the *TV Guide* and stared hard at the listing—nothing about being preempted. And then he glanced at the date. This was *last* week's *TV Guide*! Morgana must have taken the new one to look for vampire movies and forgotten to toss the old one again! Deflated, he picked up the remote. Surely with so many channels on cable he could find something that would amuse him. But the buttons on the remote wouldn't work. Not the channels, not the volume. . . . He shook the thing. He tapped it against the edge of the coffee table. Nothing. His arm dropped in despair and the remote slipped from his grasp, hitting the floor. The door of the battery compartment fell off and a small but crucial-looking plastic piece jumped up in the air at an angle, like an insect, and bounced beneath his chair. There were no batteries inside the compartment! He had a flash of Céline announcing that the batteries to the little digital camera she always carries with her were dead and she didn't feel like going to the store.

"Great!" he said to the air, throwing up his hands. He got up and switched off the TV, too defeated to manually change channels. This was turning into a very bad night. And he knew who was to blame—those three bitches!

Well, they wouldn't get away with it! He'd hunt them down, drag them back here by their dyed roots and give them what-for!

He strode to the closet for his cape. It was gone! Damn! He'd *told* Morgana to pick it up from the dry cleaner! Would they never listen to him?

Capeless, he raced out of the house and headed to the Vampire Lounge. They would *not* get away with ruining another night of his cursed eternity!

He hurried past the chic restaurants and cafés. Most of the women and some of the men noticed him, of course. Even after half a millennium, and capeless, he still cut a dashing figure. While he waited for a light to change, a little goth chick with ebony and mahogany hair, all in black, wearing a leather corset over her tiny latex dress, and sexy stiletto boots that wrapped around her spider-webbed thighs, stood next to him at the curb. He gave her "the eye," that hypnotic stare he'd been famous for even when he'd been a mortal centuries ago. She looked at him and giggled. "Cool hair!" she said, and stepped briskly across the street.

He followed her farther south, past the Humor Museum—an oxymoron if he'd ever seen one. She turned into the doorway of the Vampire Lounge. He adjusted the pointed collar on his shirt—maybe the evening wouldn't be such a write-off after all!

The cretin at the doorway stopped him with the words, "Five bucks, man."

Istvan felt in his pocket. Damn! He'd left his wallet at home. Normally, he kept some spare cash in the hidden pocket of his cape. "Uh, I seem to be without funds."

"Yeah?" the tattooed goon said. "Well, bro, I guess that's where you'll stay—without!" And he turned his back.

Istvan could see through the large plate-glass window that the joint was jumping. The little gothette stood in the middle of the room, garnering appreciative glances here and there. Suddenly, she turned, saw him at the window looking in like a starving puppy and motioned for him to join her. It was all too inviting.

Istvan touched the bouncer on the shoulder. "You *vill* admit me!" he said.

Just then, a minivan pulled to the curb. A dozen black-clad kindergoths bussed in from the 'burbs began to disembark, wearing more chain mail and noir leather than Istvan had seen worn throughout the entire Middle Ages. While the muscle began collecting hard cash and stamping bats around the ripped-lace, fingerless gloves that covered hands, Istvan surreptitiously made his way inside.

Music that on the street had been loud bass became ear-splitting on the other side of the door. His acute hearing magnified each note ten times, and the pounding reminded him of a human heart beating beyond its capacity. In the pocket of his cape he kept a pair of earplugs for just such occasions as this, but without that cape. . . . He really couldn't bear this, and turned to leave.

"Hey! What's your hurry?"

The warm gloved hand on his cold arm belonged to the goth chick, who was now standing close and smiling up at him. It had been so long since Istvan had experienced a welcoming and guileless smile from a female that he felt disconcerted.

"Come on," she said to him, and grabbed onto his arm, pulling him through the crowds and to the bar at the back of the room. En route he spotted the three bitches, each chatting up a morsel for later. They were all too busy with the business at hand to notice him, although he had no doubt they would be aware of his presence soon, just as he had been aware of theirs.

As they reached the back bar, the music dimmed a bit. Not enough for conversation, but at least the stabbing at his eardrums ceased.

The bar presented another problem. He had no cash, and mesmerizing the quick-moving bartender wouldn't be easy with so many thirsty pseudovampires crowding the brass rail. But as it turned out the girl said, "What are you having, Mr. Nosferatu? My treat."

"Vine," he said, using the accent. "I only drink vine."

"Yeah, me, too," she said, seemingly not noticing either the accent or the reference. "Red, right?"

He nodded and she leaned over the bar, signaled the bartender and ordered, slapping a bill onto the metallic bar surface.

The wine came quickly and she handed him his glass. Protruding through the glove tips were nails filed to a point and painted black as a Transylvanian night. Well, he was used to that. All three of his women preferred noir nails, for some reason, although from time to time they used crimson polish, "Just to lighten my mood," Sephora had said.

The girl took a sip of wine and looked up at him. "Where you from?"

"Transylvania." It never failed to impress—except this time.

"Yeah, cool," she said, as if he'd said Buffalo.

"I was born in the Carpathian Mountains," he went on, knowing he was trying to claim her interest, wishing he would just let it go, but unable to. "That's where Dracula is from."

"I know," she told him, scanning the room as if searching for someone.

Okay, he thought, that's my best line. Where do I go from here? But before he could think of another bit of bio that would snag her, she turned to him quickly and said, "See that girl over there? The tall one with the long ponytail?"

She pointed in the direction of Céline.

"Yes," he said cautiously, and at that moment Céline turned in their direction. She began waving furiously and he scowled, lifting and moving a hand discreetly as if to brush her away. But she was not waving at him; she was aiming the effusive greeting at the girl, who enthusiastically waved back.

Great, he thought, they know each other, and a gloomy mood descended as Céline made her way toward them. He figured he'd sunk as low as he could go, the night now being thoroughly lost, when suddenly Morgana and Sephora showed up and he was surrounded on four sides. It can't get much worse than this, he thought, forcing a fanged smile, inhaling the scent of the cheap wine—something from Bavaria, no doubt—and wrinkling his nose in distaste.

"Master," Sephora said in her singsong voice, "we have a birthday surprise for you."

"And here she is!" Morgana gestured at the gothette.

Céline laughed, which always got his radar going, but then she moved to the girl and gently but firmly pushed her toward Istvan. "Her name is Doru. She is Romanian and means 'longing.' "

"I know that," he said. It had been his mother's name. And the name of the one who'd turned him.

He stared at the girl, who seemed to feel anything but longing. Clearly she was not affected by all the attention coming her way. She glanced around the room, waved at a couple of friends, did a few dance movements that mimicked a mime pushing the air away from her body in slow motion. Maybe she's a hooker, he thought, rented for the night.

As if to confirm that, Morgana said, "She's yours until sunrise."

"Happy birthday, Master," Sephora said, and kissed him on the cheek.

"*Bonne fête!*" Céline added.

"Is it my birthday?" Istvan said, confused, racking his brain to try to remember the date of his birth, which he had a vague recollection of having been in the fall, not the spring. Perhaps it was the birth into this undead life, but he remembered it was cold outside and must have been winter. He just could not remember dates. These three were always chiding him for not acknowledging their birthdays—both living and undead—so why should they expect him to remember his own?

Morgana just stood there, arms folded across her ample chest and the hideous crucifixes that didn't affect *her* but bothered *his* eyes glaring like minisuns. She nodded at the girl, swinging her head slightly in Istvan's direction as if he were a piece of fruit in the market and Morgana was instructing her to "take that one."

Doru, with a small sigh, acted on cue. She placed her glass of undrunk wine onto the bar, took Istvan's arm and silently led him to the door of the club.

He heard laughter behind him and snapped his head around, but the three were still at the bar, smiling, waving, Sephora blowing him a kiss.

All right, he thought as he and Doru, still holding his arm, moved through the crowded streets, their feet in step though he was a good four heads taller. Maybe for once the three had gotten something right and had thought of *him* for a change! He glanced down at the girl and she looked up, her eyes twinkling like dark stars, her full black-painted lips a bit hungry-looking but nothing he couldn't deal with. She really is a cute little thing, he thought. What a shame to drain her blood.

As they strolled his thoughts moved along a familiar path and he fantasized about turning her. Maybe this was the one who would obey him. One that would love him unconditionally, and let him be. Give him peace. Meet his expectations. Maybe Doru, whose blood was from the same country as his own, would be the perfect mate. Maybe he could ditch the three bitches!

When he caught his fantasy grinding toward the ultimate perfect conclusion, Istvan reminded himself harshly that he not only had been down this road before but had suffered failure three times. He had thought the exact same thing each time he'd turned one of his "wives," and look at the results! There was no point thinking this way. Whatever good qualities this girl possessed now would alter after the change. And in truth, the change required an exchange of blood and he certainly wasn't in the mood to give up anything when he had almost nothing in his system tonight, thanks to the Furies!

Better to just drain this girl's blood and be done with it. Never look a gift horse in the mouth, his mother had always said, although they had never owned a horse, either through purchase or gift, so he did not know where she got that saying.

They arrived back at the house and the girl took

in the English garden, which Morgana, in her few moments of being industrious, tended. The house needed painting and the porch was awash in spiderwebs but otherwise the structure stood tall in its Victorian splendor. The moment he closed the heavy walnut door he was keenly aware of the incredible mess that the three had left behind. "It's not usually like this," he began, but Doru put a finger to his lips to silence him, meanwhile drawing him toward the red velvet settee.

All right! Istvan thought. These modern women are like that. He would let her lead. It would end the same way regardless and he didn't mind being passive. To a point. His eyeteeth ached in anticipation of piercing flesh, and he licked his dry lips, wanting to wet them on something thick and rich in minerals. He would enjoy a little erotic attention, even if it wouldn't, couldn't lead to what she expected. But it would lead to what he expected. What he deserved.

Once they were seated, Doru began unbuttoning his shirt, already open to midchest. She leaned over and pushed the chains aside to kiss his chest, which once had been darkly hairy and masculine but since he'd altered had become pallid like the rest of his reanimated flesh. Not very appealing, but she didn't seem to notice.

Istvan leaned back and closed his eyes, feeling her

hands and lips all over him. Yes, she was a delight. Cute. Small. Attractive. He had not fed yet and his blood receptors were fully open, providing acute sensations. He fantasized about how he would take her blood slowly. No, quickly. Maybe a combination of both. He wondered about her family name and was just about to ask when he felt a sharp prick at his throat. Instantly he knew she had bitten him. He felt blood leaving his vein like water dripping from a tap.

Istvan instinctively shoved her hard away from him. She flew across the room and crashed against the wall. Infuriated, she snapped her head up and snarled at him like a wolf; her eyes almost glowed, and her lips were smeared with red that sparkled like jewels. He put a hand to his throat and felt . . . his own blood! "What in hell do you think you're doing?"

Laughter from the doorway forced his head to turn in that direction.

"Just a joke, Master," Sephora said.

"We wanted to surprise you," Morgana said. "She's from your land."

"She is like us, no? She will *be* like us," Céline corrected herself. "She is not like us but we will all be like her—"

"No!" Istvan shouted, losing control. "I won't change her."

"Oh, you don't have to bother," Morgana said,

striding into the room and helping Doru to her feet. "We've already taken care of that."

"Are you insane!" he shouted. "You made another? You have no right! *I* make vampires, not *you*!"

"Made," Morgana said. "We've taken over the job."

"If she is like us now, will she be like us later?" Céline mused in her language confusion.

"She is like us *now*," Sephora said. Then to Istvan, "We wanted a sister."

"And you should be happy," Morgana added. "She's of your blood."

"My blood?"

"Well, from your line."

"She's *related* to me?"

Doru, who had been listening silently as the others talked about her, suddenly rose to her feet. "I'm your cousin ten or twelve times removed. I lost count. Hi, cuz!" The girl waved at him, licking her lips.

Istvan put a hand to his head as if to hold his brain in. His eyes fell on the mirror and he saw an empty room. It was true. They had already turned her. Likely she belonged to all three of them, which meant she would obey *them*, not Istvan. Now there were four! Against him! How would he survive?

The four bitches surrounded him. Sephora threw an arm around his shoulders, Morgana placed a palm on his thigh and Céline took his hands in hers. Doru knelt at his feet and looked up at him with dark flashing eyes, eyes that somehow resembled his own. "It won't be so bad," Doru said.

"Not at all," Morgana confirmed. "We can have parties—"

"And have fun and go to clubs—" Sephora added.

"And buy chic dresses and makeup—" Céline contributed.

"And go to fancy restaurants and shows—" Sephora said.

"And meet guys—" Morgana said.

"And girls, too—" Céline added.

"And—"

Istvan tuned them out. He thought for a moment of all the money it would take to add another horse to his stable, one whose mouth he should have looked into, despite Mamă's warnings to not do that. If he had, he would have seen that Doru's fangs were not plastic implants but the real deal.

But his thoughts also flitted to cold winter nights when the winds blustered outside the house. When he would be home alone with the four of them, and what that would mean to his sanity. For fleeting moments, he imagined running, hiding, getting as far away as fast as he could. Putting distance between him and the four bitches. Would he never be free? When had eternity turned into hell on earth?

As if reading his thoughts, the young Doru ran a hand up his chest and tilted his face until he was looking into those eyes, bottomless murky pools. She moved close and the others with her. He felt himself tense, as if caught in a huge spiderweb.

"No! Absolutely not!" But before he could do or say more, they each had their sharp incisors in a vein or an artery and Istvan was being drained dry. He was already weak from not feeding, and the little resistance he could muster proved futile. They drank every last drop, leaving a starving, needy shell. It was all he could do to keep his eyes open. But open they were, enough that he could see the sky lightening through a crack in the curtains. A crack that widened when Morgana threw open the drapes.

"Time for bed, my sisters," she, the eldest, said, and the other three giggled and followed her from the room like baby ducklings, leaving Istvan crumpled on the settee. As the brilliant sun scaled the horizon and its rays shot through the window like fiery arrows moving steadily toward him, he heard more laughter in the distance. And words like "boring" and "demanding" and "cramping our style" and when he heard "box of wafers," he knew that they were talking about him.

Oh, how could it have come to this! He had given them eternal life and they gave him nothing but vindictiveness! Some women would *pay* to have the blood drained out of them, but these bitches just wanted revenge!

And now death by sunlight and starvation. Oh, cruel fate! He deserved much better. But some part of his brain consoled him with the fact that soon it would all be over. His misery. The torment of those . . . those . . . creatures! The true death would free him at last!

Sounds dimmed. Light blazed through the window. His thoughts turned inward, remembering home and his mother and how at last he would be reunited with his family. Or burn eternally in hell. He wasn't sure which, and he wasn't sure which fate was worse because he had never gotten along with his domineering mother. Oh, he could see it now, how he had been set up from childhood so that he was drawn to controlling women. Well, the true death, regardless of where it led him, had to be better than what he'd been enduring. Good-bye, cruel world! Good riddance, evil brides!

But Fate, heartless as she can be, presented herself to him in the physical form of Doru, who appeared before his eyes as if materializing out of a mist. The lovely Doru at that moment seemed as pure and innocent as an angel.

Now she wore a seductive, diaphanous gown the

color of new vitae. She held out a wrist, which she or someone else had bitten into until blood—likely blood she'd taken from him—flowed along her arm. He stared, mesmerized, at the seeping liquid as it slowly wove its way along her skin, hating the waste of it.

"Here, Master. Drink," she said. "Make me your bride."

Suddenly, the arm moved closer until the blood nearly touched his lips. "No!" he cried weakly. "Let me die! I'm just about free! I want to be incinerated, to fade with hunger from this wretched world." But she did not listen. He tried to resist, but the smell of the red stuff drove his depleted, immobile body insane with blood lust.

Instantly, instinctively, thoroughly against his will, he gathered the last fragments of his energy and lunged. He slurped up the coppery elixir like a hungry baby sucking milk. Istvan had the wrist to his lips and the blood down his throat faster than a bat flying out of a dark cave at night. Energy flowed back into him with every gulp, filling his cells as if they were expanding balloons. He knew he was cementing the relationship between them, but, like an addict, he could not kick this habit and only stopped when she yanked her arm away.

He had drunk enough to be somewhat mobile again and wanted nothing more than to throttle her.

But Doru had more blood in her veins than he did, and moved faster than he could, and in truth his first movements were to get out of the path of the encroaching light.

"Now we are truly family," she said dramatically. "One big, happy family!" And then she made a theatrical exit.

The realization struck Istvan that this one, this Doru, was more diabolical than the other three combined. Now his existence would go on and on and the four of them would torture him into infinity, to the limits of his endurance, if not beyond!

Weighted down with that grim thought, Istvan staggered to his coffin and pulled the heavy lid closed, immediately soothed by the balm of total darkness. He tried to cheer himself. Tomorrow, he thought, is another night. He could always get up early, buy batteries and there was bound to be a rerun that he'd enjoy, maybe *Six Feet Under.* If only he could get the four bitches out the door before midnight. . . . Maybe he could score another pint at the blood bank without it being missed. He'd need a new hiding place, of course, for the blood and, if not more wafers, perhaps a stash of garlic as a safeguard, squirreled away someplace they would never find it. It was doable. Nothing could defeat the all-powerful vampire Prince of Darkness. Well, almost nothing . . .

The Bell . . . FROM HELL!!!

JEFF STRAND

I own a bell forged by Satan himself. With it, I can summon the Prince of Darkness to our plane of existence. I often think about doing it, but I fear my own power.

Some question the authenticity of the bell. "No way did Satan make that," they say. "If Satan made a bell, it would be, like, some big, scary-looking thing made out of black iron with pentagrams carved into it, and, I dunno, boiling blood dripping down the side and stuff. That's just a stupid little plastic bell. It still has the price tag on it."

Of them I ask, "Why would you assume that Lucifer is proficient in bell-making skills?" William Shakespeare may have been the most brilliant writer in human history, but did he know how to successfully milk a cow? Doubtful. Everybody has their own skill set. I don't see why Satan's bell must be an unholy spectacle to convince people of its origin. It was his first attempt. It's not going to be the Liberty Bell.

The price tag I can't explain. Some phenomena are beyond the understanding of mortal man, and should remain that way.

Sometimes my co-workers snatch the bell from my desk and ring it, just to tease and infuriate me. Wretched souls. "Uh-oh!" they say. "The devil's gonna be here any second! Everybody look busy!" I explain that the bell must be rung six hundred and sixty-six times for the summoning to take place. Fortunately, my co-workers do not have the patience for that much ringing.

No, I did not get the bell from Satan directly. It's ridiculous to think that I would have. I'm not so caught up in feelings of self-worth and ego to think that Satan would feel the need to personally deliver his gift to me, any more than the president of the United States has to hand deliver a certificate of commendation for it to be a thoughtful gesture. One of his minions presented me with the bell three months ago.

This is where my frustration with my co-workers

becomes almost unbearable. Yes, Satan's minion took human form. Because of this fact, my co-workers constantly insist that it was not a demon at all, but rather a homeless man selling junk he'd stolen from the dollar store. Logic eludes them. Why do they think that Satan would be stupid enough to send a scaly, red-skinned, sulphur-scented, prehensile-tail-wearing demon to wander the brightly lit streets? Of *course* the demon would have transformed itself into something passable as human. They simply don't understand this line of reasoning.

Oh, I guess I should point out that I'm not a devil worshiper. I can see where you might get the wrong idea. I'm actually a reasonably devout Christian, which is why it surprised me more than anybody when the minion sold me the bell for such a low price. I would've expected him to choose somebody who practices the dark arts, or listens to evil music, or at least reads *Harry Potter.* But, no, I was chosen.

I don't want to see Hell on earth or a thousand years of darkness or anything like that. If I do end up summoning Satan, it'll be to defeat him.

My co-workers have a great big laugh at that. I'm fully aware of how it sounds, but I wish they'd give me credit for not being a complete idiot. I'm not saying that I'm going to whip out my +3 vorpal sword and lop off Beelzebub's head for eight thousand experience points; I'm just saying that if I *did* use the bell, I could conceivably summon him under circumstances where his evil would be vanquished once and for all.

"Whatcha gonna do, trap him under a net?" asks Rick from Corporate Accounting, playing with the bell. I really shouldn't leave it sitting out on my desk.

"No," I say, trying not to let my impatience show. "I am not going to trap him under a net. His skin would burn right through it." How can he be so highly paid and yet so ignorant?

"Gonna use your martial arts skills on him?"

I sigh. "I don't have martial arts skills."

"Really? I thought you were, like, a ninja or something."

He's making my brain hurt. "I admire ninjas. I'm not one myself."

"Bummer."

"It's not a bummer. I have no interest in taking a human life."

"But you're trying to kill Satan."

"I never said I was trying to kill Satan. All I've said is that if I can figure out a way to trap him, I might summon him with the bell. That's a pretty big 'if.' I'm not trying to pass myself off as some mighty devil hunter—I'm just saying that if I figured out a workable plan, I might try to rid the world of him. Give me a frickin' break."

Rick jiggles the bell. "It doesn't even really ring. It just sort of clacks around."

"Well, gee, perhaps a fallen angel has better hearing than you do. Did you ever think of that?" His stupidity is beyond belief.

"I've gotta tell you, Howie, I'm not quite buying the whole devil bell thing."

I've never claimed to be perfect. Sometimes I suffer from the sin of pride. And on that day, I simply couldn't take the ridicule anymore. I snatched the bell out of Rick's hand and began to ring.

I rang it ten times.

Twenty.

Thirty.

Rick stood there, a smirk on his face. Oh, how I would enjoy seeing that smirk ripped off and boiled in bile by Lucifer himself.

I continued to shake the bell, counting each tinkle. Forty-six, forty-seven, forty-eight . . .

"I've gotta go," said Rick.

"You're not going anywhere," I told him. "You don't believe me? I'll prove it to you, once and for all."

Fifty-three, fifty-four, fifty-five . . .

"How many rings does it take?"

"Six hundred and sixty-six."

"Is it cumulative?"

"What do you mean?"

"Do my rings count?"

"No. One person in one session."

"What are you up to?"

"Ninety."

Sarah, who sits three cubicles behind me, approaches with a cup of coffee. "What's going on?"

"Howie's summoning Satan."

Sarah smiles. "You figured out how to vanquish him?"

I shake my head and keep ringing. "I'm just teaching Rick a lesson."

"Pretty harsh lesson if Satan *does* show up."

"I'm teaching all of you a lesson," I announce. "You never believed me. You all think I wasted my dollar fifty. Well, when I reach the six hundred and sixty-sixth ring you'll find out just who wasted what."

"How many rings is that now?" Rick asks.

"One hundred and forty-one."

"Can you call me when you're at six hundred?"

His condescending tone makes me want to watch his eternal torment even more. I ring harder and faster.

In the back of my mind, I question the wisdom of summoning Satan without an escape plan, but I'm far too annoyed to worry about that. Whatever happens, happens.

A crowd begins to gather. They all look amused. I

can't wait to see the amusement on their faces transform into a distinct *lack* of amusement.

I've sort of lost count of the number of rings at this point—I think I'm around three hundred—but the summoning doesn't require me to stop at exactly six hundred and sixty-six rings, so if I go over I won't mess things up. I just need to keep track enough that I know when to duck and cover.

"Shouldn't we make Satan a welcome banner or something?" asks Mike, who is also from Corporate Accounting. The others acknowledge that it's a good idea (though I doubt their sincerity), but nobody goes to make one. They won't have time, anyway.

Patricia, who is also from Corporate Accounting (their area is right next to mine), looks at me sadly. She's always been nice to me and I harbor a secret crush on her, despite her being thirty-two years my senior. "C'mon, Howie, knock it off. You don't have to prove anything."

If I could have taken her statement to mean "because *I* believe you," that would've been good enough and I would have ceased ringing the bell. Unfortunately, she clearly means "because nothing will happen and you'll look like an idiot," and so I must continue.

Tinkle, tinkle, tinkle, tinkle, tinkle, tinkle, tinkle.

My hand is starting to get tired. See? Even with it being a minuscule plastic bell, the ringing process is tiring. *That* is why I was provided with this particular bell and not some giant black iron behemoth that would be impossible to ring a sufficient number of times without collapsing from exhaustion. Everything makes sense when you apply simple logic.

"Was that six hundred and sixty-six?" Rick asks.

"No. We're just over five hundred," I inform him.

"This all seems kind of inconvenient."

"Oh, sure, because it makes sooooo much sense that the process of summoning the devil should be so convenient that you can do it just by grabbing the bell from my desk and shaking it a couple of times," I say, making no effort to hide the sarcasm in my voice. "Think about what you're saying, Rick!" I don't have to treat him with respect any longer. You can't respect somebody who is moments away from being skewered by a flaming pitchfork.

I switch the bell to my left hand and continue ringing.

Six hundred (approximately).

I want to cackle with maniacal laughter about what is to occur, but I have to remember that we're still in a place of business, and professional conduct is expected. I can't stop myself from grinning, though.

I ring so fast that my hand tingles.

And finally I reach the Ring of the Beast. I ring ten more times just in case.

I give a satisfied nod to my doomed antagonists . . . but then my grin vanishes.

What have I done?

Oh God, what have I done?

To prove a point to my co-workers, I have brought Hell to the offices of Tyler & Bettin, Inc. How can I call myself a Christian when I would so selfishly summon Lucifer himself for no reason but to make Rick from Corporate Accounting look foolish?

Satan may not have arrived yet, but there is still an evil presence in this room, and it is me.

I am so displeased with myself that I want to scream. Rivers of blood will flow over our keyboards and mice. Our printers will melt and sizzle in the hellfire. My co-workers ridiculed me, but did they really deserve this eternal overtime of misery?

What can I do to stop this?

Though I'd said that a net couldn't hold Satan, that had merely been an educated guess. If we have one around, it is certainly worth a shot. I want to shout for my co-workers to try to find one, but I am so terrified and appalled by my own behavior that I can't speak. I gesticulate frantically, while they stand around my desk, still looking amused.

"Hello? Satan?" Rick calls out, unaware that he is almost certainly making himself the first target.

I have to stop this! But what can I do? What could

ward off the Prince of Darkness? What does he hate most in the world?

And then I realize the answer.

Love.

The power of love can stop the Beast from invading our plane of existence. A kiss, true and pure. Upon sensing the expression of human love, the devil will be so repulsed that he might—*might*—return to his hellish plane and leave us alone.

I gaze at Patricia.

She turns and sadly walks away from my desk.

I think I can hear a rumbling sound in the distance. It reminds me of the ventilation system, but I am in no condition to accurately judge sounds and know there is no time to spare. I have to express pure love *now.*

I stand up, whisper "I love you," then pull Rick toward me and kiss him on the lips. I don't really love him, but perhaps Satan will be fooled.

The chaos is so great that for a moment I think Satan has arrived. But, no, they are merely reacting to my act of redemption. Not in a positive way. Still, they can judge me all they want as long as I've staved off the effects of that accursed bell.

Satan does not show up in the offices of Tyler & Bettin that morning. The kiss worked.

I destroy the bell by stomping on it with my foot. It is too much responsibility for one man.

I spend some time down in Human Resources, explaining my actions. I am written up for unprofessional conduct and told that it will negatively impact my raise, but that's okay. I had succumbed to the sin of pride, and my punishment is just.

And I learned an important lesson. Love conquers all . . . but in a pinch, you can fake it.

Dead Hand

Sharyn McCrumb

In stock car racing, a "dead hand" is a jack-type device with which you hold up heavy car parts (like a transmission) while you unbolt them.

I don't hold with talking to dead people. Of course, that's just a personal preference of mine. It ain't against the rules of NASCAR, you understand. And it's about the only thing that ain't.

Will they let you adjust the spoiler a couple of degrees for less air resistance? *Naw.*

Can you make the roll cage bars out of aluminum instead of steel to lighten the chassis? *Not if they catch you.*

How about putting a little nitrous oxide in the gasoline to give your car an instant boost in horsepower? *Don't even think about it.*

Cheating in stock-car racing is a time-honored tradition, an endless game of Whac-A-Mole. You find some little way to give your team an edge, and then NASCAR catches you at it, and the next day they add a new no-no to the rule book. So then you go looking for some other way to get ahead, and that works for a while, and then they catch you again, and so it goes.

I was on a team that was so far up the creek in engine sludge that we couldn't even afford to pay the fines they'd hit us with if they caught us cheating. We were dead last in points, dead men racing, dead in the water as far as being competitive in the sport. That's what got me thinking about dead people, I guess.

Trampas-LeFay used to be a name to conjure with on the NASCAR circuit, but that was back in the day, when drivers still knew their way around an engine, and when most of the guys out there racing had day jobs instead of fan clubs. Back then a race team could be located anywhere, like the Wood Brothers' shop in Stuart, Virginia, or in the garage in back of Ralph Earnhardt's little white house in Kannapolis. Back then Trampas-LeFay was a shoestring operation out of the Tennessee hills, with a lot of moonshining know-how going into their engine building, but they held their own for the better part of two decades, and they won enough races to turn a profit.

Times changed, though. Big money and national media exposure changed the sport beyond recognition, so now we were in an era of West Coast pretty-boy drivers and rocket-science engineering, all propelled by the almighty dollar.

But Trampas-LeFay had hardly changed at all. We were still the same little one-car team in the Tennessee hills with a cheesy regional sponsor and some local good ol' boys working the race shop. But now we were trying to go head-to-head against corporate racing giants who had twenty-million-dollar budgets from Fortune 500 companies, all of them located within hailing distance of Mooresville, the epicenter of NASCAR, where they had access to the wind tunnels, the state-of-the-art engineers, and the Charlotte media machine.

We hadn't won a race in a year of Sundays, but that doesn't mean we don't know our stuff. It just means we're stubborn and maybe a bit behind the times, which in this sport is the fast lane to oblivion.

For one thing, all the winning teams field three or four cars every week. We had one. So while the big boys got three times as much testing and research from pooling their multicar information, we had one car and one set of answers. We also lacked the twenty-million-dollar sponsor that paid for all those engineers and testing equipment that gave them the edge. A three-hour race is often won by just a tenth of a second, and it takes a few million dollars to buy you that tenth of a second. The way things stood now, Trampas-LeFay didn't have enough money to buy the stopwatch, much less the tenth of a second to win.

I had been the team's chief mechanic a long time—since Earnhardt Sr.'s rookie year—and I still knew a few tricks of the trade, but it would have taken a miracle to compete with those million-dollar golden boys down in Mooresville.

"I don't see us finishing out the year," J. P. Trampas told me that afternoon at the shop. He was a tall, gaunt fellow who looked older and grayer than he should have, but watching a hundred grand a week spiral down the drain will do that to a man, I reckon. His grandfather had been the original Trampas in racing, and I knew that it hurt J.P. to watch the family business sink into oblivion. He had to be wondering if there was something he could have done differently to have prevented that. His grandfather had been a tough old moonshiner who parlayed his expertise in outrunning the law into pure driving genius in NASCAR, and he had been smart enough to get out of the car early and start building an empire. J.P. was a good fellow, but he was two generations down from shirtsleeve money. He had too much culture and not enough grit in his craw for a cut-throat business like racing, and he had spent his youth in a fancy college, not in the race shop. It was hard to blame him, though, for being what he was raised to be. He was doing his honest best—which was part of the problem. The honest part. There are only two kinds of racers: cheaters and losers.

"Well, times is hard," I said.

"Indeed they are." He reached for a rag to wipe the sweat off his face, saw the gleam of motor oil on it, and put it down again. "It used to be, almost every car qualified to make a race, which would have guaranteed us a few thousand dollars participation money anyhow, but now with fifty six teams trying out each week for only forty-three slots—well, we're just throwing good money after bad. We spend thousands to get to the track; we fail to qualify by a few tenths of a second; and we then come home with nothing. Half the time we don't even get to race. What sponsor is going to pay us a hundred K a week when we don't even make the show?"

I shook my head sadly. He'd get no argument from me there. Facts is facts.

J.P.'s frown deepened into a furrow. "We're a week or so from laying people off, Rattler. I hate to say that, but I don't know what else we can do."

"We could make the race for once," I said, and he managed to laugh and still sound sad at the same time.

"Make the race," he said. "Well, that would take a miracle."

A miracle would have come in handy, but I don't hold with accepting charity from anybody—not even from folks wearing halos—so I didn't figure on going to the nearest church, lighting a candle, and asking for a handout. I figured if there were miracles needed, I'd best see about devising one on my own.

Now, my people have been in these hills a long time, and we don't run to saints and such, but I do have a streak of Cherokee blood in my veins wider than the Holston River, and I had learned a thing or two besides engine mechanics from those bootlegging, full-blood great-uncles of mine. I can do a deal of things that don't have anything to do with racing: heal wounds with a white quartz stone; talk the fire out of a burn; find water with a fork of willow branch. But I had never tried anything as big and scary as what I proposed to do now. This was messing with serious magic, and I didn't do it lightly.

No point in me trying to tell you the particulars of it. Like my granddaddy used to say, "You can't explain what you don't know any more than you can come back from where you ain't been." And likely it only worked because of my bloodlines, anyhow. But in the light of the full moon I gathered the plants I needed from a little mountain meadow near my people's healing lake, and then I took them along to the funeral home in Kingsport.

The fact that a local dirt-track driver named Eddie Taylor had just got killed last night wouldn't make the national news and didn't deserve to, but if he'd had the right breaks and a few more years to hone his skills, he might have rated a raft of tributes around the country. Eddie had wanted to be a big-time NASCAR driver, and while he had the nerves and the skills for it, he never got the chance to prove it. Last night on Highway 23, Eddie crashed into a tree, swerving to avoid a deer in the road. Now, aside from his racing prowess, Eddie was known around these parts as a keen and skillful deer hunter. It struck me as ironic that Eddie would die trying to spare the life of a critter that he would have proudly blown to Kingdom Come under different circumstances, but maybe the universe likes a joke as much as anybody. Just shy of Eddie's twentieth birthday, it was all over for him. A damn shame, I thought, him never having a chance. It sorta justified what I was doing, I told myself.

Funeral homes are not all that closely guarded, because most people would rather get rid of a corpse than acquire one. Anyhow, at 2:00 a.m. nobody was on the premises, and I managed to get what-was-left-of-Eddie off the steel table and out to my truck, because we had somewhere else to go.

Exit 67. The road to the Tri-Cities Airport, where all the drivers fly in when they race at Bristol. One icy April night about fifteen years ago, one of those planes hadn't made it to the runway. It had crashed in an open field a mile away, killing the pilot and one of the best NASCAR drivers I'd ever seen race. Oh, maybe you haven't heard of him: He didn't have a chance to win seven championships like Earnhardt did, but maybe he would have if he'd lived. He'd never really had his chance, either.

So I dragged Eddie Taylor's body out to the middle of that field—just where I'd seen the wreckage of that plane—and I laid it down in the moonlight, sprinkled my herbs, and I called life back into the dead. It's like a door opens somewhere, maybe in your mind, and you can talk through it to someone you can't see.

I said, "I know you're here, Champ. I can feel it. You died here. I came to offer you another chance to race. Over here. *Where it counts.*" For all I knew, the Champ was spending eternity racing against the likes of Dale Earnhardt, Davy Allison, and all the Flock brothers over there, but that wouldn't get him into the record books here. Even if only he and I knew it was him back doing the racing, it would mean something to him. I figured he still had something to prove.

The night breeze blew cold on the back of my neck, while I waited for him to consider the offer.

Then just as a silvery cloud swallowed the moon, the late Eddie Taylor sat up and said, "Deal."

He looked okay. Eddie was a handsome kid in that chicken hawk, redneck way that puts you in mind of Steve McQueen, and he hadn't been messed up in the wreck. Just took a whack in the chest that stopped his heart. People in NASCAR might have recognized the Champ, even after fifteen years, but nobody would be looking for the face of Eddie Taylor in a Cup car. I gave him a new name just to make sure. Victor Northstar. I planned to claim him as a Cherokee cousin.

He looked all right, by the way. Eddie Taylor had only been dead a few hours, so there had been no real deterioration, and once you put the life force back into a corpse, all the internal systems start working again, so the body doesn't decay or get a beard of moss, or any of that horror movie stuff. It just picks up living right where it left off. He just looked like a regular guy, which was kind of a shame because these days NASCAR likes its drivers to look like soap opera stars or male models. Eddie was just average. Hendricks wouldn't have hired him, but I was betting that Trampas-LeFay would take what they could get.

It wasn't hard to talk J. P. Trampas into hiring him, and it wasn't a moment too soon, either. The current Trampas-LeFay driver was a pretty-boy NASCAR star who had stooped to driving for us, because he was on the wrong side of forty and because in accent and temperament, he was a stubborn throwback to the old days. After we'd missed enough races to embarrass him, and he'd started to worry that his paychecks might bounce, he did us all a favor and quit. J.P. was about to pack it in when I introduced him to my cousin Victor.

"He's the best driver this side of heaven," I said with a straight face. J.P. hesitated, so I added, "And he'll work dirt cheap."

So we were back in the game.

I'll leave out all the parts about the phony biography I concocted: the IDs and the NASCAR driver's license and all, which took some ingenuity on my part, but just because something is hard work doesn't mean it is interesting. Maybe if we had been an important team, people might have taken a closer look, but we were so hopeless, I believe we could have put Tim Flock's monkey behind the wheel without causing much comment. Maybe the Cherokee factor helped, too. NASCAR is all about diversity these days. Well, you don't hardly get more underrepresented than "dead," so I figured we were doing them a favor, even if they didn't know it.

"Victor" came to live with me in my little A-frame back in Possum Holler, east of Kingsport, though we didn't let on about that, because people want to think NASCAR drivers live glamorous lives. Anyhow, we didn't spend much time there, because we had to make up for lost time in the racing shop.

We decided to take it easy on him at first—no fan meet and greets, and no TV. The press interviews were the easy part. Sportswriters expect clichés and platitudes from the drivers, and in these touchy times only a fool would give them anything else. I had to explain that to the Champ, but once he caught on, he could talk piffle with the best of them: *"Like to thank the sponsor and the good folks at Trampas-LeFay for all their support. We just never got it to work quite right. Maybe next week."*

Even dead people can manage to say that.

Nobody had to teach the Champ how to drive again. Some of the technicalities of race cars might have changed in fifteen years, but the sport itself was still a cross between ballet and mud wrestling, and the Champ was still a master at the technique. They're still mostly racing at the same old tracks, so he knew all his old tricks at them, as well: how to pass at Bristol, where to speed up in Turn Two at Darlington, and which groove to run for speed at Talladega.

Of course, we still had to work mechanical magic to give our driver a competitive car to work with, and, considering how many millions of dollars the other teams had that we didn't, I almost wished I'd conjured up a rich sponsor instead of a dead driver, but what with one thing and another, we did manage to get him into the race at Charlotte.

The Champ still knew how to drive, and we did a thing or two to the car that they didn't catch us at, and so his qualifying lap was good enough to get us in at a starting position of twenty-eighth out of forty-three positions starting the race. We didn't figure we had a chance to win, but they pay more than fifty thousand dollars even to the guy who finishes in last place, and that was money we needed to stay in business. We didn't expect a top-ten finish.

We didn't get one, either, because no shoestring operation can compete with the *wind-tunnel and 500 engineers* teams, not even if the Archangel Gabriel was driving for them. So we knew the car wouldn't be competitive, but we did think the Champ could hold his own.

"What the hell's the matter with him?" Kit Porter, our beleaguered crew chief, who is better than our record would have you believe, was whiter than the ghost we were currently employing.

I came to all the races to look after the Champ, but since I wasn't part of the pit crew, I lingered behind the wall, making myself useful in case they needed any repairs midrace, beyond the usual repair resource: duct tape. I had been checking out the next set of tires, and not watching the track, when Kit stormed up to me, wanting to know what was wrong with our driver.

"He's letting cars pass him like he was standing still. Every time a car comes near him, he scoots out of the way like he's terrified. Like this was his very first race."

I shook my head. That certainly didn't sound like the Champ. He didn't win a NASCAR championship by being a shrinking violet. Fifteen years ago I had seen him beating and banging his way down the track, racing against Dale Earnhardt himself, and he never gave an inch. The Champ had gone into the wall so many times he could probably tell you which speedway he was at by the taste of the dust. Why would he suddenly lose his nerve?

I walked over to the wall to observe the progress of the race. It isn't easy to watch a race from the infield, especially at a mile-and-a-half track like Lowe's Motor

Speedway. I could only see the cars for the few seconds that they swept past our pit stall on their way to the next turn in the oval, but that few seconds was enough to show me that Kit Porter had been right about our driver: He was dodging the other cars for all he was worth, and it was costing him track position with every second, as one by one even the slowest cars started whizzing past him.

"What's the matter with him?" asked Kit. "You'd think he'd never raced before."

I mulled that over. The Champ was certainly no rookie, but that body he was currently inhabiting had belonged to Eddie Taylor . . . *who had died in a head-on collision.* I wondered if somewhere deep in the muscles of that body was an ingrained fear of car wrecks. He sure had a right to feel that way, but I couldn't let that memory wreck our race team. I had an idea, though. NASCAR teams are in constant radio contact with their driver. They can advise him on tire wear and fuel mileage, and up on top of the grandstands a spotter warns him of trouble ahead or a car gaining on him out of his line of sight. So I could talk to the Champ, but since team frequencies are made public, I would have had a lot more listeners than just the Champ.

"Give me a headset," I told Kit Porter. "Our driver needs a pep talk more than he needs a spotter right now. And put us on a closed-channel frequency. I don't want anybody eavesdropping on this conversation. Not even you."

Kit Porter handed me his own headset. "Whatever works," he said. "But make it quick."

I nodded, and took a deep breath while I worked out what to say. I sure hoped the channel was on a private frequency, but I decided to be careful anyhow. "Champ," I said into the microphone. "This here's Rattler. We got us a situation here, and it's going to cost you your comeback if you don't get a grip on it. Part of you is scared of the other cars. Do you get my drift?"

Silence.

I tried again. "What I am telling you is that the body driving the car is afraid of dying in a car wreck. And that body seems to have a pretty good memory of what that was like. Next caution, bring it in for a pit stop. There's one thing we can try. Eight wheels corner better than four. You know what I mean?"

I heard a grunt in my headset, and the Champ said, "Yeah."

I went over and tapped the crew chief on the shoulder. "I told him to come in for a pit stop next caution. When he does, disable his brakes."

"What?"

"He needs to relearn racing as a contact sport. *Do it.*"

Eight wheels corner better than four. I was referring to the move in racing when you speed up on the inside of the car you are passing by, not slowing down going into the turn. You are, of course, going too fast to make the turn, so in the middle of the turn your car slides up the track, flush into the car that you are passing. Using that other car as a crutch keeps you safely on track and allows you to complete the pass. The problem is that sometimes doing that puts the other car into the wall.

The Champ had cut his teeth on that maneuver, but the *other* passenger in our driver's body would be appalled at the thought of deliberately hitting another car. I figured if we took out his brakes, he wouldn't have any choice.

A dozen laps later, one of the rookies ran out of talent and hit the wall on Turn Two, which gave us that caution lap we were waiting for. The Champ pulled in, the pit crew swarmed all over the car, and, per my instructions, they kinked the two front brake lines.

To actually sever the brake line would have been a hassle. Fluid spills everywhere, and you can't repair it quickly, but it is possible to put a kink in the brake line, or to put vise grip pliers on it. Technically, there are four brake lines on a race car, and tampering with any one of them would only affect the brakes to that wheel, but since any reduction in braking force is enough to cause a problem on the racetrack, the driver would be forced to compensate for his loss of braking power, which is exactly what I wanted.

Thirteen seconds later, the car roared back onto the track, and forty-two other NASCAR drivers were unaware that we had just sent a loose cannon out among them.

Caution laps run as sedately as Sunday afternoon freeway traffic, so nobody noticed anything amiss until they dropped the green flag again to restart the high-speed racing. The Champ worked his way past 160 mph in a couple of heartbeats, and then Turn One was looming in front of him. Poor Eddie, whose body was understandably a little confused about whether or not it was dead, tried hard to keep that car away from everybody else on the track, but going into a turn at 200 mph without brakes didn't give him too many options. He could either go into the wall, or he could use another car as a crutch to get him out of that corner. Maybe he froze from the terror of the situation or maybe the Champ just overruled the body's reflexes, but when the car started to get loose, the driver swung it a little to the right, where one of the sport's golden boys just happened to be trying to pass on the outside. *Eight wheels are better than four.* That twenty-million-dollar set of training wheels carried us through the turn and into the straightaway slick as goose grease. Unfortunately for the golden boy, the weight of our car unbalanced him and sent him sliding toward the wall, where he ended up with a crumpled right front panel, and he collected a couple of other cars in the wreck. As always when wrecked cars are cluttering up the track, they threw a caution so they could clean up the mess, and when they did, we took the opportunity to bring the Champ back in, and we fixed the brakes. I figured he had the hang of it again now, and I was right.

We didn't win, of course. In a three-hour stock-car race, the difference between first place and fifteenth place is less than a second, and as I said, it takes a few million dollars to buy you every tenth of a second, which we still didn't have, but at least we made the race and finished in the middle of the pack. That's more than we had accomplished in a long time. But, while I might have been happy just to have a half-decent season, it wasn't enough for the Champ—or for J. P. Trampas, who was still pouring fifty grand a week into this racing operation. Sand down a rat hole.

"He's a good enough driver, Rattler," J.P. told me as we were loading the car back into the hauler. "But he still can't make enough of a difference in our standings unless we can afford to provide him with decent equipment."

"I wish I could conjure up a sponsor," I said. "But there are limits even to Cherokee magic."

"I think I have an idea about that," said J.P. "Let me see what I can do."

• • •

By the time I heard the details of J.P.'s brilliant idea, it was too late to do anything about it, except hope that it wouldn't blow up in our faces.

NASCAR has changed a lot since the Champ last took the checkered flag. Back in those days, drivers were ordinary-looking fellows who knew their way around an engine, but now the sport is an international multibillion-dollar behemoth, and the drivers are expected to be movie stars in firesuits. If you are a corporation looking to pay a race team ten million dollars a year to advertise your product, then you want a lot of charisma for your money. J.P.'s idea was to turn our driver into a celebrity. After all, "Victor" was supposed to be my Cherokee cousin, and NASCAR was all about diversity these days. The Ganassi team's new Hispanic driver had brought a whole new set of fans into NASCAR, and J.P. figured he could do the same with his Native American phenomenon. So he wrote up some press release, giving the sports journalists Victor's bio, which consisted of the pack of lies I had given our official team publicist, who was also the wife of the jackman. Then, since the next race was Martinsville, relatively close to home, J.P. arranged for our driver to do a bunch of local appearances the week of the race. He'd be doing a signing in a local auto parts store, meeting with NASCAR fans at a charity event at the Roanoke coliseum, and doing local TV and radio interviews. It was a helluva schedule, but the big-time NASCAR drivers do it every week of the season, each week in a different city. It's part of the job. Didn't use to be, in the Champ's day, but it was now.

I was worried. The Champ knew how to drive, but he had never been known as Mr. Sunshine, and from what I could see, death hadn't made him any more outgoing.

"Media celebrity is part of the job now," I told him. "Making you famous is our best hope of getting a sponsor. Just give it a shot, Champ. And keep your sunglasses on."

He didn't like it much, but they assigned the jackman's wife to go along as his minder, and all week she walked him through that exhausting round of silly media questions and avid racing fans. The Champ spent a couple of hours a day in appearances, autographing a few hundred "Victor Northstar" hero cards for folks who thought that wearing a NASCAR firesuit made you *somebody*. He answered all the reporters' questions politely, but in as few words as possible, and when avid fans insisted on hugging him and getting him to pose for pictures with them, he put up with that, too, but his cardboard smile looked like he had put it on with a staple gun. He seemed a little baffled by the questions relating to his Cherokee heritage, as well he might be, but he would just say something vague, and everybody just nodded and went on, because I don't think TV interviewers really listen to people's answers anyhow.

When the jackman's wife dropped him off at the hotel after the last day's round of appearances, the Champ flopped down on the chair next to the window, closed his eyes, and let out a bone-weary sigh. "I'm glad that's over," he said.

"Until next week it is," I told him. "J.P. intends to keep up this publicity blitz until you build up enough of a fan base to land us a sponsor. And after that, of course, you'll be in even more demand for these kinds of appearances, because the sponsor will expect you to keep their potential customers happy. So get used to it, Champ. This is a way of life. It's the new NASCAR."

He didn't say anything for the rest of the evening, and when I went down for supper, he was still sitting there in the chair by the window, staring at nothing.

Martinsville is a short track where a driver's skill can actually make a difference, so we had high hopes of a good showing in Sunday's race. He qualified well, because he knew the track and he'd always been good at it, so we thought this race was our best shot at reviving our hopes for the team.

Sure enough, in Sunday's race everything went well for about seventy-eight laps, and then all of a sudden the Champ went into a spin all by himself in Turn Four, and slammed the car against the outside wall with two more cars piling into him from behind. Those wrecked cars slid down the apron next to the infield wall, and the drivers climbed out, but the Champ's car stayed where it was. I looked over that infield wall in time to see little tongues of flame begin to spiral up from the underside of the car. The fuel line must have broken; gas was spilling all over the pavement.

"It's okay," said the crew chief, seeing my expression. "See? He put his window net down."

That's what drivers do after a wreck to signal that they are conscious and functioning: they unfasten the window netting on the driver's-side window. When they do that, you expect them to climb out of the car unassisted within a couple of seconds.

But he didn't.

We watched and waited while the flames caught the gas from the leaking fuel line and leapt higher and higher, engulfing the back of the car. He didn't have much time left to escape. Soon the whole chassis would be a fireball. Yes, he was wearing a firesuit, but that term is misleading. Those things are fireproof for all of eight seconds, and after that you might as well be wearing your pajamas. Funny thing, but watching that fire melting the decals off that race car and flicking toward the driver's seat just gave me chills.

I grabbed a headset from the nearest crewman. "Champ!" I yelled, not caring who heard me. "Get out of there now! The flames are almost to your roll cage. Get out!"

There was a little crackle in my headset, and then the Champ's voice, calm as ever, like he was already a long ways away. He said, *"I'd rather be dead."*

Well, that was the end of our hopes for the current season. The car burned up so much they barely got enough of the driver out to bury. Our team made all the sports magazines for a week or so after the tragedy, and a few fan groups made up memorial T-shirts of Victor Northstar, but we were right back to square one as a team.

After that, I gave up on the thought of bringing any more of the great ones back to race again. They just couldn't handle the carnival aspect of the sport these days. It ain't much about driving anymore. So we're scouring the east Tennessee high schools for some good-looking kid who photographs well and talks like they do on the TV. Then we'll worry about teaching him how to drive. Even magic has its limits, you know.

Day Off

A Story of the Dresden Files

JIM BUTCHER

The thief was examining another trapped doorway when I heard something—the tromp of approaching feet. The holy woman was in the middle of another sermon, about attentiveness or something, but I held up my hand for silence and she obliged. I could hear twenty sets of feet, maybe more.

I let out a low growl and reached for my sword. "Company."

"Easy, my son," the holy woman said. "We don't even know who it is yet."

The ruined mausoleum was far enough off the beaten path to make it unlikely that anyone had just wandered in on us. The holy woman was dreaming if she thought that the company might be friendly. A moment later they appeared—the local magistrate and two dozen of his thugs.

"Always with the corrupt government officials," muttered the wizard from behind me. I glanced back at him and then looked for the thief. The nimble little minx was nowhere to be seen.

"You are trespassing!" boomed the magistrate. He had a big, boomy voice. "Leave this place immediately on pain of punishment by the Crown's law!"

"Sir!" replied the holy woman. "Our mission here is of paramount importance. The writ we bear from your own liege requires you to render aid and assistance in this matter."

"But not to violate the graves of my subjects!" he boomed some more. "Begone! Before I unleash the nine fires of Atarak upon—"

"Enough talk!" I growled and threw my heavy dagger at his chest.

Propelled by my massive thews, the dagger hit him two inches below his left nipple—a perfect heart shot.

It struck with enough force to hurl him from his feet. His men howled with surprised fury.

I drew the huge sword from my back, let out a leonine roar, and charged the two dozen thugs.

"Enough talk!" I bellowed, and whipped the twenty-pound greatsword at the nearest target as if it were a wooden yardstick. He went down in a heap.

"Enough talk!" I howled, and kept swinging. I smashed through the next several thugs as if they were made of soft wax. Off to my left, the thief came out of nowhere and neatly sliced the Achilles tendons of another thug. The holy woman took a ready stance with her quarterstaff and chanted out a prayer to her deities at the top of her lungs.

The wizard shrieked, and a fireball whipped over my head, exploding twenty-one feet in front of me, then spread out in a perfect circle, like the shockwave of a nuke, burning and roasting thugs as it went and stopping a bare twelve inches shy of my nose.

"Oh, come on!" I said. "It doesn't work like that!"

"What?" demanded the wizard.

"It doesn't *work* like that!" I insisted. "Even if you call up fire with magic, it's still *fire.* It acts like *fire.* It expands in a sphere. And under a ceiling, that means that it goes rushing much farther down hallways and tunnels. It *doesn't* just go twenty feet and then *stop.*"

"Fireballs used to work like that," the wizard

sighed. "But do you know what a chore it is to calculate exactly how far those things will spread? I mean, it slows everything down."

"It's simple math," I said. "And it's way better than the fire just spreading twenty feet regardless of what's around it. What, do fireballs carry tape measures or something?"

Billy the Werewolf sighed and put down his character sheet and his dice. "Harry," he protested gently. "Repeat after me: It's only a game."

I folded my arms and frowned at him across his dining room table. It was littered with snacks, empty cans of pop, pieces of paper, and tiny little model monsters and adventurers (including a massively thewed barbarian model for my character). Georgia, Billy's willowy brunette wife, sat at the table with us, as did the redheaded bombshell Andi, while lanky Kirby lurked behind several folding screens covered with fantasy art at the head of the table.

"I'm just saying," I said. "There's no reason the magic can't be portrayed at least a little more accurately, is there?"

"Again with *this* discussion." Andi sighed. "I mean, I know he's the actual wizard and all, but Christ."

Kirby nodded glumly. "It's like taking a physicist to a *Star Trek* movie."

"Harry," Georgia said firmly. "You're doing it again."

"Oh, no I'm not!" I protested. "All I'm saying is that—"

Georgia arched an eyebrow and gave me a steady look down her aquiline nose. "You know the law, Dresden."

"He who kills the cheer springs for beer," chanted the rest of the table.

"Oh, bite me!" I muttered at them, but a grin was diluting my scowl as I dug out my wallet and tossed a twenty on the table.

"Okay," Kirby said. "Roll your fireball damage, Will."

Billy slung out a double handful of square dice and said, "Hah! One-point-two over median. Suck on that, henchmen!"

"They're all dead," Kirby confirmed. "We might as well break there until next week."

"Crap," I said. "I barely got to hit anybody."

"I only got to hit *one*!" Andi said.

Georgia shook her head. "I didn't even get to finish casting my spell."

"Oh yes," Billy gloated. "Seven modules of identifying magic items and repairing things the stupid barbarian broke, but I've finally come into my own. Was it like that for you, Harry?"

"Let you know when I come into my own," I said, rising. "But my hopes are high. Why, this very morrow, I, Harry Dresden, have a day off."

"The devil you say!" Billy exclaimed, grinning at me as the group began cleaning up from the evening's gaming session.

I shrugged into my black leather duster. "No apprentice, no work, no errands for the council, no warden stuff, no trips out of town for Paranet business. My very own free time."

Georgia gave me a wide smile. "Tell me you aren't going to spend it puttering around that musty hole in the ground you call a lab."

"Um," I said.

"Look," Andi said. "He's blushing!"

"I am not blushing," I said. I swept up the empty bottles and pizza boxes, and headed into Billy and Georgia's little kitchen to dump them into the trash.

Georgia followed me in, reaching around me to send several pieces of paper into the trash, too. "Hot date with Stacy?" she asked, her voice pitched to keep the conversation private.

"I think if I ever called her 'Stacy,' Anastasia might beat the snot out of me for being too lazy to speak her entire name," I replied.

"You seem a little tense about it."

I shrugged a shoulder. "This is going to be the first time we spend a whole day together without something trying to rip us to pieces along the way. I . . . I want it to go right, you know?" I pushed my fingers back through my hair. "I mean, both of us could use a day off."

"Sure, sure," Georgia said, watching me with calm, knowing eyes. "Do you think it's going to go anywhere with her?"

I shrugged. "Don't know. She and I have very different ideas about . . . well, about basically everything except what to do with things that go around hurting people."

The tall, willowy Georgia glanced back toward the dining room, where her short, heavily muscled husband was putting away models. "Opposites attract. There's a song about it and everything."

"One thing at a time," I said. "Neither one of us is trying to inspire the poets for the ages. We like each other. We make each other laugh. God, that's nice, these days . . ." I sighed and glanced up at Georgia, a little sheepishly. "I just want to show her a nice time tomorrow."

Georgia had a gentle smile on her narrow, intelligent face. "I think that's a very healthy attitude."

I was just getting into my car, a battered old Volkswagen Bug I've dubbed the "Blue Beetle," when Andi came hurrying over to me.

There'd been a dozen Alphas when I'd first met

them, college kids who had banded together and learned just enough magic to turn themselves into wolves. They'd spent their time as werewolves protecting and defending the town, which needed all the help it could get. The conclusion of their college educations had seen most of them move on in life, but Andi was one of the few who had stuck around.

Most of the Alphas adopted clothing that was easily discarded—the better to swiftly change into a large wolf without getting tangled up in jeans and underwear. On this particular summer evening, Andi was wearing a flirty little purple sundress and nothing else. Between her hair, her build, and her long, strong legs, Andi's picture belonged on the nose of a World War II bomber, and her hurried pace was intriguingly kinetic.

She noticed me noticing and gave me a wicked little smile and an extra jiggle the last few steps. She was the sort to appreciate being appreciated. "Harry," she said. "I know you hate to mix business with pleasure, but there's something I was hoping to talk to you about tomorrow."

"Sorry, sweetheart," I said in my best Bogey dialect. "Not tomorrow. Day off. Important things to do."

"I know," Andi said. "But I was hoping—"

"If it waited until after the Arcanos game it can wait until after my da . . . day off," I said firmly.

Andi almost flinched at the tone, and nodded. "Okay."

I felt myself arch an eyebrow. I hadn't put *that* much harsh into it—and Andi wasn't exactly the sort to be fazed by verbal salvos, regardless of their nature or volume. Socially speaking, the woman was armored like a battleship.

"Okay," I replied. "I'll call." Kirby approached her as I got into the car, put an arm around her from behind, and tugged her backside against his frontside, leaning down to sniff at her hair. She closed her eyes and pressed herself into him.

Yeah. I let myself feel a little smug as I pulled out of the lot and drove home. That one had just been a matter of time, despite everything Georgia had said. I totally called it.

I pulled into the gravel parking lot beside the boardinghouse where I live and knew right away that I had a problem. Perhaps it was my keenly developed intuition, honed by years of investigative work as the infamous Harry Dresden, Chicago's only professional wizard, shamus of the supernatural, gumshoe of the ghostly, wiseguy of the weird, my mystically honed, preternatural awareness of the shadow of Death passing nearby.

Or maybe it was the giant black van painted with flaming skulls, goat's head pentacles, and inverted crosses that was parked in front of my apartment door. Six-six-six of one, half a dozen of another.

The van's doors opened as I pulled in and people in black spilled out with neither the precision of a professional team of hitters nor the calm swagger of competent thugs. They looked like I'd caught them in the middle of eating sack lunches. One of them had what looked like taco sauce spilled down the front of his frothy white lace shirt. The other four . . . well, they looked like something.

They were all wearing mostly black, and mostly gothware, which meant a lot of velvet with a little leather, rubber, and PVC to spice things up. Three women, two men, all of them fairly young. All of them carried wands and staves and crystals dangling from chains, and all of them had deadly serious expressions on their faces.

I parked the car, never looking directly at them, and then got out of it, stuck my hands in my duster pockets, and stood there waiting.

"You're Harry Dresden," said the tallest one there, a young man with long black hair and a matching goatee.

I squinted at nothing, like Clint Eastwood would do, and said nothing, like Chow Yun-Fat would do.

"You're the one who came to New Orleans last week." He said it "Nawlins," even though the rest of his accent was Midwest standard. "You're the one who desecrated my works."

I blinked at him. "Whoa, wait a minute. There actually *was* a curse on that nice lady?"

He sneered at me. "She had earned my wrath."

"How about that," I said. "I figured it for some random bad feng shui."

His sneer vanished. "What?"

"To tell you the truth, it was so minor that I only did the ritual cleansing to make her feel better and show the Paranetters how to do it for themselves in the future." I shrugged. "Sorry about your wrath, there, Darth Wannabe."

He recovered his composure in seconds. "Apologies will do you no good, wizard. Now!"

He and his posse all raised their various accoutrements, sneering malevolently. "Defend yourself!"

"Okay," I said, and pulled my .44 out of my pocket.

Darth Wannabe and his posse lost their sneers.

"Wh-what?" said one of the girls, who had a nose ring that I was pretty sure was a clip-on. "What are you doing?"

"I'm a fixin' to defend myself," I drawled, Texas-style. I held the gun negligently, pointing down and to one side and not right at them. I didn't want to hurt anybody. "Look, kids. You really need to work on your image."

Darth opened his mouth. It just hung that way for a minute.

"I mean, the van's a bit overdone. But hell, I can't throw stones. My VW Bug has a big '53' inside a circle spray painted on the hood. You're sort of slipping elsewhere, though." I nodded at one of the girls, a brunette holding a wand with a crystal on the tip. "Honey, I liked the *Harry Potter* movies, too, but that doesn't mean I ran out and got a Dark Mark tattooed onto my left forearm like you did." I eyed the other male. "And you're wearing a freakin' Slytherin scarf. I mean, Christ. How's anyone supposed to take *that* seriously?"

"You would dare," Darth Wannabe began, obviously outraged.

"One more tip, kids. If you had any real talent, the air would practically have been on fire when you got ready to throw down. But you losers don't have enough magic between you to turn cereal into breakfast."

"You would dare—"

"I can tell, because I actually *am* a wizard. I went to school for this stuff."

"You would—"

"I mean, I know you guys have probably thrown your talents at other people in your weight class, had your little duels, and maybe someone got a nosebleed and someone went home with a migraine and it gave your inner megalomaniac a boner. But this is different." I nodded at one of the other girls, who had shaved her head clean. "Excuse me, miss. What time is it?"

She blinked at me. "Um. It's after one . . . ?"

"Thanks."

The Dim Lord tried for his dramatic dialogue again. "You would dare threaten us with mortal weapons?"

"It's after midnight," I told the idiot. "I'm off the clock."

That killed his momentum again. "What?"

"It's my day off, and I've got plans, so let's just skip ahead."

Darth floundered wordlessly. He was really out of his element—and he wasn't giving me anything to work with at all. If I waited around for him, this was going to take all night.

"All right, kid. You want some magic?" I pointed my gun at the van. "Howsabout I make your windows disappear."

Darth swallowed. Then he lowered his staff, a cheaply carved thing you can pick up at tourist traps in Acapulco, and said, "This is not over. We are your doom, Dresden."

"As long as you don't drag it out too much. Good night, children."

Darth sneered at me again, pulled the shreds of his dignity about him, and strode to the van. The rest of them followed him like good little darthlings. The van started up and tore away, throwing gravel spitefully into the Blue Beetle.

Could it sneer at them, the Beetle would have done so. Its dents had dents that were worse than what that van inflicted.

I spun the .44 once around my finger and put it back into my pocket.

Clint Yun-Fat.

As if I didn't have enough to do without worrying about Darth Wannabe and his groupies. I went inside, greeted my pets in order of seniority—Mister, my oversized cat first, then Mouse, my undersized ankylosaurus—washed up, and went to bed.

The Mickey Mouse alarm clock told me that it was five in the morning when my apartment's front door opened. The door gets stuck, because a ham-handed amateur installed it, and it makes a racket when it's finally forced open. I came out of the bedroom in my underwear, with my blasting rod in one hand and my .44 in the other, ready to do battle with whatever had come a-calling.

"Hi, boss!" Molly chirped, giving my blasting rod

and gun a passing glance, but ignoring my mostly nudity.

I felt old.

My apprentice came in and set two Starbucks cups down on the coffee table, along with a bag that would be full of something expensive that Starbucks thought people should eat with coffee. Molly, who was young and tall and blonde and built like a brick supermodel, offered me one of the cups. "You want to wake up now or would you rather I kept it warm for you?"

"Molly," I said, trying to be polite. "I can't stand the sight of you. Go away."

She held up a hand. "I know, I know, Captain Grumpypants. Your day off and your big date with Luccio."

"Yes," I said. I put as much hostility into it as I could.

Molly had been overexposed to my menace. It bounced right off her. "I just thought it would be a good time for me to work out some of the kinks on my invisibility potion. You've said I'm ready to use the lab alone."

"I said 'unsupervised.' That isn't quite the same thing as alone." My glower deepened. "Much like having an apprentice puttering around the basement is not quite the same thing as being alone with Anastasia."

"You're going horseback riding," Molly said in a

reasonable tone of voice. "You won't be here, and I'll be gone by the time you get back. And besides, I can make sure Mouse gets a walk or two while you're gone, so you won't have to come rushing back early. Isn't that thoughtful of me?"

Mouse's huge, gray doggy head came up off the floor and his tail twitched as she said "walk." He looked at me hopefully.

"Oh for crying out—" I shook my head wearily. "Lock up behind you before you go downstairs."

She turned back to the front door and started pushing. "You got it, boss."

I staggered back to my bed to get whatever rest I could before my apprentice died in a fit of sleep-deprivation-induced psychotic mania.

For the first time ever, Mickey Mouse let me down.

Granted, being a wizard means that technology and I don't get along very well. Things tend to break down a lot faster in the presence of mortal magic than they would otherwise—but that's mostly electronics. My wind-up Mickey Mouse clock was pure springs and gears, and it had given me years and years of loyal service. It never went off, and when I woke up, Mickey was cheerfully indicating that I had less than half an hour before Anastasia was supposed to arrive.

I got up and threw myself into the shower, bringing my razor with me. I was only partway through shaving when the explosion rattled the apartment, hard enough to make a film of water droplets leap up off the shower floor.

I stumbled out, wrapped a towel around my waist, seized my blasting rod—just in case what was needed was *more* explosions—and went running into the living room. The trap door leading down to the lab in my subbasement was open and pink and blue smoke was roiling up out of it in a thick, noxious plume.

"Hell's bells," I choked out, coughing. "Molly!?"

"Here," she called back through her own thick coughing. "I'm fine, I'm fine."

I opened a couple of the sunken windows, on opposite sides of the room, and the breeze began to thin out the smoke. "What about my lab?"

"I had it contained when it blew," she responded more clearly now. "Um. Just . . . just let me clean up a bit."

I eyed the trap door. "Molly," I said warningly.

"Don't come down!" she said, her voice near panic. "I'll have it cleaned up in a second. Okay?"

I thought about storming down there with a good hard lecture about the importance of not busting up your mentor's irreplaceable collection of gear, but took a deep breath instead. If anything had been destroyed, the lecture wouldn't fix it. And I only had fifteen minutes to make myself look like a human being and find some way to get rid of the smell of Molly's alchemical misadventure. So I decided to go finish shaving.

Am I easygoing or what?

No sooner had I gotten bits of paper stuck to the spots on my face where I'd been in a hurry than someone began hammering on the front door.

"For crying out *loud*," I muttered. "It's my day *off*." I stomped out to the living room and found the smoke mostly gone, if not the smell. Mouse paced along beside me on the way to the door. I unlocked it and wrenched it open, careful only to open it an inch or three, then peered outside.

Andi and Kirby crouched on the other side of my door. Both of them were dirty, haggard, and entirely covered with scratches. I could tell, because both were also entirely naked.

Kirby lowered his arm and stared warily at me. Then he let out a low growling sound, which I realized a second later had been meant to be my name. "Harry."

"You have got to be kidding me," I said. *"Today?"*

"Harry," Andi said, her eyes brimming. "Please. I don't know who else we can turn to."

"Dammit!" I snarled. "Dammit, dammit, dammit!" I wrenched the door the rest of the way open and muttered my wards down. "Come in. Hurry up, before someone sees you."

Kirby's nostrils flared as he entered, and his face twisted up in revulsion.

"Oh," Andi said as I shut the door. "That smells terrible."

"Tell me about it," I said. "You two look . . ." Well. I would have used different adjectives for Kirby than for Andi. ". . . a little thrashed. What's up? You two get in a fight with a barbed-wire golem or something?"

"N-no," Andi said. "Nothing like that. We've had . . . Kirby and I have . . . fleas."

I blinked.

Kirby nodded somber agreement and growled something unintelligible.

I checked the fireplace, which Molly had lit and which was crackling quietly. My coffeepot hung on a swinging arm near the fire, close enough to stay warm without boiling. I went to the pot and checked. She'd put my cup of expensive Starbucks elixir in there to stay warm. If I'd been preparing to murder her, that single act of compassion would have been reason enough to spare her life.

I poured the coffee into the mug Molly had left on the mantel and slugged some of it back. "Okay, okay," I said. "Start from the top. Fleas?"

"I don't know what else to call them," Andi said.

"When we shift, they're there, in our fur. Biting and itching. It was just annoying at first, but now . . . it's just awful." She shuddered and began running her fingertips over her shoulders and ribs. "I can feel them right now. Chewing at me. Biting and digging into me." She shook her head and with an almost visible effort forced her hands to be still. "It's getting hard to th-think straight. To talk. Every time we ch-change it gets worse."

I gulped down a bit of coffee, frowning. That *did* sound serious. I glanced down at the towel around my waist, and noted, idly, that I was the most heavily clothed person in the room. "All right, let me get dressed," I said. "I guess at least one of us should have his clothes on."

Andi looked at me blankly. "What?"

"Clothes. You're naked, Andi."

She looked down at herself, and then back up at me. "Oh." A smile spread over her lips, and the angle of her hips shifted slightly and very noticeably. "Maybe you should do something about that."

Kirby looked up from where he'd settled down by the fireplace, pure murder in his eyes.

"Uh," I said, looking back and forth between them. No question about it—the kids were definitely operating under the influence of something. "I'll be right back."

I threw on some clothes, including my shield

bracelet, in case the murderous look on Kirby's face got upgraded to a murderous lunge, and went back out into the living room. Kirby and Andi were both in front of the fireplace. They were . . . well. "Nuzzling" is both polite and generally accurate, even if it doesn't quite convey the blush factor the two were inspiring. I mean, they'd have been asked to leave any halfway reputable club for that kind of thing.

I lifted my hand to my eyes for a moment, concentrated, and opened up my Third Eye, my wizard's Sight. That was always a dicey move. The Sight showed you what truly was, all the patterns of magic and life that existed in the universe, as they truly were—but you got them in permanent ink. You didn't ever get to forget what you saw, no matter how bad it was. Still, if something was chewing up my friends, I needed to know about it. They were worth the risk.

I opened my eyes and immediately saw the thick bands of power that I'd laid into the very walls of my apartment, when I'd built up its magical defenses. Further layers of power surrounded my lab in a second shell of insulating magic, beneath my feet. From his perch atop one of my bookshelves, Mister the cat appeared exactly as he always did, evidently beyond the reach of such petty concerns as the mere forces that created the universe, though my dog Mouse was surrounded by a calm, steady aurora of silver and blue light.

More to the point, Kirby and Andi were both engulfed in a number of different shimmering energies—the flame-colored tinges of lust and passion foremost among them, for obvious reason, but those weren't the only energies at play. Greenish energy that struck me as something primal and wild, that essence of the instinct of the wolf they'd been taught by the genuine article, maybe, remained strong all around them, as did an undercurrent of pink-purple fear. Whatever was happening to them, it was scaring the hell out of both of them, even if they weren't able to do anything about it, at the moment.

The golden lightning of a practitioner at work also flickered through their auras—which shouldn't have been happening. Oh, the Alphas all had a lot more talent than Darth Wannabe and his playmates. That went without saying. But they had become extremely focused upon a single use of their magic—shapeshifting into a wolf, which is a *lot* more complicated and difficult and useful than it looks or sounds. But that kind of activity should only have been working if they were actually in the process of changing shape—and they weren't.

I stepped closer, peering intently, and saw something I rather wouldn't have.

Creatures clung to both of them—tiny, tiny things, dozens of them. To my Sight, they looked something like tiny crabs, hard-shelled little things with oversized pincers that ripped and tore into their spiritual flesh—tearing out tiny pieces that each contained a single glowing mote of both green and gold energy.

"Ah!" I said. "Ah-hah! You've got psychophagic mites!"

Andi and Kirby both jumped in shock. I guess they hadn't noticed me coming closer, being fully occupied with . . . oh, wow. They'd sort of segued into NC-17 activities.

"Wh-what?" Andi managed to say.

"Psychophagic . . ." I shook my head, dismissing my Sight with an effort of will. "Psychic parasites. They've latched onto you from the Nevernever. They're exerting an influence on you both, pushing you to indulge your, um, more basic and primitive behavior patterns, and feeding on the energy of them."

Andi dragged lust-glazed eyes from Kirby to me. "Primitive . . . ?"

"Yeah," I said. I nodded to them. "Hence the two of you, um. And I imagine they make you want to change form."

Andi's eyelids fluttered. "Yes. Yes, that sounds lovely." She shook her head slightly and came to her feet, her eyes suddenly glimmering with tears. "Is it . . . can you make them go away?"

I put a reassuring hand on her shoulder. "I can't figure out how they would have gotten there in the first place. I mean, these things are only attracted to very specific kinds of energy. And you'd only be vulnerable to them when you were actually drawing upon the matter of the Nevernever—when you were shifted. And—" I blinked and then rubbed at my forehead. "Andi. Please don't tell me that you and Kirby have been getting down while you were fuzzy."

The bombshell blushed, from the roots of her hair to the tips of her . . . toes.

"God, that's just . . . so wrong." I shook my head. "But to answer your question, yes, I think that—"

"Harry?" Molly called from the lab. "Um. Do you have a fire extinguisher?"

"*What!?*"

"I mean, if I needed one!" she amended, her voice quavering. "Hypothetically speaking!"

"Hypothetically speaking?" I half shouted. "Molly! Did you set my lab on fire?!"

Andi, a distracted expression on her face, idly lifted my hand from her shoulder and slid my index finger between her lips, suckling gently. A pleasant flicker of lightning shot up my arm, and I felt it all the way to the bottoms of my feet.

"Oh, hey, ho-ho-ho! Hold on there," I said, pulling my finger away. It came out of her mouth with another intriguing sensation and a soft popping sound. "Andi. Ahem. We really need to focus, here."

Kirby let out a raw snarl and hit me with a right cross that sent me tumbling back across the room and into one of my bookshelves. I rebounded off it, fell on my ass, and sat there stunned for a second as copies of the *Black Company* novels fell from the shelf and bounced off my head.

I looked up to see Kirby seize Andi by the wrist and jerk her back behind him, placing his body between her and me in a gesture of raw possession. Then he balled up his hands into fists, snarled, and took a step toward me.

Mouse loomed up beside me then, two hundred pounds of shaggy gray muscle. He didn't growl at Kirby, or so much as bare his teeth. He did, however, stand directly in Kirby's path and face him without backing down.

Without blinking, Kirby's body seemed to shimmer and flow, and suddenly a black wolf nearly Mouse's size, but leaner and swifter-looking, crouched across the apartment, white teeth bared, amber eyes glowing with rage.

Holy crap. Kirby was about half a second from losing it, and he had the skill and experience to cause some real mayhem. I mean, taking on an animal is one thing. Taking on an animal directed by a human intelligence with years of experience in battling the supernatural is a challenge at least an order of magnitude greater. If it came down to a fight, a real fight, between me and Kirby, I was sure I could beat him, but to do it I'd have to hit him fast and hard, without pulling any punches.

I was not at all confident that I could beat him without killing him.

"Kirby," I said, trying to keep my voice as low and steady as I could. "Kirby, man, think about this for a minute. It's Harry. Listen, man, this is Harry, and you've just blown your willpower check, like, completely. You need to take a deep breath and get some perspective here. You're my friend, you're under the influence, and I'm trying to help you."

"Harry?" Molly called out, her voice higher-pitched than ever. "Acid doesn't eat through concrete, right?"

I blinked at the trapdoor and screamed in frustration, "Hell's bells, what are you *doing* down there?!"

Kirby took another pace forward, wolf eyes bright, jaws slavering, head held low and ready for a fight. Behind him, Andi was watching the whole thing with a wide-eyed look that mixed terror, lust, excitement, and rage in equal parts, her impressive chest heaving. Her hands and lower arms had already begun to slowly change, sprouting curling russet fur, her nails lengthening into dark claws. Her eyes traveled to me and her mouth dropped open, revealing fangs that were already beginning to grow.

Super. In a fight against Kirby, I was worried about him not surviving. Against Kirby *and* Andi, in these quarters, it would be *me* who was running against long odds.

But I try to be an optimist: at least things weren't going to get any worse.

Above and behind me, a window broke.

A length of lead pipe, maybe a foot long, capped at both ends with plastic, landed on a rug five feet away from me. Cheap, Mardi Gras–style beads were wrapped around it.

A lit fuse sparked and fizzed at one end of the pipe.

It was maybe half an inch away from vanishing into the cap.

"But this is my day *off*!" I howled.

I know that things looked bad. But I honestly think that I could have handled it, if Mister hadn't picked that exact moment to leap down from his perch and go streaking across the room, acting upon some feline imperative unknown and unknowable to mere mortals.

Kirby, already on the edge of a feral frenzy, did what any canine would do—he let out a snarl and gave immediate chase.

Mouse let out a sudden bellow of rage—for crying out loud, he hadn't gotten that worked up over *me* being in danger—and launched himself after Kirby. Andi, upon seeing Mouse in pursuit of her fellow werewolf, shifted entirely to her own wolf shape and flung herself after Mouse.

Mister rocketed around my tiny apartment, with several hundred pounds of furious canine in pursuit. Kirby bounded over and around furniture almost as nimbly as Mister. Mouse didn't bother with nimble. He simply plowed through whatever was in the way, smashing my coffee table and one easy chair, knocking over another bookcase, and churning the throw rugs on the floor into hummocks of fabric and fiber.

I leapt for the pipe bomb and picked it up, only to have my legs scythed out from beneath me by Kirby as he went by. Mouse accidently slammed a paw bearing his full weight down onto me as he rumbled past in pursuit, and got me right where the damned dog always gets a man. There was none of that delayed-reaction component to the pain, either. My testicles began reporting the damage instantly, loudly, and in nauseating intensity.

No time for pain. I lunged for the pipe bomb and nearly wet my pants as another explosion shook the floor—only this one was followed an instant later by an absolute flood of bright green smoke that billowed up from the lab.

I grabbed the pipe bomb and tried to pluck out the

fuse, but it vanished into the cap and beyond the reach of my fingers. In a panic, I scrabbled across the floor to the door and ripped it open with terrified strength. I hauled back to throw the thing out and—

A sharp burst of sound.

My hand exploded into pins and needles.

I fell limply to the floor, my head falling in such a way as to bring my gaze over to where my hand had been clutching the pipe bomb a few seconds before and—

And I was still holding it now, unharmed. Heavy jets of scarlet and purple smoke were billowing wildly from both ends of the pipe, scented heavily with a familiar odor.

Smoke bombs.

The freaking thing had been loaded with something remarkably similar to Fourth of July smoke bombs, the kind kids play with. Bemused, I tugged one plastic cap off, and several little expended canisters fell out along with a note that read: *The next time you interfere with me, more than smoke will interfere with you.*

More than smoke will interfere with you?

Who *talks* like that?

Mouse roared, snapping my focus back to the here and now, as he pounced onto Kirby's back, smashing the werewolf to the floor by dint of sheer mass. Mister, sensing his opening, shot out the front door with a yowl of disapproval and vanished into the outdoors, seeking a safer environment, like maybe traffic.

Andi leapt onto Mouse's back, fangs ripping, but my dog held fast to Kirby—buying me a couple of precious seconds. I seized a bit of chalk from the basket by the door and, choking on smoke, ran in a circle around the embattled trio, drawing a line of chalk on the concrete floor. Then I willed the circle closed, and the magical construct snapped into existence, a silent and invisible field of energy which, among other things, completely severed the connection between the psychic parasites in the Nevernever and the werewolves whaling on my dog.

The fight stopped abruptly. Kirby and Andi both blinked their eyes several times and hurriedly removed their fangs from Mouse's hide. A few seconds later, they shimmered and resumed their human forms.

"Don't move!" I snapped at them, infuriated to no end. "Any of you! Don't break the circle or you'll go nuts again! Sit! Stay!"

That last was for Mouse.

Mostly.

I couldn't see what Molly had done to my lab, but the fumes down there were cloying and obviously dangerous. I hauled myself over to the trapdoor.

Molly hadn't made it up the folding staircase, and just lay sprawled semiconscious against it. I had to grab her and haul her up the stairs. She was undressed from the waist up. I spotted her shirt and bra on the floor near the worktable, both of them riddled with acid-burned holes.

I got her laid out on her back, elevated her feet on a stray cushion from the smashed easy chair, and checked her breathing. It didn't take long, because she wasn't, though she did still have a faint pulse. I started rescue breathing for her—which is a *lot* more demanding than people think. Especially when the air is still thick with the smell of God only knows what chemical combinations.

I finally got her to cough, and my racing heartbeat subsided a little as she began breathing again, raggedly, and opened her eyes.

I sat up slowly, breathing hard, and found Anastasia Luccio standing in the open doorway to my apartment, her arms folded over her chest, one eyebrow arched.

Anastasia was a pretty girl—not glamorously lovely, but believably, genuinely pleasant to look at, with a fantastic smile and killer dimples. She looked like someone in her twenties, for reasons too complex to go into right now, but she was an older woman. A much older woman.

And there I was, apparently sitting up from kissing a topless girl, with a naked couple a few feet away, and the air thick with a pall of smoke and the smell of noxious fumes. For crying out loud, my apartment looked like the set of some kind of bizarre porno.

"Um," I said, and swallowed. "This isn't what it might appear to be."

Anastasia just stared at me. I knew it had been a long time since she'd opened up to anyone. It might not take much to make her close herself off again.

She shook her head, very slowly, and the smile lines at the corners of her eyes deepened along with her dimples. Then she burst out into a hearty belly laugh. "*Madre di Dio,* Harry. I cannot for the life of me imagine what it *does* appear to be."

I lifted my eyebrows in surprise. "You aren't upset?"

"By the time you get to be my age," she replied, "you've either worked out your insecurities, or they're there to stay. Besides. I simply *must* know how *this* happened."

I shook my head and then smiled at her. "I . . . my friends needed help."

She looked back and forth between the Alphas and Molly. "And still do," she said, nodding sharply. She came in and, as the only one actually wearing shoes, began picking up pieces of fallen glass from the broken window, literally rolling up her sleeves as she went. "Shall we?"

• • •

It took most of the day to get Molly to the hospital, gather the materials needed to fumigate Kirby and Andi's auras, and actually perform the work to get the job done. By the time they left, all better and psychophage-free, it was after seven.

"So much for our day off," I said.

She turned to consider me. "Would you do it differently if you had it to do again?"

"No. Of course not."

She shrugged. "Then it was a day well spent. There will be others."

"You never can be sure of that, though, can you?"

Her cheeks dimpled again. "Today is not yet over. You mourn its death somewhat prematurely."

"I just wanted to show you a nice time for a day. Not get bogged down in more business."

Anastasia turned to me and put her fingers over my mouth. Then she replaced her fingers with her lips.

"Enough talk," she murmured.

I agreed.

About the Authors

KELLEY ARMSTRONG is the author of the *Otherworld* paranormal suspense series. She grew up in Ontario, Canada, where she still lives with her family. For more on Kelley and her work, check out her website at www.KelleyArmstrong.com.

JOE R. LANSDALE is the bestselling author of thirty novels and numerous short stories and articles. His work has been turned into film, most notably with the cult classic *Bubba Ho-Tep* and for Showtime's *Masters of Horror* series with his story "Incident On and Off a Mountain Road." Forthcoming from Knopf is his new novel, *Leather Maiden*.

LUCIEN SOULBAN is a flight of God's fancy. He doesn't exist. He doesn't live in Montreal and he certainly didn't write for *Horrors Beyond 2* or for video games like *Rainbow Six: Vegas.* At best, Lucien is a rote, grabbing random words and sequencing them like some form of literary eugenics. By reading this, you're feeding the delusion of his existence: that he has substance. Great . . . now you've done it. Are you happy? He thinks he's real. P.S.: Lucien also never wrote four novels, including *Desert Raiders* and *Dragonlance: The Alien Sea* . . . the smug bastard.

CHRISTOPHER WELCH is a happily married freelance writer, reporter, and reviewer originally from Akron, Ohio. He currently lives in Fort Atkinson, Wisconsin, where he works for the local newspaper and news radio station. He earned a BA and an MA in English from the University of Akron, with a minor in creative writing. Welch's creative works have appeared in various small press and professional publications. His most recent fiction has appeared in *Dark Wisdom* magazine and the anthology *Catopolis.* His story in *Blood Lite* is more autobiographical than he likes to admit.

MATT VENNE received his BA in English from UCLA, and his MFA in Film from USC. His screenplay for *Near Dark* is being produced by Michael Bay (*Transformers*), and his *Masters of Horror* episode "Pelts" (based on the F. Paul Wilson short story) was directed by Dario Argento (*Suspiria*). Matt is currently adapting Stephen King's *Bag of Bones* for Mick Garris (*The Stand*) to direct and Guillermo del Toro (*Pan's Labyrinth*) to produce, wrote an episode of *Fear Itself* entitled "Spooked" for Brad Anderson (*Session 9*) to direct, and is writing the next installment of the *Rambo* franchise for Sylvester Stallone. Matt and his wife, Brynna, live in Los Angeles with their two daughters.

DON D'AMMASSA is the author of *Blood Beast, Servants of Chaos, Dead of Winter,* and four other novels, as well as three nonfiction books and more than one hundred short stories. He was the book reviewer for *Science Fiction Chronicle* for almost thirty years. Don is currently writing full-time, at least when he's not reading.

MARK ONSPAUGH is a native Californian who grew up on a steady diet of horror, science fiction, and DC Comics. He's written a whole lot of screenplays, and was one of the writers of *Flight of the Living Dead.* He knows people expect horror writers to be lurking misanthropes, but hasn't lurked since leaving LA. He lives in Los Osos with his wife, author/artist Dr. Tobey Crockett and two off-kilter cats. He hopes that, by the time this book is published, he has retired to a private island in the South Pacific.

J. A. KONRATH is the author of the Lt. Jack Daniels thrillers, the latest of which is *Fuzzy Navel.* He also edited the hit-man anthology *These Guns for Hire* and wrote the horror novel *Afraid* under the name Jack Kilborn. Vist Joe at www.JAKonrath.com.

F. PAUL WILSON is the award-winning, *New York Times*–bestselling author of *The Keep, The Tomb,* and other novels and short stories spanning horror, adventure, medical thrillers, science fiction, and virtually everything between. More than eight million copies of his books are in print in the U.S. and his work has been translated into twenty-four languages. He also has written for the stage, screen, and interactive media. His latest novel, *Secret Histories,* stars a teenage Repairman Jack.

CHARLAINE HARRIS writes the *New York Times* bestselling Sookie Stackhouse novels and the Harper Connelly series. She lives in southern Arkansas with her husband, daughter, and three dogs. The duck died. Charlaine's only consistent hobby is reading.

STEVEN SAVILE won the Writers of the Future Award in 2002. Since then he has gone on to publish novels in six different languages. He has worked with the popular *Doctor Who, Torchwood,* and *Primeval* television shows in the UK, most recently with the novel *Primeval: Shadow of the Jaguar,* and the audio drama *Torchwood: Hidden.* He has also written four novels for Games Workshop's *Warhammer* fantasy series and two Celtic fantasy novels in the *Sláine* series. He doesn't fantasize about killing his wife. Honestly.

During WILL LUDWIGSEN's adolescence, teachers and guidance counselors placed even odds on him ending up in a mental hospital or prison. He now works for the federal government, thereby fulfilling both predictions at once. When not writing horror nonfiction for them as a training consultant, he writes horror fiction for *Weird Tales, Cemetery Dance, Alfred Hitchcock's Mystery Magazine,* and other venues your mother warned you against. If you're working on a graduate thesis in sociopathology, his website at www.will-ludwigsen.com is a treasure trove of research material.

JANET BERLINER is the Bram Stoker Award–winning author of six novels, including *The Madagascar Manifesto* trilogy with George Guthridge, and *Artifact,* her four-way collaboration with friends Kevin J. Anderson, Matthew J. Costello, and F. Paul Wilson. She has sold over one hundred short stories to magazines and anthologies. She is also the editor of six anthologies, including two with illusionist David

Copperfield, and one with Joyce Carol Oates. She is a member of the Council of the National Writers Association, a past president of the Horror Writers Association, and a member of Authors Guild, and the Science Fiction and Fantasy Writers of America. Born in South Africa, Janet now lives in Las Vegas while she plans her escape to the Caribbean.

Despite taking creative writing classes in the 1980s, ERIC JAMES STONE did not begin seriously writing fiction until 2002. Since then, he has sold stories to the *Writers of the Future* Contest, *Analog*, and *Orson Scott Card's Intergalactic Medicine Show*, among other places. Eric lives in Utah, has a website at www.ericjamesstone.com, and does not eat human flesh.

Number one *New York Times* bestselling author SHERRILYN KENYON lives a life of extraordinary danger . . . as does any woman with three sons, a husband, a menagerie of pets, and a collection of swords that all of the above have a major fixation with. But when not running interference (or dashing off to the emergency room), she's found chained to her computer where she likes to play with all her imaginary friends. With more than twelve million copies of her books in print, in twenty-eight countries, she certainly has a lot of friends to play with, too. Writing as Kinley

MacGregor and Sherrilyn Kenyon, she is an international phenomenon and the author of several series, including *The Dark-Hunters, The League, Brotherhood of the Sword, Lords of Avalon*, and *Nevermore*.

Five-time Hugo Award winner MIKE RESNICK is, according to *Locus*, the all-time leading award winner for short fiction. He is the author of over fifty novels, close to two hundred stories, a pair of screenplays, and has edited fifty anthologies. His work has been translated into twenty-two languages.

D. L. SNELL is an Affiliate member of the Horror Writers Association, a graduate of Pacific University's Creative Writing program, and a freelance editor for Permuted Press. Snell's first novel, *Roses of Blood on Barbwire Vines*, pits zombies against vampires. David Moody, author of the *Autumn* series, calls it "violent and visceral . . . beautiful and erotic," and Bram Stoker Award–winning author Jonathan Maberry says, "[I]t has all the ingredients needed to satisfy even the most jaded fan of horror fiction." For more information, visit www.exit66.net.

NANCY HOLDER is a *USA Today* bestselling author who has received four Bram Stoker Awards, and has been nominated for two more. She was a charter member of HOWL and is a former trustee of HWA. The author of *Pretty Little Devils* and the co-author of the *Wicked* series (with Debbie Viguie), she lives in San Diego with her beautiful, wonderful daughter, Belle. Together they write about a magical mouse named Lightning Merriemouse-Jones, and have sold two of their short stories to DAW Books.

Award-winning author NANCY KILPATRICK has published seventeen novels and about two hundred short stories, and has edited eight anthologies. She also has written one nonfiction book: *The Goth Bible: A Compendium for the Darkly Inclined* (St. Martin's Press, October 2004). Mostly she writes in the horror/dark fantasy field, but has also penned fantasies, mysteries, erotica, and one science fiction story. She lives in Montreal with her black cat Bella and her calico cat Fedex. Check out her website for a list of current works: www.nancykilpatrick.com.

JEFF STRAND was a 2006 Bram Stoker Award finalist for his novel *Pressure*, but most of his work consists of demented horror/comedy like *The Sinister Mr. Corpse*, *Mandibles*, and *Gleefully Macabre Tales*. He's also the creator of Andrew Mayhem, who has bumbled his way through the novels *Graverobbers Wanted (No Experience Necessary)*, *Single White Psychopath Seeks Same*, and *Cas-*

ket for Sale (Only Used Once). You really should consider checking out his official website at www.jeffstrand.com.

SHARYN McCRUMB, a *New York Times*–bestselling Appalachian writer, won a 2006 Library of Virginia Award and the AWA Book of the Year Award for *St. Dale,* the story of a group of ordinary people who go on a pilgrimage in honor of NASCAR's Dale Earnhardt and find a miracle. McCrumb, who was honored as one of the "Virginia Women in History" for 2008, says: "Writing about NASCAR was a wonderful experience for me. After spending my adolescence writing term papers and avoiding proms, I am now jumping hills at one hundred mph with a race car driver on Virginia back roads, and it is glorious. The books won literary awards, are taught throughout the region, got me invited to the White House, and put the Earnhardts and a Daytona 500 winner on my speed dial. I'm having much more fun than writers usually have." McCrumb is best known for her Appalachian "Ballad" novels. A film of *The Rosewood Casket* is currently in production.

JIM BUTCHER stands accused of writing the *Dresden Files* and the *Codex Alera,* though it is worth noting that his plea of not guilty by reason of insanity has thus far withstood official scrutiny. He lives in Missouri with his wife, son, and a ferocious guard dog.

Editor KEVIN J. ANDERSON is a prolific bestselling author best known for his epic science fiction work (the *Saga of Seven Suns* series and his *Dune* novels written with Brian Herbert). As an editor, he put together the three bestselling SF anthologies of all time (*Tales from the Mos Eisley Cantina, Tales from Jabba's Palace,* and *Tales of the Bounty Hunters*). In horror, he collaborated with Dean Koontz on *Frankenstein: Prodigal Son,* and his first novel, *Resurrection, Inc.*, was nominated for the Bram Stoker Award. More information can be found at www.wordfire.com.

This page is an extension of the copyright page on page iv.

"The Ungrateful Dead," copyright © 2008 by KLA Fricke, Inc.
"Mr. Bear," copyright © 2008 by Joe R. Lansdale
"Hell in a Handbasket," copyright © 2008 by Lucien Soulban
"The Eldritch Pastiche from Beyond the Shadow of Horror," copyright © 2008 by Christopher Welch
"Elvis Presley and the Bloodsucker Blues," copyright © 2008 by Matt Venne
"No Problem," copyright © 2008 by Don D'Ammassa
"Old School," copyright © 2008 by Mark Onspaugh
"The Sound of Blunder," copyright © 2008 by J.A. Konrath and F. Paul Wilson
"An Evening with Al Gore," copyright © 2008 by Charlaine Harris, Inc.
"Dear Prudence," copyright © 2008 by Steven Savile
"A Good Psycho is Hard to Find," copyright © 2008 by Will Ludwigsen
"High Kicks and Misdemeanors," copyright © 2008 by Janet Berliner-Gluckman
"PR Problems," copyright © 2008 by Eric James Stone
"Where Angels Fear to Tread," copyright © 2008 by Sherrilyn Kenyon
"A Very Special Girl," copyright © 2008 by Mike Resnick
"Love Seat Solitaire," copyright © 2008 by D.L. Snell
"I Know Who You Ate Last Summer," copyright © 2008 by Nancy Holder
"Bitches of the Night," copyright © 2008 by Nancy Kilpatrick
"The Bell . . . FROM HELL!!!" copyright © 2008 by Jeff Strand
"Dead Hand," copyright © 2008 by Sharyn McCrumb
"Day Off," copyright © 2008 by Jim Butcher

TAKE A WALK ON THE DARK SIDE...

Pick up an urban fantasy from Pocket Books!

Maria Lima
MATTERS OF THE BLOOD
Book One of the *Blood Lines* series

M.L.N. Hanover
UNCLEAN SPIRITS
Book One of *The Black Sun's Daughter*

Stacia Kane
DEMON INSIDE

J.F. Lewis
STAKED

Linda Robertson
VICIOUS CIRCLE

Adrian Phoenix
IN THE BLOOD
Book Two of *The Maker's Song*

Available wherever books are sold or at www.simonandschuster.com

21360

VISIT THE ALL-NEW

SimonandSchuster.com!

WATCH, LISTEN, DISCUSS

Go behind the scenes with revealing author videos, interviews, and photos.

INTRIGUING QUESTIONS, UNEXPECTED ANSWERS

Check out Authors Revealed and find out what your favorite authors *really* think.

AUTHOR VOICES

Enjoy rants, raves, musings, and more.

BROWSE INSIDE

Preview and search the pages of a book.

BOOK RECOMMENDATIONS

Loved it? Hated it?
Let others know about it.

READING GROUP GUIDES

Plan your next book club meeting here.

Go to www.simonandschuster.com and connect with authors and readers from around the globe!

SIMON & SCHUSTER
SIMONANDSCHUSTER.COM